PRAISE FOR JOSIE BROWN

Secret Lives of Hus

"I loved this juicy-as-it-is-hea[...]
friendship—and sharp, manicure[...]
—Melis[...] ...e Secret of Joy

"Brown proves that a story with suburban bodies can be just as suspenseful as one with dead bodies! A probing, entertaining fishbowl of married life in a well-heeled, wayward neighborhood. Loved it!" —Stephanie Bond, author of *Body Movers*

"Poignant and funny! Josie Brown's protagonist is strong, resilient and unflinchingly honest; she has all the skills she needs to navigate the 'mean streets' of the gated community of Paradise Heights. A great read!" —Wendy Wax, author of *Magnolia Wednesdays*

Impossibly Tongue-Tied

"Brad, Angelina, Britney and Kevin may want to check out Josie Brown's new novel for its ripped-from-the-headlines plot." —*New York Post*, Page Six

True Hollywood Lies

"Brown captures the humor of working for a megalomaniac. . . . [A] well-paced, entertaining story." —*Publishers Weekly*

"The tone is confessional, the writing laced with venomous humor." —*Wall Street Journal*

"A fine piece of literary work." —*New York Post*, Page Six

Secret Lives of Husbands and Wives is also available as an eBook

SECRET LIVES OF
HUSBANDS AND WIVES

JOSIE BROWN

DOWNTOWN PRESS
New York   London   Toronto   Sydney

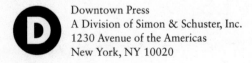

Downtown Press
A Division of Simon & Schuster, Inc.
1230 Avenue of the Americas
New York, NY 10020

First Downtown Press trade paperback edition June 2010

DOWNTOWN PRESS and colophon are trademarks of Simon & Schuster, Inc.

For information about special discounts for bulk purchases, please contact Simon & Schuster Special Sales at 1-866-506-1949 or business@simonandschuster.com.

The Simon & Schuster Speakers Bureau can bring authors to your live event. For more information or to book an event contact the Simon & Schuster Speakers Bureau at 1-866-248-3049 or visit our website at www.simonspeakers.com.

Designed by Renata Di Biase

Manufactured in the United States of America

10 9 8 7 6 5 4 3 2 1

ISBN 978-1-4391-7317-6
ISBN 978-1-4391-7318-3 (ebook)

For Martin
Always my first reader, always my first love

Acknowledgments

I will always appreciate those who have been so generous in their support.

To those dear friends and family who are there to listen to me, love me, and cheer me on: my deep appreciation to Darien and Don Coleman; Helen Drake; Austin Brown; Andree Belle; Allyson Rusu; Poppy Reiffin; Patricia Steadman and Mario Martinez; Bonnie and John Gray; Sheryl and Richard Levy; Sharon, Tim, and Rob Conn; Holly Cless; Paula Santonocito; Rita Abrams; and Sharon and Bill McKeon.

To those who are both my pals and my mentors: Karin Tabke, Tawny Weber, and Stephanie Bond, you are always there for me, and I love and appreciate you for that.

Very special thanks to Anna Brown and Allison O'Connor, whose invaluable insights shaped this book's characters and provided fodder for some of its zanier incidents.

My editor's thoughtful consideration is felt on every page of this book. Megan McKeever, not only are you a brilliant editor, but you were the book's uncompromising advocate. I feel blessed to be writing for you.

And finally, to my agent, Holly Root, who has been my tireless cheerleader from nanosecond one: Holly, thank you for your honesty, for the diligence with which you guide my career, and above all for your friendship.

Halloween

"Getting divorced just because you don't love a man is almost as silly as getting married just because you do."

—Zsa Zsa Gabor

Thursday, 7:32 p.m.

Y ou know how I hate to gossip, but . . ."

That is how Brooke Bartholomew always begins before she launches into a piece of hearsay. She knows and I know (for that matter, everyone knows) that she is the most notorious gossipmonger in our gated community of Paradise Heights.

So, yes, this will be juicy.

"Don't be such a tease," I answer. "Just spill it."

"It's about DeeDee and Harry Wilder," she whispers. "They've split up. For good!"

Her tone has me looking around to see if the leads in Brooke's drama are within hearing distance. But it's hard to tell because it is dark, and everyone, even the adults, is in costume. Witches, Harry Potters, Shreks, and vampires zigzag across Bougainvillea Boulevard, lugging king-size 300-count pima cotton pillowcases filled with all kinds of individually wrapped miniature candy bars. For Brooke, it is not just Halloween but Christmas too: her husband, Benjamin, is Paradise Heights's dentist and will reap what Hershey's has sown.

I check to see that my daughter, Olivia, is out of earshot but still within sight. To my chagrin, she and her posse of five-year-olds are racing up the circular staircase of the Hendricksons' New Orleans–style McMansion. All the girls are dressed as fairies, which in Halloweenspeak translates into gossamer wings and long tulle skirts over leotards. It is inevitable that one of them will slip, fall, and cry, so I cannot take my eyes off them, even to gauge the veracity of Brooke's raw data. For the first time tonight I notice that Temple, DeeDee and Harry's younger child, is not one of the winged creatures flittering in the crush in front of me.

The nickname given the Wilders by my very own clique, the board of the Paradise Heights Women's League, comes to mind: the Perfect Couple. Until now, it fit like a glove. Both DeeDee and Harry are tall, golden, patrician, and aloof. They are Barbie and Ken dolls come to life. Rounding out the family is their thirteen-year-old son, Jake, the star of the Paradise Heights Middle School basketball team. Our older boy, Tanner, is part of his entourage, as is Brooke's son, Marcus. Temple is exactly Olivia's age. With those gilt coiling ringlets and that dimpled smile, Temple is not just the kindergarten set's unabashed leader but beautiful as well, which is why all the other little girls aspire to be her.

While the Wilders seem friendly enough during the social gatherings that put them in close proximity to the rest of us mere mortals, they never engage, let alone mingle. In Harry's case, I presume he thinks his real life—that is, his *office* life—is too foreign for us to grasp: he is a senior partner in the international securities division of a large law firm, where every deal trails a long tail of zeros. But DeeDee has no such excuse. She doesn't work, yet she pointedly ignores our invitations to lunch, preferring to spend the precious hours between school drop-off and pickup gliding through the posh little shops on Paradise

Heights's bustling Main Street. Heck, even the Heights's working mommies try harder to fit in. The overflow crowd at the Women's League Christmas party is proof of that, as are the numerous corporate sponsorships they secure for the school district's annual golf tournament fund-raiser.

Proving yet again that mommy guilt is the greatest of all human motivators.

And now that the Wilders' crisis has been exposed to the masses, DeeDee's force field will stay up permanently, for sure.

"No way! The Wilders?" I say to Brooke. "Why, I just saw them together last weekend, at the club. He didn't leave her side even once. And I know for a fact that DeeDee was at the school yesterday, for the Halloween costume contest." Although I wasn't there, Ted, my husband, mentioned seeing her. I stayed home with our younger son, Mickey, who has a nasty case of head lice, the scourge of the elementary school set. Not fun at any time, but doubly distressing to a nine-year-old boy on a day in which all class work is suspended in honor of a candy orgy.

To get his mind off what he was missing, Mickey and I spent the morning carving two more pumpkins to join the family of five already displayed on our steps and spraying a spiderweb of Silly String on the porch banister. Ted, who is too fastidious to appreciate our haphazard handiwork, has elicited promises from us both that all of this sticky substance will be pulled off first thing tomorrow morning, before it has time to erode the nice new paint job on our faux-Victorian.

Now, as I keep watch over Olivia's raid on the neighbors' candy stashes, Ted is at home with Mickey, parsimoniously doling out mini Mounds bars. Despite having purchased forty bags of the stuff, neither of us will be surprised if we run out long before the last trick-or-treater has come and gone. That is the downside to having a house that is smack-dab in the middle of Bougainvillea Boulevard, where all things pertaining to Paradise

Heights begin and end. Because of this, poor Mickey will have to share whatever goodies Tanner and Olivia bring home. I don't look forward to the fight that breaks out over who gets the Godiva candy bar and who is left with the smashed caramel apple.

"Yeah, well, apparently it happened yesterday morning. From what I heard, he came home early from work so that he wouldn't miss the Halloween parade—and *found her in bed with another man.*" Brooke waves her little hellion, Benjamin Jr., on toward his older brother, Marcus, who has been trying all night to ditch the kid. Having been an only child, Brooke cannot accept the notion that a thirteen-year-old wouldn't want to hang with his only sibling, especially one seven years his junior.

Frankly, I think all of Brooke's energy would be better spent on some therapy over her own traumas. "My God! That's horrible! Do you think it's for real?"

"Who knows? For that matter, who cares?" Brooke arches a cleanly plucked brow. "Anyway that's the rumor, and it's too good not to be true, so I'm sticking with it. Besides, Colleen was behind Harry in line at Starbucks this morning. She overheard him bickering with DeeDee on his cell. Seems she's asked for a divorce, but he's fighting her for everything: the kids, the house—even the dog! In fact, he also told one of his partners that he planned to cut back his hours at work to prove he should be the one to get full custody. Look, I say where there's smoke, there's fire."

And they say that hell hath no fury like a woman scorned? Bullshit. What guy wouldn't go for the throat, particularly one who's just been made a laughingstock in the neighborhood?

Frankly, I can't really blame him, since I'd do exactly the same thing. Still, I wonder what he'll do if he does get it all. I'm of the theory that househusbands are born, not made. And they are certainly not made from high-powered corporate attorneys like Harry Wilder, who live for the thrill of the deal.

But I don't say this to Brooke, who wears her sistah solidarity on her silk Cavalli sleeve. If what she says is true, then there is no reason to feel sorry for DeeDee in the first place. Harry is the one we should pity, since he has no idea what he's in for. I'm willing to bet he'll reconsider his stance the first time Jake needs to be carpooled to basketball at the same time Temple has to be at ballet and it's not until they are halfway there that she tells him she's forgotten her tights.

"So, who is DeeDee's boyfriend?"

Frustrated because her reconnaissance is incomplete in this one very important area, Brooke's perfect moue of a mouth turns down at the sides. This is what passes for a frown when your social calendar revolves around standing appointments for Botox and collagen injections. "Since neither of them is talking, your guess is as good as mine. But don't worry, I've got my spies working on it." She winks broadly.

That trail might be cold right now, but she is a good enough gossip hound that I've no doubt we'll know the answer by the end of the week.

As we pass DeeDee and Harry's authentic-looking Tuscan villa, I notice that all the lights are off and the bougainvillea-wrapped wrought-iron gates are locked. The Wilders did not even leave out the requisite consolation: a plastic pumpkin filled with candy and sporting a sign that begs visitors to TAKE JUST ONE AND LEAVE THE REST FOR OTHERS.

Once again, Brooke is right: there is trouble in Paradise Heights.

2

"The great question … which I have not been able to
answer, despite my thirty years of research into the
feminine soul, is 'What does a woman want?'"

—Sigmund Freud

Friday, 1 Nov., 11:08 a.m.

As of lunchtime today, Mickey's head has a clean bill of health. Not a louse in sight. Monday he'll be back in school. To celebrate—and to rid ourselves of the cabin fever we're experiencing—Mickey and I sneak out with our Labrador, Harvey, to Paradise Park while school is still in session. I figure this is okay, since there will be no one there to infect anyway.

I'm wrong. Little Temple Wilder is playing alone on the swing set. Even before we are spotted, we can hear her plaintive plea: "Daddy, you said you'd push me! Please! PRETTY PLEASE, WITH SUGAR AND WHIPPED CREAM AND SPRINKLES ON TOP?"

Harry, the sleeves of his crisp oxford button-down shirt rolled up to his elbows, is mumbling authoritatively into his Bluetooth headset. Sunlight brings to life the glints of gold in his gently tousled hair. He places a fingertip to his lips in the hope of willing her into silence, but Temple isn't buying it. Patience is a virtue rarely found in five-year-olds.

Spotting us, he gives me a look that promises the world if I can guarantee him a few minutes of her silence, not to mention that of their Airedale puppy, Lucky, who's barking at Harvey. Harry is a novice when it comes to negotiating with a mommy who has been housebound with an antsy boy for almost a week. But knowing his plight and feeling his pain, I give Temple a push that sends her giggling skyward, and then I do the same for my son. Harry bows in gratitude.

A half hour later, Harry pulls off his headset for good to find Temple and my son playing nicely together on the climbing gym. Mickey has gotten over his wariness of girl cooties (imaginary), and Temple is reassured that Mickey's cooties (real, but gone) won't be invading her full head of sun-kissed sateen curls. All is right in the world.

Harry smiles his unabashed gratitude. "Sorry. East Coast," he says, by way of explanation. "Had to catch those guys before they go home for the day."

I nod understandingly, and then stick out my hand. "Lyssa Harper. We've met before."

Vagueness clouds his eyes. "Sure, I remember. You're the Stuckeys' au pair, right?"

I don't know whether to be flattered or miffed. True, both the au pair and I have long dark hair, although mine is somewhat curlier. Okay, make that frizzy. And yes, it strokes my ego to be compared to a mere woman-child some ten years younger (not to mention ten pounds lighter). But it's more likely that he's suggesting that I don't seem worthy to live in Paradise Heights— unless I'm in someone's domestic employ.

Only in my wildest fantasies would I assume that this was his way of hitting on me. Still, the thought of being picked up on the playground by the neighborhood DILF (the Dad I'd Like to—well, you get the picture) does give me a cheap thrill.

Then it hits me: what if he's asking because he thinks he can buy my services, which would leave the Stuckeys high and dry? Ouch! And those twins of theirs are a handful. . . .

Gee, I wonder how much he's offering, anyway?

Turns out he's not offering at all. He just doesn't remember meeting Ted and me at the Crawleys' Christmas party last year. Or sharing a picnic table with us this past summer at the Paradise Heights Annual July Fourth picnic. Or that we were the ones who found Lucky after he escaped under their fence in order to chase after the Corrigans' tabby.

My God, as oblivious as this guy is, I'm surprised he remembers his way home.

Then again, maybe he doesn't. That might be why DeeDee had an affair in the first place.

"Um . . . no. I'm just a mom here in the Heights."

As my black-and-white image of the Wilders gradates to chiaroscuro in the harsh light of reality, Harry tries to make amends for forgetting how many times our paths have crossed by complimenting me on how well my son plays with Temple.

Now it's my turn to blush. I'm not used to hearing compliments about Mickey from other parents, only pointed remarks about how much more "rambunctious" he is than their own perfect progeny. "Thanks," I stammer, then add, "I think his patience comes from having a younger sister."

"Oh yeah? My son isn't half that great with Temple. Of course, he's somewhat older, a teenager." He gives a conciliatory laugh. "You know how they are."

"I know your son." Surprised, he blinks, then leans away slightly. He seems wary of what I might say next, so I continue gently, "Jake, right? He's a sweet boy. He and my other son, Tanner, play together on the basketball team. Very few of Tanner's friends let Mickey join in when they come over to shoot hoops. You know how they can be—snubbing kids who are younger, or not as well-coordinated. But Jake doesn't seem to mind."

Harry nods uncertainly. "Well, I'm glad to hear he's not so—so judgmental all the time."

"I never thought of it that way. I just think some kids instinctively know what to do with younger children." Upon hearing this, Harry frowns. Quickly I add, "I'm not saying that that's a good thing or a bad thing. In fact, I think it shows that someday they'll make pretty good parents."

Harry stares off in stony silence. As we sit quietly, I wonder what I've said wrong.

On the other hand, what does it matter? It's my guess that he will forget our conversation the minute we gather up the kids and say our awkward good-byes. And the next time we meet, be it in the carpool line or at a school function or at a neighbor's party, he'll vaguely wonder what the Stuckeys' au pair has done with the usually caterwauling twins.

Right then and there I make up my mind that that is not going to happen, that I'm going to make a big enough impression on him that my name will finally be emblazoned on his brain, or at the very least that I crack his typically icy demeanor just this once.

Suddenly I remember another thing we have in common: our daughters.

"So, you've decided to give Temple a day off from school? My daughter, Olivia, is in kindergarten with Temple. Every now and then I let her do that too. Kindergarten can be so overwhelming for little kids, even with a year or two of preschool under their belts. It's not like they'll miss calculus or anything really important, right? And the trade-offs are some wonderful memories. To be honest, though, I hate when it's called 'quality time,' don't you? I mean, every second with your child is memorable. Even watching them while they sleep is precious—"

I've been blathering so much I haven't noticed that Harry is crying.

The tears roll down his face in two steady lines. He turns his head toward me so that the children don't see this, but my look of shock must be just as dismaying to him because he ends up burying his face in his hands.

And sobs even harder.

Harry Wilder, captain of industry, neighborhood enigma, one half of Paradise Heights's Perfect Couple, is now a puddle of mush.

And it's all my doing.

Out of habit, I still carry Handi Wipes. Although they aren't ideal in situations like this, I can tell that Harry is appreciative of anything that will sop up this mess that is now his life.

When he's able to face me again, he looks me in the eye. "My wife left me. She's left *us*."

At this point I could feign ignorance, but since we're both striving for honesty here, I have no desire to muck things up with a polite albeit face-saving (for him) lie, a "Gee! Look how late it's getting" exit line, and another year or two of polite neighborly oblivion. Instead, I nod and say, "Yeah, I heard. On Halloween. I'm—I'm so sorry about it."

"You know about it? But I—I haven't said anything to anyone yet! And she's—she's long gone, so I know it didn't come from her." He shakes his head at the thought that his personal soap opera is being bandied about at the local Starbucks. "Jesus! And I thought news moved fast on Wall Street."

"Yeah, well, you'll find out about the Heights's mommy grapevine soon enough. I mean, if you plan on sticking around—"

"I do, for sure. I'm not going anywhere." Harry's face once again realigns into a steely implacability. "This is our home. My kids love it here. We'll . . . we'll work through it somehow."

"Sure you will," I murmur reassuringly. "There's no place like the Heights for raising kids. That's why we're all here. Hey listen, really, I didn't mean to scare you off. You know, about the way we mommies talk and all. It was just such a shock to everyone. The two of you always seemed so—so happy."

"Yeah. Happy. I thought we were too." His eyes get moist again. This time, though, he shrugs, then passes a broad palm over them. I assume he's decided that the Handi Wipes give the wrong impression. "You were right when you said that every minute you spend with your kids is important. And I haven't been around for most of them."

Well, of course you weren't, I want to say. *You were out making a living! Bringing home the bacon, playing this millennium's version of caveman . . .*

And boy oh boy, your stucco palace has all the bells and whistles to prove it.

Too bad you found another Neanderthal in there with your wife.

But I keep my mouth shut. Because you don't hit a man when he's down.

Instead, I let him rhapsodize about how things will be from now on, now that he is home to nurture, protect, and defend. He has already asked his partners at his firm to cut him some slack, he tells me stoically. He'll go into the office just two days a week, and only during the hours that the kids are in school. His partners don't like the idea, but hey, they need him too badly, so they'll work around it. Besides, he can still juggle things out of his home office, after he takes the kids to school, right? At thirteen, Jake is too old for a nanny—not that Harry would ever consider that in the first place, oh no, no way in hell! That's all DeeDee would need to hear to make her case for full custody. He and the kids will muddle through together, everyone pitching in to help out. He'll position it to them as a family adventure. . . .

As for the grocery shopping, or getting Jake to basketball

practice, or Temple to her ballet and gym and acting classes, or nursing them when they have fevers, or covering them when their school is out for staff development days—not to mention showing up for parent-teacher conferences—how bad can it be? All it takes is a little planning, some adept scheduling on his BlackBerry. Heck, it'll be a cakewalk compared to flying all over the country in order to take meetings and meals with CEOs and CFOs at the Palm in DC, or the River Café in New York, or the Grillroom in Chicago—

You poor, pathetic, misinformed man.

DeeDee certainly fooled you in more ways than one.

I am so tempted to level with him about his new life, to blurt out the truth:

That suburbia is a jungle, filled with lots of vicious creatures.

Gain a few pounds, and the hyenas start giggling behind your back. Fail to volunteer for that field trip, and the silence of those usually sweet-as-lambs mommies who must pick up your slack will be deafening. Forget that it's your turn to bring the after-game healthy snacks for the Little League team, and you might as well not show up because the other mothers' tongue-lashing will shred you into human tartare.

And you, Harry Wilder, are nothing but fresh meat. So please, please watch your back.

But what is his alternative? To wallow in fear of the platoon of Pilates-pumped Amazons who commandeer the streets of Paradise Heights in their Lexus LXs or their Benz GLKs, and pray that he doesn't say or do something so DI (domestically incorrect) that his kids will be ostracized until they leave home for college?

Or perhaps it would be better to seek out the other househusbands in the neighborhood.

I wince at this thought. There are just two of them. Calvin Bullworth is a software geek, and such a hermit that he's rumored to be a cyberterrorist under house arrest. His wife, Bev Bullworth, is the Heights's number-one realtor. (Her motto: No Bull, Just Better Service!) Unfortunately, this means that she is always in other people's houses with strangers, and rarely home with Cal and their two children: Sabrina, who at twelve and a half is already a study in disaffected Goth; and Duke, her ten-year-old brother, who has the callow demeanor and social skills of his father. The poor kid gets crammed into a lot of school lockers.

And then there is Pete Shriver, the Heights's househusband extraordinaire: a trust-fund baby—yes, he's heir to the Shriver Tectonics fortune—he has immersed himself in all things Paradise Heights. As coach of the Paradise Heights Middle School basketball team, he has led the Red Devils to three undefeated seasons straight. At the annual Heights Labor Day Blazin' Barbecue Cook-Off, his melt-in-your-mouth brisket, prepared on a fifty-four-inch professional Lynx grill, brings home the blue ribbon every time. Under his tutelage, the Paradise Heights communal vegetable garden is shorn not only of errant weeds, but of any members who don't work their plots prodigiously. And as the editor of the *Boulevard Bugle*, he ran an editorial on the aesthetic advantages of authentic antique gas lamps versus newer aluminum faux versions. It inspired the community drive that anted up the four thousand dollars needed to cover their additional cost.

Oh, sure, Pete is a dynamo. . . .

Although he's rumored to be somewhat less energetic in the bedroom, which is perhaps why his wife, Masha—a Russian mail-order bride—is the neighborhood slut. And to everyone's dismay, their thirteen-year-old daughter, Natassia, is rumored to be following in her footsteps.

I don't have the heart to break the news to Harry about his new band of brothers. Not that he'd believe me anyway. No, it's best that I ease him into this new world order.

As we round up the dogs and the kids and say our good-byes, I suggest that we make a playdate for Olivia and Temple for next Tuesday. Harry, grateful, promptly says yeah sure, then flips through the agenda on his BlackBerry and thumbs that in, along with my cell-phone number.

He is now officially a househusband.

His next task: file for divorce.

"I'll never understand why this all happened in the first place," he murmurs with a shake of his head. "I thought I gave her the life she always wanted. I guess I was wrong."

3

"Don't marry the person you think you can live with;
marry only the individual you think you can't live without."

—James C. Dobson

A s I watch Harry Wilder drive away, I wonder if he's ever considered that maybe it was DeeDee who was wrong about what she wanted out of life.

Or more to the point, their lives together.

I'm guessing no. But then again, I'm speaking from my own experience with Ted.

I accepted Ted's proposal even though I wasn't really sure that he was The One. I said as much to my mother, the day after he proposed.

"What is 'The One,' anyway?" The smoke from her Kool Menthol streamed out from the high corner of her curled smirk and floated toward the ceiling like a serene genie. "Hey, nothing's perfect, right?"

It wasn't a question but a warning. During the twelve years of her own marriage, she had assumed my father was The One for her. I had, too. He'd been my first and only love.

As it turns out, Father wasn't The One for either of us. He proved it when I was ten. That was the year he left us both for his secretary, the giggly Patti-with-an-i, and the penthouse apartment where he'd stashed her.

Our consolation prize was our two-acre country-club estate in tony Atherton, with its overextended mortgage. But of course we couldn't afford the house on our own. Within a year we had downsized to a one-bedroom rent-controlled walk-up in San Francisco's Upper Tenderloin—a "transitional" neighborhood—where we crammed in as much of our large overstuffed furniture as we could fit.

The only good thing about that roach-infested hole was that it was a five-minute bus ride to the Saks Fifth Avenue on Union Square. My mother got a job at the cosmetics counter alongside the same women who, when she was married and flush, had showered her with Clinique and Estée Lauder samples as she swept by them on her way to the designer showroom. After the divorce, the Puccis, Guccis, Yves Saint Laurents, and Blasses she'd worn to the weekly cocktail parties at her country club either subbed as very expensive work attire or found their way to consignment shops, where they sold quickly at bargain rates. Whereas she was no longer living proof that you can never be too rich, she certainly proved that you could be too thin—if all you could afford to eat was canned tuna on saltines.

Like a good girl, I didn't blame my father or complain to my mother. Instead I threw myself into my other love: painting big sad canvases that made people stop, look, and react.

The best reaction I got netted me a full scholarship to the San Francisco Art Institute. Despite a few decent commissions, life as a starving artist was just as unsettling—just as scary—as life without Father. By my junior year I'd had enough of that and switched my major to graphic arts.

Within three years I'd parlayed a summer internship at a hot advertising agency into a coveted job as a senior art director, with a six-figure income along with a perk package that included four weeks of vacation time, an excellent 401(k) plan, bonuses, a shot at an equity share, and, oh yeah, the two-month "mind-cleansing sabbatical" that was encouraged for all employees after three years.

My hefty paycheck gave me the one thing that had eluded my mother: financial freedom. It also granted me enough emotional security that I didn't feel the need to jump into the arms of the first man who asked me to marry him.

Instead I played hard, making the club scene with my girlfriends. And I played hard to get, holding off from any commitments as long as I could while one after another my girlfriends found the men they considered their soul mates—or settled for guys who, at the very least, took them off the market.

Then Ted came into the picture.

Ted, the ultimate salesman, who pursued women with the same philosophy he used when wooing new business accounts: Go in for the kill. Win at all costs. Take no prisoners.

His pickup line wasn't original, but that just goes to show you it isn't the message that gets our attention, but the messenger. "See my friend over there? He wants to know if you think I'm cute."

"I find that hard to believe." I wasn't lying either. With dark curly hair and sad deep-set eyes that contradicted his playful smile, Ted had the kind of lanky physique that invited women to melt into his arms. No, this guy didn't really need my assurance at all. Every other woman in the bar would have gladly confirmed that for him. "Do you need my vote for it to be unanimous? Isn't it enough that every other woman in the room is flirting with you?"

"No one else's vote counts but yours."

"You've got to be joking." So that he wouldn't notice I was blushing, I gulped down my drink.

"I'll tell you what." He leaned in and locked eyes with me. "Spend the night with me and I'll prove it."

Of course I didn't. But I did give him my phone number. Then I proceeded to turn down his daily calls for a month or so.

In the meantime, he made sure his wingman buttered up my best friend to get a rundown of all my quirks and passions. Obviously he wanted to be The One, even if I wasn't so certain.

That is why, eventually, I took his call.

By quoting Mark Twain and wooing me with peppermint ice cream after a private tour of the Legion of Honor, did he win my heart? I convinced myself that only a man who was willing to love me forever would push so hard.

Then a year and a half later, I convinced myself that what he had to offer was good enough for me.

Slowly I found myself falling in love with a man who had a steady and lucrative job that he enjoyed as a sales manager for a software company, an undying allegiance to his hometown Lakers, an obsession with neatness, an allergy to strawberries, and a love for chocolate that matched my own. That he also had an aversion to any sexual position other than missionary style was something I hoped I could change in time.

Mother was right: nothing is perfect.

What made Ted perfect enough was his determination to turn all my noes into yeses, to whisk me away from the life I'd made for and by myself and into the perceived endgame of every woman approaching thirty: my very own picket-fenced cottage. Or in this case, a four-bedroom, three-and-a-half-bath shingled faux-Eastlake Victorian with a full basement, on three-fifths of a live oak–studded acre in Paradise Heights, a gated Silicon Valley community close enough to San Francisco to be worth the commute to any fast-tracking power ranger. In my mind, this posh enclave, with its broad sweeping streets, antique gas lamps, and well-manicured lawns, was as far from my father's lies, my mother's bitterness, and my own fear of loneliness as I could possibly get.

But Happily Ever After isn't a place. It is a state of mind.

More to the point, it's a state of heart.

Two hearts: his and yours, beating as one.

To be honest with you, our union has been fragile since day one.

He told me so himself, five years into our marriage, as we lolled, naked, late one night in our new backyard hot tub, our inhibitions let loose by the roiling steam, a pitcher of frozen margaritas, and the knowledge that Tanner, then three, was fast asleep.

"Are you in love with me?" I asked casually. I guess I was anticipating a declaration of undying devotion.

Instead he paused—only a second, but even that was too long for a woman who is always waiting for the rug to be pulled out from under her.

"Yeah, sure. I love you."

In spite of the hot water we were sitting in, a chill went down my spine. "What is that supposed to mean?"

"I don't know. It means—it means just that." Watching me blink my concern, he let loose a guilty chuckle. "Look, to be perfectly honest with you, I'm attracted to women who play hard to get. And you played the hardest. In fact, I lost a bet that night because of you."

"In other words, if I'd said yes that night, we probably wouldn't be sitting here now?"

Ted guffawed at that. "Well, I'm certainly not married to the girl who *did* take me home." Then he kissed me on the forehead with frosty lips. "Come on, babe! You were a great catch, for sure."

Go in for the kill. Win at all costs. And take no prisoners.

But nothing is perfect, right?

We didn't talk after that. Later that night, as we made love (as usual, missionary style), I wondered: *Now that I'm "caught," have I lost my appeal?*

Nine weeks later, I learned that I was pregnant with Mickey.

Yes, I could have left him . . . but I didn't. With one child and another on the way, I couldn't see myself walking away from my children's father just because my perception of the love I thought I deserved didn't match up to what he was able to give me.

Besides, I thought, maybe over time that would change. People who are in love sometimes fall out of love, so why couldn't the reverse be true too?

Now, ten years later, I've no doubt Ted loves me. And yet I know better than to presume he's finally fallen in love with me.

I can live with that. If I've learned anything at all, it's that it is more important to measure Ted's loyalty than his love.

DeeDee and Harry Wilder are proof of that.

4

"A dress that zips up the back will bring a
husband and wife together."

—James H. Boren

Saturday, 2 Nov., 2:16 p.m.

Each of the dressing rooms in the Collectors department at the local Nordstrom looks like the Apollo Room in Catherine the Great's Winter Palace in miniature. Gilt-framed mirrors line the walls from floor to ceiling. The settee is thickly upholstered and covered in silk brocade. The tufted carpet tickles underfoot so that you float, not walk, on a velvet cloud. Indirect lighting of a rosy hue gives your complexion a healthy, girlish glow. The raised panels on the doors are meant to give the impression that you are secure in this plush sanctuary.

But it is only an illusion.

In fact, the walls are paper-thin, allowing the Nordy shopgirl—or, for that matter, anyone within listening distance—to hear the murmur of zippers or the frustrated sighs that come with the disillusionment that one designer's size four is another's size six.

I have just smoothed on a Marc Jacobs sweater dress that is perfect for the event I have this evening—the board meeting for the Paradise Heights Women's League—when I hear the sobs: breathy gulps of heartache that no amount of expensive couture can muffle. They're coming from the next dressing room where, just a few minutes earlier, this very demanding customer sent her sales associate scurrying through the department in search of "whatever you have in Armani or Herve Leger, size zero, of course. . . ."

That alone would cheer me up, but not this poor soul.

Unlike my friend Brooke, eavesdropping is not my cuppa. And the very last thing I'd ever want to do is butt in when something is none of my business—

But *someone* needs to make sure this petite soul doesn't drown in her own tears.

I tap gently on her door. "Hi, just wondering if everything is okay."

She gasps before going silent. Then: "Yes, so sorry to have bothered you."

"Oh, not at all. Please don't feel you have to apologize. We all have our bad days."

Slowly the door opens. DeeDee Wilder, eyes liner-smeared and glistening with tears, stares back at me. "Would you mind unzipping me?"

Speechless, I nod and close the door behind me. She avoids looking me in the eye or staring into the mirror because she knows she won't like what she sees reflected from either point of view: pity from me, and her own despair. I made her soon-to-be ex cry yesterday. It must be Pavlovian. The Wilders get around me and they can't hold back the tears.

I look around the room. There are three other dresses hanging there. I recognize one as Armani. A mannequin out front is wearing its twin. On another hanger is an Escada that was showcased in the storefront window. The dress she's wearing is Michael Kors. I tug at the zipper but stop when I realize that it's caught on the lining of the dress. Besides, her teary hiccups make it hard for me to nudge it along without the risk of tearing $1,800 worth of wool crepe.

"I've been so damn weepy lately! It's so stupid, really. I guess that's what happens when you are going through a nasty divorce." She bites the gloss off her lower lip in an effort to calm down.

"I'm sorry to hear that." I truly am. Upon hearing this, she relaxes enough for me to grasp the fabric from the inside and try again.

"Don't be. I've never felt so—so frightened, and yet so relieved and exhilarated too." She wipes away a tear. "He's a hard worker, a good provider. He's one of those guys everyone calls 'perfect.' But if I'm not happy around him—if I feel as if I'm *trapped*—then I guess he's not perfect *for me*. I can't live someone else's ideal. So why waste time in a marriage that doesn't make me happy?"

I don't know how to answer her. Because I don't know that answer myself. For her sake, I hope she's thought it through. "You were that unhappy?"

She stares at herself in the mirror, as if seeing herself for the first time. "It took fifteen years, but it finally hit me: *I don't love him.*"

Just like that? No, it's never just like that. There is always the one thing that pushes you over the edge. . . .

Her eye catches mine in the mirror. Her smile is hard. "My God, just saying it out loud, it's like a burden has been lifted off my shoulders!"

As she breathes in again, the zipper gets the last bit of traction it needs. I guide it slowly down her back. "There, it's moving again."

She steps out of the dress, all smiles again. "Thanks. Hey, do me a favor—"

Before she can finish her sentence, her cell phone rings. She holds up one hand that stops me from backing out the door as she fishes it out of her purse with the other. "Yes? Bethany? . . . He says *he won't*? But . . . Damn him! He can be so vindictive. . . . Yes, I know it's his ego. Well, he's used to winning, to getting his way. But you've *got* to convince him that he's not thinking about what's best for the kids! My God, he won't even know what to do with them. He'll probably palm them off on an au pair. He'll have to, if he wants to stay a partner. . . . I don't care what he says, this has nothing to do with an affair. . . . Seriously, do you really want to know? . . . Ha! I thought not. Trust me, there is no way . . . Careful? Yes, *I know*."

Angrily she tosses the cell back into her purse. Then, realizing I'm still there, she scoops up the three dresses that are hanging and hands them to me.

"I don't like this one, but you can ring up the others for me, okay? I don't think he's thought of closing my account here, but just in case, you better do it fast."

It's on the tip of my tongue to remind her that I'm not her salesclerk, that I'm her neighbor; that our sons play ball together, and our daughters dance in the same ballet class.

But what's the use? The Heights is no longer DeeDee's paradise.

It's her war zone. And right now she doesn't know friend from foe from shopgirl.

That's smart on her part, because I haven't made up my mind which side I'm on.

As my salesperson rings up the dress on my back, I hand off DeeDee's frocks to her clerk with a thumbs-up, all the while wondering how many of the other dresses draped over the woman's arm will make it onto Harry's Nordstrom account before he realizes he's even got one.

5

"Love is an irresistible desire to be irresistibly desired."

—Robert Frost

6:36 p.m.

Y ou're a natural-born leader, you know? A *natural.* I've never met anyone like you! You say you were, what, in advertising? Account management, I'm guessing. . . . No? An *art director*? Well, that explains a lot. Like that natural flair you have for our big events. . . ."

Margot Hardaway, the president of the Paradise Heights Women's League, thinks she has to sell me on the idea of being her successor.

And because I love being wooed, because I long to be desired, I've been playing hard to get all year long.

But the truth is, I want it just as badly as she wants me to have it.

"Keep talking." I bat my lashes. "I can be had."

Ted, who is refilling our margaritas, chokes back a snicker that causes him to tip the pitcher precariously over Margot's head. I give him a look that says *Shut your piehole*, but he's not buying it.

"Yeah, boy, I can vouch for that." He catches his breath, puts on his poker face. "And, Margot, I'll let you in on a little secret: if you bide your time long enough, she's yours for the taking."

"Oh, is that so?" Margot smirks knowingly. "Thanks for the tip, Ted."

When she glances away, I give him a kick. That's not exactly what I want Margot to hear.

It's my night to host her, along with the rest of the Paradise Heights Women's League board: Brooke, of course, as well as Isabelle Randall, Tammy Satterfield, and Colleen Franklin. Board meetings used to take place in the tasting room of the one and only wine bar in Paradise Heights's "resident-serving commercial district": an apropos rendezvous, considering that our ironically named planned community shares a sun-drenched, mist-kissed valley with about thirty wineries. But on too many occasions, after too many sips of some trendy varietals, finding our way home through the Heights's concentric maze of streets (pitched in the Paradise Heights real estate brochure as "Another reason why it's the Pentagon of neighborhoods! It's not for everyone, but isn't that the point?") became tantamount to running an obstacle course—especially for "all you tiny women in monster SUVs," as Officer Fife, our extremely polite local police chief, put it after issuing his fourth DUI warning to as many board members.

By unanimous vote, the decision was made to cut out the driving as opposed to the drinking, which is why league board meetings now rotate among the board members' homes, each of which contains three things necessary for such powwows: a husband relegated to running interference with whatever children are home at the time, a well-stocked wine cellar, and a state-of-the-art blender, therefore expanding our beverage choices.

Thus far only one board member has been too tipsy to find her way home after a member-hosted meeting, so the system has been deemed a success.

Margot—a former senior vice president of an IBM division that got downsized into oblivion, and she along with it—views the Paradise Heights Women's League as her new executive suite. As its CEO, she has already begun to Peter Principle it to death. With just a year on the board under my belt, I'm the board's newbie as well as its provost. As such, I've taken on a lot of the grunt work that the others (especially those who have been on it the longest) abhor, like reconciling Scrip receipts from the classroom moms and organizing the Annual July Fourth picnic.

The others hold loftier board titles than mine: treasurer (Colleen), sergeant at arms (Brooke), secretary (Tammy), and vice president (Isabelle). However, their productivity leaves a lot to be desired. As opposed to rolling up their sleeves and getting their hands dirty, they prefer to strategize (Colleen), delegate (Brooke), whine (Tammy), and, when all else fails, point fingers (Isabelle).

In Margot's previous life, by now pink slips would have been handed out all around.

On the other hand, my can-do efficiency has positioned me as Margot's go-to gal.

Her girl Friday.

Okay, yeah: her bitch.

That's okay. I need to prove something to myself: that I've got style as well as substance.

That I am admired, appreciated, and beloved.

That I am desired.

If not by Ted, then by Margot and her posse. That'll do for now, anyway.

"You know, Tammy will be disappointed if I skip over her for the nomination." Margot leans in close, as if what she has to tell me is gossip gold, but I can see this for myself by all the anxious looks Tammy shoots our way. "She chaired a decent Valentine's dance, but let's face it, her handling of the Easter egg hunt was a travesty! She only dyed three thousand eggs—and in solid colors! No decoupage, no glitter, no tie-dye—nothing. I don't have to tell you how disappointed I was. And the kids found them all in eight minutes flat. How anticlimactic." She winces. "You, on the other hand, pulled off the July Fourth picnic with aplomb. The fireworks were spectacular. Those red, white, and blue wieners—sheer genius!"

"Why, thank you." There's no way I'm going to tell her that Tanner egged Mickey into putting blue food coloring into some of the pots of boiling hot dogs. That would blow her illusion of my creative flair to smithereens.

"In all fairness, though, Tammy had two projects to your one." She goes in for the close. "So, how about if you take on one more? Something easy, just to cinch it."

I brace myself: for all I know, she's sending me to collect the broomstick of the Wicked Witch of the West.

"No biggie. Something simple, like running the Thanksgiving food drive." Margot smiles. "All you need to do is inspire the community to collect a few thousand cans. A cakewalk! Not that you'll even get close to breaking my record: 2,018 cans, if I remember correctly. Of course, if you do, the presidency is yours for the taking. So, you think you're up for that?"

I'm too tipsy to say no. Besides, the presidency is nearly within my grasp.

I wonder if it comes with a tiara. . . .

7:53 p.m.

"Whoa, Tammy, look at those muscles! Flex 'em for me, babe, go on."

Tammy accommodates Ted's demand by taking off the sheer blouse she wears over her tight tank top and curling a taut, sinewy arm. When he rewards her with a wolf whistle, she feigns bashfulness by covering her eyes.

But no one is fooled. This is why she curls ten-pound barbells in twelve reps, four times each arm: so that other women's husbands will admire her.

Including mine. I hate it when Ted flirts.

It wouldn't be so bad if he weren't so good at it. Or if he only flirted with me.

But no, that would be too much to ask.

Unlike some husbands who feel awkward in a room full of women, Ted loves being the cock of the walk. And because he knows I am completely and utterly assured of his loyalty, he openly flirts with my friends.

He does it with a certain smile on his face. You know the one. It promises more than he can deliver. I know this firsthand.

But Tammy doesn't—until she sees the loving manner in which he unconsciously strokes my hair while complimenting Brooke on her last tennis game.

As Tammy follows the other women out the door, she sighs in my ear, "You are *sooooooo* lucky."

Whereas she is not. Her Charlie's bank account may be humongous, but his sperm bank is all but empty.

This gives her something else to whine about.

It also gives her the audacity to graze up against Ted on her way out the door.

If she thinks I didn't see her, she's crazy. Okay, now I *have* to be president. Just so I can kick her off the board.

9:44 p.m.

Vixen . . . I am a vixen . . . a sexy, vibrant vixen . . . a sultry—

"Hon, do me a favor and move your head a little to the right, okay? Otherwise you block the TV—What the *hell* is wrong with Kobe? That's the second foul shot he's missed!"

I sigh and open one eye in time to watch the odious Spurs

race down the court with the ball. For the past ten minutes I've been straddling Ted's cock—backward, froggy style—in the hope that all my gyrating will be just as riveting to him as the antics of his beloved home team.

As if. When will I ever learn that a close game between the Lakers and the Spurs brings him to orgasm faster than anything I can do to him?

A TV set in the master bedroom makes it convenient for Ted to watch basketball, but it has had a marked effect on our love life. His answer to this is to suggest that we subscribe to a porn channel to put us in the mood—not exactly what I have in mind for romantic stimuli.

Then again, neither is a subscription to NBA League Pass.

It's been ten years since that day in the hot tub, when Ted confessed he wasn't in love with me. Still, I steadfastly refuse to believe I can't change his feelings. I figure it all comes down to one thing:

Keeping the passion alive.

My parents didn't share that, and look what happened to them.

Since then I've been working my way through all seven parts, thirty-six chapters, and 1,246 verses of the *Kama Sutra.* Variety is the spice of life, right?

Wrong. When it comes to sex, Ted likes it missionary style. He takes that to mean he's in control. Otherwise he views it as a spectator sport, albeit not half as stimulating as his precious Lakers.

If only Ted appreciated my moves as much as he admires Kobe's. Come to think of it, maybe I should come to bed wearing nothing but a Lakers jersey.

"Hey, I've got a pretty radical idea." I mute the television. This makes Ted go wild-eyed, but at least I now have his undivided attention. "Why don't we make love with the TV off?"

He squints as if contemplating that seriously, but I know better. Watching basketball is the way he unwinds, his release, his stressbuster. . . .

Whereas I'm just an annoying distraction.

Like when the TV is tuned to ESPN with color commentary by Bill Walton, who won't shut up, I won't *give* up.

I don't need him to go soft on me to prove the point. If nothing else, at least while the TV is on I'm guaranteed a hard-on.

Then again, I have that with my dildo, sans Stu Lantz's color commentary.

I flick the TV's sound back on and take my dildo with me on the way to the guest room.

After five minutes of personal playtime, it dawns on me that I miss Stu.

I wish I could say the same about Ted.

6

Monday, 4 Nov., 10:13 a.m.

It is true that the Highlander Hybrid goes from zero to sixty in around 9.6 seconds.

However, the inverse of that—say, you're driving at sixty miles an hour down Highway 101 in a rainstorm when you blow a tire—happens a little more slowly.

I am experiencing this now, as my Highlander hydroplanes out of control as yet another rain wave rolls under its chassis.

I eat up the first few seconds with some freaking out and swearing at myself for forgetting Ted's warning about going too fast on bald tires. Then, oh, possibly another six seconds goes to slamming on the brakes and praying up a storm as the Highlander spins out of control. By the time it comes to a complete stop and my heart rate goes back down to normal, I'm guessing I've lost another twelve seconds.

Okay, I lied. My chest is still heaving twenty-two seconds later when I hear the tap on my window.

"Lyssa, are you okay?" Harry Wilder's face stares back at me, blurred and contorted through my rain-spattered window. It's been a couple of days since we saw each other in the park.

I nod slowly and roll down my window. The cold air feels great on my face because it reminds me I'm alive. "I—I was very stupid, going that fast."

"I'm just happy you're alive. Look, would you like me to call someone?"

"No, that's okay, really. I have Triple A. I've got the card here somewhere. . . ." My hands shake as I rummage through the deep, unfathomable well of my bag, but I can't find it. DAMN DAMN DAMN Olivia's been playing in my purse again.

I look up again just in time to see a raindrop roll off the tip of his nose. "Oh, my God, sorry! Why don't you get in?" I fumble with the auto-lock. When he hears it click, he jumps into the passenger seat behind me.

He's wearing a rainproof jacket, but he's shivering nonetheless. Seeing him with his hair coiled into damp curls, it strikes me how much more his daughter looks like him than like DeeDee.

"Listen, by the time you find the number, I could have already changed your tire. Do you know if you have a spare?"

"Yes, but—you'll get wet!"

He laughs heartily at the obvious. "At this point, I think I'd say that's a moot issue."

I'm happy to hear no pain in his voice, unlike the first time we met. Maybe DeeDee's shopping spree put things in perspective for him. "Okay, sure, it's there somewhere. Let's look together. The least I can do is hold the umbrella."

We both jump out of the car and head toward the hatch. After moving the kids' basketball and soccer gear, with some finagling we're able to shift the backseat forward and open the compartment, which holds a fully inflated tire, thank God, and a jack.

He heaves both out and crouches to set up by the blown tire. As I stand over him with my umbrella, I'm given a different point of view of Harry Wilder. I take note of how thin his hair is at the crown of his head, and the way his shoulders expand and roll beneath his jacket as he cranks the jack and twists off the bolts. A few moments later, when he stands up to move the flattened tire out of the way, he forgets how close I'm standing and bumps his head into the umbrella. I'm caught off guard and topple backward, but he grabs my hand before I fall into a puddle.

"Sorry!" we say in unison, then, "Don't be—" and then together we laugh. That breaks the tension. But then a mist of awkwardness envelops us again.

I find it suffocating. Apparently he does too, because he clasps my hand with his even tighter.

My hand lingers in his just long enough for me to appreciate its warmth.

And to feel his wedding band.

Yes, Harry is still in mourning.

As nonchalantly as I can, I take my hand out of his. We stand there in the rain, letting it pull us back to reality. Finally I realize that one of us should say something. My attempt is feeble but sincere. "You know, I'm forever in your debt."

"Don't be silly. I'm just glad you weren't hurt, and that Olivia wasn't with you—or your boys. That spinout was pretty scary."

I shake my head in wonder. "I don't know what I would have done if I had hurt them."

"We can't protect them against everything." He frowns. "All we can do is make the judgment calls we feel are best at any given time."

"But that's just it. We're only human. Sometimes we get it wrong. Sometimes we screw up. Ted warned me about these tires being bald. I just haven't made the time to buy new ones. Well, there's still a couple of hours before school is out. I was on my way to the bank, but I think it's best that I head over to Costco now and get them changed out."

He laughs. "Hey, do you think that place has something called Lunchables? Temple is finally burned out on my peanut butter and banana sandwiches. That's top of the list of my household duties today: bring home these Lunchables."

It's my turn to smile. "You've never been inside a Costco?"

"DeeDee did all the shopping. She even picked out my suits." He grimaces. "But, hey, I'm game for anything now."

A Costco virgin? This should be fun. "Tell you what: you follow me over, and while they're changing my tires, I'll give you a tour. And by the way, Olivia loves the idea of having Temple over. We discussed Tuesday. Does that still work?"

"Yes, and thanks again." He reaches out again to shake my hand.

I take his hand again. But why do I have such a hard time letting it go?

10:31 a.m.

The trip to Costco with Harry is like a scene out of *E.T.* "You know, I've heard about places like this," he says, "but I've never comprehended why anyone would shop here."

He changes his mind the minute we pass the Aisle of Man: the one with all the humongous flat-screen televisions at prices that have him drooling.

All of a sudden he gets the concept. Who knew there was this whole crazy world beyond the cool, sane recesses of the executive suite, one in which everything is bundled in bulk, including a twenty-four-pack of Lunchables?

As he munches on a Swedish meatball speared on a toothpick that was nudged on him by one of the genial Costco sample ladies, Harry shakes his head in wonder. "I get the quantity discount concept, but seriously, where am I supposed to store all this stuff?"

I suggest rearranging his kitchen pantry. "Make it a project with the kids."

I think it best not to remind him that, since DeeDee left, he's got at least one empty walk-in closet in the house. My new friend still has a long way to go before the empty spaces of his life are filled again.

7

"Why does a woman work ten years to change a
man's habits and then complain that he's not
the man she married?"

—Barbra Streisand

Tuesday, 5 Nov., 3:50 p.m.

The bitch called. Apparently they've run a few tests on *him*. They see something or other on a lung." Mother says this quite matter-of-factly.

Translation: Patti-with-an-i wants us to know that Dad is dying.

And if Mother has her way, even this bit of news shouldn't move me to his side.

As the kids hustle and flow around the kitchen, I can hear Mother suck hard on her cigarette, then exhale her smoke and venom in a sigh of relief. "It couldn't have been his heart, now, could it? Because he doesn't have one."

I wish that were a joke, but it isn't. She truly believes this.

By all rights, I should too. I haven't seen my dad since I was ten. It was the Saturday before Father's Day. He crushed me to his double-breasted gray pin-striped Kuppenheimer power suit and babbled a promise to be home later that night. Then he tossed his Samsonite in the trunk of our—actually *his*—brand-new BMW 725i, and drove off to his new life.

The special breakfast I made him the next morning—scrambled eggs, buttered pumpernickel toast, a cup of percolated Chase and Sanborn—sat on the kitchen table the whole week as Mother lay weeping on the California king bed in their bedroom.

Before she rose, I burned the Father's Day card I'd made him in the fireplace.

"Did we get cut off?" Mother asks now. She knows better. My silence is expected, but she doesn't dare ask if I'm okay. To her mind, I would be nothing else.

The truth is that I can't think of anything to say. It's as if I've been waiting for this all my life: the day on which I am to churn up all those feelings of anger and sadness and abandonment I've patted down deep in the fertile soil that is my life now, the one I've created with Ted and my children.

As always, the kids are my excuse to get off the phone. Olivia needs me to pour her juice. Tanner didn't see his athletic socks in the wash. Mickey wants thread for some science project. Besides, I have to prepare a report on that deadly food drive for the Women's League board meeting tonight, not to mention that any moment now Harry is dropping off Temple for her and Olivia's first playdate.

The one overexposed Polaroid snapshot I saved of my father (before my mother could find it and shred it, like all the others) shows a tall, husky man with my wide mouth and curly hair. Apparently Tanner has his height and his sense of humor. And although the camera's flash turned my father's irises into alien red dots, sometimes, like now, I spot him looking at me out of Mickey's green-flecked squinty eyes.

That's when I tear up.

• • •

4:04 p.m.

My new motto: Be Kind to Strangers Bearing Gifts.

"For you, m'lady." Harry hands me a box of Krispy Kreme doughnuts.

"Ah, my favorite!"

He smiles as I pluck the only maple-topped glazed one from the box. "Ha. I would have guessed you for a chocolate-topped cream-filled."

"With two growing boys in the house, I've learned to settle."

Although I've given Harry permission to take off and run any errands he might have, he seems to be in no rush. When I ask him if he'd care to share a cup of coffee with me, he seems relieved to have been given a reason to hang around. Gingerly, he perches half off and half on one of the high stools under my kitchen's breakfast bar.

Since yesterday's Costco adventure, I've come to realize that Harry needs a domestic Sherpa: someone to teach him the ins and outs of life in our 'hood, like which is the best dry cleaner as opposed to the one who loses all your buttons, and which drugstore has the fastest cashiers, and what PTA volunteer slots take the least time and effort.

He claims a knack for cooking, so believe it or not, he doesn't mind grocery shopping, although in the past that was also (as he puts it) DeeDee's domain. However, he has taken to heart my warning that he should do as much of the shopping as possible when the kids are in school. Otherwise he'll get coerced into buying junk food and other stuff they really don't need.

"Yeah, I learned that by default, the first week after DeeDee walked out," he confessed.

It's been raining all afternoon, so the girls make an indoor "cottage" ("It's a Craftsman," Temple informed me very seriously) by stringing a couple of faded quilts over the two couches in the family room and making domestic tableaus with Olivia's stash of Barbies. Tanner is at basketball practice. Unfortunately for Mickey, his after-school soccer practice was rained out, so he has holed up inside his room and placed a No Girls Allowed sign on his door, in silent protest of the girls' having taken over the only room with a TV he's allowed to watch. In sympathy, I've agreed to let him play games on my iPhone.

Slowly, as fine ground coffee steeps in my French press, Harry mellows as well, to the point where he now feels comfortable enough to open up in a way he never has before. This includes giving me a play-by-play of the legal bombs DeeDee has hurled his way.

"Frankly, I thought this stay-at-home dad thing would be a cakewalk. You know, get the kids out of the house by eight, pick them up at three, and use the time in between to deal with the clients. Ha! Easier said than done." He smiles wryly. "The real world keeps getting in the way. By that I mean *this* world."

"Let me guess. Life in the carpool lane is different from life in the fast lane."

"Do you know how hard it is to talk on the phone when your dog is barking at the neighbor's cat?" He gulps his coffee. "Then there's the DeeDee factor. She was the one who wanted out, not me, but she feels she's entitled to everything I've made, even part of my pension and my bonus. So what, now I'm supposed to just hand over the kids and the keys to the house, and walk off into the sunset? Forget that! I'm not paying for her decision with my home and the rest of my family."

And no, on Halloween he did not walk in on her with a lover. She just asked him for a divorce, without giving any reason other than that she no longer loved him.

But he refuses to believe she doesn't have one, so now she's taunting him to prove it.

"The truth is that this is shaping up to be one hell of a divorce." As he says this, his hands curl up into fists. "For the time being, we've agreed to joint custody. But DeeDee has already hired Bethany St. John, so I'm guessing she'll go for full to justify getting everything."

Of course I know that name. The newspapers call her "the Terminator" because of her success rate with high-profile divorces. "Will someone at your firm be representing you?"

"No. We don't handle divorces. I was referred to Edwin Worth. He's supposed to be somewhat of a bulldog, too. With what I'm paying him, I certainly hope so. And of course I'm doing what I can to help out with any of the due diligence."

I think back on some of the dirtier divorces that have taken place here in the Heights. Brenda Ravner, who lives down the street, accused her husband, Bill, of abusing their kids, and he lost his job over it. Phil Menkin, who used to live on Locust Street, ran up his wife Cindy's credit cards, then skipped town. She had to sell the house to get out of debt.

If Harry approaches his divorce as if it is some corporate merger that needs auditing, he'll be in for a rude awakening. The mud will be flying as fast and furiously as it does on the Heights's soccer field after a hard rain.

I want to pat him on the shoulder and tell him that I feel his pain, but I fear he'll close up again, like some hothouse flower that only blooms in an environment devoid of foreign elements. In that regard, I can just imagine how strange my cluttered kitchen seems to him.

Realizing that I am uncomfortable with the topic, he turns his attention to my window ledge, which is laden with pots of my favorite flower, orchids.

"Aren't they hard to grow?"

"Not if you pay attention to them. Just make sure they get the right amount of light, and plant them in the right kind of soil. Oh, and you can't forget to water them every ten days or so. For that matter, you can't overwater them, either."

"Hmm. That's much too complicated. I don't know how you do it and keep up with the kids, and your dog. And your husband, of course."

"I guess if you love something, you make it a priority."

As I say this, the look on his face changes.

I wish I'd kept my big mouth shut.

Instead I open it again, with a suggestion I hope I won't later regret: "Hey, Harry, I was thinking: with all that's going on in your life, widening your circle of friends is a perfect way to create a support system. You know, to break up carpool duty, for emergency childcare, that kind of thing. What do you say, think you're up for meeting some other people here in the Heights?"

He shrugs. "Sure. What can it hurt?"

I break a doughnut in two and hand him half. "My thoughts exactly."

8

"A successful marriage requires falling in love many times,
always with the same person."

—Mignon McLaughlin

So, what's he really like?"

That question is coming from Margot. I'm sitting with her and the rest of the board in Tammy's newly redecorated great room.

(This is the room's third renovation in as many years. You see, while workmen underfoot drive the rest of us crazy, it is a natural state for Tammy, who channels her frustration over Charlie's low sperm count and his allergies to pet fur into remodeling projects. Granted, they're not as satisfying as a baby or even a puppy, but they will certainly pay better dividends when it comes to her home's resale value.)

The reason for this week's board meeting is, ostensibly, to divvy up duties for the Heights's after-Thanksgiving potluck. In reality, it is to dish the latest neighborhood dirt. That includes any neighbor's (a) wild child, (b) obvious substance-abuse issue, or (c) spouse behaving badly.

My close encounters with our favorite Martian certainly trump the Randolphs' sixteen-year-old son's shoplifting arrest at the local skateboard store, and Activist Mom's one-woman hunger strike protesting the town council's decision to ignore her request to remove chlorine from the public swimming pool. ("She only dropped six pounds," sniffs Isabelle. "Come on already! She would have been better off doing Weight Watchers.") They even trump Brooke's suspicions that Biker Mom, who lives next door to her, is spiking her seven-year-old's Capri Suns with Robitussin DM. (She's just pissed because Marcus's new role model is Biker Dad, who sports a tongue stud, is inked within an inch of his life, and rides a Harley bare-chested in black leather chaps. Not a great look for a future dentist.)

Upon Margot's question to me, the deafening chatter comes to a halt as the pierced ears on the other women perk up and, in unison, tack in our direction.

Proof positive that Harry Wilder is, hands down, Paradise Heights's Number One DILF.

Since Halloween, Harry has been trying to stay below the Paradise Heights gosdar. (In this case, "gossip radar," as opposed to the local "gaydar," which is not so finely tuned, as we all discovered when Corey Torrance ran off with his wife's highly temperamental landscape designer. You would have thought that the time the two men spent together in the toolshed would have been a dead giveaway.)

In deference to his privacy, I've managed to duck all pointed references to Olivia and Temple's playdates—until now.

I take a deep breath to buy time before answering, knowing full well that every word that comes out of my mouth will be dissected and ruminated over for the next week, or until more illuminating facts come to light.

And I am very aware that anything I say can and will be used against him in the future.

"Frankly, I think the whole thing has him in a state of shock. I have to say that I feel sorry for him. From all he's said, he didn't see it coming. He thought that they were totally in sync—"

This evokes a snort from Isabelle. Still, it is a much, much milder response than what I would have received last year: a few choice expletives, perhaps even a backhanded slap. It wasn't too long ago that Isabelle's appearance at the Heights's mall had every shopgirl cowering in her Kate Spades. But that was before her rampage at the Nordy's cosmetics counter, when she bitch-slapped the poor beauty consultant who sold the last vial of La Mer Serum out from under her. The woman didn't press charges, but only because Isabelle was her best customer.

Isabelle's anger-management classes have taught her to channel her aggression elsewhere. Her new vice: binge eating. Still, I guess you can say that therapy does work after all.

Oh yeah, and drugs. Lots of wonderful mood-altering prescription pharmaceuticals.

Now I feel safe enough to pretend to be miffed. "I'm sorry. Did I say something funny?"

At first Isabelle just shrugs, then looks from side to side at the others for support. Margot's smirk gives her the courage to go on. "I don't know, but doesn't it strike you that his pleading innocent about his wife's affair is a bit—well, disingenuous?"

My first inclination is to administer my own sucker punch. Instead I feign ignorance. "Gee, I guess I'm not following you. Are you saying he should have been psychic? That he should have deduced what was going on here while he was at work?"

"I think what Isabelle means to say," Margot interjects quickly, "is that the guy obviously has a lot on the ball. Why didn't he pick up on the fact DeeDee was unhappy? My God, she was certainly upset enough to take a lover."

I shake my head, hoping that someone else will jump in on my side, but the others want to see where this is going before they weigh in with their own two cents.

I guess I don't really blame them. Since very little is known about either half of the Perfect Couple, their natural inclination is to side with one of their own kind.

And since DeeDee has all the right equipment, she wins their vote. At least for now.

Wouldn't I feel the same way? I ask myself. Well, yeah, I guess I would . . . if I hadn't seen this very strong, very together guy go to pieces in front of my eyes.

"Look, Lyssa, I'm sure Harry is a very nice guy and all," says Brooke gently. "But admit it: you've only heard one side of the story. You—or any of us—don't really know why she left. Heck, for all we know, he beat her every night with a stick—"

I can't believe what I'm hearing. "Oh, come on! The guy's wife leaves him, and now we have him beating her black and blue? Isn't that just a bit—oh, I don't know . . . sexist?"

"Maybe Lyssa has a point," Colleen, our resident romantic, chimes in with that breathy kewpie-doll voice of hers, all wide-eyed innocence. "I guess we shouldn't assume anything one way or the other, if we don't even know the man. Right?"

The rest of them lean forward expectantly.

Cha-*ching!* The conversation has come around to where I'd hoped. Silently I bless the fact that Colleen is once again attending our meetings (but only because she's finally weaned herself from the notion that McGuyver, her three-year-old son, still needs to be breast-fed), and I go in for the close. "Hey, I've got an idea. Why don't I arrange a little get-together tomorrow? You know, we can all meet for coffee, and you all can get to know him better."

Their slight nods are casual enough, but the sly smiles that slip onto their faces for a mere nanosecond speak volumes.

Only Margot is still wary. "Well . . . I guess that will be okay. His son is the same age as my Laurel, and he seems polite enough. Although, considering how absent his father has been in the past, I assume his manners are his mother's doing."

To keep from reacting to her remark, I look down at the marble floor and focus on its dizzying herringbone pattern. I hope I don't throw up before I can think of an answer that won't blow this for Harry. The fact that Harry is a man—and a very handsome one at that—makes him catnip to this group of women who, by the time the last mojito has been poured, will readily admit that their sex lives leave a lot to be desired.

Well, Harry is certainly desirable.

Before I have a chance to answer Margot, Tammy mutters, "If you think DeeDee is some kind of Miss Manners, you're wrong. Admit it, Margot, the only time that woman ever said two words to any of us was when she wanted something. I for one think she's a very cold fish."

"Well, she warmed up to someone. Ha! I wish we knew who he is," Brooke says slyly.

I can feel Margot's back stiffen. "That's just my point. We don't know anything at all, about either of them. So why stick our noses in their business now? I mean, for all we know, it may be one of our husbands she's sleeping with."

For the second time this evening, the room is dead silent. Warily we all glance at each other as we contemplate this crazy thought.

Then Isabelle snickers again.

One by one, our giggles join her cackle as we all hit on the same vision:

DeeDee Wilder, Paradise Heights's ice queen, trading handsome Harry for one of the other husbands whose sexual prowess at least one of us thinks she can vouch for.

Or, more honestly, couldn't vouch for if her life depended on it.

9

"Men always want to be a woman's first love.
Women like to be a man's last romance."

—Oscar Wilde

Wednesday, 6 Nov., 9:06 a.m.

I've arranged for the meet-and-greet to take place the next morning after school drop-off, at the Paradise Heights Starbucks. For some stupid reason I seem more nervous about it than Harry, who laughs off my suggestion that we rendezvous earlier than the nine o'clock appointment time so that we can commandeer enough chairs in the primo spot, a windowed nook.

"In fact," he says much too casually, "I may be running a little late. Why don't you save me a seat near you?"

I bite my lip to keep from reacting like an overbearing mother whose first-grader has made the inevitable pronouncement that from now on he plans on walking to school without her.

Unlike Harry, I fully comprehend the importance of this first impression to his future here in the Heights. Thus far, though, playing hard to get has worked in his favor, so maybe he knows what he's doing after all.

Still, my heart flutters when I get there and realize that everyone has arrived but Harry. My friends try to keep their expressions blank, but I feel an undercurrent of excitement. They are as giddy as sophomore schoolgirls on a first date with the football team's captain.

Although it has not yet been determined if Harry is friend or foe, full war paint has been applied. (What, did they all stop by Benefit for makeovers first?) And unlike me, all of them have forgone the usual morning attire—yoga pants and hoodies—for slim designer jeans and fitted jackets over tight tees. What better occasion is there to show off the results of a three-day-a-week Bikram yoga regime than a coffee date with the neighborhood DILF?

Each of my friends is sipping her usual poison. For Brooke, it's a nonfat green chai latte, while Isabelle guiltily tucks into a fully loaded mocha Frappuccino. Tammy is apparently already on her second double cappuccino; and Colleen, a follower even down to her choice of brew, mimics alpha-diva Margot's pick: a grande caramel macchiato.

I pray that Harry gets here soon, before they are too hyped up to pay him his due.

Today I am too nervous for my usual triple venti vanilla nonfat latte, and settle for a Calm tea instead. Thank goodness only Brooke notices this. I expect she'll tease me unmercifully when she and I regroup later this afternoon at after-school pickup, when we'll do our own postgame analysis of Harry's audition.

I've just sat down with my tea when Harry makes his entrance. He is a study in casual elegance: white shirt under a V-neck cashmere pullover, and khakis with a razor-sharp crease. Does he hear the involuntary chorus of admiring sighs that greets him? I'm guessing not. Otherwise he'd be running for his life instead of sauntering over with that confident grin.

As I jump up to make the necessary introductions, my cup of tea tilts and splatters my hoodie. Ever the gentleman, Harry quickly reaches for a spare napkin, but stops short of patting my breast dry.

Margot's smile is wicked. It wouldn't surprise her in the least if a burn mark suddenly appeared, shaped like the letter A.

To the other women, though, Harry is a savior, having brought with him a gift box: cupcakes from the Palo Alto Sprinkles just down the road. Ah, so *that's* why he's late! And knowing my friends' love of this particular treat, it was certainly worth the trip.

"Can't do coffee on an empty stomach. Besides, you girls are skinny enough." He serves up these guilty pleasures with a chuckle before queuing up for his own preferred brew.

I can't help but marvel at his gamesmanship. Beating DeeDee in this messy divorce may mean winning friends and influencing frenemies. And if our little coffee klatch is any indication, both are in abundance here in the Heights.

"*Mmmm*, not bad," murmurs Isabelle. By the way she's eyeing Harry's well-toned backside, I take it she's not talking about the coconut bourbon cupcake she's just wolfed down.

"Right, a real sweetie. What's that saying again? Oh yeah: 'Beware of strangers bearing gifts.'" Only Margot, suspicious as always, refuses to indulge. From her frown, you'd think the cupcakes' icing was sprinkled with polonium-210. To make the point that she won't allow Harry's interview to be, quite literally, a cakewalk, Margot flicks a glazed coconut flake off Isabelle's cheek.

By the time he's back at the table, Margot has nudged her reluctant minions into line. Now they won't dare melt under the heat of his clear blue eyes or the warmth of his smile.

The inquisition begins.

My bet with Harry was that the women would wait at least half an hour before the grilling commenced.

I am wrong. After only fourteen minutes of polite chitchat, in which Harry liberally sprinkles subtle compliments to each woman between questions about their children's ages, the care and feeding of their lawns, and the sports teams their husbands worship, Isabelle murmurs none too subtly, "A shame. About you and DeeDee, I mean."

Harry's smile turns down just slightly at the corners. "Yeah, I think so too. I guess it happens in the best of families."

Colleen takes up the baton. "Is it true that—well, that some-one else was involved?" Then, all doe-eyed innocence, she adds, "Oh! I'm sorry! Look, really, don't feel you have to answer that."

Liar.

If he doesn't answer, they won't trust him.

And if they don't trust him, they won't accept him. *Ever.*

It is Harry's moment of truth, his rite of passage, and doesn't he just know it. His eyes catch mine for a mere nanosecond, as if to say *BRING. IT. ON.*

Dear Harry, be careful what you wish for. . . .

"It's funny you should ask, Colleen." Harry shifts slightly closer to her and oh-so-gently grazes her little finger with his own, creating the kind of intimacy that this perennial sports widow with three hyperactive sons and an obsession with ro-mance novels has only dreamt about. "Since—well, since she left me, I've been wondering the same thing myself."

Brooke's perfect pout falls open. Her disappointment is obvi-ous. "Then you don't know *for sure*?"

He gives Colleen's hand a light pat before turning those pierc-ing baby-blues on Brooke.

"No, Brooke, I can't say that I do. All I know is that she—*we*—quit talking about a month ago. I don't mean that we stopped chitchatting about the usual stuff: the kids, finances, you know, those 'Hi, honey, how was your day?' comments. But one day those really deep conversations we both lived for *just went away*." As he looks down at his coffee, the women exchange glances, and I know why. Harry Wilder has just presented the ultimate fantasy:

A husband who actually wants to have a two-way conversation.

"At first I just assumed she was a bit preoccupied. Temple has just started kindergarten, and now that Jake's in the eighth grade, all of a sudden he's discovered girls." Tammy, Brooke, and I chuckle appreciatively. We all have boys in middle school, and have seen a big change in their behavior. "But DeeDee's never been one to complain. She'll ask for help only when she's done everything she can on her own. Frankly, that's one of the things I love about her. I assume you noticed that about her too."

The women smile and nod absently, then drop their heads guiltily. The truth is that none of us were ever close to DeeDee. In fact, just hearing Harry talk so lovingly about the woman renowned for her frigid air makes him even more of a saint in our eyes.

"Of course, I assumed that eventually she'd mention whatever was bothering her. But she never did. Little did I know that I was the problem."

"Surely there must have been some telltale signs. There always are. . . ." Even as Tammy says this, it's obvious to everyone at the table that she is grasping at straws.

"You know, I've thought about that. Were there times she was sad? Or angry? Did she leave me notes, asking to talk things out? No. She's always grace under pressure."

Translation: DeeDee's frozen smile was a Kabuki mask that never came off. Not even for her husband.

"As for our lovemaking—well, quite frankly, if I were to describe it, I guess I'd say we went at it like teenagers. Particularly after a business trip . . . Sorry, I'm speaking out of school here. Oh, what the hell. I'm among friends, right?" Sheepishly he looks down at his coffee. Everyone's eyes focus on the way his large, broad hands easily envelop his mug. I can just imagine what they are thinking: *Large digits, large dick . . .*

To break the spell, I ask the question that is on everyone's lips: "How exactly did she walk out?"

"It happened on Halloween. I'd had a low-grade fever that morning, so I came home from work earlier than usual. My garage door opener wasn't working, so I parked in the driveway and tried the front door, but it was locked. I let myself in through the back. At first I didn't hear anything at all. Only when I got into the bedroom did I realize that DeeDee was in the shower, with . . . with . . . ." He stops for a moment, closes his eyes, and rubs his forehead. Obviously, the memory of the day still leaves him dumbfounded.

Well, that's too bad, because the suspense is killing the rest of us. Even the ever-snide Isabelle is enthralled. I can tell because she's stopped midgobble on her third cupcake to choke out, "With whom?"

The spell is broken. He looks over at her, surprised. "*Whom?* No one. She was alone. But she was fully dressed. Crying. Sobbing in the shower. It was as if she'd—*cracked* somehow."

In her *clothes*?

That was the very last thing the others expected—or wanted—to hear. Out of her clothes would have been more like it.

And in some other man's arms.

Especially since they now know a shower was involved. . . .

No one says anything at first. It is Brooke who finally breaks the awkward silence. "So, what did she say when . . . you know, when she finally came out?"

"You mean, when I *pulled* her out? That she loved me. That she knew I loved her too, but that she was no longer—how did she put it? Oh yeah, that she was no longer *in love* with me. That she could no longer pretend that everything was just fine, or that she was living her life on terms that worked for her. That something—something *big*—was missing. And it would always be that way if she didn't get out. *Now.* Just what the hell does that mean, exactly?"

He's addressing that not to any one of us, but to all of us. If we were to be honest with him, with ourselves, we'd have to admit that we've all been there at one time or another.

"Listen, I want to thank all of you for just—well, for listening to me go on like this." We see the pain in his frown. "Maybe if DeeDee and I had had conversations like this, even a month ago, we might still be together. I guess it's not fair to blame her for something I didn't do well myself."

Harry doesn't exactly tear up, but his eyes are glassy. He is unsteady as he rises to his feet. The comforting pats he receives from Tammy and Isabelle assure him that he has won the redemption he seeks. Colleen and Brooke actually jump up and give him kisses on his cheek.

He is still their Perfect Guy. Better yet, he's now their friend too.

Only Margot is still a nonbeliever. "Truly touching. But I, for one, would be interested in hearing DeeDee's side of it."

The others flinch at her bluntness, but Harry smiles as if she's paid him a compliment. "You and me both. But I guess that's wishful thinking on my part. Because, despite what happened, I'm still in love with her."

Her response is a shrug.

Time is up. Harry has given it his best shot, but the reality is that Margot refuses to fold. And because she insists on full submission from her minions, eventually they will find reasons to dislike him too.

Just when I think all is lost, he turns to Margot with a sideways glance. "Wait a minute. You said your last name is Hardaway? Wow, then you must be the mom of that adorable kid Laurel."

Bull's-eye!

Margot blushes. A genuine smile breaks out on her lips. Truly, there is no greater sound to a mother's ear than praise for her offspring. And Harry's compliment is all the sweeter because Laurel, the leader of the middle school's posse of mean girls, nets her mother more enemies than friends. (In that regard, the nut does not fall far from the tree.) "You *know* Laurel?"

"Of course. We *are* talking about the Laurel who cheers at the middle-school boys' basketball games, right? My Temple thinks she's the cutest one on the squad. Jake is the team captain, you know. In fact, I think he's got a bit of a crush on her. Of course, he probably wouldn't like it that I let that out of the bag."

"Oh . . . yes, that's my Laurel. And, no! I won't say anything about Jake. And, um, feel free to invite Laurel over anytime. To babysit Temple, I mean." Jake is the class hunk. Even Margot knows that. The last thing she'd want to do is throw a wet blanket on her daughter's crush. How would that play out in Laurel's twice-weekly therapy sessions?

Mine is the last SUV to leave the lot. I've just pulled up to the light when my cell phone rings. I don't recognize the number, but the voice is unmistakably Harry's. "So, what do you think? Did I pass inspection?"

"I'll say." I shift uncomfortably in my seat. "As of this moment, you officially walk on water. At least as far as my board is concerned."

"Yeah? Great. Then you think they bought it?"

" 'Bought it?' Bought what?"

"The bit about the shower."

"That wasn't true?" I'm so shocked that I almost ram the BMW in front of me. "But—but it sounded so real!"

"Good, because it was supposed to. What, do you actually think DeeDee would dare jump in the tub in designer duds? No way. Total fabrication. But what the hell, I had to do something to warm up that crowd. Those girlfriends of yours are a frigid bunch. And I wasn't counting on a heckler to boot."

"Yeah, Margot can be so obnoxious sometimes. But, Harry, why did you do it?"

His pause is so long that I start to think the cell connection is broken. "Because DeeDee is going for full custody, as well as the house. I can't let her win. I *won't* let her."

Harry is right. All is fair in love and divorce. Even ugly lies, which, in this community, spread quicker than kudzu during a wet and steamy Georgia summer. Now, even if DeeDee does win in court, she'll always wonder why she's getting so many pitying sidelong glances from the neighbors she has always snubbed.

"But what if one of them runs into DeeDee and brings up what you said about her?"

"Seriously, do you think any of them would have the guts to do that now?"

No, come to think of it. Not after they saw the pain in Harry's eyes.

And certainly not now that Margot is his new best friend.

I can't help but feel just a tiny bit jealous. . . .

"I owe you big, Lyssa. I presume you want to be paid in cupcakes?"

"You wish. No, you can't get off the hook that easily. For your penance, you'll have to cover Olivia one afternoon."

He signs off with a laugh, but I know the morning has taken its toll on him too.

I glance down at the dashboard clock. What? We were sitting in there for *only forty-eight minutes*? This little outing has taken a year off my life. I am sweating as if in early menopause. A shower would feel good right about now—

I don't think I'll get into one again without thinking about DeeDee in soaking wet Phillip Lim cashmere, thanks to a standard feature in all Paradise Heights master baths: the Hansgrohe Raindance Royale 350 showerhead, with its fourteen-inch face and air-injection technology.

10

"Sometimes I wonder if men and women really suit
each other. Perhaps they should live next
door and just visit now and then."

—Katharine Hepburn

Monday, 11 Nov., 1:23 p.m.

So, what would you guess is Harry's favorite color?"

Tammy's question seems innocent enough—except that we are in Nordstrom next to a counter filled with men's boxer briefs. In one hand she holds a box of 2(x)ist's electric blue soy-fiber "comfort trunks," while the other lovingly strokes a pair of C-IN2 bamboo mesh trunks that are the color of a Mexican sunset, or *rumba*, if you go by the color on its box.

It also claims that the trunks have something called a "Trophy Shelf Pouch™ for a bigger, better profile," whatever that means. I'm assuming Tammy doesn't know either, since the word *trophy* has never crossed her lips when describing her Charlie's penis.

Inchworm has, however.

"How the hell would I know what color he likes? And why exactly are you buying underwear for Harry, anyway?" I try not to sound so upset, but really, I am disgusted. It's been almost a week since the Starbucks meet-and-greet. Since then, each member of the Paradise Heights Women's League board has made

Harry her very own pet project. While Isabelle thoughtfully picks up little items for him at the grocery store and Colleen leaves casseroles in his fridge, Margot indulges Laurel's crush on Jake by sharing carpool duty with Harry, and Brooke is his new tennis doubles partner.

Tammy, on the other hand, has become his domestic goddess Friday. Thus far this has included rearranging his kitchen and bathroom cabinets.

Obviously she has worked her way into the master bedroom too. Which makes me wonder: Does she have intimate knowledge of Harry's need for a Trophy Shelf Pouch?

"Seriously, Lyssa, I'm doing the poor guy a favor. Why, you just *wouldn't* believe the shape his briefs are in."

"Just how would you know what shape they're in, pray tell?"

"Well, um . . . yesterday I happened to be over there when he was doing laundry—"

"I thought he had a part-time housekeeper for that."

"I guess she used to do it—before he let her go." She leans in conspiratorially. "He gave her notice on Friday. Something about proving to DeeDee's attorney that he doesn't need domestic help." She giggles at this folly. "Of course, that was before he realized a blue pen had found its way into the wash with all of his white boxers and T-shirts—"

"If you really want to do him a favor, why not just replace what he had? My God, Tammy, he's a securities attorney, not a performer at Chippendales!"

"Heck, what would be the fun in that?" She puts down her packages with a pout. "Hey, what's with you lately? You seem so grumpy."

Grumpy, huh? Yeah, well, that is the least of it. More like tired (since Halloween, Olivia has refused to go to bed before ten because she is now afraid of dementors) and worried (Mickey's prim bitch of a teacher thinks his practical jokes have gotten out of hand, and has recommended that he be tested for ADHD).

And to top it all off, I'm horny. Ted has worked late every day these past couple of weeks, and usually slips into bed in the early morning hours when I am already fast asleep.

Maybe that's why I'm a little hurt that Harry's previously undivided attention has been diverted to my board. Practically overnight he has gone from pathetic gossip fodder to the DILF du jour. Not only has he made himself available for coffee klatches and carpooling, but apparently my friends have been granted an open invitation to cry on his strong, broad shoulders whenever their marital problems become too heavy a burden.

Tammy rummages through stacks of boxer briefs. "Did you know that Isabelle is finally off her diet?"

"Wow, that's great! It's about time she got the message!" *Diet* is the board's polite euphemism for Isabelle's postmeal upchucking. While the majority of Isabelle's friends follow a policy of don't ask, don't tell, and don't listen to what is happening in the adjoining bathroom stall, for some time now I've been begging Isabelle to seek help with her low self-esteem.

"Yeah, well, he certainly knew the right way to put it so that she'd listen."

"Wow, good for Lyle!" In the past, Isabelle's husband has been less than supportive. Make that passive-aggressive. Why else would he pucker up for a wolf whistle every time some lithe young body in a string bikini crosses his path?

"*Lyle?* Don't make me laugh. Silly, it was our *Harry* who turned her around. He convinced her that men love women with a little meat on their bones, and that she's perfectly beautiful." Tammy sighs. "I just *love* that man. He is *so* intuitive about the female psyche!"

Our Harry? No, he is *my* Harry.

Or he *was* mine, and mine alone, until I introduced him to these shameless hussies. . . .

"Imagine that! So he knows how men think? Gee, I wonder why that is." I know I sound sarcastic, but I hate seeing my own knight in shining armor attending to other damsels in distress.

Oh, sure, I'm glad he was able to gain my friends' approval and empathy. But I never anticipated they'd take over the care and feeding of the Wilder family.

Or that he'd take to it so eagerly, like a newborn babe to a teat.

Or, in this case, to ten cosmetically inflated ones.

Nothing I say shames Tammy from her goal: moving to the head of this pack of über-nurturing she-wolves. She asks the Nordy shopboy to ring up not only the blue and the orange trunks, but five other pairs as well, a veritable rainbow of sensual microfibers.

While she plucks ribbed pima cotton wife-beaters from the T-shirt bin (two sizes too small for Harry, I'm sure), I substitute a pair of good old-fashioned Hanes boxer briefs for the most shocking pair in the pile, a see-through leopard-patterned "bong thong."

Now, *that* is the true meaning of friendship.

2:02 p.m.

There is still a full hour before after-school pickup, plenty of time to marinade the shrimp for our dinner tonight. But just as we pass Harry's house, Tammy veers into his driveway. She can hardly wait to present her little treasures to him.

"I don't think it's a very good idea for us to barge in without calling." In truth, I feel a little uncomfortable with that concept for two reasons. In the first place, since the women's constant hovering began, Harry has been a bit distant to me, almost cold.

And second, I'd hate for Harry to think I had anything to do with Tammy's questionable gifts.

But Tammy dismisses me with a wave of a hand. Her expertly manicured nails are too long and too red, like talons that have nabbed some delectable prey and won't let go. "Oh, he won't mind. Besides, I do it all the time."

Before I can say "Count me out," she has leaped from the car and is standing at the front door. She tries the knob, but it is locked. Five minutes of leaning on his doorbell does nothing to change that fact, so she saunters over to the side of the garage where, after stepping out of her Manolos, she jumps up onto one of his garbage cans in order to peer into a window high overhead. I cringe at the thought that a neighbor may drive by.

Or, worse yet, Harry himself.

"That's funny. His car is inside—"

Just then, Colleen comes out of her pseudo-Tudor across the street, Le Creuset casserole dish in hand. But the smile on her face turns into a disapproving scowl when she notices Tammy perched on the trash can, and me standing beside it.

With as much dignity as she can muster, Tammy jumps down onto the stamped concrete driveway. "Gee, Colleen, imagine meeting you here." The sarcasm in her voice is palpable.

"Ha. Well, I'm not surprised at all that you'd be parked on Harry's doorstep. From what I hear from Brooke, you've practically moved in. I didn't realize she'd meant into the garage. Isn't it a bit crowded in there, what with Temple's puppy and all?"

Ouch.

Tammy goes bright red under her Clarins Intense Bronze self-tanning tint. "That bitch! She of all people has no room to talk. Why, she was over here all day yesterday, and the day before that too."

That's when I remember that yesterday Brooke begged off from the monthly class-mom meeting at the school, supposedly because she had a headache. "Really? She was here? Just how would you know that?"

"Because I can see Harry's house from mine." She points across the street and far up the hill where, behind a copse of leafy heritage oaks, we can barely glimpse a high bathroom window of Tammy's perpetually remodeled Midcentury Modern monstrosity.

I shake my head in disbelief. "I don't get it: you stand in your shower stall all day and spy on Harry?"

Tammy's expression changes from triumph to guilt. "I'm not exactly spying. I happen to glance out my window occasionally—"

"That window is pretty high. Wouldn't you have to climb up onto the toilet seat?"

Tammy opens her mouth to say something, then thinks twice and shuts it again.

Colleen isn't interested in any more lame excuses. Time is fleeting, especially when you have three boys who have to be shuttled to different after-school programs simultaneously. She dives under the high privet hedge by the front door, searching until she spots one of those faux rocks for hiding keys. *"Aha!"* She has struck gold.

But then something else catches her attention. She sets down the rock and the casserole in order to pull a powder blue Ladies' Schwinn bike out from behind the hedge.

We all recognize it as Margot's. Did she hide it so that we would not guess that she is inside with Harry?

Tammy and Colleen exchange knowing glances. As for me, I am numbed by shock. Is Harry having an affair—with *Margot*?

I may not want to know the answer to that, but Colleen is bound and determined to catch them red-handed. In one giant leap she's up on the stoop, balancing the casserole dish in one hand as she fits the key into the lock with the other.

She is still fidgeting with it when suddenly the door opens.

Harry peers out. He is cradling Lucky, Temple's wriggling Airedale pup, in the crook of his arm. Seeing that it's us, he forces his lips into a smile. When his gaze gets to me, he does a double take and his blue eyes cloud over.

Hey, don't blame me. This was not *my idea. . . .*

But I can tell he's not buying it. I sigh. Granted, I could just walk home from here and by doing so avoid the knowledge that my idol has clay feet. Too late. I'll just suck it up for now.

He puts an index finger to his lips and points to his Bluetooth headset, then motions for us to enter. As we troop in after him, Tammy's and Colleen's eyes scan the room for any sign of Margot. Nothing. However, I'm somewhat pleased to note that the whole living room has become a playroom. DeeDee's Ethan Allen collection now serves as a super-size Bratz showroom.

". . . Yeah, right, Edwin. . . . Yeah, sure I agree, go for it. . . . Yeah, I said I don't care, just do it." Harry shrugs indifferently as he speaks, but he is pacing the floor, a ball of nervous energy. I'm glad his divorce attorney finally has good news for him, because thus far Bethany has been wiping the floor with him. "Look, I have someone at the door. Gotta go. . . . No, I went in yesterday, but I'm working from home today. . . . Yeah, Bradley's been on my back about it, but that's the way it's got to be these days. It's my turn for carpool." The steely grin is back, for our benefit, not Edwin's, I'm sure. "If I go in for a few hours tomorrow, I'll stop by."

He clicks off the headset, then tosses it onto a cushioned chair already loaded with Barbies and stuffed animals. "Well, ladies, nice to see you—and to see you *again,* Colleen."

She colors a bit. "Oh, well, when I dropped off those strawberries from my garden, I did mention that I had something else for you to, ah, munch on later."

From her seductive tone, it is obvious to everyone that it was not the casserole that she previously had in mind.

Not to be outdone, Tammy holds up her bag of goodies. "I come bearing gifts, too."

"Oh? Gee, you shouldn't have." Warily he takes the bag, but he doesn't dare look inside. Lucky sees this as the perfect time to make his escape. He bounds out of Harry's arm and skitters out of the room.

"It was the least I could do. After our little accident in the laundry and all."

"What little accident?" Colleen can barely hide her jealousy.

Harry turns beet red. "She . . . I . . . well, I guess you could say that I got distracted. Wrong washer setting." He looks pointedly at Tammy, but he carefully avoids my eyes.

Oh . . . my . . . God. Maybe he does have something to hide.

From the kitchen comes the sound of the back screen door creaking shut. Harry must have heard it too, because he stares in that direction.

I take it Margot has made her getaway.

Ah, so that's *how it is. . . .*

The others are too enthralled with their host to have heard it. Nevertheless, I am repulsed. All I can think about is getting out of there too. "Wow, look at the time! I've got to go pick up my kids. . . ."

Despite this very broad hint, neither Colleen nor Tammy is ready to go—at least, not until Margot comes out of hiding. "You haven't seen Margot, have you?" they ask in unison.

Harry's only chance to divert them is to open Tammy's bag and pull out one of the boxes. With as much enthusiasm as he can muster, he murmurs, "Wow, look at what we have here!"

Tammy swells up with pride. "Oh, just a little something I thought you'd like." Of course Colleen is intrigued—and jealous.

The look on Harry's face as he pulls a pair of lime green Mansilk trunks from its box is priceless.

Colleen's *oohs* and *aahs* drip with acid. If Harry is to fit into them, he'll have to skip her casserole. Yep, Tammy has won this hand.

He shoots me a look of desperation, but I ignore it. When I arranged his meet-and-greet, I had assumed he was looking for friends, not lovers. Harry Wilder has made his bed—apparently both figuratively and literally—so now he can lie in it.

Alone, or with Margot. Or Colleen, or Tammy.

Or all three, for that matter.

I also slip out the door—but not fast enough to miss hearing Tammy ask: "Hey, Harry, how about modeling them for us?"

2:33 p.m.

I am just entering my house when I realize I'm being followed. I turn around to find Lucky staring up at me. "Had to get out of there too, eh, fella?"

I scoop him up and get a tongue bath by way of thanks. The boys both have after-school practice, but it's my day to pick up Temple along with Olivia. Lucky will ride along and keep me company until I drop him and Temple back at Harry's. By then my lovesick friends will have come to their senses and rescued their offspring before they are shuttled off to mandatory after-school daycare.

3:41 p.m.

I am right. Harry comes out alone, obviously relieved that Lucky hasn't been dognapped by one of his new fangirls. I try to keep Olivia from bounding into the house along with Lucky and his little mistress, but she's too fast for me.

"Don't worry. She's welcome to stay." Despite the invitation, Harry's smile is forced.

"Oh, um . . . well, I'd hate to put you out. I mean, if you are expecting more company. Or something." I couldn't help it. When I said "or something," I almost spit out the words.

" 'Or something'? Just what exactly does that mean?"

"Nothing. Nothing at all. It was a joke." I get back into the car. But before I can start the engine, he has poked his head through my window.

"Yeah. A joke. *I'm* the joke, right? Of the whole neighborhood?"

If I start the car now, I'll take his head with me. As tempting as that is, I take a deep breath instead. "Well, Harry, if that's the case, you've got no one to blame but yourself."

"*What?* Jesus, Lyssa, I can't believe you have the nerve to say that to me—"

"Nerve? *Me?* I can't believe *you* have the nerve to—*to use me the way you did*!"

Angrily he slams his fist on my hood and heads for the house. Then he stops halfway and turns around. He is not through giving me a piece of his mind.

Too bad. I've had enough. But before I can pull away, he opens the passenger door and climbs in. "You had no right to say that to me. Not you, of all people." His words are deliberate, his tone ominous. "And, lady, you've got some nerve, sitting and pretending to be so innocent when you pretty much pimped me out to that horny pack of she-wolves you call friends."

"I did—*what?* Let me get this straight: now you're accusing me of—" I can't believe my ears. "Get real, Harry. You are the one who tells them that they're pretty, and that their kids are adorable. Heck, you even listen to them bitch about their husbands! What women *wouldn't* fall in love with you? So don't blame me when they do." I can't help it. I tear up. "Oh, and by the way, when I suggested you could be friendlier, *that wasn't an invitation to sleep with them.*"

"Are you crazy?" He looks me straight in the eye. "Who said

that about me? Oh, let me guess: that nymphomaniac Tammy."

"No, not exactly—"

"Don't cover up for her. Damn it, she's not even very subtle about it. The only reason she offered to straighten out my cupboards was so that she could climb up on a ladder in those low-slung tight-ass jeans. And every time I turn around, she's trying to get me out of my clothes. I can't prove it, but I swear she deliberately put a pen in the wash with my underwear." He shakes his head wearily. "Hell, maybe I *should* take her up on her offer and screw her brains out. It might actually calm her down. At the very least she'd finally shut up about it."

That stops me cold. If Tammy were already sleeping with him, she certainly wouldn't be talking about it, to anyone.

Neither would Colleen, for that matter. Or Brooke or Isabelle. Sure, they all desire Harry. But only because he's a nice, safe fantasy, and not some dirty reality that could blow up in their faces.

"I do believe you, Harry." When I look up at him, I'm happy to see he is relieved. "But—"

"But what?"

"Well, I—really, we *all* happened to see Margot's bike behind your bushes. We assumed that she was inside. With you. Then, when the back door opened and shut while we were in the house, I thought she'd slipped out. . . ."

Harry's face is blank. Then all of a sudden he begins to laugh.

"What's so funny?"

"That must have been when Lucky got loose. As for the bike, it's still there. Go ahead, take a look."

I jump out of the car and look behind the bush. He's right.

"Did she just leave it here?"

"Margot? Hell, no. Laurel brought it over. When she babysat for Temple yesterday. When I got home from work, it was dark, so I drove her home instead of letting her ride it. She's picking it up after cheerleading practice."

Suddenly I feel like a fool. "Harry, I'm so sorry. Please, please forgive me for doubting you. And I hope you believe me when I say that I didn't know my friends would—well, that they'd be so enthralled by you."

"That's a polite word for it." He smiles finally. "Sometimes Isabelle looks at me as if I'm a cupcake. One with *a lot* of icing. And every time Colleen shoves another casserole down my throat, I feel as if I'm being fattened up for the slaughter. Lyssa, honestly, these women are *starved* for sex."

"No, Harry. Really, they're starved for love." I glance away. I could be describing myself, but I don't want Harry to know that. "Well, look at it this way. If you can keep things on an even keel with them, you'll have a wonderful cheering section at the divorce hearing."

"That's the problem. I don't think they want to be friends on my terms."

"Then that's their loss. Stick to your guns. Just be polite about it." I pat his hand gently. "I guess you should get out now, though."

"Why? We've still got another twenty minutes before basketball practice is over. Frankly, this is the most peace and quiet I've had in the past week." He closes his eyes wearily. "Your friends are relentless."

"I know. That's why I think you should go. If Tammy notices you sitting in here, I'll never hear the end of it."

"Tammy? Shit, *where*?" He looks up and down the street. "I don't see her car."

"That's because—oh, never mind. You wouldn't believe me if I told you." I peer out the window and up the hill. "You'll just have to trust me on this one."

11

"When a man opens a car door for his wife,
it's either a new car or a new wife."

—Prince Philip, Duke of Edinburgh

Tuesday, 12 Nov., 12:21 p.m.

Excuse me? EXCUSE ME? Are you going to just leave that there?" I've sidled up to Crabby Old Neighbor Lady at the moment she least expected it: as her mangy mutt takes a crap in our yard.

She's been caught red-handed. But does she apologize? No. Nor does she look away in shame or fear.

But she does nod and say, "Yep. Have a great day," before strolling away with her dog, leaving me to clean up the mess.

"Hey, I presume you know I have three kids—"

She stops to cackle. "Of course I do. I can hear your passel of brats even with my hearing aid turned off."

"What? My kids aren't brats! And even if they were, that's no excuse for you to walk your dog over here so he can do his business! *Two wrongs don't make a right, you know!*"

But I am talking to myself. She makes it a point to tap off her hearing aid as she walks off. I am left nudging dog poop under a bush with a stick when I hear my name being called.

I turn toward where the voice is coming from: the vintage candy-apple-red convertible 280SL parked across the street.

Sitting behind the wheel is an older woman, late fifties, who wears dark glasses and a scarf over a cloud of platinum curls. She waves at me frantically.

Of course, I go over.

Only when I'm halfway there do I realize that she is my old nemesis: Patti-with-an-i.

Fate has delivered me the truest test of my resolve.

Seeing me pause, she hisses, "Lyssa, please! PLEASE! It's about your father."

Of course it is. It's happened a few times over the years: she does a drive-by in the hope of cornering me, of forcing me to talk about my father.

This time I know I must.

I climb into the passenger seat; the leather is hard and cracked. Once upon a time this was the pride and joy of Patti-with-an-i. I took a few joyrides in it myself, on those few occasions when, while hanging around outside my parents' house, I'd noticed her cruising by.

Of course, now I know she'd come in the hope of running into my father. It was an ongoing effort to coerce him to run away with her. Until the day he did, I was the consolation prize: someone who, however unwittingly, gave her the scoop on my parents' whereabouts, their fights, and their frustrations with each other.

Without the ammo I supplied, would my parents' relationship have survived?

Probably not. But tell that to a ten-year-old who is mourning the loss of her father's love.

"What is it, Patti? What do you want?" I sit up straight. I realize my father sits where I am now, and even the thought of that is too close for comfort. Even with the distance of time and space separating us, I don't want to touch him in any way, shape, or form.

"Did your mother tell you?" She turns to look me in the eye. I take some satisfaction in the knowledge that Patti hasn't aged well. I remember her as a buxom free spirit. Some twenty-four years later, what was once unlined and ash-blond is now creased and tarnished. Both body and spirit are sagging, I'm guessing under the weight of my father's plight.

I am far beyond his gravitational pull and have no desire to get sucked into his black hole. "Yeah, I heard. His lung. Good luck with that."

"Lyssa, I'm here because the doctors say he won't last beyond January."

A distant memory comes back to me: the glow of his Marlboros in the dark. Once upon a time the combination of cigarette smoke and Old Spice was my security blanket. It meant Dad was home. There with me, because he loved me.

But no, he loved Patti-with-an-i even more.

I grit my teeth to ward off any knee-jerk remorse. If she expects me to tear up, she's mistaken.

"Lyssa, he loves you. He needs to see you before he dies." She shoves a card into my hand. On it is scrawled an address and a telephone number.

It's her turn to face facts. To face me. "Don't talk to me about love! If he loved me, he wouldn't have walked away from me. He wouldn't have forgotten me. But he did." I leap out of the car. "Well, I've forgotten him too."

"You're right, Lyssa. What he did was wrong." Her voice is calm, too sweet, as if once again she's wheedling trust from a ten-year-old. "But two wrongs don't make a right."

I shrug.

Then I do something I hope I won't regret later: scribble our unlisted telephone number on the magnetic notepad suspended on her dashboard and croak out: "Don't call unless it's serious."

She waits a full five minutes after I've slammed the door to the house before driving away. I don't know what she expected. For me to come back out and say I'd changed my mind? That, yes, we'd have that reunion he needed to clear his conscience, to absolve him of his parental sins?

I can't do that.

So instead, I rummage through the basket of toys on the front porch until I find Olivia's little plastic shovel. With it, I scoop the neighbor's dog poop and fling it into her yard.

Then I run back into the house, where I can cry in private. Without my neighbor's eyes peering at me through her thin curtains.

Really, I wail. Loudly, out of control.

For her sake, I hope Crabby Old Neighbor Lady still has her hearing aid turned off.

12

"We waste time looking for the perfect lover,
instead of creating the perfect love."

—Tom Robbins

Wednesday, 13 Nov., 9:22 a.m.

W hat's up with Harry?" Margot is sulking. "He hasn't
returned any of my calls."

"You're telling me. I've been trying to reach him too.
I know he doesn't have the kids tonight, so I've been leaving him
voice mails about playing tennis, then maybe having a drink afterward in the clubhouse." Brooke shrugs and takes a sip of her
'Bucks brew du jour.

Colleen's eyes grow big with concern. "Well, something's got
to be up, or he wouldn't have asked for us all to meet him here."

I bite my tongue to keep from laughing, but I can't let that
pass. "I think you're reading more into it than it really means.
Remember, the guy is juggling a lot of balls right now—"

"Speaking of juggling balls . . ." Tammy is standing behind
me. We all turn around just in time to see her unzip her hoodie.
Underneath it she's wearing a baby-blue tight T-shirt emblazoned with the words HARRY'S HAREM. "I had these made up
for us! Aren't they adorable?" She lifts up a bag filled with the
shirts and starts handing them around. "I figure we can all be
wearing them when he comes in. Whattaya think?"

While the others laugh and squeal with delight, I stare at the one tossed in my lap and think, *Hell no, ain't no way . . .*

"Girls, wow, you're all here. Thanks for coming." Harry smiles genially, but there's something different about him, an air of detachment.

"Darn, Harry, no cupcakes this morning?" Isabelle is truly disappointed.

Harry takes her hand, drawing her eyes to his own baby blues. "Darling Isabelle, the last thing you need is a cupcake. We both know that, don't we?"

The gasps from the rest of us warn Isabelle to be on her guard. Her eyes narrow into mere slits of suspicion.

As they should. But does Harry take the hint? Not on your life.

Instead, he continues as if he doesn't have a care in the world. He is in Master-of-the-Universe mode. "Look, girls, you know I love you. But I'm going to level with you. . . ."

As he pauses, the women, unsure as to where he's going with this train of thought, lean in expectantly.

"I haven't been happy with the little 'arrangement' we've got going here." He lets that sink in. "Don't get me wrong. Of course I appreciate all you've done for me. You've been super friends, caring, considerate. For that, I'll be forever in your debt. And I hope I've given as good as I've gotten"—he looks pointedly at Tammy—"so here's what I'm proposing: Carpool is a given, fine. I don't mind being on call a couple of days a week, say Tuesdays for the kindergartners and Fridays for the middle-school guys. But there are a few nonnegotiables too. For instance, no more casual drop-ins at my house. And thanks but no thanks for the offers to do my laundry, rearrange my drawers, or buy me underwear you'd find on a male stripper."

Harry's fans exchange guilty glances. As for Harry, he's emboldened and on a roll: "And, Brooke, fair warning: you break one more tennis date and you can scratch me from your dance card permanently. By the way, I heard your message about playing tonight, but count me out. Since tomorrow is my birthday, my lawyer arranged for DeeDee to take the kids tonight instead, so I'm taking some much-needed me time. You ladies can certainly appreciate that, right? Oh, and, Colleen, puh-leeze, no more casseroles. I know you mean well, but I'm losing my boyish figure, and so is Lucky, since he ends up eating the leftovers."

The muffled yelp from Colleen has everyone else wincing.

Except for Harry. He's practically glowing. "Does everybody understand the new ground rules? Super! Gee, Lyssa, you were right to encourage me to get this off my chest! It feels so good. Hey, which one of you ladies is up for a latte? I'm buying. . . ."

The others turn to me. They don't say a word, but they don't have to. Their stares say it all:

Traitor.

Tammy has something to get off her chest, too. But since she can't yank off her T-shirt in front of all of us—and Harry is making it quite clear he's not interested in a private strip show—she zips up her hoodie and huffs off.

Harry's harem is no more.

11:51 p.m.

The phone is ringing, somewhere far away from my dream about my father showing up at my eleventh birthday party. I feel almost as indignant about this rude awakening as I am about his gift to me: a miniature sports car that looks like Patti's.

Ted, who sleeps like the dead, doesn't even roll over. I sigh and pick up the receiver to hear a muffled groan. "Lyssa . . . it's Harry."

"What . . . who?" I debate whether or not to turn on the light, and decide against it. Instead I grab the phone and move into the hall with it.

"I said . . . it's Harry. Listen, there's been a little—well, I don't know what to call it, exactly. 'Altercation,' I guess."

"Harry, what the heck are you talking about? You're not drunk or anything, are you? What time is it, anyway?"

"No, I'm not drunk! I have no idea of the time. Maybe, I don't know . . . midnight? Look, please, can you come over here? I need your help!"

"You're not making any sense."

"*Just please get over here.* I'm sure the back door is unlocked."

I consider shaking Ted awake, but then I nix that idea. Instead, I get dressed to Ted's snores and slip out of the house as quietly as possible.

11:58 p.m.

Harry is right. Not only is the back door unlocked, it was left wide open. Lucky sits on the stoop. At first he growls when he sees me approach. But as I get within sniffing distance, his tail wags, indicating that I'll be allowed to pass.

I call out Harry's name. "In the foyer," he answers.

Yep, that's where I find him: shackled to the wrought-iron banister with pink fuzzy handcuffs.

"How . . . what . . ." I'm stuttering like a fool, I know.

"Please, Lyssa, you've got to find the key. I've been standing here at least since ten!"

I look around frantically. My eyes are drawn to the mess at the bottom of the stairs, where a big gift box has spilled out all sorts of wonderful things: a vibrator, a whip, a can of whipped cream, edible panties, a pink negligee. . . .

Harry must have had quite a birthday celebration planned.

And with whom? I shouldn't care, but I do.

"Hmmm. . . . Okay, now. Well, where might I find the key?"

"She ran out so fast, I didn't see where she dropped it." He jerks his hand to make the point, but it won't break loose from the banister. "Damn that Tammy! I swear, if I ever see her again, I'll—"

"Wait! *Tammy did this to you?*" I can't believe my ears.

Suddenly his eyes grow wide when he realizes the implication. "No, you don't understand! I know this looks pretty bad, but it's not what you think. We didn't do anything—although I'm guessing that was not her intention."

He tries to move forward, but can't. In frustration, he jerks his hand, only to shout out a curse when it twists painfully. For a moment he closes his eyes. When he's calm again, he looks at me as if I'm his last hope. "I can't stay here all night. And DeeDee is dropping the kids back here right after breakfast. . . . Tammy left through the back door. Maybe she dropped it somewhere in the kitchen. Why don't you start looking in there?"

I nod and do an about-face. I don't see anything that looks like a key on the countertops. Could she have left it in a drawer? I open and close one drawer and cabinet after another. "Look, Harry, I know it's none of my business but . . . why did you let her in here in the first place?"

"Believe me, I thought twice before I did. Who knew she was such a lunatic?" He shivers at the thought. "She rang the bell around nine-thirty. She said she wanted to apologize for any misimpressions she may have given me, that she really appreciated my friendship and hoped there were no hard feelings. In fact, she brought that stupid box over there"—he jerks his head, but shudders instead of looking at it—"it was supposed to be my birthday present. She insisted that I open it while she was still here. What was I supposed to say, no?"

"I guess not." My last resort is to scrounge around on the floor. Just by chance, I happen to look in Lucky's water bowl—

And that's where I see a tiny black key. Triumphantly I snatch it up. "Hey, I think I found it! Gee, Harry, I'm guessing that was an awkward moment. I wonder what the hell she was thinking."

Lucky follows me out, right on my heels. He must think it's a dog biscuit, because he's leaping to snatch it out of my hand.

"You and me both, Lyssa. It shocked the hell out of me at first. The only thing I could think of saying was 'What's this?' How lame is that? She said that she had hoped I was as attracted to her as she was to me. That maybe this would be the start of a different kind of relationship. Or, as she put it, friends with benefits." He sighs and looks at me pointedly. "Hey, do you mind?"

"What?" I've practically gotten Lucky to sit and beg. I just wish I had a reward for him—

"Lyssa, please! The key." He rattles his shackle again.

"Oh! Of course!" I reach over and shove the key into the lock. It takes some jiggling, but finally the cuff springs open.

Harry's groan is part pain, part gratitude. He massages his wrist, then his elbow.

I consider the absurdity of handcuffs wrapped in pink powder puffs before tossing them into the box. "Don't stop now. What happened next?"

"Well . . . I laughed. But she didn't laugh with me. She said she'd been fantasizing about me since the moment we met, that she thought there'd been an obvious attraction on both our parts, and she wasn't above having it include a little sex on the side. Then the next thing I know, she's backed me up against the stair and her tongue is down my throat!"

"She's got nerve!" I'm truly livid. "How dare she! What a slut! What a—*whore*!"

Okay, maybe I'm overreacting. I have my answer from the quizzical look on Harry's face. So that he can't see how hot my cheeks are getting, I busy myself gathering up Tammy's sex toys and stuffing them back in the box. "So, what did you do then?"

"Of course I shoved her off." A sad look comes over his face. "Lyssa, it was like something out of high school. *She just broke down.* When she quit sobbing, she asked me what was wrong with her, why I didn't find her desirable. I didn't know what to say, so I told her that of course she was desirable, but that I wasn't looking for an affair, just a friendship."

He sits down on the stairs and shakes his head. "Then she started talking about how lonely it is to be in a neighborhood like this, where you can see all the love and the joy in the houses around you. How she likes to walk at night, when she can look through the big picture windows at the families gathered around the dining room table or watching TV together, and how she and Charlie have been trying so hard to have kids and can't conceive. . . . Well, of course I felt sorry for her. I put my arm around her shoulders, and the next thing I know, she's all over me again. I had to push her away. That's when it dawned on me that she wanted me to be her personal sperm donor."

"Wow, so she's that desperate to have a kid!" I shake my head sadly. "But how did you get shackled to the banister?"

"At first she denied it, but she finally came around to admitting it. She said that Charlie refuses to consider adopting, or even a sperm donor. He insists on leaving it up to fate. You know—if it happens, great; if not, then it wasn't meant to be. But she can't live with that. She promised no one would ever know, and there would be no strings attached. She'd even sign an agreement relieving me of any legal responsibilities for the child. When I said I'd pass on that dubious honor, she got angry. Told me I was a fool not to take her up on her offer. Then she called me a selfish man-ho who had just been leading her on. By then I'd had enough. I told her she was too desperate and too horny to ever be my type."

I wince when he says that. Considering Tammy's pride, I can only imagine how much that must have hurt her.

"Well, then she called me a stuck-up prick and cast some pretty cruel aspersions on my manhood—none of which I feel like repeating right now. That was when I shoved all that stuff back into the box and told her to take it and get out." He shook his head at the memory of it all. "She noticed I had my hand on the banister and, stupid me, I didn't realize she still had those god-awful fuzzy cuffs in her hand. The next thing I know, my hand is shackled to the rail. I was yelling at her to let me go, but she just laughed and said, 'Good luck explaining this to DeeDee and your kids.' And that's when Lucky bit her. Grabbed hold of her ankle and wouldn't let go. I guess he realized I was angry with her, and that got him upset. The next thing I know, she's hightailing it out of here." He nods at Jake's hockey stick, which is propped up against the banister. "For a good hour I didn't notice it was within reach. I used it to knock my BlackBerry off the foyer table. It's just long enough to do the trick, but it took me another hour to nudge it within reach. For once I'm happy Jake is too lazy to put his equipment in the garage."

It's funny, and yet so pathetic at the same time. Poor Tammy! It makes me sad to think of her twisted attempt to get pregnant by using Harry.

Suddenly Harry's eyes go dark. "Oh, shit! What if she blabs about this and DeeDee gets wind of it? Tammy can spin this in such a way that I might never see my kids again—"

I shake my head. "I don't think you have to worry about that. Frankly, I don't think Tammy would broadcast this and risk having Charlie dump her over it."

"I see what you mean. And, of course, she's betting I won't say anything to anyone either. Because of my divorce." As the fear drains from his face, sadness takes its place. "I guess my speech yesterday pushed her over the edge. I'd be angrier if her actions weren't so—well, so pathetic."

I tear up. "Listen, Harry, I'm sorry about all this. If I hadn't introduced you to the other women—to Tammy—you wouldn't have been hanging from this railing all night."

"Yeah, really. So much for a nice quiet night at home. I wonder if Goodwill accepts sex toys." A sly smile hits his lips. "Hey, I've got a better idea—why don't you take them home with you? I saw the way you were eyeing those cuffs, and I'm sure you'd look great in that negligee. Just consider it a thank-you gift for coming to my rescue—"

"Ha-ha! Very funny. If you're feeling comfortable enough to make a joke, I guess there's no need for me to apologize."

Suddenly he's serious again. "You never need to apologize to me, Lyssa. I thought you knew that."

Walking home, I pass the same windows in the same houses that hold the happy lives Tammy covets. There is no excuse for what she did to Harry. But I understand why she'd try.

Well, if he can forgive her, I guess I can too.

13

"All women are angels ... as long as you are their god."

—Leonid S. Sukhorukov

Thursday, 14 Nov., 3:13 p.m.

Mother has this saying, something she has uttered ominously albeit only occasionally since the day Dad walked out on us: "Well, kiddo, the honeymoon is oh-*VAH*."

When she says this, the last syllable of that last word hurtles at warp speed, like a silver bullet, through the thin O of her lips, aimed, I presume, at the forehead of whoever has ruined her day. Or, in Dad's case, her life.

After this declaration, as far as she's concerned the culprit is Dead on Arrival. The issue: *Finito. THE END.*

I don't know why I'm thinking about this now, except that the unfathomable is happening: Brooke's iPhone is whining— *literally*—in her elder son Marcus's voice. Apparently the customized ringtone assigned to his cell number is his personal rendition of a classic P Diddy ditty: some gangsta-rap haiku incorporating *ho, shizzle, booty*, and *mo-fo*, though not necessarily in that order. It is proof positive that no offspring's digitally preserved sound bite is too nasal, self-conscious, or raunchy for his mother's delicate ears, and she should not hesitate to share it with anyone within hearing distance.

Still, there is a time and place for everything. And considering that Brooke, Tammy, and I are mid-pedicure—in other words, ankle-deep in warm, swirling footbaths of candlenut and coconut milk, our legs slathered in chocolate (me) and honey (them)—now is not the ideal moment for Brooke to hear from any of her kids.

Especially the one who, like my son Tanner, is supposedly being taxied to a very important cross-county basketball game by Harry.

Back when we were all childless, our cell phones would have been muted the moment we entered the Heights of Beauty Day Salon's labia pink walls. But these days, me time is a guilty pleasure. Sneaking off for an afternoon mani-pedi with your gal pals is the mommy equivalent of the Burgundian mercenaries leaving the Beech Bottom Dyke unmanned during the Second Battle of St. Albans. (Okay, maybe not that bad, but you get the point.)

Marcus's lament unleashes that most Pavlovian instinct of all: maternal. Without a second thought, Brooke plunges her hand into her Yves Saint Laurent suede Muse bag, paraffin dip be damned. Despite her fumbles and curses, the bag's cell-phone pocket is too slippery to unzip with mitted hands.

Realizing that someone has to come to her rescue or we'll all get booted out for upsetting the serenity of the other patrons, Tammy wrestles the purse into submission, and in the process smudges her freshly polished french tips.

To Harry, she's a psycho rapist. To Brooke, she's a friend in need.

"Jesus, Marcus! What is it? Not another front tooth!" Brooke's face mask is cracking under the stress, a veritable San Andreas of organic egg white and coarse brown sugar. Her worst fear is that, once again, a collision with some rebounder's elbow has turned Marcus's picture-perfect smile into a gap-toothed grin.

Tammy and I can't hear what he's saying, but his indignant tone speaks volumes: *Whoa, Mom, heck, don't blame me, because this time it's not my fault. . . .*

Brooke's face confirms this. Although petrified in meringue, like the moon during a lunar eclipse it moves oh-so-gradually through several phases of emotion: fear, relief, concern, disbelief, and then anger.

"What's happened?" I hiss.

Brooke shushes me. With Marcus, though, she is as calm as a kindergarten teacher during a fire drill. Panic is something we mothers share with a priest, a shrink, or friends willing to feel our pain, but never with our kids. "Okay, listen. . . . Yes—yes, I know it's a tournament game. . . . Honey, just call Coach Shriver and tell him to stall. We'll be there as soon as we can." She hangs up.

Tammy can't stand it any longer. "What's wrong? Why aren't they at the game?"

"Because Harry never picked them up from school, that's why. Seems that he went into the city today instead." As Brooke lunges toward the changing suite, her pedicure tub tips over and the milky mixture sloshes onto the floor. Tammy slips and slides as she chases after her. The honey that has her thighs practically glued together doesn't help her forward momentum.

I shake my head in disbelief, but both of them are so far ahead of me that neither can see me. "But—but that's not possible! When I reminded him this morning it was his turn to carpool the boys to their game, he told me how much he was looking forward to going."

Okay, maybe those weren't his exact words. But there is no way I'm going to tell them that his real response was an eye roll and a litany of curses: at his partners for scheduling an important meeting with one of his largest clients in the early afternoon, as opposed to sometime in the morning; at DeeDee and Bethany the Terminator for socking him with yet another court order demanding that he leave the premises and agree to her taking full custody of their children; and at himself for forgetting that Jake even had a ball game this afternoon, let alone that Temple now had to be covered too.

He'd saved his final curse for himself. "I'm some arrogant son of a bitch, aren't I? I mean, really, who do I think I am, Superman? Hell, I can't even bribe Temple to go to bed at a decent hour! Do you know what she tells me? *That she's worried about her mother sleeping alone.*" Absentmindedly he ran his fingers through his hair. It was now somewhat shaggier than usual, but that was understandable. With his two worlds colliding, these days Harry rarely had time to shave, let alone hit a barbershop.

"Listen, because we thought you had us covered for middle-school carpool, Brooke and I were going to leave Olivia and Ben Junior with Colleen and her little McGuyver while we get mani-pedis. I'm sure she won't mind looking after Temple too," I told him.

"What? Hell, no, I wouldn't do that to you—or Colleen either. Don't worry about a thing. If the meeting starts on time, I'll be home a good half hour before the boys get out of school. Temple can come with us. You and Brooke just do your thing, and don't worry about me."

He wasn't going to come out and say it, but I knew why he didn't want to call Colleen: because of his work emergencies, already Brooke and Colleen had subbed for him in carpool. If Harry ditched carpool duty yet again, brows would lift in consternation, and his worst fears would be realized:

The girls would have yet another reason to gossip about him behind his back.

"That's just it. It's not just the two of us anymore. Brooke told me Tammy is joining us." Since the handcuff incident I'd been avoiding her like the plague. I guess I was afraid I wouldn't be able to resist the urge to give her a piece of my mind.

"Harry, seriously, I don't mind bowing out. Particularly not after . . . well, you know."

"Look, Lyssa, eventually you'll have to converse with her. We both will, for that matter. You might as well get it over with. Just play it cool. Don't let on that you know what happened, or she'll feel obligated to cover it up. Then it will spread like wildfire, only I'll be made out to be the bad guy. You know I can't afford for that to happen."

I went, for Harry's sake.

Now I wish I'd followed my gut and stayed home with the kids.

Still sticky and pissed off, Brooke and Tammy run on ahead to the parking lot. While Tammy revs up her BlueTec, I toss my credit card at our mystified pedicurist and steel myself for the conversation sure to take place on the way to the boys' school. In this group of frenemies, where snide suppositions are sharper than any surgeon's scalpel, Harry's character will be sliced and diced to tiny pieces.

Tammy's remarks will be the sharpest.

Now it's payback time.

Needless to say, the bloom on the rose that was once the Paradise Heights Women's League board's lopsided love affair with Harry is withering, one petal at a time.

3:38 p.m.

Harry must have pulled up to the school just a few moments before us, because the boys are about to get into his car—that is, if they aren't run over first by Tammy, who careens to a stop in front of Harry's sedan in such a way that it's obvious she's watched too many *Law and Order* episodes.

"Humph! Nice to see you were able to make it after all." Brooke's tone is snide enough to make Harry wince. Or maybe it's seeing Tammy again that does that to him. In any case, he smiles and tries to wave us on.

But Brooke isn't having it. "I guess you don't care that this is a tournament game for the boys! Have you forgotten that they're all starters? My God, Harry, if Paradise Heights loses, I hope you realize it'll be all your fault."

"Not to mention that *our* appointments are just as important as yours, Harry Wilder." Tammy raises her smeared fingers to make her point.

To his credit, Harry is implacable. In fact, he's gracious. "You're right, ladies. I owe all of you apologies, especially the boys. Granted, blaming it on traffic is a lousy excuse, but the fact of the matter is 101 was a real—*bitch*." As he pauses, he looks Tammy right in the eye.

All the color goes out of her face, but she keeps her mouth shut. Her passive-aggressive tendencies are quelled for the time being.

Still, I shudder to think how they'll surface next, and against whom.

Although he's not being attacked, Jake turns beet red. Just like every other teen in the world, he feels his parent is enough of an embarrassment on most days. Watching Harry being accused by a teammate's mom of ruining their game is a fate worse than death.

"Jump in, guys. We're late as it is." Harry's eyes are hard enough to cut diamonds. The kids know a showdown when they see one. I give Tanner a slight nod to let him know it's okay by me.

Perplexed, Marcus glances at his mother for approval. Brooke pauses, unsure of what to do now. She has every right to be mad at Harry, and they both know it. At the same time, she honestly likes him. Her last-ditch effort to put him in his place is halfhearted at best. "Well, I mean . . . since we rushed over here, we might as well take them ourselves."

"Nonsense! But, hey, that's not a bad idea, you meeting us there. I'm sure the boys would love the support. If you think you can keep up, just follow me." It's more of a dare than an invitation, and he knows it. If Brooke and Tammy had their druthers, they'd much rather be back at the Heights of Beauty. But having been called out in this way, what else can they do?

Spurred on by Harry's sharp nod, the boys, all lean limbs and tense energy, implode into his once-immaculate BMW 750Li. The tribulations of carpool duty during the rainy season have taken their toll on the car's black napa leather.

Harry glances over at me and winks. That's his way of telling me that he's okay, but I know better. Harry isn't used to fucking up, and this incident has shaken him to the core.

Well, at least he won't have to concern himself as to whether or not Tammy can keep up with him. I'm guessing her malicious compliance will next show itself in road rage.

Just in case I'm right, I let Brooke ride shotgun.

14

"Marriage is nature's way of keeping us from
fighting with strangers."

—Alan King

5:46 p.m.

R U coming?

Right as I hit the send button, I stare down at the message I've just typed into my cell. Since it has nothing to do with any balls other than the one being tossed around here in the Bohemian Grove Middle School gym, this ain't exactly sexting. . . .

Yet I wonder if the message's recipient, my husband, will see the irony in this double entendre.

I doubt it.

Damn it, Ted, it's been too long. I need to get laid. . . .

I'm sure he's feeling frustrated too. Not about our sex life, but that he's not here to cheer Tanner on. It's not like him to miss our elder son's basketball games, especially one this important. By hook or by crook, Ted always finds a way to slip away from the tedium of courting new clients. To him, even the thrill of closing a multimillion-dollar deal is nothing compared to the swoosh of a ball falling through a net. It's even sweeter when that ball is shot by his son.

It's one of the things I love most about him.

Of course, he's not alone. Besides students and mommies, this day game is attended by the most avid fans of all: fathers who were once players themselves. The American gymnasium experience is a hotbed of neuroses. Projected onto our kids are our own shattered dreams. Each squeak of a sneaker on these highly polished wood floors is the audible reminder of a wrong turn, a missed opportunity, a woulda-coulda-shoulda moment that, for whatever reason, just didn't connect. The chance to relive our youth through our offspring is a parental perk, particularly if our kids are better at the things we never mastered ourselves. This is why our primal instincts push us away from even those faces that make our hearts go pitter-patter, if long strong limbs aren't also part of the package—or anything else indicating superhero genes that, when combined with our own, ensure the next generation's athletic achievements will be better than any Mini-Me could possibly be.

The purr of my cell can barely be heard over the crowd on our side of the gym, which is chanting for Jake Wilder, our team's captain and a starting forward, to make his foul shot. When he misses it, I pat Harry on the shoulder. After the carpool incident, he needs all the TLC he can get. I wait for his wry smile before reading Ted's response:

Big deal going down. Keep me posted, OK?

I sigh and flip my phone shut. Tanner will be disappointed. It is the fourth quarter of the Division IV play-off game that decides the first-place standing between these archrivals. For the past half hour, the momentum has swung from one team to the other, the lead tipping back and forth between the two. When the spectators' eyes aren't following the players bolting up and down the court, they gravitate to the wall holding the scoreboard, where a large banner proclaims:

WE OWN YOU!!!!!!

This is meant both literally and figuratively, as the founding fathers of this private hallowed institution were the last century's captains of industry.

If there is any doubt to the contrary, the team's name is the CEOs.

As posh as we thought we had it, Bohemian Grove puts us to shame. There is enough nonskid Paraguayan beeswax on the African hardwood floor to make it glisten within an inch (make that two) of its life. Below the scoreboard is a JumboTron that magnifies every zit on the players' otherwise cherubic faces: overkill, to say the least. Forget bum-numbing bleachers: the tiers of lumbar-control captain's chairs climbing both sideline walls rival what you'd find in the best club-level suite in the Staples Center or on the bridge of the USS *Enterprise*.

In this setting, Paradise Heights is the public ghetto school.

All the more reason why we must win this game. This is a grudge match between archrivals. A thrilla in vanilla, you might say.

Yes, Harry was right to goad us into coming. For the first quarter, these deluxe surroundings threw our Red Devils off their game. Playing catch-up was a bitch, and they needed all the support they could get. Besides Brooke, Tammy, Harry, and me, Margot is here too, in her capacity as official squad mom of PH Middle School's cheer squad. She and her girls not only attend home games, but follow the boys to their rivals' courts as well. Her Mercedes GLK SUV, laden with lithesome tween beauties who double as human jumping beans, brings to mind the slatternly caravan that followed General Hooker's Union army into battle. I'll readily admit it's their uniforms, which hug breasts, expose navels, and graze butts, I find so off-putting: certainly fitting attire for both cheering and hooking, depending on what pom-poms are being shaken. (I pray that by the time Olivia reaches puberty, the turtleneck and chastity belt will have reemerged as must-have fashion statements.) Today, though, I appreciate all they are doing on our boys' behalf. Besides ratcheting up the tension with husky-voiced chants clapped out with a robotic precision, they are a lusty distraction for our opponents. The thong-wearing flyer, launched in the basket toss, stops them dead in their tracks every time.

Isabelle is here too, in her unofficial capacity as the Red Devils' loudest fan. This makes her the bane of son John-John's existence, specifically when she warbles *"THAT'S MY JOHNNIE!"* at his every layup attempt, be it successful or not. Should he follow his father into litigation, I've no doubt she'll wangle her way into the courtroom in order to be his one-woman peanut gallery, or, worse yet, figure out how to get on the jury, whereupon she will proceed to badger the other peers into a favorable finding for her son's client. Here's hoping his partner bonuses assuage his shame.

Colleen is the only AWOL member of our momtourage. She is minding Brooke's Ben and my Olivia, along with McGuyver. I presume Harry begged her to take Temple too, since he didn't have her in the car with him. Colleen has always discouraged third-grader McAllister and eighth-grader McCawber from playing, since sports are at odds with her earth-mother sensibilities. In her universe, there are no winners or losers, just journey takers. To that end, McCawber's own path has him exploring his innate talents for makeup application and T-gurl couture. In fact, the cheer squad's uniforms are his design, so in his case Colleen's philosophy has paid off beautifully.

If only we all had the courage of our convictions.

Tensions are running sky-high, now that the Patek Philippe tourbillion clock on the wall has ticked down to the final minute of the game. Only in this last quarter have the Red Devils finally caught up. I have to give the boys' coach, Pete Shriver, credit for this. He is a true Obi-Wan who nurtures, drills, and inspires each boy to attain his personal best. "Alex, shift!" and "Connor, less Kobe" are part of his patter, a secret code between him and his team that keeps them focused and cohesive.

Today it pays off with some excellent ball handling. I'm especially proud of Tanner, who's had two successful foul shots and a three-pointer that barely beat the third-quarter buzzer (make that chimes, which are calibrated to sound like Big Ben an hour past noon).

Unfortunately, today Harry can't claim similar pride in Jake. Besides the missed foul shot, our team's captain is having an off day of epic proportions. Seems that every time he gets hold of the ball, it slips from his grasp and rolls out of bounds, or his shots skim the rim, then fly faithfully into the hands of our opponents.

I've no doubt Tammy's tongue-lashing of his father has something to do with this. Then again, Shannon Brown's mojo would have evaporated under her icy-hot glare.

Harry, on the other hand, isn't letting Tammy's cold albeit elegant shoulder kill his enjoyment of the game. He smiles and cheers and pretends he's still adored by all of us, even her. In fact, he taunts Tammy by directing most of his remarks to her. I sit between them hoping to deflect her anger, but my nervous laughter is thin coverage for the daggered glances she aims at him. I almost lose it altogether when he taps her shoulder and offers her his hot link. "Care for a bite of my dog?" he asks with a very innocent smile.

"Omigod! Did you see what that little bastard just did to John-John? *Did you?*" Isabelle, who sits on his other side, thinks nothing of shouting out Tourette's-worthy play-by-play descriptions. Harry has to yank her back down into her captain's chair before she attacks the CEO guard who dared to cross her son's airspace. Unfortunately, that puts Harry close enough for her to pierce his arm with her lavender-hued nails. "*YES! YES! YES!* My Gawd, you're DAH BOMB, JOHN! *DAH BOMB!*"

Harry's eyes widen. The horror of witnessing her Jocastian lust is reflected in his dilated pupils.

But this is just the lull before the tempest that drowns Jake in a perfect storm of shame and pain.

With only twenty-three seconds left on the clock and the score tied, he finds himself with the ball. Granted, he's got a wide-open shot, but with the luck he's been having, maybe he should consider a Plan B that's obvious even to me, and certainly to his coach and his teammates: to pass it to John-John, who is standing directly under the basket.

Jake hesitates only a nanosecond before making his choice:
Redemption.

If only.

He sets himself. Perfectly poised, he releases, letting the ball roll off the tips of his fingers toward its final destination. It has only begun its perfect arc when the towering CEO forward (a six-foot-three-inch ringer whose parents are both Russian Olympic team alums: mom was a gymnast, dad played basketball) floats high up above Jake and snatches the ball from midair—

And just a second ahead of the buzzer, it is swooshing through the CEOs' hoop.

Jake's eyes shift through a kaleidoscope of emotions: Disbelief. Horror. Shame.

So do Harry's: Pride. Sadness. Sympathy.

"What are you, some sort of idiot?" Jake may be a head taller than Isabelle, but her words, finding him over the cacophony of the CEOs' whoops of joy, cut him down to size.

Harry grabs her by the arm and spins her around. "How dare you talk to my kid that way!"

"Well, what else could he be? John-John was wide open! Jake saw that and blew it! Yeah, I'd say that qualifies him as an idiot!"

Margot, Brooke, and I freeze. If this were a clash of off-spring as opposed to parents behaving badly, the pair would be shushed and separated, and the ride home would be a Kumbaya of penitence. Instead, this train wreck of emotions leaves us all speechless. We *expect* Isabelle to go off the deep end. Each of us has been there/done that with her, too many times to remember. Not for love, but survival: keep friends close, and enemies closer, right? So, like chinchilla-swaddled starlets confronted by a PETA activist with a blood-engorged balloon, we duck and dodge her vitriol as best we can—

And keep on smiling.

But not Harry.

In a boardroom he may be Machiavelli, but his skills in playground politics are remedial at best. He's finding out firsthand that there is no beast in the corporate jungle half as fearsome as the mother tiger protecting her cub's shot at MVP glory.

But before she can pounce again, Harry uses the only weapon available to an unarmed man: his roar. "You bitch! Who the *hell* do you think you are?"

The gym goes silent. His words have choked the air like a LeBron James powder toss.

Suddenly it's a free-for-all. Pete jumps in between the two of them, trying to calm them down. I can imagine, though, that he's glad someone finally had the nerve to tell Isabelle where to get off.

Jake, ashamed of himself and for his father, can't take it anymore. He runs out of the gym before the other guys catch on that he's teared up.

Just then, my cell phone buzzes. I fully expect it to be Ted calling for the wrap-up score, but no, the number is Colleen's.

"Lyssa? Where are you guys? I thought you'd be back by now!" Even when Colleen is miffed, her voice is barely above a whisper. Between all the screaming going on around me and little McGuyver's rebel yell on the other end of the line as he shoots some imaginary gun at Olivia, it's surprising I can hear Colleen at all. McGuyver bucks her peacenik teachings with a vengeance, which just goes to show you how strongly nature trumps nurture.

"So sorry, Col! Really I am! We—well, we thought we'd take in a few minutes of the boys' game. You know, for moral support."

"Oh, you're at the game? Is Harry there too?"

I hesitate before answering. Tammy's crush on Harry may be over, but Colleen is true-blue through and through. "Yeah, he's here. Why do you ask?"

"Miss Judith called from the preschool. She was wondering if I'd seen him, because Temple—"

"Wait. Isn't Temple with you?"

"No, silly! Why would you ever think that?" Colleen's giggle is the trill of a Disney princess high on life. "I told her that Harry was at the game, and that maybe Harry asked DeeDee to do pickup for him today. . . ."

As if.

To make his implosion complete, I yank him off to the side to give him the bad news: that, inexplicably, he's forgotten his daughter.

When he hears that DeeDee has been called, the color drains from his face, as does his anger. It is replaced by an ashen dread. "Great! Just . . . great. Why the hell didn't Judith just call me? Why did she go and do that?"

The way he's flexing his hands, I know he feels like strangling someone. If I tell him it was Colleen's doing, I know who his victim will be, so I stay mum.

"Do you realize how DeeDee will spin this in court?" Harry shrugs helplessly.

SECRET LIVES OF HUSBANDS AND WIVES | 99

"Look, if we leave now, maybe we can get there before she does."

He hears me loud and clear. Without another word, Harry shoves his way through the crowd and out the door, to his car and his son. Realizing that this was Tanner's ride home, I shout out to Brooke that Tammy should give him a lift back to the Heights; that after picking up Temple, I'll have Harry swing around to Colleen's, where we'll grab her Ben and Olivia.

Tammy clucks her tongue in mock despair. "No wonder DeeDee left him! What kind of man forgets his own kid?"

15

"Marriage is an adventure, like going to war."

—G. K. Chesterton

6:11 p.m.

G ame face.

We all have one. It takes your smile and sharpens it into a grimace. Rocked by an emotional earthquake, the gentle planes of your face shift into stone. The happiness once beaming from your eyes is now refracted inward, focused with laser-sharp concentration on the dark matter at hand.

Harry's is one I don't recognize. I'll admit it: for the past few weeks his dimpled smile and courtly manners have been the icing on the cake of my day. And while courting the league board, he was sweetness and light. Now, though, devoid of any joy, his smile has curdled into a snarl.

What I'm seeing now sends icicles through my veins.

He is ready to do battle with DeeDee the Ice Queen.

Temple won't be the only collateral damage. In the side-view mirror, I see Jake. He sits silently in the back, just staring out the window, his damp red-rimmed eyes as wide as those of the ghoul in *The Scream*. I can only imagine what he's thinking: that all of this—not just the lost game, but his father's fall from grace, even his parents' breakup—is his fault.

If I could, I'd reach back there and hold his hand. And yet, as the mother of one of his friends, the only place I hold in his life is that of an abstract acquaintance.

What *am* I doing here, anyway?

Almost as if reading my mind, Harry places his fingers on my arm and pats it absentmindedly. That tells me what I need to know: I'm here because I'm the only friend Harry has in this gated, well-landscaped corner of the world.

We pull up to the front of Paradise Waldesorri Preschool and Kindergarten just in time to see DeeDee walking out with Temple and Miss Judith, the head of the school. DeeDee's silk blouse and cashmere slacks look almost militaristic next to Miss Judith's gauzy flowing skirt and Birkenstocks. If Miss Judith's attire isn't the broadest hint that she is the community's one and only holdover from the days when Paradise Heights was a hippie commune (hence the first portion of its name, before the place was elevated into the economic stratosphere), her head scarf, tied over flowing gray curls, is a dead giveaway. Whatever DeeDee is saying has Miss Judith shaking her head in dismay. This causes the beaded fringe on her scarf to jiggle. She glances sympathetically at Temple, whose eyes are starred with tears, her pillowed lips bitten into a pout.

The way the car screeches as it comes to a halt undermines Harry's attempt at indifference. Jake slumps down when his mother comes into view. Either he's hoping she doesn't see him and ask him to recap his inglorious day, or he has his own bone to pick with her.

"Stay here," growls Harry. I don't know if he's talking to me or to Jake. But in the mood he's in, neither of us plans on disobeying him.

He's out of the car in a flash. Because he's keeping his voice low and level, I can't hear every word, but I do catch the phrases "very sorry" and "won't happen again." Miss Judith nods sympathetically, but tired uncertainty shades her pale gray eyes; it is obvious that whatever DeeDee has been telling her has colored her view of Harry.

Temple slips her hand into her father's, but does not let go of DeeDee's either. In fact, she squeezes it even tighter, as if to prove, if only to herself, that they are still joined in some way.

This only seems to amp up their feelings toward each other— and their voices. "I've told you, I've got it under control," Harry insists.

"My God, Harry! I wouldn't be here now if that were the case. And if Temple feels more comfortable going home with me . . ." The way DeeDee's voice trails away makes the offer seem so inviting, I'm surprised her daughter doesn't leap at it. When it comes to their parents, most children possess innate neediness.

Not Temple. She knows a game is afoot. Her way to change the rules to suit her needs is brilliant. "*No*, Mommy, no! You can just come home with us," she states matter-of-factly.

The adults stare at her as if she's just landed from another planet.

Harry's game face, dampened by tears he can't wipe away quickly enough, softens into doubtful hope.

DeeDee's, on the other hand, frosts solid with determination. Her teeth are tiny daggers, more a snarl than a smile.

"Damn it, Temple!" Jake's eruption echoes with pain. Opening his car door, he yells, "Don't you get it? She doesn't want to come home. NOT EVER. Aw, just get in the car! NOW!"

All eyes now turn toward us. Temple's emotional Geiger counter has picked up on her brother's anguish as only a sibling's can. Unlike the adults, who patronize her with cheery half lies that never pay off with the only golden ticket that counts—her mom and dad together again—Jake's bellow tells her what she needs to know, even if it isn't what she wants to hear:

Her parents will never love each other again, ever.

In Jake's opinion, it's all DeeDee's fault. Can't his sister see this too?

This sudden realization is too much for the little girl. As if she's letting go of all hope, a rivulet of urine runs down Temple's leg, seemingly at the same pace as the tears streaming down her face. Despite this, Harry scoops her up into his arms and heads for the car. Miss Judith clucks soothingly beside him, hoping to hush her student's heart-wrenching howls.

All mothers break apart when confronted with their children's grief, and DeeDee is no exception. Fault lines of anguish transform her flawless veneer of a face from haughty to sorrowful. She runs after her child—

But stops cold when she notices me in the car.

DeeDee realizes this battle is lost. But the war is still to be won. Her eyes narrow and her frown inverts into a smirk. "You've hired some shopgirl from Nordy's? Oh, now that's rich! Why couldn't she have picked up Temple? Doesn't she drive?"

At first Harry doesn't catch on that she's talking about me, but Miss Judith does. Relieved at the chance to set something straight, she trills nervously, "DeeDee, that's Lyssa Harper, Olivia's mommy."

After what I've just seen, I don't expect a cheery hello. Still, even a stiff nod of recognition would go a long way to clearing the air.

But no. DeeDee isn't apologetic. She's shocked.

Suddenly it dawns on me that hitching a ride with the soon-to-be ex is not the best way to reintroduce yourself to a woman who never remembers who you are no matter how many times she runs into you.

From DeeDee's granite stare, I am assured she won't forget me ever again.

I can't help but watch her in the rearview mirror as we drive off. She, too, keeps me in her sights.

DeeDee has a new target.

16

"I have great hopes that we shall love each other all our
lives as much as if we had never married at all."

—Lord Byron

Friday, 15 Nov., 4:42 p.m.

Tanner and Jake won't let me in the playroom." Olivia's
mouth is pursed, the first sign that thunderstorms of tears
are on the way. "And I need to get Mrs. Wiffle!"

Nurturing that oddly named plush lump of threadbare terry
cloth is one of Olivia's daily rituals, reason enough for the paint-
brush I'm brandishing to stop midstroke. Sadly, the only painting I do these days involves adding yet another coat of white
high-gloss to any household surface that needs it. In this case,
it's the door that leads from the kitchen to the backyard. Tanner
opens it by slamming his basketball against the wobbly knob,
while our little karate green belt, Mickey, uses a roundhouse
kick. Harvey the Labrador hasn't figured out that scratching it
with muddy paws, as opposed to bounding through the built-in
dog door, is what earns him those smacks on his rump. In fact,
this door has been whitewashed so many times that if the Mona
Lisa had been painted anywhere on it, a forensics X-ray would
miss it entirely.

"The boys have locked the door?"

"Yes! And they're laughing at me! And no matter how nice I ask, they won't let me in. They tell me to go away! Mrs. Wiffle hates being in there with them, I just know it."

I put down the brush and follow her downstairs to the basement. She's right: they're guffawing about something. Even my light tapping doesn't catch their attention. Then it hits me: there is another way into the room, through the half bath at the foot of the steps.

"Wait here, sweetie." I give Olivia a kiss on the forehead before stepping into the bathroom.

The boys don't hear me as I come up behind them. They are too engrossed in whatever is on the screen of Jake's cell phone. Only when I'm right behind them do I see what it is:

Laurel, naked from the waist up.

In the photo, she strikes a practiced pose, legs spread apart and hands lifting her thigh-grazing flounce of a skirt for a peek-aboo view. But it's not her come-hither pout that has the boys all hot and bothered. Her breasts, with their large and perky nipples, draw your eyes instantly.

Ashamed for her, I glance away. With one swipe, I grab the cell out of Jake's hand.

"What—" If possible, his eyes open even wider when he realizes I've seen what all the fuss is about. His eyes blink his annoyance, then narrow with defiance. "What the hell, Mrs. Harper? Give it back! That's . . . *personal*."

"Yeah, I'll say it is." He looks so much like Harry when he's angry, it makes me want to laugh and cry at the same time. I cross my arms, protecting not just Laurel's image but my own vision of this boy who, over the past couple of weeks, has gone from being sweet and gracious to sullen and disrespectful. "Really, Jake! How could you take a picture like this? It's—it's such a violation of her privacy!"

He smirks at my naïveté. "Hey, can I help it that she sent it to me?"

Watching my mouth open in shock, Tanner tries to soften the blow. "Yeah, but dude, you *did* ask her to do it. And she's so freaked about you dumping her—"

"What?" I look from one boy to the other. "You're no longer dating Laurel?" Jake's ongoing relationship with Laurel ensures Margot's support of Harry. These days, that gives him an invisible force field that deflects Tammy's scornful venom and keeps Isabelle thinking twice about punching him out.

"Yeah, well, you know how it is: so many girls, so little time." Jake's smile is forced. "Besides, it's only a matter of time before she dumps me first, right? They all do. This way, at least I have a little something to remember her by."

"You're wrong. Every girl is different, just like guys are all different. You can't let—you know . . ."

"Let what? Who?" His eyes beg me to say it, to tell him that he's wrong about Laurel.

About DeeDee.

But it's not my place to say it. I shake my head with a sigh. "Look, Jake, this picture of Laurel—well, it's not just 'a little something to remember her by.' It's her last-ditch effort to hold on to you, so that she won't be hurt." *Like you are now*, I want to say, but I don't. "Tell me the truth: has this made the rounds?"

Jake shrugs as he shakes his head.

Thank goodness. I hit the cell's delete button, and toss the phone back at him. "I have to say I'm very disappointed in you. In fact, I think it's time you head home."

By now, Olivia is pounding on the door, demanding entry. As I make my way over, Jake growls, "I guess you're going to tell my dad about this."

"I think we both know he'd prefer to hear it from you."

Jake winces at the suggestion.

I'm sure Tanner is expecting repercussions for the role he played in these shenanigans. His penance comes from Olivia: as I open the door, she runs past me to grab Mrs. Wiffle, and on the way out she catches Tanner off guard with a roundhouse to the belly.

Obviously she's been taking lessons from Mickey. I guess the next shoe print I'll be painting over will be a girl's size one.

Saturday, 16 Nov., 11:05 a.m.

"Thanks. I owe you," Harry hands me one of the two sacks he's carrying, the one sweating glazed doughnut sugar. Yum.

Temple and Olivia's ballet class has just started. I sneak a peek inside the bag, but forgo doing a happy dance, despite finding it filled with my poison of choice: two chocolate-topped Krispy Kremes.

I shoot him a thumbs-up. I've been up since sunrise, but with all my running around—chauffeuring the kids to their activities, not to mention collecting and distributing the barrels to every classroom for the board's annual Thanksgiving Homeless Shelter Food Collection—this is the first bite of anything I've had all day. However, munching snacks in front of the studio's glass partition is verboten, something about little ballerinas getting the wrong message if they see their parents gorging themselves on pastries. Adhering to ballet mistress Nadia's rule, I motion for him to follow me outside, where we can enjoy a guilt-free pig-out.

We settle on one of the benches in the little park beside the studio. "Hey, no coffee to go with this?" I don't know if Harry can make out what I'm saying, what with my mouth stuffed with doughnut. As he frowns, his dimples deepen. Lord help me, I can't stop my cheeks from heating up. Does he notice? Nah, he's too busy dodging the spittle hurtling out of my mouth.

He bats a pellet of fried dough off his cheek, then flicks one off mine as well. "I'm boycotting the 'Bucks these days. If I run into Margot and her posse, I'm sure she'll have me shot on sight."

That stops me mid-munch. "Ah, so Jake broke it off after all!"

"Yes, last night. Thanks to your urging, he and I had a heart-to-heart about it. He feels he's being pressured into going steady, and he's just not ready for that. My God, they're not even fourteen yet! Last year he was the shortest kid in his class. Even the girls were taller." Harry crumples up the bag and hurls it into the garbage can by the street. "Laurel took it pretty hard. But it could have been a lot worse, if Margot had gotten wind of that sext message." He stops and gulps. His doughnut remains untouched on his napkin, so I know the catch in his throat isn't from that. "Knowing her, I'm sure she'd be threatening to sue. That's one less brouhaha I need in my life." He rubs his eyes wearily. "Not that, legally, she'd have a leg to stand on."

"How's that?"

"Because Laurel sent the message to Jake. She's the one who broke the law, not him. They're both minors, and that's the legal concern. But still, *he asked her to do it*. As far as I'm concerned, it's the principle of the thing. Of course, I read him the riot act. I think I got it through his thick skull that nudity and sex, no matter how tempting, aren't things he should be rushing toward. Not for a few years, at least." He gives the parental salute: a genuflection. Seeing my smile, he allows himself one too. "Seriously, Lyssa, it's a good thing you waylaid the boys before they did something we'd all regret. So you see, I owe you a lot. And by that, I don't mean a couple of doughnuts." He opens the other sack and pulls out a beautiful little plant in a glazed pot. It boasts one small flower, white streaked with red, which has yet to fully open.

"How beautiful, a candy cane amaryllis! Wow, Harry. Really, you didn't have to do this. You don't owe me anything. I mean, you would have done the same thing if you'd caught Tanner in the same predicament."

He looks at me strangely. "Yes, I guess I would—now. But before I knew you, before all of this"—he waves his hand beyond the cluster of businesses, toward the neighborhood unfurling beyond it—"I could not have cared less. I would have just laughed it off, just chalked up it as, you know, 'boys being boys' or some such nonsense."

"Why would you say that? The last thing you are is callous, Harry."

"Then you really don't know me so well. Before DeeDee left me, stuff like this just wasn't important to me. It fell under DeeDee's purview, not mine. I didn't care to hear about the kids' fights with their friends. If something was bugging them, I'd let her handle it. I was too busy carving out my own place in the bigger universe beyond here. And for what? Seriously, Lyssa, nothing—and I do mean *nothing*—is as important as my kids' lives at any moment. I didn't realize that until Temple's accident the other day."

"Harry, you can't blame yourself for that—"

"Oh no? If I was in tune with her feelings, then why didn't I pick up on her angst? Because I've been an absentee father, that's why." His voice cracks. "Do you know that I missed Father's Day with my kids this year? I was stuck in a messy merger deal out of town where I was working twenty-four seven for over a month. But I promised them that, come hell or high water, I'd make it home that Saturday night. So the two of them took their allowances to buy us all seats at a Giants game." He shakes his head sadly. "I didn't get home until late Monday. Their hand-made card was on my bureau—with the tickets inside. I'm quite a dad, aren't I?"

"Those things happen. Besides, Harry, everything you've done is for them."

"Not really. Up until now, my ego was more important to me than my kids. I had it all: beautiful wife, great kids, power position at a prestigious firm. Now look at me."

"You've still got your kids."

"For now. But I'm not going to pretend that things are perfect. Temple is still wetting the bed at night. Says she doesn't want to sleep alone. And Miss Judith has asked that I pack an extra pair of underpants in her backpack. In fact, it's a struggle to get her to go to school in the first place. Miss Judith has suggested a shrink for Temple." He shakes his head sadly. "I wonder if I can get a family discount. Jake is sullen, too. I miss that sweet cocky kid in him. It's this damn divorce! I guess I've let both my babies down. But I swear to God, I'll never let that happen again."

I tap his hand with my sticky fingertips. Does that gross him out? Apparently not, since he covers them with his other hand.

"Look, Harry, we all wish we could freeze time, turn back the clock. Sometimes I stare at my kids' faces while they sleep, just so I'll always be sure to remember them at every age: you know, like when they were three and had those sweet apple cheeks. Or right before they can walk, and you can't stop squeezing their fat little legs, or kissing their instep because it's so smooth and soft. Do you remember that?"

Memories haze his eyes for a moment. Hearing the hum of a jet high over our heads, he follows it as it disappears into the sun.

"Lyssa, I'll let you in on my dirty little secret: Sure, I have all those same images, but before the divorce I *don't remember ever kissing them when they weren't asleep.* I left for work while it was still dark, or I came home late, usually after they went to bed."

As he stands, he pulls me up with him. "But that's okay, because now I'm making up for lost time. Just think—if DeeDee hadn't left, I would have never realized what I've missed all these years. I guess she did me a favor after all."

17

"Men kick friendship around like a football, but it
doesn't seem to crack. Women treat it like
glass and it goes to pieces."

—Anne Morrow Lindbergh

Monday, 18 Nov., 9:10 a.m.

She's devastated! Simply DEVASTATED. She hasn't quit crying since he broke the news!" Brooke, who is usually a loudmouth, barely speaks above a whisper. For the first time since I've met her, I have to lean in to hear one of her proclamations.

Hell, yeah, this is serious.

Harry may have deserted Starbucks, but I still need my vanilla latte fix, which is why I've joined the board at its usual school-morning coffee klatch. Besides, I'm doing reconnaissance on Jake's breakup with Laurel, if only to cover Harry's back.

And if what Brooke says is true, the knives are being sharpened.

"I took over a casserole, and the poor thing wouldn't even have a bite," Colleen chimes in. "I doubt that she has eaten since it happened."

"Well, of course not," sniffs Tammy. "What he's done is a cruel betrayal of their relationship, the *cad*!"

I feel the color leave my face. Did Laurel's sext message

somehow re-pixelate and float back out into the ether, forever branding her a slut and Jake a boy ho?

I'm almost afraid to ask, but I know I must. "Was it something . . . irreversible? Maybe it was a mistake—"

"Mistake? Yeah, well, he'll find out what this 'mistake' will cost him," growls Isabelle. "She's on the warpath, and rightly so. But no, it's not irreversible. Not if he does the right thing by her."

Exhaling again, I feel my upper lip quiver as I smile. "Well, then, that's something, at least! I'm sure this will all blow over in a week or so, and then they'll be friends again."

Isabelle snorts at my naïveté. "Ha! Fat chance! It should never have happened in the first place. Hell, she wants him back."

"Whoa, whoa! It was puppy love! You know, a first crush. Seriously, someone has to help her put this into perspective. What does Margot have to say about it?"

Dumbstruck, all three of them turn and stare at me. Colleen is the first one out of her trance. "Just who do you think we're talking about, silly?"

"Laurel, of course! Wait—it's *Margot* who's so upset? But—why?"

All eyes shift slightly to my right. I don't have to look to know what I'll find there:

Margot, apparently having risen from the dead.

I turn slowly, expecting to be hit with the wrath of a woman scornful of those who doubt her abilities to get even.

Instead I find a listless, hollow-cheeked shell of a woman. I pat her arm in sympathy, but she's not having it. She shrugs me off with a shudder. *"Because no one dumps my daughter,"* she hisses. "Certainly not some delinquent like Jake Wilder."

Give me a break.

"Bad boys." Tammy smiles wryly. "You know how it is: like father, like son."

Harry—a bad boy? So that I don't laugh in her face, I look down at my feet—but not for too long, because the three toes with the smeared polish remind me of the pedicure debacle. "He's just a sweet kid who's going through a rough patch."

"Some rough patch," murmurs Brooke. "Marcus tells me he's been skipping school. And he's talking back to his teachers too."

"That's exactly what I mean. Of course he's preoccupied with his parents' divorce." I turn to Margot. She is sniffling like a baby whose pacifier has been taken from her. "Look, I know it hurts. I'm sure Laurel is broken up about it—"

"Ha! Not my baby! She's a trouper, that one."

"Good for her, for snapping right back!" My cheeriness is met with an icy silence. "I mean, everyone gets dumped at least once, right? It's a rite of passage."

"I never did. And I reserve that right for my daughter, too!"

"I don't think there are any take-backs in breakups."

"Oh no? Let's see what Harry has to say about it." Margot whips out her phone and hits speed-dial.

"You're calling him now, while he's at work?"

Isabelle nods adamantly. "What difference should that make? This is an emergency!"

That won't be good for Harry. He only goes in once every two weeks now, and his partners have taken to ribbing him about it. He's caught them calling him Mr. Mom. "Margot, your kid falling out of a tree is an emergency. Your kid breaking up with his girlfriend at the age of thirteen is just a fact of life—"

Margot lifts her index finger in order to shush us. "Yes? Harry Wilder, please. . . . In a meeting? Well, get him out. It's about his son. . . . Yes, I'll hold." She smiles triumphantly.

I shake my head in disbelief. But before I can say another word or yank the phone out of her hand and toss it into the barista's whining coffee grinder, Harry's concerned voice can be heard through Margot's BlackBerry. "Yes, hello, this is Harry Wilder. Is this the school?"

"No, Harry, this is *Margot*." Her sneer could disable the satellite transmitting it.

"Oh." Harry pauses. "Look, I'm in a client meeting now. Can I call you back?"

"No. Our children's futures are at stake! Isn't that more important than any meeting?"

"Margot, I'm serious. Now is not the time. I'll be glad to talk to you when—"

"I'll make this short." Margot purrs her threat. "Just ask Jake to apologize, to tell Laurel he made a mistake."

"I can't do that."

Margot's voice wavers. "You have a daughter! How would you feel if some boy broke her heart?"

"I'm sure I'd feel as you do. I'd be upset at anyone who hurt my daughter." Harry talks slowly, soothingly, as if he's trying to talk a lunatic off a ledge, which in this instance is not far from the truth. "But I'd also explain to her that what she's feeling is temporary, that there will be other relationships in her life, and that we grow from such experiences, even when they don't turn out the way we want them to."

"But—*but it's what she wants*!"

"Well, tell her life doesn't always turn out the way she wants. That love isn't perfect. That she should be playing the field, not clinging to some kid who isn't ready to settle down."

"Oh. I see," says Margot coolly. "Is that what you told DeeDee? Is that why she left you?"

Her jibe catches Harry off guard. There is a long silence. When he does speak again, he sounds worn out: "Margot, I don't know why she left. But now that you mention it, yeah, okay: if we hadn't married so young, maybe we wouldn't be divorcing now. People change, along with their priorities.

Seriously, doesn't it bother you that your daughter is so boy-crazy? And why do you encourage it? Why are you so anxious for your kid to get her heart broken?"

She doesn't bother to answer him, but taps the phone off in frustration.

Harry's honorary membership in the Paradise Heights Women's League has officially ended.

18

"A true friend never gets in your way unless
you happen to be going down."

—Arnold H. Glasow

3:23 p.m.

Mommy, do I have to invite Temple to my birthday party?"

Olivia entered our world on New Year's Day. We've always combined her party with a New Year's open house. Our Christmas tree is still up, and the invitation list is large: not just Olivia's pals, but our closest friends and neighbors too. Also, we arrange for Santa to make a post-Christmas drop-in. He totes a sack of goofy gifts for all the children. "Christmas leftovers," he claims. Since Olivia was three, she has presumed Saint Nick and she share the same birthday. We can't convince her otherwise. And so, at her insistence, whatever poor fool we hire to play him must help her blow out the candles. Everyone leaves filled with one more shot of holiday cheer and the resolve to treat others with kindness in the New Year.

Or maybe not, as I realize now from Olivia's question.

"Hmmm . . . Well. Are you and Temple mad at each other right now or something?" I pause the TV's DVD player. We're snuggled up in my bedroom, watching *March of the Penguins,* a homework assignment from Miss Judith. Tomorrow during magic circle time, the children will be encouraged to express their fears for the poor penguins left sitting on the eggs for months at a time while their mates go off in search of food. The mothers and fathers trade off these duties, with the sole purpose of feeding and protecting their babies.

Heavy stuff for kindergarteners, but Miss Judith, still concerned about Temple's home life, knows exactly what she is doing.

Olivia frowns and sucks her thumb. This is a prime indication that the topic at hand is not one she relishes. "We're not mad, Mommy. She still likes me, but I just don't like her anymore. Her hair is falling out, and sometimes she stinks. And if she gets mad at you, she bites you."

So, she's still wetting herself, and pulling out her hair to boot. Poor Temple.

Poor Harry. "I think Temple is very sad now, don't you?"

"Yes. She hates her mommy." Olivia stares at the television screen. Freezing the DVD has smeared the penguin colony into a blur of black and white polka dots. "She hates everybody."

I scoop her up into my arms and kiss her hair. Shampooed just an hour ago, it is still damp and smells as sweet as soda pop. "But she doesn't hate you. And friendship is about helping people when they need you the most, not just when everything is happy."

I let that sink in for a moment. Olivia winces as if shot squarely in the eye by the acidic pulp of her unpleasant dilemma. "What do you think, does Temple need her friends to hug her and hold her hand right now?"

"Yes, I guess so. Okay, I'll invite her to reading hour today."

She takes the remote from my hand and clicks the waddling penguins back to life. Noting that one of the male penguins has broken his egg, Olivia shakes her head with a sigh. "Poor penguin! Daddies never know what they're doing." She burrows deep down into my lap. "When Temple's mommy comes home, will her daddy have to give Temple back?"

I don't know how to answer that. My stuttering attempt is interrupted by our ringing telephone. Saved by the bell.

Or not. From the caller ID, I see it's Patti with yet another update on Dad. I let it ring through. Patti is used to this and leaves another stoic message detailing his deteriorating condition.

I'll play it later, after the children are in bed.

Just then Olivia screams at the top of her lungs for me to look quick, as one of the daddy penguins is getting eaten by a polar bear.

Before I do, though, I dry away a tear and put on a happy face.

4:38 p.m.

"Hey, thanks for bringing Temple with you and Olivia to story time. I got out of the city as fast as I could, but with the traffic and all—"

Harry's loud apology earns him a sound shushing from the librarian who is supervising the after-school story time. At least the passel of kids listening to this week's story are ignoring us. They are too enthralled by the reader, an out-of-work actor who serves up each rhyming verse as if it were Hamlet's soliloquy. But several of the mommies, perched on the room's tiny chairs, second her demand with stern nods and pursed lips. At this stage of life, me time is catch-as-catch-can: perhaps just a few minutes to speed-read the *O* cover story entitled "Ahhhhhh! 16 Ways to De-Stress Your Life." Something as time-consuming as the latest Jennifer Weiner will have to wait for late at night, when the kids fall asleep.

And, of course, there is no time for sex.

I wave sympathetically at these women even as I push Harry

out the door. He still has time to tip his baseball cap to them. He's in a playful mood, heaven knows why.

Even before we reach the curb, he nudges my sunglasses just enough that they fall off the top of my head and over my eyes, and says, "Hey, don't you know you're not supposed to be seen in public with an Undesirable?"

"You're a smart-ass, you know that?" I move the glasses back onto their resting place, the nest of curls crowning my head.

He learned that term from Brooke one Saturday, when the three of us were people-watching while minding our little ones in Paradise Park. Noticing that Biker Mom, rainbow-haired and decked out in tight leather, was there swinging her toddler, Brooke started in on yet another tirade about her theory that Biker Mom is blatantly courting Marcus's crush.

"Just what we need: a son who wants to be a skinhead! Did you know he wants a Harley theme for his bar mitzvah?" She bit her lip in frustration. "Benjamin is going to blow his top when he hears what Marcus wants for the party favors."

"Okay, I'll bite," said Harry. Before Margot sent him into exile, his approach to Brooke and the other members of the league board was similar to how you'd treat zoo animals: while it is interesting to observe them in a realistic habitat, if you're smart you'll keep your distance, considering the sharpness of their claws.

Brooke rolled her eyes. "Something very secular: leather motorcycle jackets embroidered with Marcus's name and the event's date." As she gave a friendly wave to her nemesis, she muttered under her breath, "Biker Mom's idea, of course. Convinced Marcus it would be, and I quote, 'awesome.' "

Harry whistled. " 'Awesome' is that Maserati she drove up in. Not your typical mommy-mobile. Considering that and the cost of a home here, how do you figure Biker Mom pays the bills?"

"In that getup, I wouldn't be surprised if she were a dominatrix. Or maybe Biker Dad holds the region's franchise on pot."

"Brooke, cut her some slack! You really aren't giving her the benefit of the doubt." So that he'd quit staring, I snapped my fingers in front of Harry's face. He came to with a start. "I, for one, enjoy the fact that we're not all cookie-cutter out here."

"You would." Brooke laughed. "Demographics is a numbers game, and the Heights is a big place, so I guess it's inevitable that we have our fair share of Undesirables." In another life— that is, BC (before children)—she was a media buyer at an advertising agency. So to her, everything is a statistic that boils down to cost-per-person.

And to hear her talk, we don't all cost the same.

In her opinion, Activist Mom makes the Undesirable list, as do the old-timers whose rambling ranches, with their shabby yards and grand old oaks, were grandfathered in when the developers made their bid for the surrounding prune orchards. While not exactly Undesirables, to Brooke and the others on the board, most of the working moms are also marginalized: they are too harried with their careers, and feel too guilty about it. On the other hand, work-at-home mompreneurs are given some slack—but not too much, because if they could, they'd lean on those whom they consider less ambitious.

The Heights's househusbands and their spouses are also on the list: Pete and Masha, the neighborhood slut, and the dysfunctional Cal and Bev Bullworth.

And now Harry is on it too. Right there at the top of the list.

Well, I'm not going to let him feel sorry for himself. Not about the board, anyway. "You're right. Just standing here beside you could get me blacklisted. Except—"

"Except what?" He's barking, but I'm not biting, because I feel his pain: his not-quite-ex is a hardball-playing banshee, his kids are acting out, and his partners are grumbling about his shortened work schedule.

"Except that right now the board needs me more than I need them."

He raises an eyebrow. "How do you figure that?"

"I'm this year's Thanksgiving food drive chair."

"Oh yeah? And how's that coming?"

Right now we're down 90 percent from last year, but he doesn't need to know that. "Slow but steady," I say coolly. "Why do you ask?"

"No reason . . . except yesterday I noticed two boys using the barrel in Miss Judith's classroom as a fort."

"Darn it." I flop down on the curb. "I don't think I can take Margot playing puppet master for yet another year. But if the drive is a dud on my watch, I'll have no choice."

"What does the food drive have to do with her role as the queen bee around here?"

"Just about everything. The food drive is the most important thing the board does each year, not to mention the most un-wieldy to coordinate. If I end up chairing a successful drive, I'll be the board's next president."

"Talk about a hollow victory." He shakes his head in dis-belief.

"It's a matter of pride. So what if Margot used to be some sort of expert in employee productivity! So what if last year she doubled the previous record! So what—"

"So what if you're so jealous that you've bitten off more than you can chew." He tilts the brim of his cap so low that all I see is his smirk.

He's right, but not about the food drive. *It's you that's got me concerned.* I almost blurt it out, but I know better. Would he admit he's lost control of his life?

No, not even to me.

No, *especially* not to me. He wants me to keep him on a pedestal, even as the others are now slinging mud at him, left and right.

The rumors will start immediately, now that Margot has lifted the embargo on all gossip concerning the Wilders. Like leaves kicked aloft in the now-chilly afternoon gusts, the whispers—all hearsay, "they say . . ." innuendo, and blatant lies—will skitter from cell phone to cell phone, from block to block.

They'll say DeeDee left because he was cold and unfeeling; that his children are wild and uncontrollable since she has been gone.

That the proof is the anger in his children's eyes.

Harry's eyes have dulled, too. I know he's angry at himself for his inability to control the one thing out of his reach: his children's feelings for their mother. Unlike him, they can't bury their emotions in a merger. Nor do they have the guile that would allow them to smile and pretend everything was hunkydory. And they certainly haven't yet learned the art of tamping down their emotions, or channeling their hurt into some other activity—although it would be interesting to know how Jake's been spending his afternoons lately.

"Tanner says Jake has skipped the last few practices." I try to keep my voice nonchalant, but by the way Harry frowns, I know he hears my concern. "Coach Shriver says if he misses another, he's off the team."

"But . . . that can't be. Jake told me—I mean . . ." Harry's eyelids close under the weight of his pain. "Aw, jeez. Damn it, Jake—"

"Hey, look: Pete may be a bit of a blowhard, but deep down he's a pretty nice guy. I'm sure Pete would understand, if he knew what Jake is going through." Pete Shriver comes off somewhat gruff, but if anyone knows the grief of a disconnected marriage, he does.

Harry Wilder and Pete Shriver have more than their dysfunctional marriages in common. So why shouldn't they know each other better? The third househusband, Calvin Bullworth, is a bit strange, but maybe that's just shyness. Anyway, it's worth a try.

"Hey, speaking of Pete, you two have a lot in common."

Harry looks at me sharply. "What makes you say that?"

"Well, you both work out of the home—"

"From what I can tell, that dude doesn't work at all."

I shrug. "From what I hear, he doesn't have to."

"Lucky slob."

I'm surprised to learn that Harry really doesn't miss the office as much as I had thought he would. "Yeah, but that's not the point here. What I mean is that you're each your family's primary caregiver."

"That term sucks. Why don't you just come out and say it? We're both lonely guys in a neighborhood filled with silly, bored housewives."

"Hey, watch it there! I resemble that remark."

"Granted, you keep a nice, albeit a bit messy, home—"

I frown. "Hardee-har-har. I don't think that's what you meant to say, now, is it?"

"And I know you're bored, or you wouldn't have taken me under your wing."

"I had an ulterior motive: I heard they're looking for a replacement for Mother Teresa."

"Well, you still have a ways to go before I'd call you a saint. To your credit, you aren't half as silly as all the other women in this neck of the woods."

I smack him on the biceps. "I'll take that as a compliment. So, what do you say? Why don't we invite Pete out to coffee tomorrow? Hey, you know, I'll bet Calvin Bullworth would be up for a cuppa joe, too—"

"Whoa, whoa, hold up a minute! That strange dude they call the Cyberterrorist?"

It's on the tip of my tongue to say beggars can't be choosers, but I think better of that. "That's somewhat cruel. Why don't we give the guy a chance? One day he may be someone you'll be glad you know."

Harry sighs deeply. "Yeah? Okay, you're right. Set it up, if you feel like it. Besides, if he really does know how to build a bomb, at least we'll have him on our side."

19

"Fear makes strangers of people who would be friends."

—Shirley MacLaine

5:27 p.m.

So, you say you think you can get my forward back on the team?" Pete ducks just in time to miss being slammed in the head by one of the many basketballs hailing down upon us as they ricochet off the school gym's backboards.

I'm not so lucky: one wings me in the arm, knocking my purse strap off my shoulder. The contents of my purse scatter under the Red Devils' shuffling feet. Just in time I pluck my brand-new Benefit lipstick out from under Marcus's size-thirteen sneakers. However, my own son has pulverized my new MAC compact.

"Sorry, Mom!" yells Tanner, now in a full-tilt boogie toward the other end of the gym.

Pete is desperate to entice Jake back on the team. Since the kid went AWOL, the Devils have lost two games, both by around eight points, which just so happens to be three points lower than Jake's average per game. Not only that, he's always been the heart and soul of the Red Devils.

Whether his teammates still feel that way about him is debatable. According to Tanner, Jake has discovered that his quick wit can be used to be cruel as well as funny. His choice of victims has no rhyme or reason. Depending on his mood, they are geeks, freaks, or his jock buds. In fact, Tanner no longer considers Jake a friend, but an "asshole."

Laurel still adores him. Go figure. Needless to say, it's eating Margot alive.

"Look, I can't promise he'll show up at the next practice, but it's certainly something his father wants to see happen and is willing to discuss."

Pete nods grudgingly. He wants me to believe that he's doing Harry the favor instead of the other way around.

To get Harry some domestic backup, I'm willing to play ball. "You know, Harry says you're the best coach Jake has ever had."

"Oh! Well, that kid has a lot of potential. In the right hands, he could be the next Kobe."

"Yes, Harry agrees. He also feels you deserve a lot of credit for the big leap in the whole team's play-off potential." As I say this, I bat my lashes. It's no secret that poor Pete doesn't get much flirting at home. His wife is too busy making eyes at practically every other man in the neighborhood.

Pete shrugs, but his pinkening cheeks give him away. "Okay, I'm up for a Jake confab."

I can't help but feel giddy. *I love matchmaking!* "So, listen, are you free for coffee, say, after school drop-off tomorrow?"

"Yeah, that should work. The 'Bucks?"

I can feel my smile slip a bit. Hell, no, not Starbucks! Not with the board there, passing judgment, snickering, shaking their smartly coiffed heads in pity.

"Harry—well, I think he'd much rather go where you guys can grab a bite. Maybe pancakes or something. How about the IHOP by the expressway?"

He nods, then jerks me out of the way before I'm wiped out by another storm of balls. "Yo, Parker! Balls like that will keep you on the bench. Challenge yourself! *Challenge!*"

One down, one to go. Right, Coach. I'm inspired. I'm up for my next challenge. I think.

I hope. . . .

5:56 p.m.

"You're not selling Tupperware, are you? Sorry, but we don't believe in plastics. Too toxic. You know, PCBs and all. It's the reason my generation will be barren."

Paradise Heights's only disaffected Goth girl, Sabrina Bullworth, peers out of the peephole of the Bullworths' massive front door, which looks eerily similar to the one that welcomed the damned hotel guests in *The Shining*. It took Sabrina five minutes to answer my insistent gonging of the Bullworths' version of a doorbell: chimes that sound like the ringing of Big Ben on the half hour. "No? Um, let me guess: Avon calling, right? Well, sorry, we don't use products for which animals were mutilated, and which are sold through multilevel networks."

The Bullworths moved into the neighborhood when Sabrina was only five. Even back then, what with her dark pigtails, large sad eyes, and deadpan countenance, she could easily have passed for Wednesday Addams. This resemblance was enhanced by her parents' choice of a home: the oldest of the original Victorians in Paradise Heights—"because it was a steal," her realtor mom, Bev, proudly reminds everyone.

Well, of course it was. Besides squatting on a dark, lonely street far from the center of town, it had been a stronghold of refugees from the Summer of Love, with all that implies. Even after the last tenants finally grew up and got real lives, their old crash pad stayed vacant for decades.

Whereas a systems renovation has finally been completed on the inside, apparently the Bullworths ran out of money before they were able to do any interior decoration, let alone scrape what was left of the peeling original paint off the exterior fretwork. No matter, since not much of the house can be seen through a choke-hold of bushes and vines. If none of this leaves the local Mary Kay representative quaking in her kitten heels, the fact that the property backs up to a century-old cemetery will certainly have her turning pale under her creme-to-powder foundation.

Yep, a real steal.

"Sabrina, wait! Don't you remember me? I'm your class mother. You know, Tanner's mom, Mrs. Harper." As my cheeriest Mary Poppins lilt echoes through the massive foyer, I squelch an involuntary shiver. "I'm here to see your dad. Is he around?"

Sabrina opens the door just a sliver. The darkness inside is barely penetrated by the sunlight pushing its way in. She gives me a wary look. All of a sudden I realize she's wondering if my introduction means this is in some way official school business, which perhaps puts her in the one position she and every other odd-kid-out innately hates:

Anything that might bring her odd-parents-out within gawking distance of her peers.

"No. He's . . . out of town. Europe, I think."

But before she has a chance to shut the door in my face, Calvin's voice drones out through some tinny intercom: "Sabrina, please invite our guest in and send her back to my study."

Sabrina sighs. Resigned to her fate, she yanks open the massive oak door with all the solemnity of a crypt-keeper. "He's in the last room down the hall."

She disappears into the indigo darkness before I can thank her.

For what, I'm sure I don't know, since she hasn't left me a flashlight to find my way back out.

The eerie glow that leads me to Cal's office turns out to be from a wall of large flat-screen computer monitors. The digital centipedes crawling across each screen seem to have no rhyme or reason. Calvin doesn't even turn around to see who has invaded his secret lair. Why should he, when there I am, larger than life (yeah, really: video is not a friend of anyone over a size four) on the far right screen?

When he finally does turn toward me, I hope he can see me better than I can see him, since he's the one who's looking through Coke-bottle-thick glasses. "I'm sorry, you say you're with Sabrina's school?"

"Huh? . . . Oh! Well, not exactly." It takes me a second to come back into the real world, as opposed to the virtual one up on Calvin's giant computer screen. "I was just pointing out to her that she might remember me from school. Really, I'm here to talk to you about a nonschool matter. Just a fun, friendly, neighborly gathering. Um . . . do you mind me asking: what are those things crawling across your computer screens?"

"Computer code. I helped design the government's satellite surveillance system." Calvin blinks twice. "And why would you want me there?"

It's on the tip of my tongue to answer, *Because you're a lonely guy, and now there are enough of you in the 'hood to be doing three-part harmony. . . .*

But I come to my senses before I blurt that out. "Another couple of the Heights's stay-at-home dads were hoping you'd join them for breakfast tomorrow. They thought you could work out carpool backup, hang out—you know, guy stuff. You all have kids around the same age, so who knows?"

Calvin thinks about this for a very long moment. I imagine he has never been asked to join a team that didn't involve computer code, and certainly no one ever asked him to a prom.

So, yes, I wait patiently as he enjoys his moment in the sun. As it is, the only light emanating in this, his cave, comes from several thirty-inch TFT-LCD computer monitors.

Finally he breaks the spell with a gentle smile. "Sure, okay. Getting out of here would do me some good." Calvin follows my eyes back to the big screens. "It's mesmerizing, isn't it?"

"I'll say." New friendships usually are.

Tuesday, 19 Nov., 9:18 a.m.

The true-blue roof of the International House of Pancakes glistens under a sheen of dew. Harry pulls into the spot closest to handicapped parking. I presume he's preparing for a quick getaway in case this playdate ends up being a bust.

He turns off the engine and lets it gasp to a stop before giving me a sidelong glance. "Okay, the truth now: how bad is this going to be?"

"Personally, I like the pancakes here. The thin Swedish ones are my favorites. I think it's the lemon zest they add to the batter."

He sighs and steels himself to get out of the car. But as he helps me out my door, he mutters, "Glad to know. By the way, breakfast is on you."

Frankly, it's a small price to pay for my guilt over the board debacle. Where I went wrong was my presumption that the girls could be just friends with Harry, despite the fact that apparently he's a live version of their *Mystery Date* dreamboat.

Then again, fantasies require less maintenance than friendships.

The realization that it takes a village to be a single parent dawned on Harry last week, around the same time his kids devoured the last of Colleen's casseroles. Since then, they've lost a pound or two, and they've been grousing about the number of times they've had to eat his signature dish, tuna mac.

Worse yet, yesterday they were rhapsodizing out loud about their mom's homemade beef stew. Lucky the Airedale is now the proud recipient of a six-pack of Dinty Moore as Harry, not to be outdone, attempts the impossible: to follow his wife's grandmother's recipe, which is written in Norwegian.

Desperate times call for desperate measures, even if that means carpooling with the neighborhood outcasts. I fully realize that this thing can break one of two ways: either kisses and giggles, or farts and *merde*.

I'm not making book on either.

When you place a low-priced national chain restaurant at a busy exit off one of America's superhighways, it shouldn't surprise you that its patrons look as if they'd be at home inside the *Star Wars* bar. I'm just saying that there is no genteel way to wolf down a tall stack of Butterscotch Rocks pancakes with a chaser of link sausages, is all.

We find our party in an alcove booth. Both men are studying large, glossy menus, as opposed to conversing or making eye contact. They view us warily, and immediately Harry does the ultimate 'chismo move: you know, the glad-hand-and-backslap, which is accompanied by a far-too-cheery "Coach! Cal! Been too long! Great to see you again!"

To men, is insincerity the sincerest form of flattery? Hey, I know we women fall for it, but guys do too? Go figure.

Or maybe the goal of the flatterer is to put the flatteree off his game. Pete shuffles to his feet and grumbles something that sounds like a cross between "Good morning" and "Don't get the eggs here, they are too runny," while Cal swallows a whole wedge of toast, as if stashing away evidence before the breakfast police come to haul him away. Unfortunately, he doesn't take the time to wipe his greased fingers before Harry pumps what little life there is from them.

The look of doom on Harry's face is priceless.

The waitress is hovering the second we sit down. She has us pegged as the biggest tippers in the group. I guess that's because

Pete has only ordered tea, and Cal refuses to take the bait and stare at her breasts. Since now Harry expects me to order the Swedish pancakes, I do, along with coffee and a side of bacon, under the assumption that I'll seem more like one of the boys.

That illusion is blown to smithereens when Harry orders a typical Master of the Universe breakfast: a bowl of fruit.

That's it.

Oh yeah, and an ice water.

Great. Now with my "hearty breakfast," *I* feel like a refugee from the palace of Jabba the Hutt, particularly with Calvin, he of the amazing toast-vanishing act, sitting at my side.

The men sit in silence for almost five minutes before Pete finally breaks the ice. "So, when is Jake coming back to the team?" Obviously, he is not one for beating around the bush.

"Your guess is as good as mine." Harry stares into his glass of water as if searching for the answer in the sole crystalline ice cube floating in it. "Truth is, I didn't know he was skipping practices."

"Since that game with Bohemian Grove, in fact," Pete murmurs absentmindedly.

Harry is staring at Pete, but it's so hostile that it stops the waitress from refilling our blueberry syrup pitcher. That's okay. I'm not a fan of the blue stuff anyway. "I don't get it. You're his coach! Why didn't you just pick up the phone and call me?"

Pete glares back. "I did call. I called the only number I had. *Your wife's cell.*"

Harry closes his eyes in dread. I know what he is thinking: that this is just one more thing DeeDee can use against him in court.

This is not going at all like I'd planned. Sure, I expected some male posturing, but nothing like this. I use a tried-and-true trick learned in my years of mothering three competitive siblings:

Focus all parties on a joint goal.

"You see? This is just what I'm talking about: *communication*. I'll just bet that, among the four of us, we can come up with a way to ensure the safety of Jake and all of our kids." I look helplessly at Calvin.

He blinks twice, then takes a deep breath and goes for it. "You know, it's simpler than one might think: satellite surveillance for the whole neighborhood."

That catches Pete's attention. "How would that work?"

"It would take some doing, but that's just a matter of plotting coordinates and syncing them to video satellites already in use."

Harry looks up, impressed. "How do you know all this?"

Calvin studies his eggs modestly. "I've consulted with the Feds on satellite security issues. I'm retired now. Ideally, we'd create a secure zone through and around Paradise Heights; you know, so that we can stop break-ins and the like before they happen." He looks over at Harry. "Or help our kids, before they get into trouble."

Harry downs his water in one gulp. "What's that supposed to mean?"

"I'm just saying, we can't be everywhere we need to be all the time. And . . . well, my son, Duke, gets picked on a lot. If he gets in trouble, this is one way I can be of some help."

Harry fidgets with his fork. He's now well aware of Jake's new form of acting out. I can just imagine him wondering, *Is he talking about Jake?*

Calvin turns and stares at a guy who's just poured a whole pitcher of syrup over his French toast. "In fact, I suggested to the Paradise Heights Women's League board that they introduce a measure to the city council so that this surveillance system can be added as an amenity for the town. The price is negligible, really, when compared with the security benefits. But those women didn't think it was important enough."

"Really?" I put down my coffee cup. "Because, personally,

this is something I would have supported, and I'm on the board. Who turned it down, exactly?"

Cal shrugs. "The bitchy one."

Harry laughs. "Well, that could be any one of them. Oh, um, present company excluded." He winks at me.

"No, not the catty one. And not the schizoid, either. And not the one who thinks she's hot shit on the tennis court but can never make her first serve. And the one who still breast-feeds, she's harmless, anyone can see that. It was the *really, really* bitchy one."

"Margot," Pete and Harry say in unison. They look at each other and snicker in solidarity. Suddenly they are long-lost brothers.

And Cal—well, he's the strange cousin with a few screws loose. But family is family, right?

Especially when you've all been abandoned in one fashion or another by the women in your lives.

Pete looks at Cal, as if seeing him for the very first time. Which, I'm guessing, is not far from being the case, since his son isn't on Pete's team. "Hey, so this SATCOM thing. How long would it take before it was up and running?"

Cal thinks for a moment. "Maybe a week. That includes the beta testing period, of course. But the whole 'hood would be covered, from every angle. And its zoom capability would be awesome! Seriously, the system can pick a gnat off an elephant's ass." Cal is enjoying the admiration of his new BFFs.

I know this should spook me, but instead I'm elated. It's the answer to every tween parent's dream. I think of all the times I've called Tanner to ask what he's up to and gotten a mumbled "nothing" through the wail of sirens.

I turn to Calvin. "I'm still trying to figure out why the league was so against it. Are there any legal issues with personal privacy?"

"There aren't any," says Harry. "Surveillance via webcams is used in both public and private buildings, and in communities all over the country. Not to mention on public streets. This just takes it to another level."

"Man, I could get behind that!" Pete beams, just thinking of the possibilities for his neighborhood watch program. "No more dealing with volunteers who flake, or who fall asleep on the job. Too bad that idiotic city council is a social club. Just a bunch of hobbyist deadbeats who kowtow to that pack of witches—"

"Why is the league board's approval necessary, anyway?" Harry's question stops the other guys dead in their tracks.

"It's a symbiotic relationship, sort of like the alligator and the scorpion," I explain. "The board lobbies for the changes it sees fit to support, but the council has to vote them into law. And because it's easier to just put up and shut up than to have the board make your life miserable—"

"By dissing you at all the town's social functions," says Cal.

"Or spreading rumors about you and your wife." Pete slams down his tea mug. "Do you know how often my wife has cried herself to sleep because of those women?"

Having sat there as the board ground Masha Shriver's reputation into coarse gossip grist, I can only imagine.

Suddenly it hits me that I never stood up for her. Or any of their other targets, for that matter.

Instead, I nodded, or giggled, or simply kept my mouth shut.

And certainly I never challenged them, because that would have been social suicide.

That would have enticed them to talk about Ted and me.

As if they don't already. . . .

Pete shakes his head in wonder. "It's a shame it got voted down, for sure. But I'm not opposed to making a case for it in the *Bugle*."

The men seal their newfound friendship by turning seamlessly to the universal language of sports.

The waitress finally appears and slides my fully loaded plate in front of me. But by now, I'm no longer hungry. Thinking about Margot's power over our lives will do that to me.

Harry, on the other hand, must have found his appetite, because he reaches over and snatches up one of my pieces of bacon and devours it with gusto. Never realizing that what's stuck in my throat is the crow I'm eating, he waves the waitress back over and happily announces, "Hey, I'll have what she's having!"

20

"The 'Wedding March' always reminds me of the
music played when soldiers go into battle."

—Heinrich Heine

Wednesday, 20 Nov., 9:07 a.m.

The crash of trash cans out back means one of two things: either Harvey, our perpetually ravenous Lab, has a hankering for last night's leftover lasagna, or the family of raccoons that once lived under our house is back and has brought a few cousins along. I grab my tennis racket as backup, and pray it's one of those scenarios or the other, but not both, since I don't have time to squeeze a trip to the vet in between Olivia's ballet and Mickey's piano lesson—

That's when I see the Wilders' dog, Lucky, gnawing on the puppy version of an after-dinner mint: one hundred twenty-eight dollars' worth of vintage red leather boots, girl's size one.

I wasn't pleased when Ted brought them home for Olivia, who had been begging for a pair for a week. "Hey, it's only money" was his excuse.

"But these are Romagnolis! They're vintage leather! Trust me, Ted, she won't appreciate them!"

"She's my baby. Let me indulge her."

"But I could have gotten the Disney princess boots at Payless for a fifth of the price—"

"You're just jealous."

As my daughter danced an ecstatic jig in her new boots, I wondered if maybe he was right about that. I couldn't remember the last time Ted had bought me a gift that wasn't a cooking or cleaning gadget, let alone a simple bouquet of flowers.

In three weeks' time, the boots were so last week. Caked in playground mud, they've sat on the back stoop. Until now, when one is getting a second life as Lucky's new chew toy.

Nope, not going to happen. Not as long as children go barefoot in Africa. It's the principle of the thing.

"Out again? You're a regular Houdini, aren't you? Lucky, *come*—" I fall to my hands and knees and inch closer to him. My game plan is to distract him so that I can snatch the boot away. But no, Lucky takes this as a sign that I want to play with him and his new little toy. Immediately he crouches low too, taunting me to grab it out from under his nose. Instead, I pause. Then, very slowly, I lift one hand into the air, far away from him. While his eyes follow it, the fingers on my other hand crawl within inches of the boot—

Only to be nipped before he grabs it with his teeth. "Damn it, dog! Give me that!"

As if. Instead, he prances away, teasing me as he tosses his head from side to side.

Show-off. "So, you want to play tug-of-war, eh?"

I grab hold of the toe and pull with all my might. But his teeth, the end result of several millennia of wolves-mate-dogs, aren't going anywhere.

If I let go, he wins. Well, sorry, I'm not going to let that happen. There is a reason why we humans don't walk on all fours: unlike the rest of the animal kingdom, we've got to be able to open refrigerator doors.

I shake my head at him, then turn and walk away slowly. He stops, perplexed, then follows me into the kitchen, the boot clamped in his jaws. But before he gets there, I've already grabbed a leftover chicken breast from the fridge. "Yummy! Want a treat?" I crouch down, placing it right in front of me . . .

And wait for the trade-off: Olivia's muddy boot for cold KFC Original Recipe.

As the jaws of strife open to take the bait, I make my move with the kind of speed possessed only by a mom whose toddler has waddled onto a four-lane highway.

It's the kind of sleight-of-hand motion that David Copperfield would appreciate. But I don't have time to pat myself on the back, because I have to give Lucky the Heimlich maneuver instead. Chicken bones are certainly tastier than vintage leather but, as it turns out, more dangerous, too.

9:21 a.m.

Lucky's escape was no feat of derring-do, just a matter of one of the kids leaving the back gate open. . . .

Or not. Yes, the gate is open, but whoever opened it is still in the house.

DeeDee.

At first she doesn't see Lucky and me because her arms are piled high with clothes, knickknacks, and file folders. She maneuvers her Christian Louboutin booties around a floor strewn with toys, sneakers, and dirty laundry, trying not to trip over the flotsam and jetsam left in the wake of a single dad raising two kids on his own.

I know that this is one of the rare days on which Harry has gone into his office in the city. Apparently she does too, and is taking advantage of his absence. I'm so angry that I forget my pledge to myself not to get involved. "Excuse me, but I don't think you're supposed to be here."

Just as I say that, Lucky leaps out of my arms and runs over to her. He's pawing her legs so hard that she can't help but drop the boxes. "Damn it, Lucky!" She pretends to be mad at him, but it's me she's glaring at.

She bends over to pick up the files, now scattered about her. "Maybe I should say the same to you. What are you doing here? What's this obvious fascination with my family?"

"None. Your dog—the *kids'* dog—got loose. I found him raiding my garbage can. I guess he got out when you broke in."

"Despite the rumors that I'm sure you'll spread about me the minute I drive away, I did not break in. These things are mine, and I have a right to get them."

"So, Harry does know you're here?"

"I don't think that's any of your business—that is, unless you and Harry are . . . Oh, my God, he's not fucking you, is he?" Her laugh could curdle milk. "That would be a pip, for sure!"

"Me—and Harry? No! We're just friends." My mortification creeps up my neck in a hot rash of embarrassment. *But why? It's not like we have anything to be ashamed of. . . .*

She stares at me for so long, she could be made of stone. Finally, she shakes her head. "Yeah, sorry. My bad. As if you'd be Harry's type."

That does it. I park my foot on the pile of folders, whip out my cell, and hit 911. "Yes, I'd like to report a break-in: 56 Inman Circle. . . . Yes, right now. Thank you, as soon as possible."

"That wasn't neighborly." DeeDee smacks my thigh in the hope that I'll move my leg.

No go. In fact, I nudge her back with my knee, and step on her arm to show her I mean business. "You're no longer my neighbor."

DeeDee shakes her head, as if it's all a joke. "Oh yeah? Well, that's for the courts to decide."

I hit Harry's cell number on speed-dial. I imagine he's on his way to work, but if he knows about this, he'll want to turn the car around and confront her.

I can hear Harry's voice, but it sounds a million miles away. "Hello? Anyone there?" DeeDee wrenches a file from under my foot, and it tears in half. Taken off guard, I fall on the floor next to her.

I grab for it, but DeeDee kicks it out of reach.

"Mom! What—what the hell are you doing here?" Until now, neither of us saw Jake standing there. Of course, he's not supposed to be home at this time of day. But having been caught playing hooky only emboldens him. "Dad said you're not supposed to come here—"

"Help me pick this stuff up. Seriously, Jake, I don't have all day."

He wavers, looking from her to me, and back to her again. "No! Please get out of our house."

" 'Our' house? Is that what your father is telling you? That the house is yours and his, but not mine?" She stands up. Even as tall as he is, with her back ramrod straight and in three-inch heels she hovers over him. "How dare he turn you against me? How dare he—"

They are almost nose-to-nose now. "Mom, he didn't turn us against you. You did! You ran away, not Dad."

She opens her mouth to say something, but stops. For a moment, it hangs there, open: the dark O of her bow-shaped lips is the abyss into which DeeDee the mother has fallen, in order to protect the secrets of DeeDee the woman.

Besides, what can she say, when she knows he's right?

Nothing. And that's why, instead, she pushes past him, but stops to hug him to her chest, before walking out the door empty-handed.

Whereas she has nothing to say to him, her tongue loosens up as she brushes brusquely past me: "Don't gloat. We aren't the only broken family in the neighborhood. But I guess you already know that."

9:48 a.m.

Her car has just turned the corner when the police drive up, siren blaring, with Harry on their tail. Neighbors peek out from windows and doors, but shake their heads knowingly when they realize all the hullabaloo is coming from the Wilder household. Seeing Jake being questioned by the police, of course they presume the worst: that his truancy has finally caught up with him. More than likely he's committed an even bigger crime.

He has. And, sadly, crimes of the heart are self-imposed life sentences. With a hollow-eyed sullenness, Jake shrugs off the cop's questions as to whether he's the culprit or the victim.

Harry, both a concerned dad and a lawyer, covers for Jake's truancy in light of the circumstances. "Officer, I gave him permission to stay home from school today. He's had a toothache, and the dentist can't see him until tomorrow." Harry's no-nonsense tone puts any doubt to rest. "What happened was a domestic matter. . . ."

Harry takes the police officer aside, reassuring him in sotto voce manspeak and with a firm but gentle grip on his shoulder: now that he's home, things are under control. The cop smiles and nods. His pitying glance at me, the supposed troublemaker, would normally incite me to commit a 243—assault on a police officer—if I weren't trying to set an example for Jake. Finally the officer gets in his car and drives away, growling his siren once for good measure at an au pair with a baby carriage who dares to stroll outside the crosswalk.

Harry waits until the police car is completely out of sight before turning to Jake and me. "So, who wants to tell me what happened?"

Jake studies his Nikes, which leaves the floor open to me.

"I found Lucky rummaging in our garbage can. When I brought him here, the back door was open and DeeDee was inside, so I called the police, then you, too. Jake insisted that she leave. I don't think she had time to take anything. I mean, what she was carrying, she dropped when I . . . when we . . ."

"Yeah. I think I heard something to that effect."

"Oh . . . yes, I guess you did." Even as I let that trail off, I wonder if I've now left Harry with the notion that DeeDee and I had some kind of hair-pulling catfight in his kitchen.

Harry looks Jake in the eye. "And what were you doing home?"

"Like you said. Toothache."

Harry frowns. "Don't be a smart-ass. Listen, Jake, I know this is hard on you. I know you're angry with Mom and me right now—"

Jake shakes his head, throwing his hands up in the air. "You don't know anything! If you actually did know something, Mom would never have left!"

That earns Jake a slap to the face.

As I look on, mortified, I wonder if I'm the only one who saw Harry blow his stack.

Unfortunately, I know I'm the only one who sees the regret cross his face, because it does so just as he turns to follow Jake, who has already run inside.

Harry is too late to reach Jake before he has a chance to slam the door to his room and lock it behind him. I watch as Harry shakes his head in frustration. But so that he doesn't see me pitying him, I glance down quickly, shoving the items that fell from DeeDee's arms back into the boxes scattered to and fro on the floor.

Harry, noticing the files on the floor beside me, breaks out in a raucous laugh.

I stop, dumbfounded. "What's so funny?"

"She fell for it. She thought the files she was stealing would prove I was hiding money from her."

Perplexed, I pick up one of the manila file folders. It's labeled as last year's tax return—but the forms inside are for Minnie and Mickey Mouse. Another file, tabbed "Partnership Contract," is nothing more than a printout of what looks to be the first twenty pages of *Moby-Dick* hole-punched at the top and bound with a gold bracket.

"Too bad she didn't take them." Bitterness ruins his smile. "It would have been priceless to imagine her face when she got these home. Oh, well. I've got to remember: first thing tomorrow, a locksmith."

21

"A man's growth is seen in the successive
choirs of his friends."

—Ralph Waldo Emerson

7:07 p.m.

Whom did you say? *Harry Wilder?* He's keeping such a low profile, you'd think the poor dumb bastard had disappeared off the face of the earth . . ." Brooke's voice trails off casually. In truth, she's fishing.

But I'm not biting.

It's my turn to host the league board's meeting. Since Ted is working late yet again, I've bribed Tanner to keep Mickey and Olivia busy upstairs while I play host to my own firing squad.

We're only a week away from Thanksgiving. You'd think that, by now, the drive was on its way to being a success, that I'd be coasting to a sure victory as the next president of the board—

Wrong.

Thus far, the drive has been an unequivocal disaster. Most of the barrels in Paradise Heights's schools sit empty, except for the handful of cans that rattle the death knell of my dreams of being Margot's successor as board president.

Most of my class chairs have flaked: too many volunteer activities, so little time. And the smiley face–shaped notes I've been stuffing into the children's knapsacks have rallied few parents to my cause. E-mails—pinging parents' in-boxes weekly at first, but now daily, and soon to be hourly—are apparently being junked without even being opened. Is it the frantic subject line (HELP! PLEASE! GET OFF YOUR CANS) that scares everyone off?

Well, subtlety has never been my strong suit.

Needless to say, the board thinks I have a lot of explaining to do.

To prolong the inevitable, all night long I've been shoveling out my patented lobster salad canapés to the board, along with avocado dip and salty chips by the bagful, then pouring pitcher after pitcher of margaritas in the hope that this will sate the board's thirst, if not its hunger to eat one of its own.

That one being *me*.

All because I dared to take on the neighborhood's one-woman juggernaut, its female whirling dervish of productivity, its queen bee.

What a fool I am.

It is only because Colleen is more than just a wee bit tipsy that she has wondered out loud about the One Dad Whose Name We Dare Not Speak. Despite his banishment, deep down she has not given up hope that the board's prodigal DILF will once again be clasped to its ample if augmented bosoms (hers being the amplest of all, thanks to her covert nursing of three-year-old McGuyver).

Hearing Harry's name being bandied about, Isabelle bares her veneered fangs. "That guy? Believe it or not, I saw him just this afternoon with—well, you'll *never* guess who!" Isabelle is so smug about trumping Brooke with this latest piece of hot gossip that she doesn't notice I missed her glass completely when I tried to refill it. Quickly I grab a handful of napkins to sop up the puddle by her sleeve, resisting the urge to cram them down her throat.

"Oh, I saw them too," exclaims Tammy.

Not to be outdone, Isabelle joins her in blurting it out: "With Pete and Calvin." Then they both cackle with laughter.

Margot looks up from the notes she's been preparing since she darkened my doorstep. "My, my, how the mighty have fallen. So now there are three stooges. That's fitting, I guess."

"Yeah, well, it doesn't surprise me in the least," gloats Tammy. "We all find our own levels, don't we?"

Watching me bite my lower lip, Brooke puts her hand on my arm to caution me, but I can't take it anymore. Instead of giving in to the temptation to pour what's left of the margaritas down the back of Tammy's Lilly Pulitzer halter dress, I blurt out, "Frankly, that's pretty great company, if you ask me."

"You've got to be kidding!" Isabelle's head snaps around.

Seriously, she's got nothing on Linda Blair. If I weren't wearing the tiny silver cross Ted gave me last Valentine's Day, I'd be more worried. "No, I'm not! It just so happens that Calvin is a really sweet—and *very normal*—guy. In fact, he's a security consultant with the government."

"Hah! Is that what he told you? Are you sure he didn't say the witness protection program?"

Colleen snorts at Isabelle's joke. Seeing my glare, she ducks in shame.

"And as for that other lonely guy, Pete Shriver, I can certainly see what he and Harry have in common: wives smart enough to go AWOL." Margot raises her glass to Isabelle at their mutual wittiness.

"Gee, Lyssa, sounds like you've been cavorting with these losers too." Suddenly suspicious, Tammy gives me the once-over. "What, are you their new mascot or something?"

"Who, me? No! I—I just . . . well, I just don't see the harm in having a wide circle of friends, is all."

"With all the socializing you're doing these days, it's no wonder our food drive is in the crapper."

I flinch as Margot's declaration hits its target succinctly. "That's not fair! I've been working my ass off—"

"Oh, really?" As she says this, she glares pointedly at my bum before flipping open the MacBook she brought with her. "If that were the case, productivity wouldn't be down 78.4 percent." Her nod is barely perceptible, but Colleen catches it, and is scurrying to hit the TV remote. The family room television screen comes alive with a bar graph of three rows made up of graphics of cans. "As you can see from this analysis of the past three years' drives . . ."

And for the next hour, instead of the usual gossiping and mommy one-upmanship we enjoy so much, I and the rest of the board are treated to a fully animated HDTV PowerPoint presentation showcasing the intricate details of running a boffo off-the-charts school event, Margot Hardaway–style. You can take the girl out of the boardroom, but you can't take the boardroom out of the girl. Corporate America's loss is Paradise Heights's gain.

The theme from *Rocky* crescendos as each page melds into the next. One shows fifth-graders stacking cans into a pyramid that reaches the ceiling. I recognize the voice-over on the presentation: it's an actress from a sitcom that's been off the air for at least eight years. She's now a full-time mommy here in the Heights, so I'm guessing Margot got her on the cheap.

"Each successive year has had a quantum leap over the previous year. Your event manual explains the primary cause for this phenomenal success: simply put, it's KPE! That is, Kindergarten Parent Enthusiasm. The social anxiety these parents feel for their children is channeled into hyperactivism within

their children's new classrooms—which in turn translates into enough cans—"

"Manual? But I never got a manual!" I can feel the beads of sweat forming on my brow.

Margot sighs and shakes her head in annoyance. "Sure you did. I handed it to you myself. Don't you remember? It has a burgundy binder."

Ah, yes, I remember now: a 486-page tome filled with footnoted analyses within sections labeled "Creative Sales Techniques," "Classroom Incentive Programs," "Post-Program Analytics," "Data Management," "Manpower Analysis," and on and on . . .

Yes, I did try to read through it, but by page 73 I was sporting one whopper of a headache. And I guess I should never have left it open on the kitchen counter, because the whole section on "Team-Level Analysis" was smeared with jelly when Mickey made a sandwich over it, and is now stuck together.

Quickly I turn around to make sure the laundry room door is closed. Otherwise, Margot may notice it's being used to prop up the washing machine so that it doesn't rumba across the floor when Tanner stuffs too many of his and Mickey's dirty towels into the wash.

Damn it, I hate being put on the defensive. Time to turn the tables. "You know, the purpose of a volunteer event is grass roots. Everyone is supposed to pitch in and help. Margot, if you actually got in the trenches with me, maybe it wouldn't be floundering right now."

"We're—that is, *you're* floundering because you don't know how to inspire anyone to action. I guess we aren't all natural-born leaders." She pauses the presentation and scans the room. "You have a point, though. Someone's got to bail you out. Any volunteers?"

Except for a hiccup out of Colleen, the room is silent. These women may share a lot of things—recipes, babysitters, doctors, sometimes even vacations—but when it comes to screwups, it's every woman for herself.

"Ah, well, busy schedules all around, I guess. Sorry, Lyssa, dear. You're on your own. It'll just take a little extra planning on your part, is all."

But her tone says it all: I've already failed.

Margot's crown is safe for yet another year.

As she takes a sip from her glass, the frozen presentation page dissolves to her screen saver: a picture of Margot, lying out by the pool at her palatial Maui beach house with her hubby, Gerard, a cardiologist.

"Oops, sorry, girls!" But she's not really. She just wants us to remember that her picture-perfect life is the result of more than a little extra planning on her part.

It also has to do with marrying well.

As her friends ooh and aah over Gerard's toned, tanned, and hairless chest, Margot boasts that he's hairless all over, even under the postage stamp–size Speedo that rises, like the Barnum and Bailey big top, over his obvious bulge.

In fact, she manscapes his twigs and berries herself, as part of their lovemaking ritual.

Yeah, right.

Margot is no subservient geisha, and we all know it. Truth be told, Gerard used to go to the Heights of Beauty for a little waxwork around his package—until Margot caught the waxing technician throwing in a free hand job.

Her best friend, Tammy, leaked that little tidbit to Brooke, which in Paradise Heights is the equivalent of giving Brian Williams a late-breaking news item.

To our frenemies, indiscretion is the greater part of malice.

As Margot informs us as to why plucking is much more meticulous than waxing, I just tune out—until she comes to the part about "first aid." "Every now and then, even I miss the hair. Just goes to show that no one's perfect. . . ."

Ouch.

Yes, she's a sadist. Not that this is news to anyone. That her tweezers grab hold of skin instead of hair . . . well, chalk it up to Margot extracting her ounce of flesh from Gerard, literally as well as figuratively.

Or to holding on for dear life, with all its imperfections.

8:53 p.m.

The meeting finally wraps up just as Ted saunters through the door. Instinctively all eyes move in his direction. In the space of a nanosecond, their brains have processed his vital statistics: tall, handsome, swarthy good looks, taken . . . but is he smitten?

He, too, assesses the situation: six women, of whom five are stoically married, if not out-and-out unhappy about it.

He doesn't presume he should count me among them.

He gives Brooke a wink as he reminds us of the results of their last tennis game, and massages Isabelle's neck, which has her practically purring. When he compliments Tammy on her tan, she demurely nudges her halter top in order to show that her golden glaze is full-bodied.

Had he challenged that claim, I've no doubt she would have squeezed out of her jeans and yanked down her thong too, in order to prove that she meant what she said.

Then we could have seen for ourselves if she waxes, shaves, or plucks.

And if she does it as well as Margot.

One of Tammy's straps is relaxed enough to give Ted and the rest of us a quick peek at a nipple. Her "Oops! Sorry . . ." convinces no one that it was an accident.

Ted feigns missing her little striptease. "Damn, Tammy! Next time give me some warning." I know better. His smile is too wide. When we play Go Fish with the kids, it's his tell.

As he helps the women into their coats and gives them each a peck on the cheek, Tammy turns and gives me a hug that almost strangles me. "We miss you, girl! Don't be such a stranger."

Ted looks at her strangely. "Why do you say that? Lyssa is here all day long."

"Is that what she tells you? Boy, I wish my Charlie were as gullible! Harry Wilder is Lyssa's new best friend. She'd much rather hang out with him than with us."

Before I have a chance to call her on this, Brooke murmurs just low enough for me to hear, whether I want to or not: "Sweetheart, you can't play Switzerland. Choose a side. For your sake, I hope it's the right one."

22

"There is no disguise which can hide love for long where it exists, or simulate it where it does not."

—François de La Rochefoucauld

10:17 p.m.

L et's fuck," says Ted.

Seriously, this is his idea of foreplay.

I look up from the bathtub I'm scrubbing—the one between Olivia's bedroom and the guest room. Its scum ring is the result of our daughter's newfound love affair with mud pies and all other primal faux baked goods. I barely had time to throw her into the tub before the board arrived, and certainly had no time at all to wash it out immediately afterward. So to ensure that my guests' powder-room visits were limited to the downstairs lavatory, particularly Margot's (why is it that those with the tiniest bladders are the biggest clean freaks?), I locked the hall door to this bathroom and barricaded it with Olivia's Imaginarium Glitter Suite Dollhouse.

With this gossip-hungry group, I've learned to take no chances.

Whereas I avoided this shame, that last little jibe from Tammy was the cherry on the cake of this seventeen-hour-long day. I was fully prepared for a fight as opposed to a love tussle, so Ted's reaction to her remark is a surprise.

Relieved, I smile wanly and rise from my knees—only to feel

Ted's arm around my waist. As he yanks me close, the canister of Comet I'm holding is crushed, and a green mushroom cloud has us choking midkiss.

But even this doesn't deter him from the task at hand:

Nailing me.

The only thing I can figure is that Tammy's taunt about Harry has made him jealous.

Well, what do you know! Ted has a new turn-on. . . .

"Hey, babe, what say we do it, like, right here in the tub?" He eyes my handiwork with a nod. No, it's not that Ted feels cleanliness is next to godliness, and certainly not as it pertains to booty calls. "You know how I like to watch you get all lathered up. Or, hey, you can hike up there on the vanity." Without a second thought, he backhands Olivia's Disney Princess toothbrush, tumbler, and soap dish into the sink, patting the counter in anticipation.

Ah, so that's how it's going to be: whoopee is to be made, but not anywhere as mundane as our bedroom suite. We are to live dangerously, even if that means doing so within yelping distance of the innocents who have sprung from our loins.

This should bother me, I know. I am truly bone tired. The fact that Ted just got in from yet another late-night sales meeting, and that his eyes have that undeniable Glenlivet glaze, is the prime indicator that I can expect snoring as opposed to snuggling after our little lovefest.

Then again, beggars can't be choosers, and our sex drought has gone on too long. So instead of bombarding him with the battery of naked Barbies that form Olivia's in-tub swim team, I pause, pretending to seriously consider his interesting offer but all the while thinking, *Dude, ain't no way in hell I'll risk waking Olivia with my fake moans, which I do only to keep you stoked enough that I can come too before you peter out, or having her walk in to go potty only to see us going at it like two hot, horny bonobos—*

Whoa. Just think how much those shrink bills would set us back. . . .

Instead, I whisper back, "Mmmm, *love* it! So naughty! But I have a better idea. . . ."

Taking his hand in mine, I lead him out into the hall, down the stairs, and out into the backyard, far away from the eyes and ears of our offspring.

Beyond the pool, silhouetted in full moonlight, is the tool-shed.

The name is a misnomer. It holds anything but. Instead it is a repository of past lives, both Ted's and mine. Two whole walls are filled with his old high school and college basketball trophies. In some alternate universe, one in which he has two good knees and no tendinitis, the Ted Harper he was meant to be has just re-upped with the Lakers, having accepted a contract befitting the league's top scorer. Are we married? I doubt it. Unlike this Ted, that one has enough challenges on the court. Somewhere in that new life, scoring has to be easy, right? For both Teds, the issue is never quantity. But in the eye of the pop tart, the supermodel, or the celebutante, there is nothing sexy about software sales, so advantage: Laker Ted.

On my side of the shed is a tall bookcase filled with coffee cans that hold paintbrushes and quart-sized cans of acrylic paints arranged by hue. An avalanche of some of my old paintings has slid below the sill of the shed's window, where they were propped. On an easel is a portrait of Mickey. It is my latest attempt at rediscovering the talent I once believed in so fiercely. It is how he looked at three: full-cheeked and sloe-eyed, nodding off with his head against a windowpane as he waits for his big brother to come home from school.

Ted ignores it even as he scouts the perfect place to ravage me. I'm praying he settles for the room's only soft surface, a daybed. It is covered in a pink sateen duvet and laden with stuffed animals. I'd hoped this dainty tableau would induce Olivia to make the shed her playhouse, but she's not having it. Not yet, anyway. She's still too young to feel comfortable playing alone this far from the house.

So that Ted will take the hint, I fall back onto it with a come-hither chuckle and rip open the buttons of my blouse, but he's not buying it. He pulls me up. From behind me, he unzips my jeans, then yanks them down to my ankles. He kisses the insteps of my feet as he untangles them from denim.

His hands roam gently between my legs and beyond the silk panel of my panties, his fingers stroking and probing until he elicits a groan and a shudder. "You want it, don't you?"

"Yes, I want it." My voice trembles just enough for him to think I really mean it.

But what I really want is the one thing he's not willing to give me:

His undying love, for as long as we both shall live.

In the meantime, I'll settle for being the best fuck he's ever had.

No amount of gusto on my part can trump that one thing I know turns him on: the thrill of the chase.

Well, today I've discovered another: jealousy.

Thanks, Harry. Next time, the doughnuts are on me.

Tonight, though, what Ted has in mind entails no rubbing, straddling, probing, pumping, sucking, or Cirque du Soleil acrobatics on my part. He is on a mission: to earn back my lust.

My job is to sit back and enjoy the ride.

Or stand, as the case may be. He walks me over to the window, kicking aside the canvases that get in his way. As they slide like dominoes over our feet, he curses me under his breath: "Damn it, Lys! Why do you keep these around anyway? Can't you unload them on craigslist? There's got to be a starving artist who'll take them off your hands for a few bucks."

It's on the tip of my tongue to ask him if he can ditch his stupid trophies on some starving athletes, but he shuts me up with a face-suck, then flips me around so that I'm facing out the window.

"There. Hands on the sill." Ted's hot breath dampens the hairs on the back of my neck, but it's the index finger that hooks onto my panties and slowly pulls them down to my ankles that makes me shiver. So that I can spread my legs, he raises one foot, grazing the arch with his hand, then does the same with the other, before repositioning me, arched and straining on tiptoe. To steady himself behind me, he holds on to my hips. I hold my breath, waiting for the plunge.

Finally, when he enters me, I moan. Each time he drives himself deep inside me, my breasts jiggle. At the same time, the loosest pane in the window shakes, rattles, and rolls as his fist hits the sill. He's in the zone, and he just assumes I am too.

So why aren't I? I should be feeling joy, lust, gratitude, happiness; I know it.

But I don't.

I feel used.

To put myself into the moment, I try to think of something that makes me happy. What immediately comes to mind is the newest blossom on the crimson candy cane amaryllis that Harry gave me. This in turn has me remembering Harry's admiration of my green thumb. Next thing I know, I'm thinking about Harry's thumb. . . . Oh, all right, I'll admit it: it's not just his thumb that comes to mind, but those long, thick fingers too—

And what that implies about any appendage he might stuff into a leopard bong thong. . . .

My moan jolts me out of the fantasy, but Ted takes it as a cue to up the ante. The locomotion in his love train is moving us full steam ahead in unison. So that my thoughts don't end up back in Harry's underwear drawer, I open my eyes and stare out the window. The full moon is not kind to the sycamores lining the street. In its glow, the shadows of their branches, shorn of all leaves, become an army of grotesque goblins rampaging over our lawn. The street beyond is lit up like a stage in the glow of the antique streetlamps Pete fought so hard for—

And that's when I see Harry.

He is out walking Lucky, who is sniffing the ground before making the pit stop that will have Harry scooping poop with the plastic bag already over one hand.

But no, instead he glances over—

Oh, my God, he sees me.

At least, I presume he's seen me—seen *us*, that is, or perhaps heard us, what with the way the window is shaking, as if we're in the middle of an earthquake or something—because he does a double take, then slowly walks in our direction, as if to get a better look.

It suddenly occurs to me that Harry has seen enough of my jubblies. I want to duck below the windowsill, but Ted has me pinned. "Ted! . . . *TED*—"

My whispers fall on deaf ears. Ted keeps pounding away at me. As he climaxes, he roars ecstatically.

Harry, now fearing the worst, is looking for a way to jump the fence so that he can check things out.

"Ted, stop, *please*!" To make my point, I reach back and smack him on the rump.

He moans loudly. "Aw, honey, give me a minute to catch my breath! I'm not a machine, you know."

But he's willing to give it the old college try. He pulls me close again. This time, to get him to listen, I slap him—*hard*—in the face. "No, listen! Someone—*someone is out there*."

"Fuck it. . . . *What?*" My hit has deflated him, both

figuratively and literally. I'm now allowed to duck below the window. Realizing his own exposure, Ted crouches, too.

"Jesus, it's that Wilder guy! What the hell is he doing out there anyway? What is he, some sort of pervert?"

"No! No . . . he's just walking his dog." I untangle myself from Ted. Crablike, I crawl over to where my pants and panties have been tossed and grab them, then tuck and roll to the bed, where I've left my shirt. I'm not about to prance around and give Harry yet another cheap thrill. "I guess that damn loose pane caught his attention."

"Yeah, right. I wouldn't put it past your new boyfriend to be some sort of Peeping Tom."

"Harry is *not* a Peeping Tom. And he's not my boyfriend. He took his dog out, then heard the noise, so he walked over to investigate. Quit making a federal case out of it."

"Why are you defending that loser?"

"You don't even know him! Why would you say something like that?" I hope I don't sound too indignant. Or, worse yet, guilty. I peek out the window, but Harry is long gone. Evidently having figured out the score, he is dragging Lucky back down the street.

I've still got my back to Ted so I can't see his smirk, but I can hear it in his voice. "Oh, sure, I know him all right. He's one arrogant son of a bitch."

"You've got him all wrong. Frankly, he's a nice guy. And despite what Tammy said, he's been a total gentleman. There's nothing wrong with being neighborly."

"How sweet. So he's finally meeting the neighbors." Ted stares out the window, but no Harry. "Well, I guess he's hoping that 'better late than never' pays off."

"What does that mean?" It's been a very long night. I toss him his boxer briefs in the hope he will take the hint and cover himself up.

"Get real. Is he stupid enough to think he'll get to keep the house, once the divorce is settled? Fat chance."

I don't want to debate him on this topic. Not while he's plastered and jealous.

Not ever, really.

Suddenly I feel guilty that Harry and I are friends. I glance over at Ted, only to see he's turned his back on me and is already out the door.

So much for snuggling.

Sometime in the middle of the night, in the middle of our bed, a thought hits me:

During our impromptu shed shag, I wasn't wearing my diaphragm.

I try to remember the number of days since my last period, but I'm so tired, and it's too much like counting sheep. Not to worry, I assure myself. My ovulation rarely occurs during the only other constant in my life: league board meetings.

Realizing how predictable my life has become, I cry myself to sleep.

And dream about Harry.

23

"Love is a gamble, it's a chance that you take.
You lay your heart down and you bet it won't break."

—Hugh Prestwood

Thursday, 21 Nov., 4:08 p.m.

W e need a fourth for poker tomorrow night. Are you in?" Harry's cheeriness seems forced. We haven't talked since I last saw him. Or I should say, since he last saw me: through the shed window.

Maybe I'm just reading him wrong. Maybe, like me, he's catching his breath from another hellish week.

Just maybe he didn't see Ted and me after all.

Of course, that's it! Otherwise he wouldn't be calling, inviting me over, just like one of the guys. And certainly he'd be teasing me unmercifully. . . .

"Yeah, sure. I don't really play, but I'm in."

"Great! Oh, and no need to worry. It isn't strip poker." He hangs up laughing.

Yep, okay, he saw us.

But he's wrong. Strip poker is just what we need to even the score. . . .

Or not. Seeing Pete without his skivvies and validating Masha's excuse for catting around on him would not give me much joy.

I'll settle for a very large cash pot.

• • •

Friday, 22 Nov., 7:04 p.m.

The judge ruled that DeeDee is allowed to take the kids to her apartment on Sundays, Mondays, and Tuesdays, while Harry gets them on Wednesdays, Thursdays, and Fridays. They'll rotate Saturdays. Since he won't get to see his kids for the next three nights, they are allowed to stay up until the game ends.

The kids accompany me. We wouldn't be here at all except for the fact that tonight Ted's company is playing a basketball league game. By the time he gets home, the kids and I are already in bed. Just once I want him to come home to an empty house. Then maybe he'll actually bother to ask where we were.

But I wouldn't bet on it.

Somehow Cal has convinced Sabrina and Duke to come along, but Sabrina's scowl is proof that she's here against her will. In order to avoid any human contact, she is concentrating on a tall wall of books in the Wilders' living room. Finally she plucks a thick tome from one of the shelves: *The Hite Report on Male Sexuality*. I've no doubt she'll get more out of it than the Wilder it was meant for.

Pete came early for his pep talk with Jake about rejoining the team. It must have worked, because the two of them are shooting hoops in the driveway. And from the way Natassia is sizing up Jake, I'm guessing Pete didn't need to twist her arm to tag along. Like mother, like daughter.

Olivia runs off happily with Temple to her fairyland of a bedroom. At first Mickey and the middle-schoolers aren't so eager to play nice. It's like watching three Mafia families meet to divvy up a new territory. Natassia and Sabrina circle and sneer at each other. Tanner and Jake ignore them as well as Duke— that is, until they realize that Duke's obliviousness to them and his fascination with his iPhone are due to the fact that, by some miracle, he is tuned to the video feed of the Golden State Warriors' coaches while he watches the basketball game on the phone's screen.

"Wow! Is that coming from some new ESPN app?" Tanner moves in for a closer look.

"No. I made it." Duke ducks his head shyly. "The picture is coming from the stadium's JumboTron feed, and the audio is coming off the licensed network's mike."

Jake, too, is mesmerized. "Duke, dude, think you can make it work on my phone too?"

Duke nods, but Harry shakes his head. "Remember the rules, kids: homework first. Jake, if you don't pass your French test Monday, you won't even own a phone."

Jake rolls his eyes. Something tells me he's skipped that class more than he'd like to admit to his dad.

Sabrina looks up from her book. "I'm in your class. I'll quiz you if you like." Her glare dares him to take her up on the offer.

Either Jake is desperate, or he likes what he sees: another rebel without a cause, not to mention a 36C chest in a tight Grateful Dead T-shirt.

As they head off toward Jake's bedroom, Tanner suddenly realizes he has Natassia all to himself. "I've got a test on Monday, too. How are you at math?"

"Lousy." Her sigh is accompanied by a flip of her long blond hair.

"Oh. That's too bad."

"It doesn't have to be." She picks up his book and riffles through it. Am I the only one who notices that it's upside down? "Want to study together?"

"Yeah, sure!" He follows her into the kitchen.

Harry laughs. "Natassia is a real boost to Tanner's ego."

"Yeah, among other things. Well, here's hoping she doesn't decimate my son's GPA." I point to the deck of cards in his hand. "Now, shut up and deal."

9:37 p.m.

"So, are you going to take a card or what?" Pete's voice drips with venom. Well, what do I expect? He hates to lose, and for the past two hours I've been beating the pants off of him—and Harry and Cal, too—in five-card stud.

"Sure, why not, I'll take a card." I say it as if I couldn't care less, and for a good reason: I've already got two pair. Since the card I draw gives me three of a kind, I've got myself a full house.

And the rest of Pete's stack.

Too bad it's not wired into his bank account.

Seeing my hand, the guys groan and fold. Harry looks over at me suspiciously. "Hey, I thought you said you don't play."

"I lied."

All three men give involuntary nods. It suddenly occurs to me that I've said the wrong thing to redeem their faith in women.

So that I don't completely wipe out my poker buddies, Harry uses a bit of psychological warfare to put me off my game: he asks me how the Thanksgiving food drive is going.

I groan out loud. "Well, if it's any indication, I'm exiled from the board's morning coffee gatherings. Until I prove myself as a leader, Margot feels my mornings would be better spent, and I quote, 'focusing on the task at hand.' "

"What a bitch!" Pete frowns. "Seriously, how many cans do you need to get back in their good graces?"

"More to the point, why would you want to be there any-way?" Harry says this just loud enough for me to hear him.

I kick him under the table. "Somewhere in the neighborhood of twenty-one hundred. Even two thousand would be considered a respectable showing. With that, I'll be within spitting distance of her record."

Cal blinks twice. "That's doable. Between all three schools, there are eight hundred kids in the Heights. If every kid brought in three cans, you'd knock the smirk off her face."

" 'Doable'? Ha! You try wrangling eight hundred kids and their parents for a worthy cause."

Pete nods. "Okay, you're on. I'll tell my team that the guy who brings in the most cans stays off the bench permanently for the rest of the season."

"My partners and I own a vacation home in Tahoe," says Harry. "DeeDee can't get her hands on it, since it's owned by the firm. If you want, you can offer a weekend there as a contest prize: everyone who brings in at least four cans is eligible, or something like that."

"That can go in the next online issue of the *Bugle*, if you want," adds Pete. "It launches at midnight tonight."

"Wow! Both of you are awesome to do this for me, seriously." I start to tear up. They barely know me, but they're willing to do more than my own board.

I have a new definition of friendship.

"I can't speak for Bev, but . . ." Cal looks helpless. He wants to offer something, but he can't think of anything. "Well, to tell you the truth, Bev and I barely talk these days."

Pete smirks. "Welcome to the club." He slings his cards so hard that they hit the wall some four feet away.

We all sit there, stunned. Then Cal does the same.

Harry takes the rest of the deck and, one by one, flicks the cards onto the table.

Yeah. O-*kay*. I get it. I'm sitting in the midst of three very angry men. "I can imagine how hard it is, to want to get through to someone you love who doesn't hear you. But you have to ask yourself: are you truly making every attempt to tell her how you feel?"

All three men stare at me. "What's that supposed to mean?" Harry spits out his words.

"I'm just trying to say that women appreciate it when you verbalize what your feelings are—and when you ask them to express theirs too."

"Oh yeah?" Pete glares at me. "What, now we've got to model our lives on a *Redbook* cover? 'Is He Giving You What You Really Want? Five Ways to Tell Him How to Do It Right.' That stuff is such bull!"

I laugh. "Well, if those headlines sell, then they must be hitting some hot button with women. Can you say the same?"

He flinches. *Ouch.* I didn't mean to hit him below the belt.

So that it doesn't seem as if I'm picking on him, I turn to Cal. "The one thing I've noted about Bev is that she's a very hard worker. I'm sure you are too, but obviously something is driving her to accomplish even more than her fair share. Perhaps she's expressed financial concerns, or she has a professional goal? Whatever it is, if you acknowledge this drive, show her you appreciate how hard she's working for you and the family, it may make her realize that she's already got what she's looking for: your love and approval."

Cal looks at his feet. "I'm not great at saying 'I love you.' I know that."

"Well, admittedly, it is the first step. Even 'Honey, thank you for all you do' will go a long way." I pat him on the shoulder. "Hey, better yet, call in a maid for a day to get the house shipshape. Anyone who works as hard as Bev would appreciate that. Then surprise her by taking her out to dinner, just the two of you. I don't know what woman wouldn't love that."

"I do." Pete looks me in the eye. "Don't you think I know what everyone—especially your girlfriends—says about Masha and me behind our backs? Okay, Oprah, since you have all the answers, what am I supposed to do, mainline Viagra?"

"Viagra? No, I don't think so." He's caught me off guard. "Look, I don't have all the answers, believe me. I wish I did. But if the issue you have with Masha is, um, personal, then maybe you need to stop thinking like a guy and think like a woman. She's a stranger in a strange country, and whatever issue she has with love—or for that matter, with sex—more than likely finds its root in some emotional pain she's never even mentioned to you." I take a deep breath. "Keep another thing in mind: as much as we women love sex, romance is our biggest turn-on."

Pete shrugs, but I know I've hit on something when he takes out his cell phone and texts a message. I'm hoping it's to a sex therapist. Or some romantic B and B.

The fun and games are over. Cal and I round up our kids and head out. Seeing that I've got a drowsy Olivia draped over my shoulder, Harry takes her from me, murmuring to Jake to get his sister to bed while he walks us around the block.

The boys race home, but I walk next to Harry. Only when we reach my porch does he break the heavy silence that hangs between us. "I've never talked to a woman the way I talk to you. Ted's a very lucky guy, in more ways than one."

He leaves it at that, and so do I. What can I say?

Frankly, I don't know how he'd feel to learn that I've told him things I've never said to Ted, and possibly never will.

I talk a good game, but I'm just like him and the other guys. I can't handle the truth if it means finding out that I'm living a lie.

24

"If there is such a thing as a good marriage, it is because
it resembles friendship rather than love."

—Michel de Montaigne

Tuesday, 26 Nov., 1:27 p.m.

Y ou know, right now Margot is pea green with envy! She
never in a million years thought you'd get even this close
to PULLING IT *OFF*!" Brooke's whisper ends with a
shriek, not for emphasis but of pain: Geraldo, her masseur here
at Serenity Now, has found yet another knot in her neck and is
pushing, pulling, and tugging it into submission.

Or else the former Green Beret and black ops mercenary may
finally have snapped and made good on his threat to shut her
up once and for all. He claims her ongoing chatter defeats the
purpose of getting a deep-tissue massage because she never gives
her mouth a break.

He also insists that her constant yammering is worse torture
than what he inflicted on our enemies.

For this reason alone, I forgo his flying fingers for those of a
small Asian Zen master, Mr. Qi. Qi may be blind, but he reads
muscles as if they were lines of braille, and he certainly doesn't
mind it when I converse with Brooke through the high partition that separates us. Granted, Mr. Qi may not be as strong

as Geraldo; then again, I'll never worry that what I say might induce a flashback that gets me waterboarded under specially oxygenated, rose-petal-infused water.

"But I haven't 'pulled it off.' At least, not yet. I still have another two hundred or so cans to go." I flip over so that Mr. Qi can work my forehead. Nothing he does will remove the lines there, forged deeper from all my worry that I'll blow this opportunity to show up Margot. We are in the last twenty-one hours of the food drive. Despite my efforts and those of Pete and Harry, victory is slipping from my grasp. "I know it's petty of me, but I *really, really* wanted to beat her, just this once. Then Thanksgiving would be perfect."

Even without breaking Margot's record, I've got a lot to be thankful for. To start with, Mother is spending Thanksgiving with her sister, down in Carmel.

"Hallelujah!" said Ted when I told him that bit of news, last night while we—well, *he*—watched the last few minutes of the Lakers game in bed. "Do you know how hard it is to swallow with her sour puss staring at me from across the table?"

"Hey, it's not all that bad. . . . Okay, yeah, it's a downer." At his behest, I was straddling his back in order to massage his shoulders. But my nuzzling him behind the ears didn't seem to arouse him half as much as Kobe's two consecutive three-point shots, so I gave up and hopped off. "Best yet, with Mother out of our hair for the weekend, you won't have to pretend you have to go into the office on Friday."

"Yep, we'll get to sleep in for four whole days in a row." He flipped over to face me. "When was the last time we did that?"

"You tell me." I turned and muted the sound using the TV's remote so he could see I meant business. "You're serious, right, about taking off Friday? You've been working so many nights and weekends lately that I can't believe my ears."

"Cross my heart, babe, I'm all yours. Why, what did you have in mind?" He kissed me hard, but his eyes were following Derek Fisher down the court.

"Absolutely nothing. In fact, I think we'll skip the potluck open house at the club, too." Really, I hadn't planned on going anyway. Not if I had to hear Margot feign sympathy over my failure to lead the troops to victory in our Thanksgiving food drive.

Now I realize that Brooke has given up on me too. Some pal.

"Hey, you can't say you didn't give it the . . . ol' . . . college . . . TRY! *Ouch!* Way to go, big guy!" Brooke caresses each syllable in sync with Geraldo's smacks to her tush on the pretense of massaging her upper thighs. If he thinks he can beat her into submission, he's sorely mistaken. She's admitted to me that part of the thrill of going to him is coming *through* him. (Being married to a dentist says a lot about your threshold for pain.)

"Your phone is vibrating." Mr. Qi's whisper tickles my ear like a sweet breeze. He's right: my purse is dancing a jig on the small stand beside the massage table as my cell buzzes away. I flip it open to a cryptic text message:

Paradise Heights Market, 2pm in back. Mojo knows.

The caller ID says *CyBerGuy.*

I am intrigued, to say the least. "Gotta run! See you at pickup!" There's no guarantee that Brooke heard me. The smacks are now coming fast and furious, as are her yelps of pleasure.

Mr. Qi can't see my concern for my friend, but he can feel it in my aura. "Not to worry. You know what they say: 'No pain, no gain.'"

• • •

2:06 p.m.

Behind the Paradise Heights Market is the part of the shopping experience few ever get to witness: the shuffle and jive of produce delivery via big trucks and beefy men. Most of them are swarming around a small balding guy who sports a full-body apron embroidered with the market's logo. After perusing the goods being delivered, he begrudgingly signs the bills of lading handed to him.

I stand behind the last deliveryman, not knowing exactly what I should say to him. When it's finally my turn, he gives me a cool once-over with one eye shut. "You lost or something?"

"I was told to pick something up here, something called, er, 'mojo'?"

His guffaw covers a bad cough. "I'm Mojo. So, you're Lyssa?" Reassured by my nod, he points to a small trailer. "Then that's for you."

"What is it?"

He sighs, then nudges me over with him, swinging one of the doors open in the back. I can't believe my eyes. On one side it's stacked to the ceiling with cans, while the other side holds bags of rice, boxes of stuffing mix, and about twenty turkeys.

Yes! I am now *so* beyond my quota!

"For your little cause. I had the stock boy pull cans that are close to their expiration dates, or are too dented for the swells. And we overbought on Butterballs. Your crowd prefers free-range birds anyway. Now, if you'll sign this donation receipt . . ."

I do so with a happy flourish. "Oh, my goodness! Thank you, thank you! But how did you know?"

"Bev Bullworth called. She's our biggest advertiser"—he points to a row of abandoned shopping carts; all of them have

Bev's face, name, and motto plastered on the back of the toddler bench—"and we appreciate it. When she asked if we could help out, of course we said yes."

"This is so great! Well, let me give you the address for the delivery—"

"Nope, sorry, lady. You'll have to tow it out of here yourself."

"But . . . I don't have a hitch."

"Your husband has already taken care of that."

"My . . . husband?" How did Ted know about this? Except to complain about "all the junk"—that is, the cans—filling the garage on the side where I usually park, he didn't even seem to be aware of my project.

"He said to tell you he'll be back with the U-Haul. That was an hour ago, so he should be—yeah, okay, here he is now."

It's not Ted behind the wheel of the rental truck, but Harry. He waves with one hand while turning the steering wheel with the other until the truck is positioned perfectly in front of the trailer, then jumps out to hitch the vehicles together.

"Isn't this your day to be in the office? You took off to help me?"

"No, not exactly. I was home anyway, when Cal called to tell me about his score." He shrugs. "My partners feel I'm too distracted to be in the office. They've asked that I consider a sabbatical."

"That doesn't sound like a good thing."

"Financially, it's not, really. But better now than later, right? At least I can enjoy all of the Thanksgiving break with the kids."

"Wow! That's super you've got them for the four days."

"Yeah, well, DeeDee needs to 'find herself.' I presume her journey of self-discovery will take her somewhere she can get an allover tan." He jiggles the door of the trailer. Finding it unlocked, he slams it closed with more force than is needed. "I hope she and her secret lover get a bad case of sunburn."

Obviously Harry has had a change of heart over the issue that has stymied the rest of Paradise Heights:

Did DeeDee take a lover before she left Harry?

"But you said you're sure it had nothing to do with anyone else. The breakup, I mean."

"That was before Temple walked in on DeeDee and some guy doing the nasty, one night when the poor kid was staying over there. At least, that's what she told Jake. DeeDee insists it was just a bad dream. And she blames me for our daughter's reversion to a baby bottle. Apparently Temple swiped one from a toddler when Miss Judith wasn't looking."

"Wow, that's pretty darn serious!" I feel sorry for Harry. "Well, if you need any tips on roasting a turkey, I'm at your disposal. . . . Hey, speaking of turkey, why don't you and the kids eat with us?"

I don't know what I'm thinking. The words just came out before I had a chance to consider the consequences. Not that the kids would mind. In fact, they'll probably appreciate the company. But Ted still takes Tammy's point of view on Harry, no matter what I say.

"No, I could never put you out that way." But the way Harry licked his lips shows he's tempted. "Besides, you've inspired me to greater heights of volunteerism. Thanksgiving morning the kids and I are going to help prep the meals in the homeless shelter. I think it will be good for them to see that, even with the divorce, they have a lot to be thankful for."

"You're absolutely right. Collecting food makes you feel good, but it's still an abstract experience." I look at the trailer. "In fact, maybe we'll join you. We can eat our own meal afterward. And I insist that you and the kids join us for that."

"Well . . . okay, yeah, that sounds like a plan. I look forward to meeting Ted, finally."

Oh yeah, Ted.

I turn away before Harry can see my frown. As much as I want to tell myself that watching a few bowl games together with their sons is the perfect way for Ted and Harry to get to know each other better, I'm kidding myself.

I don't know which will make Ted groan the loudest: my invitation to get up early to feed a bunch of people whom he feels deserve the hand fate dealt them, or the news that he'll be breaking bread with the one guy in the neighborhood he can't stand.

25

"Where there's marriage without love,
there will be love without marriage."

—Benjamin Franklin

10:41 p.m.

Y ou're kidding me, right? You've invited that guy here, for THANKSGIVING?" Ted is so shocked that he quits brushing his teeth and sprays me with a fine sheen of toothpaste. "Just what the hell were you thinking?"

"Well, actually I was thinking how much fun it would be for Olivia and Tanner to share Thanksgiving with two of their closest friends. And how sweet of you to be neighborly to a very nice guy who just so happens to be going through a pretty bad divorce." I wipe off his spittle with deliberation in the hope that he will take the hint that I'm just as miffed at his reaction as he is at my invitation to Harry. "What's the harm in that?"

"It's an invasion of my privacy." Ted is brushing so hard that I'm surprised his gums aren't bleeding.

"Oh, get real, Ted." I could easily have ambushed him into this decision by mentioning it at dinner in front of the kids, who would be ecstatic and beg him to change his mind. But no, I waited until we were alone, until after we had made love—with the television on, so that he could watch the Lakers trounce the Clippers, again. I even pretended to believe that his groan during our lovemaking had everything to do with him being in sync with my faux-orgasm, and nothing at all to do with Pau Gasol missing an easy layup. "Seriously, what is your problem?"

"*My* problem?" He stares at me as if suddenly I've grown two heads. "Look, let's just call it what it is: Harry Wilder's got a crush on you, and for whatever reason, you're egging him on."

"Harry . . . and me? *What?* Oh, boy! You're crazy."

"Tammy didn't think so."

"Well, Tammy is a horny bitch! She just said that because Harry Wilder wouldn't ask her to go to bed with him. Spreading cruel, petty rumors is her way of getting back at him." My brush is stroking my hair so quickly that a few strands have taken flight.

"Why won't he sleep with her? He's separated, so that's not an issue."

I pause with my strokes. "He won't sleep with her because . . . well, because—"

"*Because he's got the hots for you.*" Ted's eyes meet mine in the bathroom mirror.

"No! That's not it at all. Harry . . . well, if you must know, Harry is still in love with his wife." I let that sink in. "So you have nothing to worry about, you see?"

He thinks about that for a moment, then gives me a curt nod. "Yeah, all right, I'm fine with you inviting your new friend." He trades his toothbrush for his razor. "But if you think I'm getting up at the crack of dawn to feed a bunch of drunks and druggies, you've got another think coming. I'm sleeping in. End of story."

I should be happy about finally getting the two of them together, but suddenly I feel hollow: not because I lied to Ted about Harry's feelings for me, but because I didn't.

I truly believe Harry is still in love with DeeDee.

If you're looking for proof, all you have to do is look at the wedding band he still wears on his left hand.

So, no, he's not in love with me. Not even a little.

Wednesday, 27 Nov., 1:06 p.m.

I am no Martha Stewart, but when it comes to Thanksgiving, I make a mean pecan pie, if I do say so myself. How bad can it be, with a little Tia Maria splashed in?

When it comes to this holiday, I am its queen. To me, it is the epitome of the word *family*, and I work hard to make it perfect for my own.

It's the day before Thanksgiving, which means my day is fully regimented for the prep work that goes into this meal. Right now in my kitchen, the turkey is brining, pies are baking, and I've been one with my Cuisinart since daybreak. Veggies of all shapes, sizes, and harvest hues are being chopped, diced, sliced, grated, or zested for side dishes that will leave my family—oh, yes, and Harry's—as stuffed as the turkey they will have just devoured. Idaho potatoes have been whipped into a frenzy and flavored with garlic, while the top of my sweet potato soufflé has been liberally sprinkled with marshmallows, which will be crisped to a golden brown in the broiler just before the turkey is presented.

All is well in my world.

The aroma of pies permeates the air. Perfect half-moon slices of apples, scented with cinnamon, simmer under a browning lattice crust, while the allspice, which was sprinkled liberally in a pumpkin pulp drenched with dollops of triple sec, lives up to its name.

If we weren't passing on the Paradise Heights Women's League's Friday-After Potluck, I would have baked a second pumpkin pie.

Or perhaps a pie stuffed with crow, specifically for Margot. And while she ate it, I'd remind her that I beat her record by twenty turkeys and eighty-six cans. *YES! YES!*

My kitchen duties are timed right down to the second I'll leave for after-school pickup, at which point the pies will be cooling on a large rack and the vegetables arranged in casserole dishes of varying sizes and shapes, depending on whether they've been grilled, roasted, blanched, toasted, sautéed, or creamed.

Last week I purchased a bottle of a very nice Gloria Ferrer Sonoma Brut for us to toast at the gathering. Maybe we'll allow the older boys to take a sip too. What a perfect way to cap off a perfect holiday event. . . .

I have my head deep in the oven, where I'm wrapping aluminum foil around my pumpkin crust so it won't brown too fast, when I hear the phone ring. I burn a finger on one hand as I reach for it with the other. "*Shit!* Ouch . . . Sorry! Hello?"

"Lyssa, it's Carla Liotta."

Ah, Tanner's principal. I await her accolade, one of many I've received since word got out about the food drive's success—

"You have to come down to the school immediately. I've got Tanner in my office, and—well, he's drunk."

"I . . . I beg your pardon?"

"Unfortunately, your son is looped. I think you should come and get him. Of course, this means suspension, through the full week after Thanksgiving. A shame, what with exams and all the following week—"

"But—but that can't be! He doesn't drink—"

"Tell me: are you missing a bottle of champagne?"

I run to the fridge. Yep, the Gloria Ferrer is AWOL, so she's got me there.

"What, he finished a whole bottle by himself?"

"Oh no, he's in fine company. Jake Wilder helped him out. His parents are on their way, too."

I grab my keys and run out the door.

1:33 p.m.

Even before I open the door to Principal Liotta's office, I can hear DeeDee pricking Harry with well-placed barbs. "This is exactly what I'm talking about! You are absolutely oblivious to the needs of our children!"

"Me—oblivious? How dare you, DeeDee! It sure is easy passing judgment from where you are, which is essentially out of their lives—"

"No, I'm not out of their lives, Harry. I'm out of *your* life. And you just better get used to it."

"Oh, I'm used to it, all right! At this point, I have no regrets about your desertion."

"Why did you say that? Just because our son is here with us?"

"Blah blah blah, 'our son' boo-hoo, blah blah!" Jake's impression of his mom sets Tanner off into convulsions of tipsy giggles. Both he and Jake fall to the floor laughing.

Tiny Carla is a woman who, by nature, is as demure as a dewy-eyed Southern belle, but fully in touch with her inner middle-school principal. In one second flat her voice drops an octave and a half, leaving her young charges in no doubt that she means it when she tells them to cease and desist with all their drunken tomfoolery.

Unfortunately, Harry's next instincts are his worst. He lunges at Jake, yanking him to his feet and drawing him close, so close that the two are nose-to-nose. "You stupid little jerk! How dare you say that to your mother—"

"Harry, NO!" Somehow I've leaped between him and his son. Jake, frozen in fear, trembles into sobriety. As he registers me, Harry's anger deflates and he falls back. Unconsciously he places his hand on my shoulder.

He needs me to prop him up in so many ways.

DeeDee sees this too. Her eyes dampen in the realization that she truly has what she wants: she is free of Harry.

And he is free of her.

With death come the five stages of grief for the survivors: denial, anger, bargaining, depression, and acceptance. For DeeDee, stage two has my name written all over it. She doesn't know my role in her soon-to-be ex-husband's life, but whatever it is, she has already made up her mind she doesn't like it.

So that she will see I'm not a threat to her, I hold out my hand. "I want to apologize for Tanner's stupidity. He raided our fridge and brought the wine to school. I'll make sure that he's punished."

"Mom, really it was Jake's idea—" He shuts his mouth when he reads the look in my eye.

DeeDee smirks. "Your hooligan son has the nerve to blame it on Jake? Now, that's rich!"

I can feel my head shaking in anger. "My son is not a hooligan! Look, I've already apologized—"

"Gee, Lyssa, how big of you." DeeDee practically spits out my name. "But you don't need to cover for him. Or for Harry, either."

"I'm not! Why would I cover for Harry?"

"Oh, come on already!" She laughs out loud. "It's so obvious. You're one of those lonely little housewives who prey on any man within flirting range—"

"I beg your pardon—"

"Ladies, please!" It has suddenly dawned on Carla that she

may have a grown-up fight on her hands. To put her at ease, I sit down.

Harry puts his hand on my arm. "DeeDee, quit being such a bitch. Lyssa and I are friends. There's nothing wrong with that."

"Just friends? Frankly, Harry, I don't care who your friends are, but I do care about who our children hang out with." She glares at Jake. "And the Harper boy shouldn't be one of them. Come on, Jake, we have to get your sister."

"The kids are spending Thanksgiving with me, remember? You have plans to go out of town." Harry motions Jake to his side. Jake stands there helplessly.

DeeDee laughs raucously. "And what were you planning on feeding them, frozen turkey dinners?"

"Hell, no, Mrs. Wilder. My mom's a great cook." All eyes turn to Tanner. Realizing how much he doesn't like the attention, he shuts his mouth quickly and stares back down at the floor.

"You're taking them—to *her house*?"

"Yes." Harry's smile is not triumphant, but weary. "Lyssa—and Ted—were gracious enough to invite us. We'll be serving at the shelter first—"

DeeDee's gaze turns to stone. "No. The kids are going with me. NOW."

"You have no right—"

"Don't I? Principal Liotta, did you not just witness my husband threatening my child with bodily injury? Shouldn't you call Child Protective Services?"

"Well—I think, in the heat of the moment—"

DeeDee turns on her, teeth bared. "I'd hate for you to lose your job just because you broke state law and didn't report the incident." She flips a hand in my direction. "And I'm sure Mrs. Harper won't lie under oath about what we all saw, either. Not even for a 'good friend.'"

Harry shakes his head in defeat. "Why are you doing this, DeeDee?"

"You put it so well, Harry: my children need me." She pushes Jake toward the door, but looks back at Harry. "Don't worry. You'll get them back on Friday. Come on, Jake, you can help pick out the turkey. Just try not to throw up on it."

Thanksgiving

26

"Love: A temporary insanity curable by marriage."

—Ambrose Bierce

Thursday, 28 Nov., 7:11 a.m.

Olivia has found the king of all puddles in her journey from the driveway of the All Saints Homeless Shelter to its front door. Its depth can be measured from the muddy watermark left high above her ankles.

She bursts into tears. "I'm wet! I'm cold! I'm sleepy! I WANT TO GO HOME!"

This could all have been avoided if her galoshes weren't buried somewhere in the back of the van, underneath the boys' sneakers and sports equipment.

Or if I had reneged on my promise to help Harry at the homeless shelter.

But I couldn't do that. Not after I saw the look on his face when he realized DeeDee was once again getting her way.

Of course, he offered to let me off the hook. "Your kids won't be as excited if their friends aren't around. And besides, you've got a big meal to prepare—for your own family."

"Nonsense! This isn't about them hanging with their friends. It's about helping someone who needs it."

Like I'm helping you, Harry. If you'll let me.

"Besides, our whole meal is on autopilot. Everything will be done ahead of time. All I have to do tomorrow is stick the turkey into the oven and set the time to bake. Then, *voilá*!"

"Well . . . if you say so." He watched as DeeDee drove out of the school's parking lot with Jake. Soon Temple would be with them. He was returning to an empty home.

An empty life.

"Aw, fuck it. It's just one day, right?" he said, more to himself than to me. "I'll see them on Friday, and take them for leftovers at the potluck."

"You'll have leftovers from our dinner too." I gave him a look that said I wasn't taking no for an answer.

With all we have to do today, I'm not taking it from my kids, either. "Please Mom, can't we just go home?" Tanner, who is still nursing a killer hangover, has yet to open his eyes since I roused him out of bed.

"No, we can't." I snap my fingers in front of his eyes. "People are counting on us. Now, pick up your sister and carry her inside before she drowns in one of these puddles."

Only Mickey seems up for our grand adventure. He's already bounded out of the van with one of my pumpkin pies. While I grab another bag of groceries, he counts the number of people standing in the line that snakes around the building. "Cool! Hey, what are the chances that I'll catch scurvy from a homeless guy?"

"More than likely it'll be fleas." Tanner lets loose with a prolonged burp. It is, I hope, the last vestige of his unfortunate incident. "Those guys sleep outside, and they never take showers."

"Yuck!" Olivia wrinkles her nose. As disgusting as her brother's burp is, I'm sure she is referring to the thought of going without a bath. One of her joys in life is splashing around in her tub. For her, roughing it is doing without a Little Mermaid bubble bath for even one day.

"Kids, be nice! Not everyone has a roof over their heads like us. This is why we give thanks today—"

"Pecan or pumpkin?" yells a greasy-haired guy with one eye covered by a patch. "Hey, I'll let you touch me if you hand it over!"

"Whoa, cool!" Mickey starts over.

I grab hold of his jacket. "No! I mean . . . he'll get a piece of it when he's inside."

Mickey shrugs. "Yeah, but then they'll probably make me wear gloves."

"Listen up! This isn't a petting zoo. These are real people—"

Real people who want pie. Suddenly the line is moving in our direction. They chant "PIE! PIE! PIE!" as if calling for the head of a despotic king. Mickey looks at me helplessly. I take it from him and thrust it at their leader, One-Eyed Jack.

Not one for formalities, he sticks a grubby paw in it before passing it down the line.

The kids and I have almost made it to the door when I hear him yell: "Love the triple sec. Great touch!"

I now have all the validation I need that this will be the most awesome Thanksgiving ever.

12:19 p.m.

Free food brings out the best in people, even those serving it. Olivia's wariness disappears when she hears all the sincere thanks and "Aren't you a little sweetie!" from those who take a piece of the sliced French bread from her serving basket. Mickey's job, which is to hand out plates and plastic utensils wrapped in paper napkins, is done with a cheerful patter that earns him grateful grins. That many of his patrons are toothless doesn't seem to bother him. Even Tanner loses his surly attitude when he realizes one of the kids lined up for the mashed potatoes he's ladling is wearing a jacket he'd tossed in the Goodwill bin at school just a month earlier. It is too loose for the boy to button snugly around his skinny waist. Tanner gives him two helpings of the potatoes, having already given him the jacket off his back.

I have now had my Thanksgiving and an early Christmas gift, too.

I'll thank the shelter's director for any muscle mass I gain after this morning: she's had me lugging large pans of collards to and from the stove for the past hour. Harry, who has been slicing turkey all morning, pauses for a moment. His eyes scan the room, looking for each of us. When he catches my eye, he wipes his hands on the full-length apron he's wearing and saunters over. "I'm impressed. You and your brood have really gotten into the groove."

I shrug. "They've enjoyed a very soft life. It's good that they see this. Already I can tell it's changed their perspective."

He gives me a sidelong glance. "I'm guessing you didn't have it so easy, growing up."

Despite the fact that we're standing in a chilly room, I feel my face heating up. "We had our ups and downs."

"Really? So did we." He puts his hands in the pockets of his apron. "DeeDee and I met on an upswing. My parents were dirt-poor, but I'd wangled a full scholarship—for basketball—to Berkeley: I majored in finance, then went to law school afterward. DeeDee was a women's studies major."

I can't hide my smile. Seeing it, he laughs. "Yeah, I know. Hard to believe, isn't it?" He shakes his head in wonder. "There was a time when she would have been the one pushing for the kids to be a part of something like this, if you can believe that."

"Well, we all change. I'm not the same person either."

"Remember your chemistry? Change is a reaction to some event, usually one that's beyond our control." His eyes sweep the room. "Everyone here has had the rug pulled out from under them in some way, either financially or emotionally. Their response to it is why they're here now." He unties the apron and folds it into a neat square. "I guess the same could be said about DeeDee. The easier things got for us, the more emotionally aloof she became. It's almost as if the fight went out of her, as if she quit caring."

"People get lazy, I guess. That's when the little things seem big. We need the big things to remind us that they're not, to put things back into perspective."

"No, I think it's more than that. I never told her to give up on her dreams, her goals. On us. Before she did, I wish she'd talked it out with me first. I would have been open to counseling, if that's what she had wanted." He shakes his head in disbelief. "And certainly she could have volunteered for any cause that interested her. Hell, she got enough requests. This place, for example."

I wince. "I truly feel that there is such a thing as post-marriage depression. You know, like the depression that sets in with some women after a baby? Only it happens right after the 'I do's' when we realize that marriage isn't all it's cracked up to be."

"Like buyer's remorse, right? Only take-back's a bitch. Especially in our tax bracket." As he backs into the table behind him, I grab his hand and pull him forward just before he tips over a large pan of stuffing.

He holds on to me, as if for dear life.

For the longest time, he doesn't make a move to let go. I pretend not to notice.

Until it's too obvious, to both of us, how good it feels.

Finally, he lets his hand drop. "Hey, look, the second shift has arrived. I guess we can round up the troops. I'm famished! Think that turkey's done by now?"

"What time is it? Two o'clock? It'll be crisp and golden. I

owe it all to my Electrolux convection oven with all the bells and whistles. One of Paradise Heights's many great amenities." I pray my laugh doesn't sound too giddy, too stupid. *Too hopeless*. "What more could a girl want?"

That one little question is all it takes to wipe the smile off Harry's face. "If I had the answer to that one, I'd still be married."

27

"Marriage is a feast where the grace is sometimes
better than the dinner."

—Charles Caleb Colton

2:46 p.m.

The turkey is raw.

Yes, it was in the oven, and yes, I'd set the timer.

I just forgot to set the oven temperature, and to hit
Bake, is all.

I am trying to think of a gentle way to break the news to my
family and our guest that it will be another four hours before
dinner is served, but nothing comes to mind that doesn't include
massive tears and hara-kiri.

It wouldn't be so bad if the kids weren't already dead tired
and starving.

Or if Ted weren't acting like such a dick.

That is not to say that he isn't being polite to Harry. In fact, if
you didn't know better, you'd think they were old college buds.
It helps that they were in the same fraternity, if not at the same
college: Chi Phi's, within two years of each other, UC Santa Bar-
bara (Ted) and UC Berkeley (Harry). There are acquaintances in
common, and unshared memories of renowned gatherings that
one or the other attended. For all of five minutes, they exclaimed
over the discovery that they might even have dated the same

woman. Ironically, neither of them could remember her name. But hey, how many philosophy majors from UC Santa Cruz with butterfly tattoos on their left butt cheeks could there have been?

I hate to break it to them: *more than they'll ever know.*

Both schools are in bowl games this year. This gives Harry and Ted something else to talk about. They've compared players and coaches and scrimmages, and done so in a gentlemanly manner. But eventually Harry takes takes the hint: Ted's force field is up. And it isn't coming down anytime soon.

Usually I'd be out there in the family room with them, massaging any and all awkward silences into bonding opportunities ("Oh, Ted, Harry's got one of your competitors on his client list. . . ." or "Harry, didn't you say your firm renegotiated the Lakers' contract with the City of Los Angeles? Ted loves the Lakers. . . ."), but I'm too busy hyperventilating over my ruined meal.

And thinking about what Ted will say to me the moment Harry walks out the door:

"Hope your boyfriend was impressed with your Mother Teresa act, 'cause you blew it with your cooking."

He'd be right. I have been trying to impress Harry. Some guy shows me a little attention, and I'm just as bad as Colleen or Brooke. Or even Tammy.

Harry walks in just in time to see the first tear roll off the tip of my nose. It stops him cold. Looking for a graceful out, he sniffs the air—

But there's nothing there. Perplexed, he says, "Something . . . smells good?"

And that's when I start to cry so hard that I'm laughing.

When I'm done, I point to the oven. "I forgot to set it. I'm guessing we've got another four hours."

"Oh yeah? Watch this." He picks up a couple of oven mitts.

Opening the oven door, he grabs the pan holding the turkey and puts it on the kitchen island. "Got kitchen shears? If not, a boning knife will do."

I rummage through the knife drawer until I find a utensil that meets his approval.

"Okay, very simple—although I'd suggest that, next time, you do it *before* you put the bird in the oven." He takes the knife and saws through the turkey's back on both sides of the backbone, then pulls it out of the carcass. Next, he uses the knife to separate one side of the bird's rib cage from the meat, then does the same to the other side. The breastbone cartilage is next to go, all the way to the thighbones, but he leaves the wings intact. "We still want it to look like a bird, right?"

"Oh, my God! Deboning the damn thing, that's brilliant! Why didn't I think of that?"

"It's why I get paid the big bucks." He takes a bow, then completes the last step: easing the flat bones of the bird's thighs out of the carcass without breaking the skin.

I can't help but marvel. "Where did you learn this?"

"I worked my way through college in the backs of a lot of East Bay restaurants." He flips the bird back over into the pan and arranges it back into its form, then adjusts the temperature to the right setting. "Beats flipping burgers. This will be ready in two hours. What say we take some of those veggies and make a few appetizers? That should hold back the angry mob for another hour."

When he wipes his forehead, unknowingly he stripes himself with a thin line of turkey grease. I pick up a dishrag and motion toward his forehead, but he doesn't get it. Standing on tiptoes, I swipe his forehead. His eyes don't look up, but seek out mine instead.

But I pretend I don't see this. Because if I look at him now, he'll get the wrong message.

Of course, he knows this too, which is why he finally glances away.

That's when he notices the orchids on the windowsill. The candy cane amaryllis has two little blooms.

"Wow! Is that the orchid I gave you? Well, look at that—"

"You gave my wife flowers?"

Neither of us heard Ted come in. How long has he been there?

Harry looks up, but I can tell from the look on his face that his antennae have not yet picked up that he's treading on thin ice. "Yeah. The last time I was here, I noticed that Lyssa has a real green thumb. I so admired one of these—"

"You were here . . . before?"

Ted is smiling, but Harry has just caught on: he has said something terribly wrong.

Both of them turn to me, as if seeing me for the very first time.

My friend suddenly realizes my marriage isn't as happy as he thought.

My husband has just learned how unhappy our marriage really is.

5:22 p.m.

"It must be nice, hanging out with all the hot MILFs in the neighborhood, right, Harry? That's one way to get over the pain and sorrow of DeeDee leaving you."

Ted is tapping the larger piece of the wishbone on the table. He's been doing it since the coffee was poured and the kids were excused from the table after each one had packed away pieces of both the pumpkin and pecan pies.

He can see from my face that I wish he'd stop, because it's ruining the table's finish.

Okay, really I wish he'd stop because he's doing it to taunt me, even as he jibes at Harry.

Still, I resist the urge to stab his hand with my knife, because that would send the wrong message to the children about the right way to hold their utensils.

But Ted would certainly get the point.

"Daddy, what's a MILF?" Olivia looks up from the pillow house she's making for Mrs. Wiffle.

Tanner snickers. "You want me to tell her?"

"You know?" I stop stacking dishes and glare at Ted, then give Tanner a warning glance. He goes back to humming gangsta obscenities in sync with his iPod.

But Ted won't back down. "It's just a very pretty mommy, honey. There are lots of pretty mommies around, aren't there, Harry?"

Olivia puffs the pillow beneath Mrs. Wiffle's head. "But Mommy is the prettiest of them all."

"That's right, baby girl." Ted glares at Harry. "What do you think, Harry? Is Lyssa the hottest mom in our little 'hood?" He wraps his arm around my waist and pulls me toward him so fast that I almost drop the dessert plates in my hand. "I do know how to pick 'em, don't I?"

To his credit, Harry has kept his cool through all of Ted's little barbs during dessert: like when he asked Harry if he thought "Colleen's were real," or if he ever wondered why Brooke's dentist husband hadn't seen fit to fix her obvious overbite ("He must find it comes in handy for—well, you get my drift. . . ."), and how Tammy was clearly "all talk and no action."

But now, watching Ted mark his territory on my best holiday sweater, Harry leans back in his chair and stares Ted right in the eye. "I get hit on a lot more at work than here in the Heights. Isn't that your experience, Ted?"

Ted's smile dissolves. "Yeah . . . I guess."

"No, but seriously: have any of Lyssa's friends come on to you?"

"Her friends?" Ted looks over at me sheepishly, his face now bright red. "No! Of course not. They wouldn't be any kind of friends if they did, now, would they?"

"I wouldn't think so, no." Harry smiles slyly. "But on the other hand, I've had women come on to me in my own office. And in a client's office. Or at a convention. And certainly when I'm on the road. How about you?"

Ted shrugs. "Yeah, sure. So? What's the big deal?"

"My point exactly. If you want to play around, it's more likely you'd do it where you're less likely to get caught. Like, say, the office. Doing it in your own backyard is just plain stupid."

Ted's response is a frown and a shrug.

But Harry is not through. "And if you're smart, you'll keep it in your pants altogether. *Because you've got too much to lose.* Hell, you lose if she walks out on you just because she's bored. Or because she realizes she doesn't like you anymore." He stands up to stretch. "Hey, Tanner, how about shooting a few hoops? It's getting warm in here."

Harry doesn't know it, but he has just thrown down the gauntlet: there is no way Ted is going to lose at the game in which he was once king.

It starts out friendly enough: Ted and me against Tanner and Harry. I am supposed to be Ted's "handicap," but I don't see it that way. That is, I don't want it that way, but soon I am being outmaneuvered by my madman teammate, who grabs every rebound and rushes every ball. Eventually I quit trying. What's the use? Ted has something to prove.

To himself. To Harry. To me.

Yes, I'm loving it. I am the prize.

It's about damn time.

Tanner, too, drops out after fifteen minutes, not because he's being outplayed but because there is no point in hanging in: Harry is also seeing red, and playing as if he's on fire.

The ball goes back and forth, and so does the score. Within an hour, both men are huffing and puffing. As much as they'd like to pretend that pickup games happen every day of their lives, for the most part they're a thing of the past for these desk jockeys.

That's proven when Ted glances a shot off the backboard that pounds Harry in the face. Harry glares back at Ted, who shrugs with a smile. Not smart. Harry takes this as a slight and goes for payback: a ball to the gut.

This puts Ted on the ground. Even in pain, though, he has a few dirty tricks up his sleeve—or I should say, in his feet: he kicks Harry's knees out from under him. Both men come up flailing. Olivia, alarmed, is now crying, and Mickey is jumping up and down—

Until he gets knocked over by two men who have forgotten that they are supposed to be setting a good example for my children, even as they fight for the right to . . .

To what? I can only go home with one of them: the one who now has a bloody nose, a busted lip, and two bum knees.

And a son who is bruised and sobbing. I wrap my arms around Mickey and usher him away from the killing fields. They say you can't kick a good man when he's down. I am tempted to kick two crazy ones, and at this point, I don't think anyone would think any less of me.

11:12 p.m.

"Hey, hon, let's kiss and make up." Ted pats me on the rump.

I feel as if I've just been branded.

Despite the fact that my eyes are squeezed shut and I'm pretending to snore, he is not fooled. This is why I've given up my dream of becoming a soap star.

"Believe it or not, I'm just not in the mood."

He processes that for a moment. Then, in my ear he whispers: "Gee, I guess you're too tired, after spending the day with your *boyfriend*."

My slap sends him reeling backward. Once again his nose is a gusher, red and slick. He groans in pain, then wipes the blood away with one hand, but pins me, face down, to the bed with the other.

Even as I struggle, my body responds to his hard, deep strokes, to his whispered curses and the smell of blood that suffocates me as he presses his cheek to mine.

Our climax is simultaneous. Afterward he drops over me, a dead weight holding me down in so many ways.

Finally he shoves me to one side, grunts himself up from the bed, and stumbles to the door.

"Where are you going?" The passion I've craved all these years—Ted's—is a full-bodied elixir. I feel like coming and throwing up at the same time.

"The guest room. Oh, and by the way, I've decided I'm going in to the office tomorrow after all. So feel free to invite Lover-boy over. For my leftovers."

28

"Marriage is a mistake every man should make."

—George Jessel

Friday, 29 Nov., 12:33 p.m.

My contribution to the potluck is turkey soup.

And grace.

Unlike Margot, I'll be a benevolent winner. I won't walk in as if I own the joint. I won't gloat or preen. And I certainly won't use this social gathering to proclaim the changes I plan to implement during my year as the Paradise Heights Women's League president.

All in good time, dearie. All in good time.

Tomorrow, in fact, at the next board meeting. It can wait until then.

Humble is as humble looks. To that end, I'm dressed simply: dove gray cashmere turtleneck and slacks.

Another humble touch: a soup stain on my pants, which is what happens when you juggle a hot tureen with a large purse.

The kids have already jumped out of the car and rushed into the Paradise Heights clubhouse, so they miss hearing their mom curse like a sailor. But I can't go home and change, since we're already here. It's against club rules to leave our children unattended.

Just then Harry pulls up. Temple spots Olivia at the door and runs in after her. But Harry is slow to get out of the car. Seeing me, he gives a hesitant wave, but turns back toward Jake, whose scowl is evidence that the conversation isn't going so well.

When they finally emerge, they head in my direction. Harry is limping. After the way Ted kicked him, no surprise there.

So that I don't put him on the spot, I turn to Jake first. "Hi, guy. I hope you had a nice Thanksgiving."

He nods, but looks just beyond me. "Yeah, I guess. Hey, listen, Mrs. Harper: I just want to apologize for the . . . you know, for the champagne. I made Tanner take it."

"Thank you for that, Jake." I put my hand on his shoulder to encourage him to look me in the eye. When he finally does, I reward him with a smile. "We all make stupid mistakes. That's part of growing up. The goal is to learn from them."

He nods uneasily. I look over at Harry. His forehead shows a bruise from where the basketball hit him. I resist the urge to reach out and touch it by shifting the tureen so that no more soup will leak out.

It does anyway, splashing onto one of my brand-new Lacroix flats. "Damn! Ah . . . sorry about that, Jake."

To save me from myself, Harry grabs the tureen from me. Unfortunately, he doesn't realize why I've got it wrapped in a towel: without it, the damn thing is too hot to hold. He scalds his hands, but has the wherewithal to keep his swearing sotto voce.

Instinctively I grab the tureen from him, but this only makes him shout out in pain.

He blows on one palm. "I bruised this hand when I fell."

I shake my head furiously. "You mean, when Ted tripped you. He can be such an ass!" I give Harry a sidelong glance. "I should never have let you guys play ball."

Jake looks from one of us to the other. "You made me go with Mom, and then you had dinner with *Tanner*? And then you guys *played ball*?" His eyes glass up. "I guess your own family doesn't rate, huh?"

Harry turns to answer him, but Jake is already heading to the clubhouse. He disappears beyond the throng gathered at the door.

I'm now caught red-handed. "Ouch! Damn it, Harry! Look, give me the towel and go follow him in. I'll be okay, I swear."

"Jeez, sorry, Lyssa! No, I think he needs to do some cooling off." He shakes his head. "I would have said something to him earlier, but you told me you and the kids were skipping this shindig."

"Yeah, well, Ted and I aren't speaking after yesterday." I bite my bottom lip, if only to keep from cursing my scalded hands. "He thought it best to go in to work, and frankly, I'm glad."

"Why do you say that?"

Because I need to clear the air between us. Not that I can say this to Harry.

"I think we need time to cool off too." Noting his guilty look, I quickly add: "I mean, Ted and me."

"You and—Ted? . . . Oh! Of course."

Is he disappointed or relieved? Because he's looking away, I can't tell.

"Frankly, I don't think you should be too hard on him," he adds.

"But—but he was trying to kill you out there! He was acting like a boneheaded—"

"He was acting like a guy who felt threatened. Like a husband who suddenly realized how easy it is for another man to be attracted to his wife"—

Another man, meaning you, Harry. Are you attracted to me?

—"and he doesn't want to lose you." I feel exposed in his gaze. "I know I wouldn't."

I don't know how to answer him, or if I should even try. It

would be too hard to convince him that his illusions about Ted and me are far off base; that jealousy and lust—and certainly habit and convenience—aren't the same as love.

Harry thinks he's reading remorse in my face, but before I can set him straight about that, he beats me to the punch. "Look, Lyssa, I—"

"Well, well, well, what have we here? I swear, if you two were standing any closer, you'd be well-advised to get a room!"

Tammy's words may be sugar sweet, but her tone is anything but. I don't know how long she's been standing beside us. The fact that her cranberry-walnut-pineapple Jell-O mold still quivers from side to side gives me no hint, since everything about her (at least, from the waist up and the neck down) jiggles constantly, thanks to her propensity toward three-inch heels and balconette demi bras with straps too slender to cantilever her D-cup breasts.

"You're a regular at the Holiday Inn, right? Can we use your quantity discount?" Harry murmurs just loud enough for me to hear, thank goodness. I swallow the urge to snicker.

"Excuse me? What did you say?" Tammy's nostrils flare. Harry may not realize it, but she's ready for open warfare.

"We were just talking about how wonderful the Heights can be, *in* the *holiday* season." I muster an innocent smile.

"Yeah, well, that's why we're all here. It's so warm and welcoming, yada yada. Ooooh, Lyssa, you know you have a stain on your pants, right? On cashmere, no less. What a shame! *Hmmm*, I don't see Ted. Is he already inside?"

But of course Tammy knows the answer to that. If she hasn't already gotten a play-by-play of yesterday's basketball grudge match from some neighbor who caught it live, I've no doubt one of her early-bird scouts tonight has already texted her the full roster of attendees.

"He went in to work after all." I could kick myself for

making such a big deal of how we'd be skipping the potluck. Well, too late now. I try a tactic I use on the kids, with varying degrees of success: flattery. "Charlie will be leading the sing-along again this year, right? The children always look forward to that!"

It's not often you hear a natural contralto; I say natural, but that's only because I've never believed the ugly rumor that Tammy castrated him on their wedding night.

Until now.

Tammy nods reluctantly, but she's still suspicious. No one pays compliments to her Charlie. That is a precedent she set when they first moved into the Heights.

Emasculation is a rare art form. And while it's hard to admire, it's certainly awe-inspiring.

By the way Harry holds her elbow and steers her toward the clubhouse, I'm guessing he feels the same way. It gives new meaning to the phrase "Keep your friends close, and your enemies closer."

The clubhouse is buzzing with polite laughter and forced cheer. Everyone is there, even the Undesirables. What better way to elicit envy than to open the red velvet rope to the wannabes every now and then?

Crammed onto the tables in the center of the room are a myriad of leftovers, which are more than the sum total of a few carefully chosen, specifically measured ingredients. While these dishes are served up with pride, they are also leavened with memories both fond and wince-worthy.

I speak for myself. Yesterday left a bittersweet taste in my mouth.

I'm only here to eat up time until Ted and I can talk things out later this evening. Does he have reason to be jealous? Not on Harry's account. I appreciate Harry's friendship, and I know this feeling is reciprocated. But let's face facts: *he has never come on to me.*

Okay, yeah, I'll admit it. That disappoints me. It's not that I'm looking for an affair. I wouldn't trade the friendship and respect Harry and I share now for that.

But, hell, if Ted is going to accuse me of it anyway . . .

Not to mention Tammy and the others on the Women's League board.

Just what the hell are they staring at, anyway? Seems they can't keep their eyes off us.

But of course not. Because they want validation that what they suspect is true.

This is why they assess—make that obsess over—every move we make.

They take note of the way Harry hovers over me protectively. How his asides are addressed to me alone. How he scans my face appreciatively.

Then they wait for my reaction. I'm fully aware that, if I dare lean toward him, eyebrows will be raised. If I laugh out loud, they'll poke each other knowingly. And heaven forfend I should allow my eyes to meet his! If that happened, rumors would race through the room almost as quickly as the children, who are hopped up on soda, pie, and ice cream.

"You haven't heard a word I've said, have you?" Harry says this as if it is a joke, but the sadness in his eyes is proof he knows he's right.

"Sure I have! You were—something about . . . Okay, sorry, I give up." I force a smile onto my lips.

"Hey, if I'm boring you, feel free to play with your girlfriends. I won't be jealous." He flashes a knowing smile, but I rein in my urge to punch him in the arm for it. Instead, I shake my head. Anything more obvious will give them reason to presume they're on to something:

That what we have is more than just wishful thinking on their parts.

And on mine.

"Go up to Margot and her court? Thanks, smart-ass, but I'll pass on the honor." Oddly, that thought is liberating.

"Eventually you'll have to say something. In a month's time, you'll be their new queen. Won't it help if you cozy up to Margot?"

"You know, I could say the same to you. Shouldn't you two kiss and make up?"

His derisive guffaw has them all aflutter. "The price is too high."

Yeah, well, I feel the same way.

"Go mingle. I'm going to see if I can take care of this stain." I head off to the lavatory, but when I get there, I find the door locked. I hear a weird pounding on the other side, so I wait a few minutes before knocking again.

Finally it opens. Masha Shriver struts out. Her crass brass locks flare out from her head like Medusa's snakes gone wild. Her winter white dress defies gravity. It's strapless and boasts a neckline that plunges below her navel. Considering the amount of rain we've been getting, her deep tan is unexpected, not to mention unusual in color. (For the record, I am of the opinion that bruised papaya is not a good look.)

Masha is not alone. Despite his guilty look, I recognize the man who is still zipping up his pants as he maneuvers past me as one of our friendly neighborhood bankers.

Apparently the Shrivers' account is paying off with some unexpected dividends.

"Oh—I'm sorry. I just needed to . . . You're Masha, right? I'm Lyssa. I'm a friend of Pete's." At a loss for what to do next, I stick out my hand.

Very awkward. Pete's name does not elicit the response I'd

expected. Instead, she glares at me as if I've just cursed her first-born. (Despite the hickey Tanner received the night of the poker game compliments of her daughter, Natassia, I don't feel that would be necessary. It was bound to happen sooner or later.)

"Pete? Ah, LYZZA. Yez, I know of yooouuu!" I don't know if it's her Slavic accent or her vodka intake that has her slurring her words, but I'm willing to guess the latter. The fumes from her breath have me reeling. As she grabs me by the shoulders with both hands and hugs me to her chest, she whispers in my ear: "Streep poker, yez? Not to worry. I not mad. You see, I have 'hobby' too! But, hey, not one verd to my Pete, dah?" She pushes me away.

I stumble into the bathroom, bruised from where she gripped my shoulders. I'm sure I have two contusions on my chest that match whatever nipple armor she's wearing.

I've been marked in another way: thanks to Masha's spray-on tan, my brand-new sweater has been tagged with her finger-prints and a faint V that matches her neckline.

"Damn it! Damn it!" The soup has already dried into a dark, impenetrable shadow, while dabbing at the new stains only spreads them into a treacly Orangina.

My new outfit is ruined. Would it help if I banged my head against the wall? Nah. But if I died, they'd have an obvious clue for a murder suspect.

Then there's the issue about Pete. He is a buddy, after all. If he were a girlfriend, of course I'd speak up. But what is the mancode about such things?

Harry knows the code. And since I don't need any more enig-mas in my life, tag, he's it.

I find Harry chatting up Biker Mom. When he sees me, he waves me over. Instinctively I glance around to see if Brooke is anywhere nearby. Oh, great, she's glaring at him from across the room. Between this and my most recent introduction to a supposedly friendly face, I don't need a frantic call later from Brooke, questioning our friendship.

Seeing my concern, Harry excuses himself and casually meanders over. "What, you're not into making new friends?" As he plucks a cookie off a dessert tray, he does a double take at the new stains on my sweater. "She promised me a ride in her Maserati. I was going to ask if you could tag along, but now I don't know. I mean, what if you stain her seats?"

"Forget the joyride, Andretti. We have bigger fish to fry. I just caught Masha in the ladies' room with First National Bank of Paradise Heights." I tilt my head in the direction of Masha's boyfriend, who is now scurrying after her into the clubhouse's coatroom. Even from where I'm standing, I can see a large orange streak on his sweater. He is a marked man. "What's the protocol? Do we tell Pete?"

"Jesus." Harry closes his eyes for a moment, and shakes his head. "Yeah, well, I'd want to know. Wouldn't you?"

"Of course!" Harry's right. Yesterday's tiff with Ted now seems silly. I can't wait for him to come home.

Harry tosses the last crumb of cookie into his mouth and wipes his hands. "Well, when you tell him, be gentle—"

"Whoa, whoa, wait—who, me? Think again, Slick. You're his closest friend."

Harry groans. "If I remember correctly, that was your doing." It takes a while, but he nods. "Okay, but I don't think this is the time or the place."

"I leave it to your discretion." I give him a thumbs-up. "Oh, great, Brooke is coming over, I guess to call you a traitor."

He laughs. "Is that better or worse than an Undesirable? I forget."

"In your case, it's one and the same." I glance around the room for our salvation. It comes in the form of Cal, who is standing uncomfortably beside Bev. True to form, Bev is oblivious to this.

She has trapped the Emersons in a corner. No doubt she's giving them a pitch about a house she knows would be perfect for them, now that they're pregnant again and will need the extra space.

"Why don't we save Cal instead? The girls are downright afraid of him, so that should keep them away for a while."

Immediately I move in, tapping Bev lightly on the shoulder. "Hi, Bev! I just want to thank you for putting in that call to the Heights Market regarding the food drive. It's what made the drive an over-the-top success."

As Bev turns to me, the Emersons find their opportunity to scurry away. I see by the look in her eyes that she's tempted to run after them, but realizes this is bad form, even for her. "Oh yeah, hi, Lyssa! Glad I could be of some help. Really, it was Calvin's idea, but hey, all in the family, right?"

"You know Harry Wilder, right?" I move to the side so that Harry can shake her hand.

"Yes! I mean, of course I know *of* you." She looks at him curiously. "Well, about the . . . *you* know . . ."

"My poker games? I hope Cal attending doesn't interfere—"

"*Cal?* Oh, yes! Not at all! So sweet of you to have him over! But what I meant is that, with the way the divorce is going and all, you'll probably need this—"

She pulls a refrigerator magnet from her purse. On it is her profile and name, with that patented Bev Bullworth slogan: No Bull, Just Better Service!

Harry stares down at it. "Thanks . . . I guess."

"It's so you'll remember to call me! You know, when you're ready to buy your condo." Her tone conveys just the right amount of sympathy. "Cal tells me you'll want to stay in the neighborhood and keep commuting in, so that you can be close to the kids. You know, one of those new units they've built off Main has come available. It isn't so roomy, granted. But the condo fee is very small—"

"Why would I want a condo? I already have a house." He glares at Cal, who backs away from Bev, horrified. Whatever hole she's digging for herself, he is not going to jump into it with her.

"Yes, but not for long. You know how these things usually go. DeeDee's got the natural edge—"

"Is that what you think? That just because she's a woman, she's a better mother than I am a father?"

"Well . . . I . . . No, of course not!" Bev's backpedaling is insincere despite her cheeriness. "But it never hurts to be prepared, right? Eventually, when the court rules on the situation, you'll have to give up the ghost—"

I put my hand on Harry's arm so that he will remember where he is, but he shrugs it off. I'm too late anyway. Slackened jaws, including many stuffed with leftovers, hang open as everyone tunes in to our little drama. Margot smiles triumphantly. To her mind, Harry's comeuppance—at the hand of Bev Bullworth, no less!—is just deserts.

"Thanks for your concern." Harry's words are brittle and empty. "But do me a favor and give it a break, at least until the court ruling. Better yet, here—" He hands her back her magnet. "Save it for the next time you see DeeDee."

Before she can say anything else, Harry walks off in the direction of the front door. I follow him out, as does Cal.

"Wait, Harry! Look . . . I'm sorry Bev said all those stupid things." Cal hangs his head. "Sometimes she speaks before she thinks."

"She's just parroting the party line around here." Harry shrugs. "Ah, shit, here comes Pete. I guess we should tell him about Tanner's and Jake's suspensions." Harry shifts uneasily, but waves our friend over anyway. "Do you want to do the honors, or shall I?"

"Judging by that long face, maybe he already knows."

I'm poised to verify this, but Pete brushes me aside. "Anyone seen Masha?"

Harry gives me a warning nudge. He doesn't have to worry. Since I'll have to break the news about the boys' tomfoolery, the last thing I'm going to mention is Masha's too.

"Damn! She asked me to go home and get her sweater because she felt a chill. I guess she forgot that her mink is right here in the coatroom." He rushes off down the hall.

Harry and I look at each other, then take off after him, with Cal trailing us.

But we're too late. We get there just in time to see him freeze over his wife, who is in a love tussle with the guy who doles out the cash from his trust fund.

In a flash he yanks Masha's boyfriend up by his hair, which comes off in his hand. Those who suspected FNBofPH sports a toupee can now collect on their bets.

Livid, the guy flails back at Pete. Unfortunately for him, Pete's daily workouts give him a leg up. Pete's lip may be split, but it's FNBofPH's nose that's pushed out of joint.

Cal and I brace for what Pete might have in store for Masha as he lifts her, naked, out of the coat nest she and her lover made on the floor. Seeing her that way only confirms what I suspected since our run-in: yep, she does indeed have an allover tan.

At this point a good smack won't make up for my stained sweater, but I have to admit it would give me some satisfaction. Instead, Pete cradles his wife in his arms. "Did he hurt you? I swear, if he did—"

She shrugs, but the look on her face reflects what we're all thinking:

You poor, pathetic fool.

Closing the door behind us, Harry shakes his head in disbelief. "Unbelievable! Now, that's what I call denial. Doesn't he see what's happening?"

It's on the tip of my tongue to say, "No, because he doesn't want to," but I keep quiet. What's the point? I'm guessing we've all been there at one time or another.

Even Harry.

Especially Harry.

29

"Sometimes it's hard to be a woman
Giving all your love to just one man."

—Tammy Wynette

Saturday, 30 Nov., 10:37 a.m.

Brooke is hosting the league meeting at which I'm to be voted in as president. That is fitting, since it was she who pushed to get me on the board in the first place.

"It seems like eons ago, doesn't it, that you were just another of those newbie mommies who came into the Heights without a clue as to what was what." Like a mother who's just found out that her child has won a first-place ribbon in the science fair, Brooke beams with pride.

"You're telling me. Hey, just to set the record straight: I forgive, but I *never* forget."

She knows I mean it.

To make it up to me, Brooke is treating me to a morning of primping at the Heights of Beauty. Besides a face full of avocado and the high-gloss shellacking of my finger- and toenails, she's talked me into trying out a new do that our stylist insists will "rock my world." It's a drastic cut that tames my frenzied curls into something sleek and edgy. What I see in the mirror shocks me a bit. I can't decide if I look sultry or just cruel. If Olivia breaks into tears when she sees me, I'll have my answer.

"I'll be leaning on you heavily, you know." I skipped break-fast, and my stomach is growling. To make matters worse, the avocado in my facial smells good enough to eat, but I resist the urge to lick it off my cheek.

"Sure! I like being the power behind the throne. You know that." She's practically giddy. "Besides, I live vicariously through you. Speaking of which, how's your new best friend?" That's what she calls Harry these days. I don't know if she's jealous of him or of me.

"I'd say he's holding it together okay."

"It didn't look that way at the potluck. *Ooob*, he's so hot when he blows his stack!" She smiles and licks her lips at this mental catnip. "The drama king thing sure does become him."

Why are we so fascinated with other people's emotional car wrecks? I shake my head in wonder. "You know, Brooke, just because the others are treating him like a pariah doesn't mean you have to. He really enjoyed your friendship. And I thought you enjoyed his."

At first I don't think she's heard me because she's so busy scrutinizing her face in a magnifying mirror. Her nose has al-ways bothered her, and a day doesn't go by when she doesn't threaten to go under the knife. The problems that are skin-deep are easy to fix, but not the ones that pock our souls or balloon into tumors of insecurity. "Yeah, well, I like Harry too. But in all honesty, Lyssa, there are certain friendships that just aren't worth the hassle. Besides, if I alienate Margot, I'll be marked as an Undesirable."

"I'm not marked." She doesn't say anything, so I have to ask: "Or am I?"

"Don't be silly! Of course not. After what you pulled off, you're golden. You know that." Her smile wavers. "Hey, to-night's your night, so enjoy. In fact, show up fashionably late. We can't start the party without you, right?"

She looks back down into the mirror. I wonder if she likes what she sees.

"A toast, to our golden girl." Margot raises her martini glass in the air.

On cue, the laughter dies down, gossiping is suspended, and the eyes of my peers—Margot, Brooke, Colleen, and Isabelle—turn to me. Even Tammy wipes the smirk off her face.

Colleen, reveling in this rare moment of gal-pal détente, shouts out, "How about a speech?"

Wow. Wow, wow. I am aglow. I am living the dream. I have the adoration of my peers.

I'm also a little tipsy.

"I'm honored. I'd just like to say that I couldn't have done it without—well, without . . ."

I pause here, because it's just hit me:

There is not one person in this room who was there for me when I needed her most.

Instead, I should be thanking Harry for donating his firm's Tahoe cabin, which motivated donations of a couple of hundred cans. And Pete, whose plea in the *Boulevard Bugle* netted more than four hundred cans, not to mention the fifty others that came in from his basketball team (which will have no more benchwarmers for the rest of the season). And, of course, if Cal hadn't strong-armed Bev into calling in a favor from the Paradise Heights Market—

But I know if I bring this up, I'll be asking for trouble.

If I keep my big mouth shut now, then later I'll be able to smooth things over between the league board and the guys. Just think: if I can pull it off, future generations will liken it to

Nixon's meeting with Mao Zedong. How symbolic would it be for the two sides to reconcile over Chinese food?

Silly me, I'm getting ahead of myself. This is painfully obvious as Margot intones: "Of course, as our new president, you'll have to adhere to the prime directive already established under our bylaws. Because you've been under a lot of pressure this last month, we've let it slip. But no better time than the present to set things straight—"

"What? I don't get it. You say I'm breaking some rule?"

"Section 14, paragraph A-6: 'Behavior deemed unbecoming an officer or an officer-elect is reason for termination. This includes, but is not limited to, any action that may be construed as illegal, indecent, lascivious, lecherous, salacious, obscene, wanton, or libidinous.' "

"Huh? What are you talking about?" To my disappointment, her words are sobering me up. "When have I been *any* of those things?"

"That's a good question, Lyssa." Tammy looks me straight in the eye.

"Just what *are* you inferring, Tammy?"

"Oh, come on! Cut the Little Miss Innocent act. You and Harry Wilder are in each other's company at all hours of the day and night. Well, of course people are going to talk—"

" 'People?' " I can't help but laugh out loud. "Listen to yourself! You're the only one who thinks anything is going on between Harry and me!"

"Oh yeah?" She scans the room. "Let's see a show of hands: how many of you think that Lyssa and Harry are too cozy?"

Of course Margot's hand shoots up. Isabelle's is not far behind. Colleen raises hers guiltily. I look over at Brooke. Her eyes plead for my forgiveness, but slowly she lifts her arm too.

Et tu, Bruta?

Brooke tears up. "Look, Lys, you're among friends here. All we're trying to do is help, before you—well, before you do something that you regret."

Tammy smothers a smirk. "You mean, if she hasn't already."

"I regret nothing! Harry and I are just friends."

Isabelle snorts. "Don't you mean 'friends with benefits'?"

"No, of course not! How dare you!" She's lucky I'm not within spitting distance. I'm not one to hock loogies, but I can make an exception—

"Lyssa, Harry is cute and sweet and kind and fun to be around. We get it, believe me, we do. So it's got to be tempting." Colleen looks me in the eye. "Be honest, not with us but with yourself: aren't you tempted, even a little?"

It would be so easy for me to proclaim my immunity to Harry's numerous charms. . . .

But I'd be lying.

And unlike pecan pies, that is not one of my many talents.

"I would never be unfaithful to Ted." It comes out as a whisper. That's what happens when you've had the wind knocked out of you by your supposed BFFs.

Brooke gently pats my arm. "Honey, no one is saying you've slept with Harry. We know you too well. That's exactly the point we're trying to make here. You see, if the relationship looks, well, *awkward,* to us who know you best, how can it look to others?"

"Frankly, I don't care."

"Great. Fine. Then let me ask you this: what does Ted think about your new boyfriend?"

I open my mouth to say something, but then close it just as quickly.

Tammy, the bitch, mouths *I told you so* to Margot.

Colleen picks up the baton. "Lyssa, even if nothing is going on, none of us can even *look* like a floozy. Or we get kicked out of the club. Isn't that what the rule means, Margot?"

"To put it somewhat bluntly, yes." Margot's eyes narrow even as she bares her teeth. "In this case, I think we've made it clear that your behavior can easily be, and I quote, construed as both 'wanton' *and* 'libidinous.' "

Isabelle furrows a brow. "No, Margot, I beg to differ. It was the 'lascivious' part that rang true to me."

"Yeah, but hey, what nails it is 'behavior unbecoming an officer or an officer-elect.' I mean, am I right? Not to mince words, or anything." Tammy looks over at Brooke for support.

"You guys, don't be so silly!" Colleen's lashes flutter in distress. "This isn't an inquisition! It's an *intervention*, remember?"

"An intervention?" I close my eyes in disbelief. "Oh, brother! And I thought I'd heard it all!"

Suddenly everyone is talking at once. Margot raises her hand to silence us all. "No, now, Lyssa is right to feel put out. We're all jumping on her for something that is completely innocent"—

My heart palpitations begin to slow.

—"which is why she'll drop Harry immediately. She knows she has too much to lose." Margot has the smile of someone who is used to being obeyed. "Am I right, Lyssa?"

Yes, she is right. We both know it.

If I stay, I have too much to lose.

And I have so much to gain by leaving.

"Go to hell," I say as I head for the door.

I'm almost down the block when I hear someone panting after me. It's Brooke. I've never seen her move so fast, especially in heels. It's impressive enough for me to cut her some slack and slow down. "What is it?"

"You know, he wouldn't want you to do it."

"Ted and I have already had this discussion."

"I'm not talking about Ted. I'm talking about Harry."

This stops me cold. "Why do you say that?"

"I know him too, remember?" She smiles. "And I know that the last thing he'd want is to be the reason why you're suddenly an outcast from the rest of us."

"No, you don't know him. If you did, you'd realize he doesn't see it that way. And guess what? *I* don't see it that way, either. I consider it expanding my horizons. There's a whole big world out here, Brooke. Don't be afraid to step outside of Margot's concentration camp."

She backs away. Without thinking, she gives me a tiny wave good-bye. "Okay, have it your way. He's the king of the Undesirables, and you're now his queen. I hope he's truly as good a friend as you think he is."

Christmas

30

"The best proof of love is trust."

—Joyce Brothers

Saturday, 7 Dec., 3:41 p.m.

Hey, I like your new haircut. It's kind of sexy."
This is the first compliment Ted has paid me in over a week, since our fight on Thanksgiving.

In fact, it's his first attempt at any real conversation at all.

Don't think I haven't tried in the meantime to make amends. Yes, I'll admit that it took me a few days to come around. But let's face it, being in a marriage is a lot like being a thin-skinned fruit: you get bruised easily, but in the end you go all soft anyway.

Ain't love grand?

So I reward him with a shy smile. He reaches over and squeezes my hand, which I regard as his way of saying *I'm sorry for being such an ass, for doubting you.*

"Yea, yea, yea! Mommy and Daddy love each other again!" Unlike Ted and me, Olivia, who is wedged between her brothers in the backseat, is not too proud to sing it loud, sing it proud. He and I exchange glances heavy with shame. How many reminders do we parents need that every emotion is transparent to our children?

Today of all days we should be happy. We are on our way to

our favorite Christmas tree farm in Santa Cruz, where we'll cut down the Douglas fir that will be the focal point of our entry foyer, and our lives, for the next four-plus weeks.

We started this tradition the year Tanner was born. I remember Ted traipsing up and down the rows while I followed at a slower pace, trying to maneuver Tanner's state-of-the-art stroller around loose pebbles and protruding roots. The second year I got smarter about the whole thing and carried my little guy in a sling. Only three years ago, when Olivia was almost three, was I freed from the position of pack mom.

Now I huff and puff after the kids, who scatter through this planned forest. Finding the perfect tree is the equivalent of taking down the great white whale. It must have a thick petticoat of branches rising from the base, its layers coquettishly shorter albeit in proportion all the way up to its needled crown. As if projecting his own fears of a thinning pate, Ted cannot tolerate bald spots between layers. I, on the other hand, abhor crooked bases. Between three rambunctious kiddies and a clumsy dog the size of a Shetland pony, our tree can't have the posture of a Tilt-a-Whirl. The one thing we both agree on is that it must stand at least thirteen feet tall, so that it will not be dwarfed by the double height of our entryway, the place of honor.

The search for the tree is a highly charged competition. The winner is the first to be photographed with it. The picture is then mounted on the first page of this year's Christmas photo album, validating a full year of bragging rights.

Tanner is old enough to carry the bowed safety saw, while Mickey drags the tall PVC pole that is marked as a measuring stick. Every now and then he attempts to vault from one row to another. Olivia is charged with holding the twine that Ted will use to tie the tree to the sleigh he'll use to haul it back to the cashier, who will ply our children with Christmas cookies, candy canes, and warmed cider while I peruse the wreaths on display.

Eventually I'll settle on three: one for the front gate, and two for our double-wide front door.

"Mommy, why not this one? Or this one?" Olivia loses all sense of discretion when she's within sniffing distance of ginger-bread men.

"No, sweetie. That one is not tall enough, and the other is much too bare on the back side."

"Hey, Mom! MOM! OVER HERE!" For this task, Mickey has always had a great sense of focus that consistently leads him to the right tree. When he was younger, it frustrated him to lose to his brother. Ted's way of mitigating it was to lead our younger son to a potential winning candidate. Now that Mickey's developed a connoisseur's eye, Ted no longer has to do that.

The tree Mickey has spotted for us has all the necessary criteria. Ted whistles for Tanner to trot on over with the saw, but Tanner tries for an end run. "Wait, wait . . . what about this one over here? It's hella taller."

Ted looks down at his cell phone for the time. "Nope, we've got to call it a day. Warriors and Lakers tonight, remember?"

"Wait—aren't we going to decorate the tree when we get home?" Mickey's look is incredulous. We all look over at Ted.

He knows he's outnumbered. He smiles weakly. "Sure! Of course! It's our tradition, right?"

As we head back to the cashier with our find, I give him a kiss on the cheek. He stops short in order to draw me to him and give me a real kiss, the kind that should melt away any lingering doubts about love and fidelity.

His doubts, not mine.

5:10 p.m.

"I didn't know Margot's big shindig was tonight." Ted murmurs this just loudly enough for me to hear.

I wince, then nod nonchalantly. It took us so long to patch up our spat that I've yet to tell him about my resignation from the board. Now isn't exactly the time, either. "Yeah. No biggie. I need a break from her anyway."

Stupid me! I'd asked Ted to stop by the Paradise Heights Market on our way home, and that means going by Margot's place, which is lit up like the aurora borealis. An overflow crowd is milling around her front door.

Her Christmas party always takes place the first weekend in December, which naturally positions it as the very first party of the holiday season. This is done on purpose; in her mind, it is the equivalent of the Queen of England's appearance at Ascot, heralding the first leg of Britain's Slayer's Cup.

"Huh," he says, looking over at me after my breezy dismissal of Margot's big night. It's dark enough now that I'm in silhouette, so he can't read my face. "When does your term as president kick in, anyway?"

Ah, hell. Busted.

I take a deep breath before answering. "Well, it doesn't, exactly. I resigned from the board."

"What?" He stops short. I can hear the tree sliding forward on top of the car. "What the hell happened?"

"Seriously, it's no big deal! I just figured out that it takes up too much of my time."

He lets loose with a loud guffaw and shakes his head. "What else do you have to do?"

"Just what do you mean by that?" I'm trying to keep the anger out of my voice, but I already feel as if I'm on the defensive. In the back of the car, the kids have quit their jabbering. All ears are tuned to us as they hear the rising tension in our voices.

"Look, I know you've got a lot happening here." Ted, too, is aware of the little-pitchers-have-big-ears situation. "I just mean that the league has always been your—you know, your release. Something to do to catch up with your girlfriends."

We've reached our driveway just in time. The kids tumble out of the car and swarm into the house for phase two of our grand adventure: decorating the tree. I work in tandem with Ted to untie the twine that holds the tree to the roof of our car. "It's truly annoying how cruel they can be sometimes."

"To you?"

I gulp before answering, "No, not necessarily."

"To him." He stops to gauge my reaction.

"Yeah, okay. It's the principle of the thing. I don't like what they say about Harry."

"You mean, about Harry and you." He yanks the tree onto the ground, stands it up, and shakes it, too violently. Loose needles rain onto the ground. He bites his lower lip.

Damn it, here we go again. "Why should we care? Why should *you* care? Ted, whatever they think, you and I know it's not true."

"No, Lyssa, I don't know." He holds my gaze. "I want to believe you, but it doesn't make any sense to me. What is it between you and this guy, anyway? Tell me the truth!"

"Ted, you know the truth! I would never—my God, I can't believe we're even having this conversation!" I slam the car door shut. "Let me ask you a question, Ted. Would you, if you were me?"

"What? I don't get what you're asking."

"Just answer the question. If you were in my shoes, would you be tempted to make a play for a nice guy who just so happened to be cute too?"

He gives me a strange look. "Get real. I can't think like a woman."

"Sure you can. You just did. That's why you don't trust me.

So tell me: Why is that? Do you perceive I have any reason to want to be—you know, that way, with Harry?"

He knows what I mean. I can tell by the way he hesitates. "If I weren't happy, yeah, I'd make a play for him. Or I'd fall for any play he'd make on me."

He moves in close. "So, you want to play truth or dare? Okay, I've got one for you: Has he made his move yet?"

That's just it. He hasn't.

And that's what hurts most.

I start to say something, but my hesitation is all Ted needs to presume he's right. "You're in over your head, Lyssa. That guy is poison. Everyone but you sees it." He lifts the tree with one hand and heads for the door. "You're going to be his rebound lay, don't you see it? Drop him now, before it's too late."

"Everyone—even you, Ted—thinks they know him, but they don't. They put themselves in his shoes, and they don't like what they see." I reach out to stop him. "That's it, isn't it? If you were him, that is what you'd do, right? Tomcat up and down the street?"

Now it's his turn to think of a safe answer, but he knows I know him too well. "Yeah, okay, I'll admit it. I'd go for it. I'd see it as getting even."

I let this roll over me. "Gee, nice to know. To get even for what?" Then it hits me. "Oh! So I take it you think she had an affair, too!"

"Huh?" Realizing I mean DeeDee, Ted stops cold. "I—how would I know?"

"That's just it. You're presuming the worst, of both of them." I push past him, into the house. "And of me."

"Damn it, Lyssa! Look, enough of this! Okay, let me make myself clear: I don't want him anywhere near you! Okay?"

"No. It's not okay. I should be able to choose my own friends. And you should trust my judgment."

"Sure, then, have it your way. You've now made your choice. I hope you can live with it." He dumps the tree sideways in the foyer and stalks off to the bedroom. A moment later I hear the Warriors game play-by-play.

No surprise there.

The kids stare at me, then disperse to their favorite pouting places.

My anger gives me the strength I need to pull the tree upright and move it into place at the base of the stairway.

Then I cry.

Not because he doesn't trust me, but because I don't trust myself.

31

"Love is a gross exaggeration of the difference
between one person and everybody else."

—George Bernard Shaw

Monday, 9 Dec., 3:18 p.m.

Your kid makes a cute snowflake," murmurs Biker Mom.
She points over at Olivia, who is positioned in front of
her seven-year-old daughter, one of the stately sugarplum
fairies rehearsing for Madame Nadia's production of *The Nut-
cracker*, albeit the only one with a diamond stud in her nose.

I smile my appreciation, but shake my head at the white
chocolate drops she proffers. "Sorry, as tempting as those are,
they aren't on my diet."

"What, yogurt-covered raisins?" She stares in mock astonish-
ment.

"Oh, is that what they are?" Still, I hesitate before sticking
my hand out. Old habits die hard, and I've been warned about
taking candy from strangers.

And according to Brooke, there is no one stranger than Biker
Mom.

"Yum! These are pretty good."

"Yeah, and addictive. I think I've gained five pounds since I
discovered them. You can find them at Trader Joe's. It has much
better prices than what you'll find at the Heights Market." Biker

Mom tries to pinch an inch through her tight, shiny purple jeans, but no go. "You're Lyssa, right? My name is Summer."

I stop licking my fingers in order to shake her outstretched hand. "Nice to finally put the name with the face. Your reputation precedes you."

She breaks out in a raucous laugh. "Aw, jeez! I can just imagine what that Brooke person has said about me! Hey, don't worry, Cody and I don't eat the heads off of snakes or anything. It's not on *our* diet. We're vegetarians."

"Oh—no! Not Brooke. I meant Harry Wilder. He'll be happy we've finally met. But I know what you're saying. Brooke can be a bit of a snob."

"Try 'bitch.' " She wrinkles her nose. "Semantics aside, welcome to the other side."

"Huh? What does that mean?"

"You know: to the land of the Undesirables." She gives me a knowing smile.

"Oh, so you know about that? Harry shouldn't have told you." I feel my cheeks flame up.

"He didn't. I'd already heard about it. Marcus let it slip." She shakes her head. "He's a sweet kid. Not half as insecure as his parents, so they must be doing something right."

Suddenly it hits me that Temple isn't here. "Where are Harry and Temple, anyway?"

"In court. DeeDee is making a big play for the house and child support. I guess she's hoping Jake's suspension works in her favor. But the judge wanted the kids' input too."

"That makes sense." Of course I'm concerned for Harry, but I'm somewhat put off that I have to hear about this from Summer instead of directly from him. If she knows this much about his schedule, then apparently their friendship is closer than I presumed.

It makes me wonder what she thinks about my relationship with Harry. Brooke, my so-called closest friend—and let's not forget my husband—thinks the worst about Harry and me. So why not this perfect stranger?

I hate being paranoid. But I'd also hate being a pariah to both sides of the Heights—the self-described Desirables and the Undesirables.

So that she won't think I'm too curious about Harry, I think it's best to change the subject. "Listen, Summer, about Brooke: she really doesn't mean any harm. Frankly, I think it's a self-defense mechanism."

"I can see that." Summer gives a spot-on imitation of Brooke, arched brow and all.

I can't help but laugh. This earns us a cross look from Madame Nadia. Between the clumsiness of the sugar canes and the ADD of the ten-year-old boy recruited to play the village burgermeister in her annual holiday show, she has her hands full, and we both know it. Summer nudges me to follow her outside, to the same bench where Harry and I often take refuge.

"I'm not going to apologize for Brooke. She is who she is, that's all there is to it. And I hope I've never given you the wrong impression—you know, that I didn't think well of you or anything—"

Summer bursts out with a guffaw. "You? Nah. We knew you were harmless. At least, compared to the rest of the Coven."

"What did you say? The . . . Coven?"

"Yep. That's what the rest of us call your old pals, because they're all so great at practicing bitchcraft." She studies her nails, which, except for the rainbow glitter sprayed across her middle fingernail, are lacquered the same shade of purple as her jeans. "In fact, Mallory Eisenstadt—she's the one the Coven calls Activist Mom—she actually named each of you, I mean *them*, after fairy-tale witches. Your queen bee is Maleficent. The horny one who's always got workmen at her house is Bellatrix Lestrange, and that psycho one is called Ursula. You know, like in *The Little Mermaid*."

I feel the raisins rising in my throat. "Man, that's harsh!"

"Really? Think so?" She stops for a moment as if contemplating that. "But you didn't think it cruel to call me Biker Mom."

"Of course I did." What I don't say, but we both are thinking is, *Not that I ever said anything to shut them up.* "I'm almost afraid to ask. What was my nickname?"

"You really want to know?"

"Yeah. Go ahead, I'm bracing myself."

"Hah. I'm surprised Harry never told you. It was Sleeping Beauty."

I'm confused. "But she isn't a witch."

Summer smiles. "That's the point."

4:41 p.m.

"Your hair. You cut it." That's Harry's way of telling me that he doesn't like what he sees.

We've run into each other at Trader Joe's. Since eating Summer's yogurt-covered raisins, I've been craving them. Besides, it's easier to shop where I know I won't run into the Coven. Okay, yeah, that nickname works just fine for me.

In fact, I wish I'd thought of it first.

"Yep, I let my hairstylist go for it. Chop, chop, chop. It was a spur-of-the-moment thing. I was going for something sleek and sophisticated." I give my hair a self-conscious pat. "I guess you can't win over all of the people all of the time. At least Ted likes it."

"That's what counts, right?" Harry busies himself squeezing a few of the melons from the bin in front of us. He's trying to be casual, but his tone tells me that this is too much information for him.

That's fine. I have no desire to talk about Ted. I wonder if he feels like talking about DeeDee with me, or if that's a privilege he reserves only for Summer.

Damn it, now I'm thinking like Brooke. Still, there's one way to find out if that's the case. "How did court go?"

"Oh, you know about that?" As he shrugs, he tosses the melon he's holding into his cart. "But of course you do. You and your girls know everything."

"If you're referring to the Coven, let me assure you that I'm no longer its official mascot."

He lets out a surprised chuckle. "So you know about that? Wow, you really do have great sources."

"Just one. Summer. She's my new best friend." *And apparently yours too,* I want to say, but I know better. Friends aren't jealous of other friends.

Of course, rivals are a different story.

I break open the container of the coveted yogurt raisins and gulp down a handful before offering it to him.

"Thanks, but no thanks. In my book, the term 'healthy snack' is an oxymoron." He picks up the canister and stares at the ingredients. "But I may have to change my mind between now and the next court date. When the judge asked Temple what was her very favorite meal her dad ever made, she said, 'Kellogg's Variety Pack.' I guess nobody will confuse me with Wolfgang Puck."

I consider this. "You're right. What else did the judge say?"

"Let's put it this way: if Jake strikes out once more, it's me who's out—on the street. Bethany's mantra is that I'm an unfit dad. She says it so loud and so often that I'm starting to believe it myself."

"Why would you, when you're doing your best? Yes, you're the provider. But you're more than that. You're their father, too!" I shake my head in wonder. "I'm beginning to think DeeDee is one of those deadbeat moms."

Just then, Temple and Jake come around the corner. Harry puts a finger to his lips. He doesn't have to. I've already shut my big mouth.

"Hi, guys. Care for some yogurt raisins?" I hold out the container to them.

Temple digs in, but Jake wrinkles his nose and waves them away. Like father, like son.

"Mrs. Harper, would it be okay if I come over and study with Tanner tomorrow night, after practice? He's better at geography, and we have a test the next day." Jake's concern is impressive. Apparently the court proceedings sobered him up.

"Yes, of course."

"Great! . . . Aw, I forgot. We have to be at the gym early that day. Coach Shriver wants us there for our team photo."

Count on Pete to choose the most ungodly hour for that. Something about the natural light at that time of morning. "Look, I have an idea. Why don't you just sleep over? I know it's a school night, but I have no problem dropping you both off at school early that morning. That is, if it's okay with your father."

Harry nods his approval. "Sounds like a plan. But remember, study doesn't involve Wii."

Jake nods solemnly, then reaches down and picks up his sister, who has been climbing his legs for attention.

For once the tension goes out of Harry's shoulders. He sees the future, and it might actually be okay.

I hope Jake sees it too.

I am convinced this is the case when, later that evening, Jake calls to tell me he won't be coming over after all. Apparently he's already memorized the names of the South American countries that were tripping him up. And besides, Temple is so fussy lately. . . .

Don't worry, I assure him. Family comes first, with study a close second.

As I hang up the phone, I wonder if Tanner will ever be as mature as Jake.

32

"Only choose in marriage a man whom you would choose as a friend if he were a woman."

—Joseph Joubert

Wednesday, 11 Dec.

The crash outside my window has me bolting upright in bed. My eyes go to the clock on the nightstand, where the digitized numbers *1:13* stare back at me. My first thought is to shake Ted so that he can see what damage has been done to the live oak in the front yard.

But he isn't here.

Then I remember he was working late. Again.

Or maybe he's sleeping in the guest room. Again.

I'm wrong. Ted isn't sleeping at all. He's in the kitchen, helping himself to the leftovers from our dinner. He too has heard the crash and is headed for the front door, a roasted chicken leg still in hand.

The car wrapped around the tree is Harry's. The front end is smoking ominously.

Behind the wheel, unconscious and bleeding from his head, is Jake.

"Call 911! Call Harry! His number is on the fridge." I rush to open the car door, but the frame is too bent up to give way.

Ted runs inside, but is back out by the time I've moved the poor kid out through the passenger door. Then I wonder if I should have left Jake alone, in case he has any broken bones. When the flames roar out of the hood, I realize I've done the right thing.

Ted rushes back into the house to pull the fire extinguisher out of the kitchen. By the time he comes back with it, a police car, a fire truck, and an ambulance are already here.

But no Harry.

"Didn't you call him?" I glare at Ted. Of course he knows whom I'm referring to.

"I forgot." He feigns interest in the medics, who are strapping Jake to a stretcher.

Liar.

I snatch the cell out of his hand and dial Harry's number. Harry's voice comes out as a faraway murmur. "Who is it? . . . Lyssa? What's up?"

"Harry, you've got to come over here now! It's Jake! He's crashed the car."

"What?" He's loud, anxious, and angry. "What time is it? Lyssa, why would you let him drive your car?"

"Not my car, Harry! *Your* car. He was driving your car."

"But . . . that can't be. My car is in the driveway—" I hear the receiver drop. A moment later, he's back on. "I don't understand! Did you send him home? Why didn't you let him stay at your place?"

"*My* place?" I feel as if I'm talking a different language. "Harry, Jake never came over here after practice. He called and said he'd changed his mind."

His silence is long, his words heavy. "I'm beginning to wonder if we'll survive this divorce."

"Ted and I are leaving now to follow the ambulance to the hospital. We'll swing by your place and pick you up."

He groans anxiously and hangs up.

• • •

1:52 a.m.

Jake is conscious by the time we get to the hospital. He stares at the wall, but I know he's listening to the doctor's conversation with his father.

"Your son is shaken up, but no broken bones. He's groggy from a concussion. I'd like to keep him overnight."

"Of course." Harry looks pale in the hospital lighting. He signs the papers proffered, then watches the doctor as he goes down the hall. This gives him a few more minutes to collect his thoughts.

"It's nice of Summer to watch Temple for you."

"She came right over." The thought of her puts a wry smile on his face. "Only she can laugh off something like this. Says she can see her future just by watching our kids. She and Cody fully expect karmic payback when that hellion toddler of theirs, Elvis, gets into his teens."

"At the very least, he'll rebel over that name."

Ted shakes his head. Absentmindedly he puts his hand on Harry's arm. Maybe it has taken something like this for Ted to realize that Harry is just like him: a dad putting his kids first.

We hear the click of heels on the linoleum hall floor before we actually see DeeDee. Harry recognizes the sound first. His eyes go dark and glassy at the realization that he has to explain how their son has ended up there, in that hospital bed, under his watch.

She looks at each of us, but stops short at the vision of her son, black and blue and bandaged all over. "How did it happen?"

"He left the house under the pretense of studying with Tanner. He must have pocketed the extra set of car keys. I'd given him permission to sleep over at the Harpers'—"

"On a school night? And you let him drive over? My God, Harry—"

"Don't be ridiculous, DeeDee. He *stole* the keys." Harry shakes his head in shame. "And the sleepover was a special circumstance. They were to study together for a test, then get up early for the team photo—"

"But instead, he's out joyriding! Isn't that just perfect." She strips the scarf from her neck in frustration. "Wait until the judge hears about this! Wait until—"

"Wait until the judge hears we don't want to live with you." Jake sounds groggy, but he is adamant. Everyone turns to him. In a flash, both Harry and DeeDee are at his side.

Even as she pats his hand, DeeDee is firm. "I'm sorry, Jake, but that may not be up to you. Especially after tonight."

"Jake, I know you're angry. At us both." Harry tries to keep the despair out of his voice, but he's doing a lousy job at it. "But misbehaving only takes away what few options you have. That *we* have, as a family."

"I'm not going to live with Mom. She doesn't love us." He turns his head away from DeeDee, but she's not having it.

"Who told you that? Is that what your father says?" She swings back around toward Harry.

"Quit blaming Dad! It's not him. He never says anything mean about you at all. It's how you've been acting, and you know it!"

At that, DeeDee rears back as if she's been slapped in the face. But Jake isn't through with her. "Mom, did you leave him for that guy you sleep with? Did you leave *us* for that guy?"

Almost as if time is standing still, everyone freezes.

"I saw him, Mom. Tonight. That's why I took the car." Jake lets that sink in. "I thought he might come over, since you don't have us on Wednesdays. And I was right. I wanted to confront him, to tell him what he's doing to our family. What he's doing to me."

"You don't know what you're saying! *You don't know what*

you're doing." DeeDee's already pale face suddenly looks translucent.

"Who is he, Jake?" The urgency in Harry's voice should break the trance between Jake and DeeDee, but it doesn't.

Finally Jake turns to him. "I don't know. I just couldn't do it, not in front of Mom. So instead I followed him home."

Harry frowns. "You know where he lives?"

"Well—no, not exactly. It was dark, and he was driving too fast." Jake tries to raise his arm, but he winces in pain and puts it back down. "I lost him when he turned on Bougainvillea. I figured I could drive around in time to see him walking into his house, but I guess he parks in his garage. Or else he'd already turned another corner. If the Conovers' cat hadn't jumped in front of the car, I wouldn't have driven into the Harpers' tree." A tear rolls down his cheek. "Dad, I'm sorry I took the car. It wasn't the first time, so I thought I'd do okay—"

"I tell you, he's got it all wrong. I have a right to have friends, too." She looks at all of us—Harry, me, and Ted—before confronting Jake. "You're making all of this up because you're in trouble. Don't dare blame me. Taking the car was wrong. And once again your father was negligent on your behalf. You see, Harry? Another reason why they should be with me full-time."

"Mom, I'm not lying! Oh, by the way, I've taken your car out too. And I'll be sure to let the judge know it."

DeeDee opens her mouth to say something, then thinks better of it. Instead she glares at her son, but he takes it in stride.

For the longest time, no one says anything. Finally DeeDee breaks the silence. "Harry, I presume you're staying here tonight?"

"Yes, I'd planned on it." Then quickly he adds, "Temple is covered."

"I would hope so! I can only pray it's someone who's too old for joyriding." Without another word to anyone, she walks off.

Harry blinks twice. I know he's contemplating Summer and her Maserati.

I pat Jake's foot. "Well, I guess we should go too."

Harry reaches over to give me a hug. I feel awkward taking it, especially in front of Ted, but Harry needs it now, so Ted be damned.

"I guess you had to call DeeDee about this, so thanks . . . I think."

I shake my head. "But I didn't call her. I just didn't think about it. Frankly, I thought you were bold to do so." We stare at each other, stymied.

Ted shuffles uncomfortably. "I called her, after I called 911."

Taken aback, we both turn to him.

He stares us down. "I found her phone number in the school directory. I thought she should know too. I mean, if it were me, I'd certainly want to know. You'd feel that way too. Am I right?"

Harry nods grudgingly.

I, on the other hand, am less convinced of Ted's empathy for DeeDee.

We drive home in silence. Only after we climb into bed does it dawn on me that while he thought to call Harry's soon-to-be ex, it was actually me who called Harry, because Ted had so conveniently forgotten to do so.

And if I hadn't, she would have arrived at the hospital first.

Is that what Ted had wanted?

I now know how much he hates Harry.

33

"The best thing to hold on to in life is each other."

—Audrey Hepburn

Thursday, 12 Dec., 8:53 p.m.

Where is my daddy?"

This is the fifteenth time Temple has asked me that same question in the past three hours.

I've got her and Jake with me at my house. I know my smile is wobbly, but it's better than giving in to the impulse to frown. "You know, sweetie, he didn't realize how late they'd keep him at work."

"But it's bedtime. Why isn't he home yet?"

I pause to contemplate other excuses I can give her. The only one I can think of is the lamest of all parental fallback positions: "Maybe he stopped off to get you and Jake a surprise."

She doesn't want to come out and call me a liar, so instead she sucks on the baby bottle that is her constant companion these days, and goes back to finger-painting a black cloud over a family of stick people.

Temple has given up on adults telling her the truth.

I don't want to let on that I'm concerned about him too. He was supposed to be home by four, and it's now going on nine. After the eighth time she asked, I tried his cell phone and got a very terse, "Not now! I'll call you as soon as I can . . . like in half an hour."

That was three hours ago.

Jake, who finished his homework sometime before dinner, sits silently in the corner with his eyes half shut, trying hard to ignore Mickey's incessant chatter, which meanders from his baseball card collection to his prowess on the soccer field. He's more patient with his idol than his big brother, who gave up on engaging Jake after they had a falling-out during a one-on-one game of b-ball. Jake's foul shots might be off, but he's learned the skill of tripping up those whom he perceives as opponents with scathing taunts that leave no insecurity unturned. In Tanner's case, his shorter stature is ridiculed, along with his growing infatuation with Natassia—or in Jake's words, "Little Miss Skank."

This last is it for Tanner. He walks away, not bloodied but emotionally bruised. "What's with you, man? You've become an asshole. A real sadist."

At least during dinner we had détente.

I guess it's a good thing that Ted is on a business trip. After Jake's collision, he's made it clear that he's not too thrilled about Jake and Tanner's friendship.

Not that he'll come out and say that. Mention of any of the Wilders is off-limits for us these days.

Apparently lovemaking is on that short list, too. At least, as far as Ted is concerned. We haven't had sex since Thanksgiving.

If that's what you call what we had that night.

I call it payback sex. He was paying me back for daring to make him jealous.

I wasn't trying to make him jealous. Still, I have to admit it was nice to feel he desired me again. Make War, Then Love seemed to be our motto.

But no more. Jake's crazy joyride has me realizing how precious life really is, how we all do things we later regret. How we hold on to the hurt and the pain when we really don't have to.

Just like Jake. And Harry.

And, yes, me too.

Well, no more. I have turned over a new leaf. It means giving others the benefit of the doubt, and making new friends, even if they were formerly viewed as enemies.

It means making a truce with Ted. And certainly adopting a new motto.

From now on, I'm nice to everyone: the mean, the bad, the crazy.

Even the Coven.

Yeah, okay, even DeeDee.

The tap on the glass is so soft that I don't hear it at first. I look up to see Harry staring at me through the window, an apparition half in shadow. He puts his finger to his lips, then beckons for me to come out. I glance around to see if the children realize he's there, but no, they have finally settled into the malaise that comes with being guests who are embarrassed for having overstayed their welcome. Sullen solitude is appreciated on all fronts.

I slip out the back door into the velvety darkness broken only by the light streaming through the kitchen window. I hear Harry humming, but at first I don't see him. "Harry, where did you go?"

He stops midstanza. "I'm over here by the love shack!"

Perplexed, I follow his voice, which is now singing off-key, "'*Shot through the heart, and you're to blame! You give love a bad name. . . .*'"

"Harry, keep it down! You don't want the kids to hear you."

"It doesn't matter anymore." He flops onto the stoop of the shed.

"What doesn't matter?"

"Everything. Anything." His head drops onto his chest. It stays there for such a long while that I think he's fallen asleep—

Until he starts with the awful crooning again.

Harry Wilder is drunk as a skunk.

"You're killing me, Harry! Have some respect. It's Bon Jovi, for God's sake."

He processes that for a moment, then concedes with a nod. "I'll bet you didn't know that, back in the day, I used to look like him." He pours the rest of his beer onto the grass. "Yeah, really, Bon Jovi. Do you see the resemblance?" He turns and stares me down.

"Nah. Brad Pitt, though, for sure. Especially around the eyes."

He shrugs to give me the impression that he couldn't care less, but I know better. "What the hell do they know, anyhow? Those assholes used to tell me a lot of things."

"Let me guess: they told you something you didn't want to hear today. Am I right?"

"Jesus, Lys, you're practically . . . *psychic*." He pulls me down beside him. "Yep, that they did, loud and clear: 'Sayonara.' Just like that."

"Who . . . your partners?"

"You're battin' two for two, girly-girl." As he hugs my shoulders, I catch a whiff of his breath and recoil. At least, I try to, but he's holding me too firmly, as if I am his lifeline.

But of course I am. I wish I could say I don't like it, but I do.

"How did they do it?"

"Oh, it was all very well thought out, I can assure you. They built a case for my 'erratic behavior,' not to mention my 'client negligence.' Toss in the economy, and it's a solid triple play. Of course, they're blowing it out their asses, but I'd have to take them to court to prove it, and that's time and money that, seriously, I don't have. They know that, and they're counting on the fact that DeeDee and Bethany have beaten me down so far that I'll just take their shekels and run. They had papers already drawn up that give me a tidy little cash settlement for being a good boy and walking away from everything: the department I built from the ground up, my partnership—my firm, goddamn it! IT'S MY FIRM!"

I can hear the tears in his voice, but I don't dare look over at him.

"What about your clients? They're there because of you. They won't hang in there if you take your shingle and hang it somewhere else."

"That depends. Yeah, I'm sure a handful will stay true blue, no matter where I end up—if I can even talk my way into another partnership, that is. But the majority of my clients are wonks: they're buying the name of the firm, first and foremost."

"Will you fight it?"

"Of course!" He relaxes his hand on my shoulder. "Oh, I don't know. I went by Edwin's office to break the news to him. He turned a little green around the gills, let me tell you. Having zippo income is going to make it tough for me to pay his fee, let alone get the approval to hang on to the kids and the house." He crushes his beer can. "On the other hand, whoever gets it may have to sell the house anyway."

His head drops again, but this time it lolls over toward me. I don't know what to do when I feel it land on my shoulder.

So I do nothing at all but listen to errant dogs barking and the occasional car rolling down the street.

This close to him, I take note of the rhythm of his heart.

And the heat of his tears on my neck.

"She's going to get the kids, you know."

"*Shhhhh*," I whisper, as if he's Mickey fretting over monsters in his closet and just hearing this from me will give him all the assurance he needs to stand free of his fear, to see things in perspective.

But he is not Mickey, and DeeDee is not a monster.

She's just a mom, like me, who wants her kids with her always.

That's why I can't hate her.

I know he doesn't either. I know he loves her.

"Thank you," he murmurs, "for being here for me."

It is an innate reflex, one we mothers have, to brush our lips on the forehead we are comforting. I don't realize until it's too late that I've just done that to Harry.

Of course, immediately I pull away.

At first he doesn't react. But then he does what I hope—what I fear—he'll do:

He finds my lips in the dark.

The kiss is gentle at first. When it turns hungry, I can't help but give in, let him probe my mouth with his tongue for a little compassion—

Then I realize what I'm doing, and it hits me that Harry may wake up tomorrow and not remember that any of this happened.

Or worse yet, he'll wake up and hate himself even more, because it did.

And despise me too. He doesn't need the complication.

And I don't want us to prove Ted right.

I shove him off with both hands. He knows better than to fight me. Instead, he rises unsteadily to his feet. "You're right! You're right. I . . . aw, hell, I fully and completely apologize. Lyssa, I'm sorry—"

"Forget about it, please!" I'm glad it's too dark for him to see how red my face is right now. "It's getting late. Let's round up your kids so I can take you home in your rental car and walk back."

I ignore his outstretched hand to help me up because I know that, if I take it, I'll never want to let go again.

34

"The language of friendship is not words but meanings."

—Henry David Thoreau

Friday, 13 Dec., 10:24 a.m.

P*sssst!* Lyssa, it's Colleen!" my old friend whispers frantically in my ear.

I remove the cucumber slice from one eye before addressing her. "Colleen, FYI: despite being banished from the Coven—I mean, the board—I still recognize your voice."

Lucky, lucky me, I've chosen the same day and time as the Coven to get a facial at the Heights of Beauty.

Thus far everyone's been civil; that is to say, I've yet to be pierced by Tammy's, Margot's, or Isabelle's daggered glances.

"Oh! Good. . . . What did you say? 'Coven'?"

Her stare has the innocence of a lamb's. For a second I debate whether I should tell her that, outside Margot's very exclusive clique, her cluelessness has earned her a nickname she may actually appreciate: Glinda, the Good Witch. "Nope, sorry, I was thinking of something else."

"Listen, before Margot and the others come out of their massages, I just want to say that I'm sorry, and—well, that I miss you."

"That's very sweet of you, Colleen. Really, I'm touched." For someone like her, it takes guts to break ranks.

"If there's anything you ever need, I'm here for you, Lyssa. Covertly, of course."

I stick the cucumber back over my eye in the hope that she will take the hint.

"I mean it. That goes for Harry, too."

I lift the slice again. "Well, I'm sure he'll appreciate it. Covertly, of course."

"You know, Lyssa, he's the only straight man I've known who didn't look right through me. Or specifically at my breasts. He actually talked to my face. It was . . . nice."

I think about this for a moment. "Yeah, Harry keeps it real."

"When I thought about it, I wasn't really upset that he didn't like my casseroles. It's just that I wanted to endear him to me. I never felt I offered anything that was a fair trade for his friendship."

I envision Colleen's bland, gooey concoctions and frown. "I don't get you."

She puckers her lips in thought. "With Brooke he could play tennis, while Margot gave him power and connections, and Isabelle watched his back—at least, until he crossed her at the basketball game. And . . . well, you know Tammy."

I pretend to be intrigued by my new nail color. "What about Tammy? What do you think she offered him?"

Colleen breaks into a nervous giggle, then remembers where she is and with whom, and covers her mouth. "Gee, Lyssa, how naïve can you be? I don't have to spell it out for you, do I?"

"Just say it, Colleen."

"She wanted to jump his bones! Gosh, I thought everyone knew that."

"Did she succeed?" Does she hear the waver in my voice?

"The way she turned on him, are you kidding?" She snickers. "Nah. Harry's true blue."

"I know. Despite all DeeDee's done to him, he still loves her."

"No, silly! Not to DeeDee. To *you*."

"What?" I jerk up so fast that I've cracked my lavender mud mask. "But we aren't—we haven't—believe me, Colleen—"

"Lyssa, don't worry! All I mean is that he's got a crush on you. Everyone knows that."

If my face heats up, I'll have an avalanche of purple goop in my lap, so I try to keep cool. "But we're just friends. It's all very innocent—"

"Oh, I know you and Harry aren't having some sort of lurid affair." She looks over her shoulder, then whispers, "So please don't think I'm the one spreading the rumors. Remember, you didn't hear this from me. . . ."

3:30 p.m.

"What's your favorite Christmas cookie: gingerbread, sugar, or macaroons?" Harry's voice sounds hangover-raspy, but he's trying to keep things casual.

Of course, he doesn't mention last night's kiss at all.

I wonder if he even remembers it.

Okay, I'll play it cool, too. "You had me at gingerbread."

"Ha! I could have guessed as much. So, what are you doing right now?"

"Folding laundry. It is the bane of my existence."

"Temple and I would like to offer you what I'm sure you'll agree is a more delightful alternative. How about you and Olivia coming over and making Christmas cookies with us? It's going to be our new old tradition. Cursing our mistakes should lead to some great father-daughter bonding, don't you agree?"

I do, totally. I love the fact that Ted, too, has created one great tradition with our kids: sports movie marathons. "It's all about the team and the dream," he explains to them. At the start of baseball season, they watch *The Lou Gehrig Story* and *Field of*

Dreams. Of course, at the beginning of basketball season, there's *Hoosiers, Hoop Dreams,* and *The Air Up There.* And when the football season rolls around, there is *Brian's Song, Remember the Titans,* and the ultimate sports movie tearjerker of them all, *Rudy.*

On those nights, watching Ted and the kids snuggle on the couch with a big bowl of popcorn, I realize we are Ted's team.

We are Ted's dream.

I'm so happy for Harry that he is creating this for his own family.

Even if Harry and Temple's cookies come out like cardboard, the effort will have been worth it. My laughter tells him so. "You're not giving yourself enough credit. Maybe the cookies will actually be good. But today may not be good for me. I have to pick Mickey up from soccer practice by four-thirty—"

"Oh, heck, the cookies will be long-burnt by then, along with the rest of the house—unless you come on over and save us from ourselves. What do you say?"

Of course I say yes.

There's a lot about Harry I find hard to refuse.

By the time we get there, Harry has already placed all the ingredients and a large mixing bowl on his kitchen's marble-topped island. I've brought with us some things I know Harry and Temple will appreciate: a rolling pin and a box filled with cookie cutters shaped like men in various poses. Immediately the girls take turns divvying them up.

"Wow! Sharing! I hate to admit it, but there's a concept I rarely see in practice in the Harper household." I shake my head in wonder.

"Hey, join the club. I guess the boys need to go back to Miss Judith's for refresher classes."

The girls are in charge of adding ingredients. Soon the flour, sugar, and baking powder have been sifted together, then cut with Crisco and molasses. Harry divides this bounty into two large balls of cookie dough and places one in front of each of our girls. I watch Olivia as she carefully rolls out her dough, pushing out from the middle, like I've taught her.

Temple is watching too, fascinated. "Daddy, is this how they do it at the store?"

"No, sweetheart. They buy their cookies from a bakery, then sell them to us."

This gives her pause. "Maybe that can be your new job, Daddy! Making pretty cookies for the store."

Harry's game face slips for just a moment before he catches himself. "That's a thought. But don't you worry about Daddy. He has lots of irons in the fire."

We make small talk as our daughters line their baking trays with ginger people. When they are done, they run off to play in the den until the cookies have finished baking and have cooled enough to be embellished with generous squirts of colored icing.

There is something soothing about the aroma of spice and molasses. Even Harry now feels comfortable enough to ask the one question I'd hoped he'd never broach:

"When are you going to listen to Ted and dump me?"

"Why should I? Just because he's jealous? I have a right to choose my own friends." So that I won't have to face him, I busy myself cleaning up the baking paraphernalia.

It's certainly much easier than tidying up the mess I've made of my life.

"If I were him, I'd be jealous too."

"No, you wouldn't. You'd know better. You're more trusting."

"If I 'knew better,' I wouldn't be going through a divorce right now. Before DeeDee fell in love with someone else, she had to fall out of love with me."

"Not necessarily." That just slips out.

"Why do you say that?"

"Well . . . she may not have been in love with you in the first place."

I wasn't with Ted.

The weight of this theory staggers Harry to the point that he sits down hard on one of the plush barstools that butt up against the island. "That's cruel. Lyssa. Wow. Why would you say something like that?"

I could put his mind at ease and explain that I'm talking about myself, but I don't, because he's the one in mourning, not me. His marriage is dead, not mine.

At least, that's what I tell myself.

"It happens a lot. You know, people marrying for the wrong reasons." I take the dish towel I've been knotting through my fingers and fold it into a little square, just so that I don't have to look him in the eye. "They do it because it's the safest bet. But I guess that's better than falling out of love."

"You'll never have to worry about that. Ted is still very much in love with you."

I laugh at that. I mean, really, what am I supposed to say to him? That Ted only loves me when other men threaten his hold on me? That I didn't find out until it was too late that Ted never loved me to begin with?

That I'd never have married him had I known this?

DeeDee would certainly understand. She told me so herself.

Okay, not me exactly, but her Nordstrom shopgirl.

But Harry would never understand that, not in a million years.

Because he still loves DeeDee, despite the fact that she left him. He won't admit it to himself, let alone to me, but he wears his wedding ring in the hope that the last couple of months have all been just a bad dream—

For the first time, I notice Harry isn't wearing his wedding ring.

Harry's eyes seek out mine, as if he might find the answer to DeeDee's desertion there after all.

Okay, Harry, if you really want to know the truth, here it is—

But DeeDee's confession-by-proxy will have to wait, because Harry's cell is moaning. "Aw, hell, it's Edwin." As he flips it open, he turns his back to me. "Yes? . . . WHAT? Today? . . . Well, why didn't your office call to tell me? Who . . . JAKE?"

He rushes to the refrigerator and scans the pieces of paper stuck behind the multitude of magnets there. "No, he left me no note. Look, stall as long as you can. I'll leave right now."

He slams down his phone and grabs his coat from the hook. "They're in court now. One of my asshole partners let on to Bethany about my dismissal. She got the hearing moved up to this afternoon by telling the judge that my erratic behavior is stressing out the kids 'in the same way it stressed DeeDee.' They're making an end run on the kids, the house—"

"Go! Go *on*! I'll be here with the kids. Just GO!"

He hauls out through the house, to the front door. He doesn't even bother to shut it on the way out.

I follow and watch him peel down the street.

"Mommy! The cookies are burning!" Olivia is screeching at the top of her lungs.

I rush back to the kitchen and pull the hot tray out of the oven. The girls stare at their handiwork. Temple reaches for one of them, but Olivia slaps her hand back. She knows better. If you reach out to these sad, hard men, you may get burned.

She is smarter than her mother.

35

"Lots of people want to ride with you in the limo,
but what you want is someone who will take the
bus with you when the limo breaks down."

—Oprah Winfrey

8:30 p.m.

I say you sue everybody! Your ex, your partners, even your damn lawyer. Hit me again, Cal." Pete is all talk. That's because it's poker night, and he's feeling flush.

And that's only because I'm letting him win.

Because he's still too stunned from his court appearance this afternoon, Harry is sitting this one out. To busy himself, he's been doling out plates of the leftover meat loaf. "Ground turkey. Eat up! Bought fifty pounds of the stuff at Costco for next to nothing, and I'm not leaving any of it in the freezer for DeeDee. She can buy her own damn ground turkey."

His chatter is light, but he doesn't fool any of us. He's depressed as hell. In two days he's got to move out, and DeeDee gets possession of it all for now: the house, the furniture, the kids, and the dog. Harry takes a swig of his water. "You know, I may just move into Costco. I can live in one of those tents they leave open for display. Do you think anyone will notice?"

I'm relieved to see that he's not drinking now. It's a positive sign that his binge the other night was a one-of-a-kind abomination.

Except for the kiss, of course.

An abomination, I mean. I have to be honest with myself that it was anything but.

But, yes, it was one-of-a-kind, because I know it won't ever happen again.

Or I'm doomed.

Cal has taken Harry's Costco question to heart. "Security guards, probably. Don't forget security cams. Oh, and they may have sensor devices."

"To hell with the tent." Pete throws down a bad card. "Without any money coming in from you, DeeDee will have to put the house on the market anyway. I'll buy it from her, and you and the kids can move in and pay me rent."

Harry's water glass freezes in midair. "You're joking, right?"

"Nope. I like real estate. Particularly in the Heights. Great 'hood, great investment."

"Thanks, Pete. I'll keep it in mind. I hope it won't come to that, but let's face it: the writing's on the wall. Between Jake's shenanigans on my watch and the loss of my job, DeeDee has all she needs to make her case against my having full custody. And she's right about one thing: the kids come first." He grimaces. "Even if that means I'll be supporting two households: my tent, and hers with her boyfriend."

I sigh. "So, Jake is right about what he saw?"

"I believe him over her any day of the week." Harry takes the dirty dishes to the sink. "He may be having a rough time, but he's not a liar."

"That sucks." Pete picks up another card. "You're the better parent. Even the kids have said that."

"Well, no one is listening to any of us. And in this case, actions really do speak louder than words."

"You'll build up your practice again in no time," insists Pete.

"In fact, we're looking for someone to help on my company's merger with ICA Tech. That's right up your alley."

"Hell, yeah, it is. Are you for real?"

"As real as these two pair." He throws down his cards with a flip of his wrist.

I fold.

Cal follows. "What if you prove that she's, you know, unfit? Will that help?"

"I think that, at the very least, I'd get partial custody. And that's only fair."

It's Pete's turn to shuffle. "Even if it turns out she was having an affair the whole time, and that's the reason she walked?"

"She's not the only wife who's left during an affair. According to my lawyer, what the judge is trying to determine is who'll provide the best home for the kids. And in the majority of cases, the mothers win." Harry turns toward the sink so that we can't see his face. "In that regard, I'm not out for blood. And I certainly don't want to start a war. If I failed DeeDee in any way, then what happened to us as a couple was meant to be, and nothing I do now will stop the divorce. But I'm not out to destroy the mother of my children in order to hold on to them."

"Jeez, guy, that's turning the other cheek, for sure. Boy, if it were me . . . I'm just saying I wouldn't let any guy get the better of me." Pete shakes his head in wonder.

All three of us stare at Pete, but no one wants to point out the obvious. We all know he wouldn't see it anyway.

Harry turns to Cal. "So, what are you suggesting, that I play I Spy? Detectives aren't cheap."

Cal frowns. "A lot of it is simple deduction, even without electronic surveillance. Of course, it would be easier if we knew more about her regular habits, like when she goes out, where, and why."

"Or her lover's." Pete throws down the deck. "If what Jake says is true, we do know that he lives here in the Heights. Maybe there's a way to narrow the field."

Harry quits drying the dish in his hand. "How do you propose doing that?"

"Simple process of elimination. Comings and goings. Phone calls and e-mails. You know, that kind of thing." Now Cal's excited. "I could certainly write a program that tracks cars leaving the Heights and memorizes their known characteristics—you know, make, model, color, license plates. If any of them move toward her place, then I can train a SATCOM eye to stay on the most obvious suspects. Even if this dude is smart enough to stay away from her place, another program for the satellite will track her comings and goings as well. Eventually their two cars will be at the same place at the same time." He pauses, lost in thought. "Another consideration is cross-referencing any calls made to her, or e-mails sent."

Why do I feel they're getting carried away? "But isn't that kind of tracing illegal without a search warrant? The last thing Harry needs is to do something that gets him in dutch with the bar, not to mention the law. Then he'll never get custody."

"Don't worry. They'll never be able to trace it back to Harry. Or to any of us."

I start to open my mouth again, but the looks on all three of their faces—determination on Cal's, excitement on Pete's, desperation on Harry's—tell me it's no use to try to talk them out of any harebrained schemes.

They are on a mission. And as far as I'm concerned, it's lead, follow, or get out of the way.

I will pass. I have no choice. DeeDee and I have the same equipment.

And I certainly don't have an ulterior motive.

So that they can plot and scheme without my angsting over them like some mother hen, I take what's left of the meat loaf into the great room so that the kids can finish it off.

Don't ask, don't tell. Works for me.

While they eat, I busy myself straightening up the room. I can just imagine what DeeDee would say if she saw it now, what with Temple's toys tossed helter-skelter around the room. As I gather my children's coats and hats, I notice that Jake's have been carelessly tossed on the floor, followed by a pair of muddy sneakers. When I move the coat onto a hook, a baseball cap falls out of its pocket. It is a replica of those of San Francisco's original baseball team, the Seals. I hang it on a hook beside the coat.

It will be interesting to see how fast DeeDee can retrain her children.

Not that I'll be privy to life in this house, ever again.

36

"Marriage is like a bank account. You put it in,
you take it out, you lose interest."

—Irwin Corey

Tuesday, 17 Dec., 11:38 a.m.

It isn't until our yoga instructor has barked out the next pose—downward dog—that Brooke notices me folded awkwardly behind her. She lifts one hand to wave, and almost topples over.

I snicker at this, and that starts her giggling, and the next thing we know we're being shushed by all the yoga Nazis in the room, but that only makes us laugh all the harder.

By the time we've snatched up our mats and our hoodies and headed out of the studio, I realize how much I've missed Brooke.

And I know the feeling must be mutual, because it's she who suggests we grab a bite to eat. I'm all for that, Margot be damned. Besides, I want to hear if Colleen is right, and someone is spreading rumors about Harry and me.

12:05 p.m.

The Max's Diner by the expressway has a great matzo-ball soup and tall booths: perfect for our rendezvous. No, I don't mind that we're meeting on the sly. As of this moment, I view this as a covert op, and I need an inside woman.

I need Brooke.

And apparently she needs me too, if for nothing else than to grouse about Margot's rabid imperiousness. "You got out right in the nick of time. I tell you, Lyssa, it's a bloodbath! Besides you, Tammy was her most natural successor. But Margot doesn't want to turn the presidency over to her. Behind her back, Margot calls her 'power-hungry.' Ha! Now, is that the pot calling the kettle black or what?"

"I'll say."

"But instead of just coming out and saying that, she's been meeting with each of us on the sly, trying to sweet-talk us into running against Tammy. Do you know how she wants to choose her successor? Get a load of this: each of us is supposed to come up with a strategic plan—on PowerPoint, no less—for how we'd personally run next year's events!" She sticks a manicured finger down her throat. "Yeah, well, she can whistle 'Dixie' for that one. I came onboard for the cocktails and gossip, not the grunt work."

"But what do you think is her endgame? I mean, someone has to be president, right?"

Brooke rolls her eyes. "Frankly, I think she wants us all to vote her in for another term, but she's trying to come off as being democratic about the whole thing."

"She's pitting you all against each other so that she'll become the logical choice yet again? Man, that is brilliant." Margot truly is a Machiavellian genius. "If that's the case, I'm surprised she was even going to nominate me in the first place."

Brooke looks up from her matzo ball. "*Au contraire, mon amie.* You were the perfect choice. First off, you're an uncomplaining workhorse. And besides, with you she could play puppet master. You know, be the power behind the throne. Heck, you're so starved for attention that all she'd have to do was give you a pat on the head every now and then, and you'd be good for another event or two."

I almost choke on my soup. "Oh, get real! I'm not *that* needy . . . am I?"

"Like a puppy. If someone scratched your belly, you'd never leave their lap." She examines a nail. "Speaking of delectable laps, how is our sweet boy Harry?"

I pause too long for any lie I could tell at this juncture to be credible. "He's moving. Today, in fact. DeeDee's attorney did an end run for the house, based on Jake's latest transgression and the fact that Harry's lost his partnership at his firm."

Brooke nods. "Yeah, he was spotted tossing a few suitcases into his car this morning. An hour later, DeeDee's car pulled up."

Why am I not surprised that Brooke already knows this? Suddenly I have my hackles up. If they're still stalking Harry, then surely I'm on their radar too.

Smile pretty for the cameras. . . .

"Will he be staying in the Heights?"

I try to make my nod as nonchalant as possible. "He was looking at a couple of places, yes."

"I hear he's going to rent Pete Shriver's cabana house. I guess that will put a damper on Masha's poolside trysts." She scans my reaction to this. "Unless Harry's her type. Ha! What man isn't?"

Brooke proves once again that she's put together the best network of spies in the Heights. I don't know whether to be impressed or repulsed.

One thing I am for sure is determined to identify DeeDee's lover before Harry and the boys do something stupid that costs him his kids for good. "If DeeDee is having an affair with someone, it's going to make it easier to spot the guy, what with her living here in the 'hood again."

Brooke's demure sip of her wine doesn't fool me. Apparently she's already thought about that.

However, the couple now being seated in one of the corner booths may make her reconnaissance a moot point:

It is DeeDee with local realtor Max Karloff, better known around the Heights as the Listing Lothario.

His motto isn't Satisfaction Guaranteed for nothing.

I nudge Brooke, but she's already spotted them in one of the restaurant's many dizzying mirrors, which turn its nooks and crannies into a Peeping Tom's paradise.

"Well, well, well! I guess DeeDee's already figured out that it's not going to be easy to make the house payment with Harry being unemployed." Brooke twists her neck to get a better view. "I've always liked that tricked-out media room. I wonder what the asking price will be? Oh, my God!"

"What? WHAT?" From where I'm sitting, I can't really see a thing, now that they've sat down.

"He's got his arm around her shoulders . . . and he's playing with her hand! But she doesn't seem to like it. Maybe she really is frigid."

Brooke is poised to jump up for a better look, but I yank her back down. "I don't think you should let her see us."

"Yeah, darn it, I guess you're right. If I get whiplash, I guess this is worth spending a week in a neck brace." Even as she rubs the back of her neck, she is smiling. "Well, this is certainly the scoop of the year! What do you say we order some champagne to celebrate?"

37

"Sometimes the heart sees what is invisible to the eye."

—H. Jackson Brown, Jr.

1:03 p.m.

My heart jumps into my throat when I see all the police cars blockading my street. I pull over as close to home as I can, what with all the neighbors standing in the middle of the street, trying to figure out what's happening at the Lonely House.

Mickey came up with that name, and it hits the nail on the head. Rarely does anyone come or go. In fact, I've only seen the owners once, while walking Harvey at night—a young couple who drove up in a van with dark-tinted windows. They never park in the driveway, but pull into the garage. In the fleeting few seconds when the garage door was open, I noticed that the interior of the garage was empty except for their van.

The house, too, usually has its blinds down, and they never entertain there. I'm guessing they're both workaholics, or that they travel all the time. Or maybe it isn't their house at all, but belongs to some relative who's on an extended stay somewhere else, and they just check up on it periodically. A yard service shows up every other week to trim the grass and the shrubs.

In other words, the house is lonely.

Now it seems we'll know why.

The house is swarming with men in black zip-up sweatshirts with the letters DEA stamped large on the back. The sidewalk is taped off so that pedestrians have to cross the street in order to keep moving forward. Not that anyone wants to do so. Why should they, when the action is right here?

Our chief of police, Officer Fife, is using his bullhorn to detour cars that, like mine, need to reach the other end of the street. When he gets to me, I give him a wink and a smile in the hope that it will loosen his tongue. It should. The world of rumor and innuendo is free. In the world of fact, however, deep-dish apple pies are the coin of the realm, which I gladly tithe twice a year: July Fourth and Christmas.

The timing is fortuitous. I hand him one of the candy canes I snitched off the Max's counter. "So, what gives?"

"A big ol' drug bust. Apparently your neighbors there were running a grow house."

"You're kidding! Right here on my street?" I crane my neck to take in this new point of view of the Lonely House. "They've owned it, what, for three years now?"

"Yep. And never a peep from the neighbors about anything suspicious happening." As always, Fife is the last to know, but the first to cover his butt.

"So, what gave them away?"

"An anonymous tip was sent in. Even gave info on where the suspects sell the stuff. I guess someone had it in for them. Oddly, no one is stepping up for the reward."

"Maybe it's just some upstanding citizen."

"Hope so. Considering the number of break-ins we've had over the past week, we can use some more of them."

"Wait—what break-ins? I haven't heard of any."

"It's a fact. They haven't really been taking anything, just moving things around. We're guessing it's a smart-ass kid or two. Tomorrow Pete's putting a warning in the *Boulevard Bugle*'s online edition. We're going to reinitiate a neighborhood watch." He turns just in time to see Mallory-formerly-Activist-Mom accost a DEA agent with her petition about weapons control. "Aw, heck! Mallory's about to get herself arrested. Gotta run. . . . *Mallory!* Just let the man do his job, please."

Going home can wait. I U-turn so that I can hit the next place on my list: Pete Shriver's paradise on the hill, where Harry is the new cabana boy.

As befitting the scion of the family that owns one of the biggest tech conglomerates in the world, Pete Shriver's pad is a veritable Xanadu. In fact, that is its nickname within the Heights. This stucco miniature (albeit not by much) of Hearst Castle sits on five very lush acres on the one lofty peak that gives our community its name. The view from the house takes in the whole valley. The streets of Paradise Heights uncoil from the base of Pete's hill.

The cabana house, which flanks the Shrivers' infinity pool on one side of the property, enjoys this vista too. A telescope has been set up beside the huge picture window. Harry is playing voyeur, scoping out his old house. When he sees me trudging through the gate and up the slope, he waves me over.

"*Mi cabana, su cabana.* The pool's a nice touch, wouldn't you say? Speaking of which, did you bring your bikini?"

"You wish." I peek through the scope to see what's holding his attention. Apparently it's Lucky, who is busy chasing a squirrel around the backyard.

"I want my dog back. I miss that little pain in the ass. DeeDee shouldn't get too comfortable in the old homestead, since neither of us can afford it now—unless this new guy she's seeing is going to be her sugar daddy." He frowns at the thought. "What do you think are the odds of that? Be honest."

"Considering the commissions he's known to pull down, I'd say pretty good."

That gets Harry's attention. "Are you trying to tell me something?"

"Yeah, sort of. Unless my eyes are lying, I'd say there's a pretty good chance that I've cracked the case." I plop down on one of the cabana's rattan chairs and prop my feet up on one of Harry's two unopened suitcases. He has packed light. He's making it apparent he doesn't plan on staying. "I just got back from lunch with Brooke. We went to the Max's Diner by the expressway. DeeDee was snuggled up in one of the booths—with Max Karloff."

"The realtor guy with the billboards all over the place?"

"The one and only."

"Well, I guess that makes sense. If she can't afford the house, she's going to need someone to sell it." He goes back to looking through the telescope. "Bev Bullworth is certainly going to be disappointed. She thought she had that listing in the bag."

"Sure, they may have been meeting about the sale of the house, but . . . well, I have to tell you, it looked a little cozier than that."

"Oh, you're just trying to make me laugh, right? DeeDee with *that* slime bucket?" He shakes his head in disbelief. "My, how the mighty have fallen."

"He's got quite a reputation, you know."

"Yeah, yeah, I know: Satisfaction Guaranteed. The way he lets it all hang out in the men's locker room at the club, I can see how that might be the case. The dude is hung like a horse. I guess we now know the attraction."

"Harry, I'm sorry you had to hear it from me."

"Really? Well, I'm not. I'm glad I was forewarned." He smirks. "If you'd told me two months ago that DeeDee had anything in common with Masha, I would have said you were crazy."

"Masha's seeing him too? How do you know that?"

"Cal loaded in the SATCOM program two days ago. Pete pulled together all the baseball, basketball, football, and soccer league emergency info—you know, names, telephone numbers, e-mail addresses—and cross-referenced them with DMV records of license plates, as well as what the camera has picked up over the past forty-eight hours." He shakes his head sadly. "Let me tell you, the Heights is a regular Melrose Place! But hands down, Masha is Slut of the Year. She's got it going on with at least four guys, from what we can see."

"Wow. . . . How has Pete reacted to it?"

"Let's just say that my divorce won't be the only one rocking the Heights. It should be interesting, to say the least."

"Listen, Harry, whose satellites is Cal using anyway?"

"From the way he talks, I'm guessing it's the Feds. Why?"

"Well . . . isn't that against the law?"

"Let me worry about that—if and when the time comes that we actually have to."

"What you're doing is very foolish, Harry. It could mean you'll never see your kids again. Have you thought about that?"

"Yeah, sure, I've thought about it. But that worry is outweighed by what I can get back if we take this chance: my life."

Harry's wrong. That life is gone. It went out the door on Halloween, with DeeDee.

It suddenly dawns on me how much superior Cal's system is to Brooke's, and that's saying a lot. The CIA could certainly make it a part of their ongoing study as to whether human intelligence is better than image intelligence.

I'll suggest to the boys that they submit a full analysis to the Feds before being sent to prison. Maybe they can use it to negotiate an early release date.

38

"Marriage: A word which should be pronounced 'mirage.'"

—Herbert Spencer

Wednesday, 18 Dec., 2:45 p.m.

Christmas break officially begins after school ends today. The kids have been restless all week in anticipation of our annual trip to Cabo San Lucas, the four days after Christmas Day. Of course, we'll be back by New Year's Eve.

The call from Ted comes right as I'm heading out the door to pick them up. "So, listen, hon . . . I'll just come out and say it: Cabo is off this year."

"You've got to be crazy! The kids have so been looking forward to this! Why—"

"Sales are way off, Lys. You know that. And the boss wants next year's projections on his desk by the second of January. He's just looking for an excuse to cut some fat. And we don't want that to be me, now, do we?"

He hears my anger in my silence.

Ted softens his tone. "You and I both know that a lot of our friends aren't traveling this year. The kids are already spending one week in the PH recreation department's holiday camp. Why not just sign them up for the second week, too? Besides, this time of year in the Heights is always a fun time to hang in the 'hood. Isn't there something going on tomorrow night?"

"Yes, the lighting of the big tree, in the park at seven o'clock. You know, with Santa and an elf, the whole works. Then Christmas caroling around the neighborhood afterward."

"Well, there you go. Ho, ho, ho."

I feel a headache coming on. "Look, I've got to go pick up Olivia at Miss Judith's. Since you brought it up, I presume you'll be home in time for all of this?"

"At the very least, in spirit."

Bah, humbug.

3:06 p.m.

"I have a peace offering." DeeDee Wilder leans toward my car window, one hand clutching Temple's and the other holding out a small basket.

I pause before taking it. Of course I'm wary. These days, anyone can make a bomb. The information is all over the Internet.

As if reading my mind, she gives a shaky chuckle. "Look . . ." She unfolds the napkin that covers the gift within, to reveal gingerbread men, perfectly iced and nary a one burned to stone.

But of course not.

"Gee . . . thanks." I put the basket on the floor of the passenger seat, but that doesn't stop Olivia from begging for one. My look to DeeDee says: *These better not be poisoned or I will hunt you down and make your death slow and painful. . . .*

She gives a confident wave, so I grab two. But before I pass one back to Olivia, I sing out: "Temple, sweetie, want a cookie?"

God forgive me for making this child the canary in the mine. . . .

It's a good sign that DeeDee doesn't slap it out of my hand before it reaches Temple's lips, so I pass the second cookie back in the direction of Olivia's car seat, where it is eagerly plucked from my hand and devoured.

DeeDee's shoulders relax visibly. "Temple told me how much fun she had, making gingerbread men with you and Olivia and . . . Harry." This last word is so crisp I'm surprised it didn't crack a tooth coming out of her mouth. "I thought, since those didn't come out as planned, she and I could make it our own little mother-daughter project. Right, Temple?" She pats her little one's mop top. "I'm sure it would have been more fun if you and Olivia had joined us."

I let my silence speak for me, along with a look that reads *Not on your life, bitch.*

"Listen, Lyssa, I know we got off on the wrong foot. I know I haven't been exactly—well, fair to you. You've gone out of your way to help my children through this very trying time. They've both told me how kind and welcoming you've been to them. That means a lot to me."

"Oh . . . thank you for that. They're sweet kids. I know it's been wearing on all of you."

"Yes, all of us." She closes her eyes and sighs. "The tree-lighting ceremony is tomorrow. I was thinking—well, if you want, why don't we take the girls to see it together? And perhaps go to the caroling event afterward? It would give us a chance to get to know each other better."

"Mommy! We get to sit on Santa's lap tomorrow, right?"

"Yes, Olivia, that you will." If I say no, I'm a bitch.

If I say yes, I'm a traitor. To Harry.

"Great, Mommy. I want to remind him about our party."

"Oh yes, your party!" DeeDee chimes in. "New Year's Day, isn't it? We've already got it circled on our calendar. We're really looking forward to it. You know, Olivia is Temple's closest friend." Her eyes, starred with dampness, beseech me to absolve her of all past transgressions, to bury the hatchet.

Preferably in Harry's back.

"Let me think about it, okay?"

272 | Josie Brown

She nods, resigned to the obvious: it ain't gonna happen. "In case you've forgotten the phone number at the house, I've put it in the basket with the cookies."

Is that supposed to make me feel guilty, that I know the number to her house as well as I know my own, thanks to her ex?

Whether it is or isn't, it does.

In my rearview mirror, I see Temple waving good-bye to me.

4:15 p.m.

"You're being foolish. Seriously, you should go with her. You know the girls would have fun." Despite being bombarded by Miley Cyrus caterwauling through our den's television, Harry sounds as if he means it.

He also sounds tipsy. Make that drunk.

And that makes me nervous. Or at least, it gives me an excuse to down three of DeeDee's gingerbread men in one sitting. It pisses me off that her recipe is better than mine.

"Of course the girls would enjoy it, but I'd hate every second of it. And I'm guessing DeeDee would too. So why put ourselves through the misery of it all? Just to keep up appearances?"

"Exactly."

Relief flows through me along with my sugar high. "Good. I'm glad you feel that way. Now I don't feel so bad about blowing her off—"

"Whoa, hold up, cowgirl. I mean, yes, you *should* go with her, even if it's just for appearance's sake."

"But—"

"Listen, Lyssa, I know it won't be easy for you. But I think we should face facts: both of us will always put our kids first. And that's the way it should be. It also means making every attempt we can to get along with the others in our lives—you know, Ted *and* DeeDee."

Of course he's right.

"I do appreciate you putting up with Ted. So . . . yeah, okay, I'll make an attempt with DeeDee."

He rolls with laughter. "At least she won't give you a black eye."

"Hey, the week's not over."

"Even so, my money's on you."

Of course it is. I'm the heavyweight in that ring.

I sigh. At this point, one more gingerbread man won't hurt. I bite headfirst. It feels great.

"Lovely! Wonderful!" DeeDee sounds downright exuberant.

"Well . . . okay then. It's a date."

"Yes. . . . But just one little thing." I hear her suck in her breath. After a long pause, she lets it out again. "I had planned to do some last-minute Christmas shopping in the city before the tree lighting. As you can imagine, Harry hadn't even put up the tree with the kids. Oh, sorry, I guess that was cruel. . . . Look, would it be too much of an imposition to ask you to pick up Temple from rec camp at the same time you get Olivia? I'll meet you there as soon as I get home."

The nerve of this bitch!

But if it had been Harry who'd asked, I would have said yes.

So I say yes to DeeDee.

"Thank you, Lyssa! You're a lifesaver. I'll come as quick as I can! I promise."

As I hang up the phone, I wonder if I should have suggested she take her time. Not that I can put off the inevitable.

The phone rings. I'm willing to bet it's DeeDee calling again. Now that she knows I'm such a pushover, I'm sure she's thought of at least one more little favor I can do to cement our BFF status.

But no, the phone's caller ID shows me that it is yet another update from Patti on my father's rapidly deteriorating condition. It should only take her a minute to leave a message, but I don't check my voice mail until later that night, when the children have gone to bed and Ted is unwinding in front of the tube. I have to play it several times to realize she has spoken only three words between all those hiccups and sobs: "Any . . . day . . . now."

Santa has come and gone, which is more than I can say for DeeDee. Olivia and I are keeping Temple busy so that she doesn't ask for the millionth time, "When will my mother get here?" She has a right to have separation-anxiety issues.

She also has a right to be with her father when her mother wants to run errands. In fact, I'm surprised I don't see Harry here at the Annual Pacific Heights Caroling Extravaganza—

But of course, he doesn't want to run into us.

I've been scanning the crowd for Ted, too. I was hoping he'd get here to see Olivia tell Santa what she wants for Christmas. Then, as she's done every year of her young life, she handed Santa an invitation to her birthday party. "We'll have fun," she promised. "Just like last year."

Temple was not as bold. In fact, Olivia had to nudge her toward Santa. I can only imagine what wish she whispered in his ear. If it was for the reunion of her parents, she'll be sorely disappointed.

I know from experience.

Even at nine, Mickey is now too old for Santa. I have to poke him to keep him from snickering at his sister's idolatry of a fat man in a fake beard and a red velour suit. Tanner and Marcus are flirting with Natassia and some of her lustful gal pals. I don't see Jake anywhere, though. Since DeeDee never mentioned his tagging along with the boys, I presume she's letting him hang with Harry.

How big of her.

I am duly snubbed by Margot, Isabelle, and Tammy, although Colleen and Brooke give me reserved nods. So much for the Christmas spirit.

Finally Santa reappears and throws the switch that lights up every limb of the park's most majestic Douglas fir, and three local church choirs take turns singing it out in the name of the child in the manger. As I stand there mouthing the words to songs always identifiable even if most of their stanzas cannot be remembered, I wonder if DeeDee is still fighting the 101 traffic home or is in fact still terrorizing some couture-shop clerk and in the emotional frenzy of the experience has lost all sense of time.

Yeah, okay, it's Christmas, so this once I'll give her the benefit of the doubt.

The kids and I are walking back from the park when I spot Officer Fife coming out of our house, his partner not far behind. Seeing the concern in my face, he meets me in the driveway while the other policeman gathers up the kids for a few questions.

"Your silent alarm went off. From what we can see, nothing was taken, but it looks as if somebody sure made a quick exit from the house."

I follow him inside to verify his presumption that our valuables are still in place. Yes, there are the television and the computer, but I don't remember having left it on prior to leaving with the girls. Neither Tanner nor Mickey remembers doing so, either.

Mickey runs upstairs to confirm that his baseball card collection is safe and sound, and that Ted's favorite sex toy, the TV, is still pinned to the wall.

I start to ask him to check on my vibrator too, then think better of it.

Then I see it: the San Francisco Seals baseball cap.

So the burglar is Jake.

Boy, oh boy: the last thing Harry needs is Jake going into juvenile court for theft.

I do get some satisfaction that it happened on DeeDee's watch.

The proof of this is the cap.

As Officer Fife checks yet another window, I kick it under the couch before Tanner or Mickey can see it and ID it as their good buddy's. But if he's going to stay a friend, he's going to have to be reeled in as soon as possible.

DeeDee glides up the steps just as the policemen are walking out the door. "My God! Is everything okay?" She looks around frantically for Temple. Since Halloween, she's come to expect the worst.

"There was a break-in. Our silent alarm went off."

Relief puts color back in her face. "Anything stolen?"

"Apparently not. They're figuring it's a kid's prank." It's on the tip of my tongue to ask about Jake, but I don't want her to think that I just presume he's the villain anytime something bad happens around here. If and when the truth comes out, she'll be on the defensive anyway.

DeeDee tries on some apologies for size, but my reaction is a shrug. "The girls had fun. That's all that counts."

She sweeps Temple into her arms. Glancing around, she notices her basket on the coffee table, beside my cup of tea and an issue of *Vanity Fair.* "That's mine, isn't it? Oh! Already empty. . . . Well, I guess you liked the cookies after all! Addictive, aren't they?"

As she says this, she looks pointedly at my backside.

It wouldn't hurt so much if it weren't true.

She smothers a grin. "Yes, well, we'll have to reschedule our little bonding date. The holidays are crazy. Maybe one afternoon on the back end of Olivia's party . . ."

That's when I figure out her no-show was all a big fix.

My guess is that she rendezvoused with Max Karloff. With all his listings that are currently vacant, finding a place to fuck shouldn't be all that difficult.

If she did go shopping like she said, I hope she bought herself some very expensive pairs of shoes, and that Lucky finds one and makes a good meal of it.

39

"Friendship often ends in love;
but love in friendship—never."

—Charles Caleb Colton

Friday, 20 Dec., 11:08 a.m

Harry won't answer the door, even though I know he's in
there.

   I don't want to make a nuisance of myself, but I keep
tapping on it because he's not answering his cell phone either,
although he can see on his caller ID that it's me.

What the hell is up?

I move from the door to a window and peek in. He's still
standing at the door, listening for my knocks. He's in scrubs
and a T-shirt. There is a dark shadow of a beard on his face. I'm
guessing he hasn't shaved since I last saw him, let alone brushed
his hair, which now waves out like wings from behind his ears.

Something certainly has him worried.

I rap even harder, and startle him enough that he jumps. He
swivels around to see me, and breathes easier.

"What are you waiting for?" I tap the glass once more for
good measure. "It's cold out here. Let me in."

He wipes his face with an open palm, then with a shrug motions for me to come back over to the front door.

He doesn't greet me with a joke, let alone a smile. He doesn't even ask me to sit down. What's wrong? Does he already know the worst about Jake?

Now that this moment has come, I don't know what to say.

So I say nothing. Instead I toss the Seals baseball cap on the sofa bed, which still has not been made up.

He stares down at it. "So . . . you know, I guess."

"Oh! You know, too?"

All of a sudden, he's on his guard. "Know what?"

"You tell me."

"Nope, you know the rule: ladies first."

This game is getting old fast. "Okay, sure." I take a deep breath. "I know about Jake."

He nods but says nothing, as if he's mulling that one over. Finally: "What about Jake?"

"Harry, quit playing games! I know it's Jake who's been doing the break-ins all over the neighborhood." I stare him down. "You must know about it too, right? Hell, I know Pete knows, because Officer Fife told me so himself—"

Worry pierces Harry's brow. "What else did Fife say?"

"Are you asking me if he knows who owns this cap? No, don't worry, I didn't tell him."

Relief floods his face. "Thanks, Lys."

"Seriously, did you think I'd squeal on Jake? Give me some credit!"

For some reason he finds this hilarious. His snicker soon roils into a full-blown belly laugh.

"What the hell is wrong with you, Harry? Don't you know what this means? If he slips up again and gets caught, it could mean jail time!"

"You're right Lyssa. I shouldn't be laughing. I guess—I guess it struck me the wrong way. But please believe me when I say that Jake has nothing to do with the break-ins. In fact, Pete will agree because—"

"Oh, right. You're telling me that Jake was with you guys last night? And what, were you all playing poker—during the lighting of the Christmas tree? Cut me some slack, Harry! I'm not *that* gullible!"

"Lyssa, you've got to trust me, even if I can't tell you everything right now. Do you get that? But one thing I can tell you in all certainty is that Jake wasn't in your house. And . . . there won't be any more break-ins."

I can't believe my ears. "How can you be so sure? Look, I get it. No parent wants to believe his child is capable of anything like that. But, Harry, you have to face facts: Jake hasn't been the same kid at all since your breakup. This is no time for you to be in denial—"

"Me—*me* in denial? Boy, you've got nerve!" His face turns to stone. "You don't know what the hell you're talking about! Maybe it's time you quit butting into my business and take care of your own."

"You say *I* don't know what *I'm* talking about?" His words hurt worse than any fist could. "Okay, yeah, all right, I'll mind my own business. Heaven knows I've neglected my own life because I've been so concerned with yours. Well, that stops right now."

I would have made it to the door before he grabbed me, except that the tears are falling so hard and so fast that the whole room is a blur. I guess he's afraid I'll bump into something because he holds me close and whispers how sorry he is that he hurt me, that he never meant to make me cry ever, not in a million years, but that he's so angry now, about everything, especially what he couldn't stop, and now everyone will get hurt and will feel the pain—

Even me.

Especially me.

This time, when he kisses me, I don't pull away. I can't.

I won't.

His tongue opens my lips gently, but moves through my mouth with a ferocious hunger. I want to eat him too, body and soul, to lose myself in his touch. . . .

But first things first. I place his hand beneath my shirt and shiver as his fingers roam over my belly, light feathers that tease my skin. His tongue follows, working its way up to my breasts, where his palm cradles my heart while his index finger, with a few gentle strokes, stiffens my nipple so that it aches for the feel of his lips around it. . . .

He groans, torn between the desire to do what we both want and awareness of the consequences that we both know will come with this one act. We risk shattering our friendship . . .

And perhaps creating something better in its place.

Something that will change our lives forever.

And our children's.

And Ted's.

I feel him staring at me. I open my eyes to find in his the very last thing I'd ever want to see there:

Pity.

I bolt from his arms.

There is only one thing I can think of saying to him. "Why?"

"Do me a favor and just don't ask me, okay?"

Because he'd never do to another man what was done to him.

Because I'd be his rebound fuck.

Because, despite what I'd like to presume or what he's willing to admit to himself, let alone me, he's still in love with DeeDee.

Yeah, okay, I get it. Let's keep things friendly, no more.

Well, there will always be carpool and playdates. "See you later, Harry."

"No, Lyssa, you won't," he says very seriously, although he can't say it and look me in the eye. "I don't think we should see each other. Ever. Again."

That stops me cold. I can't feel my heart. I can't feel anything.

I've just lost my best friend. I've lost the man I know in my heart I love.

Because, despite loving him as I do, I can't be like DeeDee. I can't break up my family. Not even if it means losing Harry.

Slowly I turn back to him. It takes five steps to reach him. I count them, yes: five. When I get to him, I take his face in my hands so that he can look me in the eyes and measure the meaning of my words:

"Yes, we will see each other again, Harry. In fact, I'll see you on New Year's Day. At Olivia's party, remember?"

I don't look back as I walk out the door. I already know he can't take his eyes off me.

But this time, I know his eyes hold no pity. That's the way I want it.

He is in love with me. I know that now.

And because he loves me, he won't let me down. He knows I'll need him there beside me at Olivia's party, sharing whatever memories are made that day.

Sharing laughter and glances, and perhaps a touch or two.

Even if we can't share anything else, that will be enough.

I hope.

I pray.

40

"Never feel remorse for what you have thought about
your wife; she has thought much worse things about you."

—Jean Rostand

Monday, 23 Dec., 10:10 a.m.

I've started painting again.

This time, it's for real.

Each day, after dropping the children off at the Paradise
Heights Recreation Department's Christmas camp, where Olivia
is making ornaments out of foil paper and glitter and whole egg-
shells blown empty of the essence of life, and Mickey trots the
boards in yet another version of *A Christmas Carol*, and Tanner shuffles up and down the rec center's gym in pickup games
(basketball) and games of pickup (girls), I head out to the shed.
There I prep the large canvas with warm undertones: amber and
poppy and goldenrod for the background, blush and sunny yel-
low for skin and hair. Then I dip a thin brush in black in order
to outline, from memory, three faces I know so well: Temple's,
Jake's, and Harry's. Only now they are devoid of the pain and
anger that has been so finely etched in their features these past
months. Instead, I take joy in dabbing their eyes with the traits
we identify with love and adoration. Happiness is projected on
the broad dimpled smiles I glaze onto their faces.

This is my Christmas gift to Harry.

When it's time to pick up the children, I move my easel into the corner farthest from the door and tent a canvas over it. Not that it will be disturbed in here.

Once this shed was the graveyard of my past. Now it is a peephole into Harry's future.

3:30 p.m.

Evermoor, the "adults-only/active community" where Mother now lives, has all the bells and whistles: a resortlike setting with flat, velvety green lawns crisscrossed by smooth pathways edged in a rainbow of annuals shaded by large swaying trees.

Its brochure, filled with photos of happy, healthy seniors eating well and keeping active, does not really do it justice. Tango and yoga are the most popular classes, Eudora McClatchy, Evermoor's administrator, informs me as she escorts me down the hall to my mother's door.

Then, in a knowing whisper that ensures my antsy, sullen children can't hear her, she adds: "And our in-house pharmacy sells the most Viagra of any drugstore in the county."

"Really, Eudora, that is too much information."

"You're telling me! Hey, I'm the one who has to look these horny old sods in the face." She stops in front of Mother's door. "Not that you have to worry about that with your mom. She likes them to look, but they can't touch, if you get my drift."

Believe me, I know: once burned, twice shy.

We're both paying for it.

Eudora's sharp rap on Mother's door is ignored. She waits a moment before knocking again. "She knows you're coming for her, right?"

"Yes, of course." Mother has a motto: Let Them Wait. If They Really Want to Put Up With Me, They Will.

No, we don't really want her grief. Particularly not for three days before Christmas and two days afterward. But we wait anyway.

Finally the door cracks open. Mother peers out with a frown. "You're early, Lyssa." Even as she says this, she waves Eudora away. Eudora gives me a sad smile. Mother is now my problem, not hers. At least for the next five days.

Well, it is only five. This is why Ted is so willing to come through with the monthly stipend that keeps her here.

"The kids can sit down." She points to the couch. The boys run to it, but Olivia, her favorite, reaches up for a hug first.

"Ah! Missed you, my baby." Mother cracks her first smile. I count to see how many will follow, but know those smiles will be few and far between.

"I have something for you, Grandma!" Olivia nudges me for the gift, which is buried in my purse. I rummage until I find it, then hand it to my proud gal: an eggshell ornament, wrapped in tissue and tied with a thin gold ribbon. She made it at Christmas camp. Glued into a pipe-cleaner frame is a photo of Mother holding a baby Olivia. The rest of the egg is dipped in gold glitter.

"You can open it now, if you want . . . but where is your tree?"

After Father left, our Christmas trees went from real to fake, and from towering to tiny. By the time I left home, Mother had pretty much given up the ghost of Christmas altogether. Why bother? She spent the next decade of holiday seasons traveling with other bitter women to sultrier and, I hope, friendlier climes. Only after Ted and I had Tanner, and after one of her few girlfriends convinced her that a place like Evermoor was a happier hunting ground, did Mother purchase a small artificial tree, if only for appearance's sake.

Like Olivia, I look around, but I don't see one.

Mother shrugs. "The bedroom. On the dresser. I like the lights. They show me the way to the bathroom."

Olivia runs in there. I follow, to make sure it's not something she can topple over. What we find is a pre-decorated artificial tree only two feet high.

"Oooh," sighs Olivia. But of course. It is the perfect size for anyone under seven or over seventy. She runs back to the living room and hands over the ornament. Mother rewards the current love of her life with a hug and a pat. "Go hang it on the little tree, near the bottom."

"Do you have a hook?" Olivia holds it up to show its missing link to perfection.

"That's a luxury, little one. Poverty is the mother of invention. Right, Lyssa?" Mother grimaces. "You'll find a hairpin in the right-hand drawer of my dresser. When you do, bring it to your mother. She'll show you how to bend it so that it stays on the tree."

She pats Olivia to send her on her way. "What, Ted couldn't make it?"

"He's trying to catch up with work. Sales are down and his whole team is scrambling. But he'll be home by dinnertime." Lately that has been the case. For the kids' sake, I'm glad.

Not that it has made a difference in our lustmaking. It seems that his desire for me died around the same time he got wind of Harry's misfortunes. He doesn't know that Harry and I no longer see each other, but he does know that our children are seeing less of the Wilder kids, so maybe he's put two and two together.

Maybe he thinks that everything is back to normal.

He's right. And that's the shame of it all.

"He's a hard worker, your Ted. And a good provider. You're set for life. How many women your age can say that? All those divorces! A pity. 'Starter marriages.' Ha! No such thing when kids are involved. You can't just start over."

She looks at me sharply, daring me to disagree. But I won't, because she's right.

"I've got cake for everyone. But not you, Lyssa. You've put on a little weight."

I open my mouth to say something, but what's the use? She meant to hurt.

Besides, she's right. I have put on a pound or two. Or three. All the stress, I guess, not to mention the doughnuts. But still . . .

Mother nods me toward the kitchen. "Let's set it up. Then one cigarette for the road."

I frown. "Where, here in the apartment? But what if they catch you?" Mother has been warned repeatedly about Evermoor's no-smoking policy. Her darling Ted's big fear is that they'll kick her out and we'll have to take her in.

"I'm safe. One of the old lechers here disconnected the smoke alarm for me." She points at the one over the kitchen alcove. "I only smoke here in the kitchen. I run the fan and dump the ashes down the disposal. No one's the wiser."

I nod, and reach for the plates while she cuts the cake. The boys scramble to her small dining room table as if some catchy tune has stopped midway in a game of musical chairs.

"Grandma, whatever happened to our grandpa?" From Mickey's chocolate-smeared lips comes this blasphemy. I hold my breath for her answer.

"He left me. No one wants to be around me, little guy. Not even your mother."

Tanner, who like me must have been thinking that very thing, tries not to choke on his milk and spews it across the table's high-gloss mahogany finish. Mother lets loose a curse and grabs a dishrag to mop up the drops.

"Mommy, isn't this your name?" Olivia crawls into my lap. She is holding a letter, yellowed and musty.

Miss Judith's kindergarten spelling lessons have paid off. She is right: that is my name on it.

What she can't know, but I do, is that the block lettering is in my father's hand.

"Honey, where did you find these?"

"In Grandma's drawer. There were no hairpins, but there are a lot of these—"

I stumble past her, into Mother's bedroom. The drawer that is open is the one below the shallow drawer in which she keeps her hairpins. Within it is a towering stack of letters, all in the same hand but postmarked with dates that go back years.

All the way back to that Father's Day, so long ago.

That letter at the very bottom of the pile has no postmark, just my first name, along with a handwritten date for that day. I rip it open and begin reading:

> *Dear Lyssa, I had promised to be back last night. But*
> *Mother has asked me to stay away. It breaks my heart,*
> *being gone from you a minute, let alone a day, but I will*
> *honor her wishes. . . .*

I smell Mother standing behind me. It's not just her stale nicotine breath that repulses me, but the stench of her deceit. "Why didn't you tell me?"

"You know why." This confrontation has given her a great excuse to light up a cigarette. She taps it into the ashtray she carries with her. "You would have left me, too. You would have chosen him over me. Him . . . and *her*."

She's wrong. She needed me the most. I knew it then, just like I know it now.

But because of what she's done, she robbed me of my chance to prove my love to her.

She has robbed me of my love for her.

I walk past her, out the front door. My children scramble after me, too shocked even to call my name. Tanner is shushing Olivia, who wants to know why Grandma isn't coming too.

Because Christmas is going to be spent with Grandpa instead.

If he can forgive me. If he is even still alive.

41

"Forgiveness is the final form of love."

—Reinhold Niebuhr

4:50 p.m.

The home bearing the address on the card that Patti shoved in my hand is not at all what I'm expecting: trim but modest, a midcentury Eichler on a cul-de-sac filled with them.

My father sleeps in a hospital bed that has been set up in the center of the living room. The layout of the house provides a view of an interior courtyard from every room. After my children get over the shock that they've finally met their grandfather, they fixate on the courtyard and its gushing fountain. It is much more pleasing to look at than an old prune of a man, gray and wan like the clouds overhead, tethered to a respirator that beeps out his final wispy breaths.

They know they should love him, but that's hard when you don't have any history of doing so.

I know this from experience.

Now, in my father's presence and seeing his reality, I can honestly say there is no way to make up for lost time.

And because time is of the essence, I start our visit by introducing each child to Father by name, age, and the kind of asides that are the shorthand of parental pride: obvious physical traits, such as Olivia's silvery eyes; the activities in which each excels, such as Tanner's basketball; and character-istics my father will recognize in himself, such as Mickey's love for baseball stats.

This is my way of proving to him that out of sight does not necessarily mean out of mind, that I haven't forgotten all those little nuances that made him my first love.

That I love him still.

Afterward, Patti rounds up the kids to take them to get a pizza. I tell her she really doesn't have to, but then I realize this is her gift to my father and me.

All this time he has held onto my hand and won't let go. His voice is no more than a soft whisper, but his eyes speak volumes with each piercing stare.

"So, all these years, she hid them from you." He smiles wanly. "I was afraid of that."

"I found out today. I thought it was your choice not to be there for me all those years. Not to contact me." My sobs are making it hard for him to hear me, I know, but I can't help it. "Dad, I want to say I'm sorry. For not being mature enough to look beyond her bitterness all these years. I was torn. I thought I was being loyal to her, and that you were making it easy for me."

When he sighs, his throat gurgles. His life is flowing out of him quickly now. "You were a kid. You didn't know. If you had, that would have been different. Then the decision would have been yours to make."

Yes, oh yes! Mine to make . . .

And what would I have done?

Would I have let my mother's tears and pleas sway me?

Would I have found my own reasons to hate my father and Patti?

It's easy to pretend that I would have had the maturity to

recognize his unhappiness in the relationship he had with my mother, and to forgive him for leaving her.

At least, now that I know he didn't plan on leaving me too.

"Lyssa, maybe I didn't try hard enough to stay in your life. Maybe I should have followed you to school, or the park. Maybe I should have heard it straight from your lips."

"I would never have told you I didn't want to see you."

"I know that now. But back then, maybe I was afraid you'd say the opposite." He stops to gasp for breath, to grasp my wrist. "I had my pride. I had a new wife. God bless Patti, I love her dearly, but she would say anything to stroke that ego of mine. Even suggesting that everyone else was at fault." His eyes tear up. "But I know better. It was much easier to pretend you were far away than to hear that you hated my guts." He turns his head away so that I can't see him cry.

I can't think of anything to say. So instead, I watch his chest rise and fall beneath his pajama top.

It is a long while before he speaks again. When he does, he says, "Tell me about him."

That startles me. *How does he know about Harry?*

And then I realize he means Ted.

Ted, with whom I've spent the last fifteen years of my life. With whom I have three children, and who's kept a 3,200-square-foot roof over all our heads.

Ted, who is a loving and caring father.

But what can I tell my father? That my husband wooed me only because I played hard to get?

That he only wants me now because he's worried I'll leave him for another man?

That our love life stinks?

No. Instead I tell him what he really wants to hear: "Ted loves me. He is a wonderful provider. He gave me three beautiful children. We live the life I always wanted."

"That's all I ever wanted for you. Lyssa, my love, that is all you can ever hope for in life." These are his last gasps before he falls asleep.

I think about DeeDee and Harry, how hard both are fighting to hold on to the lives they had before their breakup. In DeeDee's case, that means everything as it was, sans Harry.

As for Harry, I now know that he's accepted DeeDee's desertion and is ready to let her go, but not his children, or the home he's worked so hard for.

Yes, he's doing the right thing to fight so hard for it. If my father had done the same, my life might have been different.

What about me? Is Harry willing to fight for me, too?

As he would say, it's a moot point because I've already made up my mind that I won't let him.

My father is right. Ted has given me my life. It's time we started living it together.

42

"Love means never having to say you're sorry."

—Erich Segal

Tuesday, 24 Dec., 2:20 p.m.

Ted's office is always a hornets' nest of activity. The day before Christmas is no exception. The sales floor is a crazy maze of cubicles where the phones buzz constantly and the computers chirp and trill with instant messages from colleagues and clients alike. Unlike the majority of visitors, I have no problem with security clearance. Ted was one of the original employees. Although that number is now in the hundreds, the security guards still ask after the once-towheaded tyke named Tanner and his two younger siblings.

I've decided to surprise Ted by showing up with an offer to buy him lunch. It's part of my new resolve: to be the kind of wife Ted will always want to come home to.

Or in this case, go home with, especially on Christmas Eve. Day.

As the company's director of sales, he rates a corner office and the accompanying perks, including a sweetheart of an assistant: Vanna, who after a decade of listening to his shuck and jive is oblivious to his rants, ruminations, and flirtations. She hugs me when she sees me, but shakes her head when I ask if he's in.

Seeing my disappointment, she quickly adds: "He took a late

lunch today. But, hey, feel free to take over his office until he gets back."

At first I hesitate at this very generous offer. As in every other situation, Ted will be balls to the wall when he comes in, fully focused on whatever bit of business is driving him crazy right now.

Damn it, it's the day before Christmas! If he's not going to stop and smell the roses today, then when?

He needs me in his life, for that alone.

I nod and head on in, closing the door all but a crack.

The chair across from his desk is loaded down with files, leaving me no choice but to take his chair behind his massive desk, on which papers, contracts, and files have been divvied up into several messy piles.

Poking out from under one stack of papers is a box from Tiffany.

Hmmm.

I look up to see if I'm somehow being observed by anyone out in the hall, but no: Ted's team is scurrying around like rats chasing down any crumbs of green cheese they can get their paws on. Still, I get up and nudge the door shut, just in case.

The box is too large for a ring and too wide for a bracelet. I recognize the design of the necklace inside: two bottom-heavy hearts—one silver and one gold—hang together on a silver chain. The design is renowned: it's by Elsa Peretti. I remember admiring it in the glass case once, when Ted walked me into the store. He'd just landed an account and was feeling flush, but the next day we found out that Tanner needed braces, so that was the end of that.

I guess not.

From what I can recall, the price tag was something over five hundred dollars. I now see it in black and white: almost seven hundred dollars.

I love Christmas.

I love Ted, for remembering.

His deep chuckle at one of Vanna's jokes is my warning that he's back from his lunch. Quickly I slip the box and its receipt back under the pile of papers and walk in the direction of his picture window. Since my back is to him, he doesn't think I see him when he enters. He comes up behind me and places his hands over my eyes. I pull them down toward my mouth and kiss them tenderly.

He's surprised by this. Yes, it's been too long. "Been waiting forever?"

"Nope, not at all. Sorry I missed you."

"With that kind of welcome, the feeling's mutual." He walks over toward his desk. "So, you came into the city for some last-minute shopping or something—"

Then he sees it: the Tiffany box.

The strangest look comes over his face. It moves from shock to concern.

I know he's wondering if I saw it.

To put him at ease, I start chattering like a magpie. "In fact, all my shopping is already done! Really, this was all for you." I feign interest in the building across the street, where Christmas lights flicker in a multitude of colors. "Hey, I just want to say that I appreciate all the hard work you've put in this past month. And I know you were just as disappointed as the kids and me about skipping Cabo this year. And let's face it, we've been under a lot of strain since—well, since Thanksgiving."

He nods absentmindedly. I watch his reflection in the window as he takes the jewelry box and slips it into the deep inside breast pocket of his overcoat.

"So, what say we let Christmas be our New Year? You know, have a mutual resolution, starting tonight: more little random acts of kindness, like a lunch date every now and then"—I'm back at his side with my arm around his neck, pulling him down to me—"and a random act of passion too. Something like this. . . ."

My kiss is heartfelt, and long enough for him to get the message: he's forgiven for all the little petty head games over the past few months.

I expect his response to be relief, maybe even a chuckle that, yes, he too is ready for bygones to be bygones.

What I don't expect is outright euphoria.

It drives him to pick me up in his arms. He presses my lips to his and gives me kisses that are hard, probing, while he leans me back onto the desk. . . .

"Whoa, guy! You've got a whole office of people out there—"

"The door is shut. If anyone knocks, I'll tell him to get lost. You want to be my priority, you want my full attention? Well, you've got it."

His hand drops to the hem of my dress, which he hikes up in order to inch his fingers up along my upper thigh. When he gets to my panties, he yanks them to one side so that his finger can penetrate me. I'm wet enough, despite my apprehension at being my husband's afternoon delight in his very busy office.

Not that he hasn't already guessed how concerned I am by the way I try to stifle my moans.

For him, that's part of the thrill.

And don't we both know it.

43

"Men who have a pierced ear are better prepared for marriage; they've experienced pain and bought jewelry."

—Rita Rudner

Wednesday, 25 Dec., 5:43 a.m.

Olivia is bouncing on our heads to wake us up. "Can we go downstairs now? *Please?* To see if Santa has been here?"

Mickey's voice chimes in from the hallway. "Olivia, of course he's been here! Just look over the banister, for crying out loud! The whole floor is covered in presents."

Ted peels our daughter off his chest, tossing her onto the foot of the bed. "Yeah, sure, go! *GO!* . . . Hey, you can look, but don't touch—not until your mom and I get down there too."

"How long will that take?" Olivia tries to pull the covers off the bed, but I hang on fast to my end.

"It will take longer if I don't get my first cup of coffee." I know I sound grumpy, but that's the breaks. It's been a long, stressful week. We put out the gifts after midnight, and I'm dead tired.

Besides, I don't do crack of dawn too well.

"I'm on it, Mom!" I hear Mickey tromping down the steps to push the button on the coffeemaker.

Olivia flies down the steps too. "Wait for me! WAIT! . . . Oh! It's bee-*U*-ti-ful!"

The tree, she means.

Well, more honestly, the field of dreams that surrounds it.

Tanner, too old and too cool for such a show of unfettered giddiness, growls from his room for everyone to shut up. "I'm an atheist! I don't believe in Santa, so shut up!"

"Santa is secular, you moron!" Mickey yells from the kitchen.

I know, though, that the minute Tanner hears Ted and me stirring, he'll be right on our heels.

"Are you up?" I nudge Ted, because he looks as if he's falling back asleep.

"Hell yeah. You know that Christmas always gives me a woody." He reaches for me and pulls me close. "So does the thought of more office sex, by the way."

"I'll remember that. Only next time, let's wait until everyone leaves for the day. I didn't like the fact that Vanna couldn't look me in the eye when I left."

"I'll make it part of her job description." He stretches as he rises from the bed. "All right! *Showtime . . .*"

I make sure to hand Ted his Christmas gift first: it is a mini digital camcorder, which will be used to capture every *ooh* and *aah* that happens over the next thirty minutes. When Ted is not manning the camera, it goes to Mickey, our budding auteur. I'm not sure he can edit out each and every time Tanner shoots a bird at the camera, but with my prodding, I know he'll do his best.

The kids make out with quite a haul. Besides video games and more sports paraphernalia, Tanner and Mickey have been gift-carded to the hilt. Better safe than standing in the return lines at the mall, is my motto. Olivia's stash includes several dolls and, of course, a few more costumes for her make-believe alternate universe.

And lots of books, books, books. A few more Harry Potters

for Tanner, another gift box set of Lemony Snickets for Mickey, and a few simple readers for Olivia.

Last but not least, it's time for my gift from Ted. Mickey steadies the camera as Ted rummages around the back of the tree for the last box there, and hands it to me with a hug.

"Oh . . . what is this?" I feign ignorance.

"Go ahead, open it." He's just as excited as I am.

I tear open the wrapping paper. "Ah, Tiffany! Nice."

He nods modestly.

For dramatic effect, I open the box slowly—

"Oh . . ." Yes, it is a necklace; but no, it's not the one with the two hearts. Instead, on the sterling silver chain is a key anchored by a turquoise enamel heart.

"I remembered you like it, so . . ."

I recognize it, too, from our Tiffany shopping expedition: when Ted whistled in shock at the price tag of the double heart necklace, he asked if I'd settle for this more modestly priced piece.

Of course I said yes. Because it's the thought that counts.

Obviously, he thought so too, and returned the double heart necklace before he came home last night. . . .

My eyes tear up. Seeing that, he hugs me all the harder. "Hey, not to worry, babe! It's not like it broke the bank or anything."

He leans back and pats his belly. "Okay, everybody's on wrapping-paper cleanup crew while Mom hits the kitchen to make our Christmas pancakes. Oh, and, Lys, I'm taking off around twoish, to go in to work—"

"Wait . . . what? You're working today?" I look down at the necklace in my hand. "But . . . that makes you the only person on the planet."

"Next week the big boss expects sales projections on his desk. And suggestions for budget cuts. I don't want him to add me to that list because I've decided to stay home." He reaches down for a handful of wrapping paper, bundles it into a wad, and takes a layup shot. When it lands in the trash can across the room, he pumps his fist in triumph. "And he *scores*!"

Not in my book. "Mickey, please, turn off that damn camera now!"

I wonder if I can figure out how to delete those last few bytes of the camera's memory.

If only it were that easy to do the same to my own.

44

"Love is a canvas furnished by nature and embroidered by imagination."

—Voltaire

Thursday, 26 Dec., 1:15 p.m.

I come to Xanadu bearing gifts: a chocolate heartache cake for the Shrivers, and Harry's painting.

The gate is open, so I roll right up to the garage. I knock on the front door of the big house first, but no answer. Out of courtesy, I leave the cake box on the bench with a Christmas card from our family to theirs.

Since Christmas was yesterday, I don't know if Harry is sharing a belated get-together with his family today or not. In a way, I'm hoping he is, because he's always happier with them beside him.

I'm disappointed when there are no signs of life coming from the cabana. There is no rain in the forecast, and the painting is wrapped up tightly. I could just leave it beside the door, but I've been looking forward to seeing the look on his face when he opens it, so I nix that idea. I know, it's selfish of me. Too bad. It's the artist's prerogative.

I'm about to leave when I hear a splash.

Harry just dove in.

I don't know what his reaction will be when he comes up for

air and sees me here. No matter. I lean the painting up against the door, then mosey over to one of the many double chaise longues scattered beside the Shrivers' pool. Might as well make myself comfortable as I wait for him to pop through the steam floating over the pool's heated surface.

Because his back is to me, at first he doesn't see me and goes under with a flip. I can't help but laugh, since that's something Mickey would have done if he'd been in the pool.

When Harry resurfaces, he coughs up the water in his lungs. It sounds like a dolphin in heat.

This only makes me double up in laughter.

He looks around. Finally spotting me, he swims over.

"Well, well. What a great Christmas present!"

I feel myself blushing. "I'm glad you feel that way. I've been missing you too." I reach over and grab one of the towels that have been left on the teak table beside me. I'm almost afraid to ask, but I do so anyway: "How was your Christmas?"

"Somewhat decent, I'm happy to say. The kids came over here yesterday afternoon." He stands over me as he dries himself, blocking out the sun and putting himself in silhouette with a halo. Although I can't see his features, already I know them so well.

By heart.

"How about you? Everyone pleased with their Christmas bounties?"

"For the most part, yes." I know he's not asking about me. And even if he were, I'd have no reason to complain. A gift is a gift is a gift.

It's the thought that counts.

I smile as I shade my eyes against the bright aurora that glows around him. "I left a cake for the Shrivers. Are they due back soon?"

"Nope. Pete and his wayward mistresses left for Tahoe this morning. He wants to give his marriage one more shot. Frankly,

I think it's a waste of time." He frowns. "Unfortunately, they'll still be up there on the day of Olivia's New Year's party."

"I'm sorry to hear that. But you're coming, right?" I look away, afraid of how he'll answer.

"Lys, I told you before that I don't think it's a good idea." He wraps the towel around his waist and sits down in the chair next to mine. "It would just complicate things."

"How so? Because DeeDee will be there too?"

He pauses as if searching for the right words. Finally he settles on a shrug. "Yes, quite honestly. I don't think it would be fair to the kids."

"Children like to see both their parents in the same place at the same time, even when they're not happy together. Believe me, I know from experience." I'm being stubborn, but suddenly I don't care.

"Lyssa, *it wouldn't be fair to me.*"

There, he's said it.

"How can you say that? Of course it's fair to be with those who love you, no matter what others think!"

His laughter comes out with no joy, just pain. "Oh, that's rich! No matter whom it hurts, right?"

Our children.

Ted.

Stalemate.

"Lyssa, you have to trust that I know what's right for all of us."

Suddenly I'm very tired. It's time for me to go. I get to my feet unsteadily. With a wave, I turn and walk back toward the house. As I pass the cabana, I see the painting I left by the door.

It's my Christmas, too, and I want to give myself the one gift that will make me happy.

I pick it up and take it over to him. "From me. Merry Christmas."

304 | Josie Brown

He's taken aback at first. Slowly he unwraps the paper taped around it. What he finds underneath brings tears to his eyes. "This is incredible. It's beautiful! You did this—for me?"

I nod. "It's how I see you: always at your happiest. And Jake and Temple too."

He thanks me with a kiss, but when our lips meet, neither of us can stop there.

He is hungry for me. His mouth lingers on mine, gently at first, then with abandon as he sets it loose over my neck, my face, my hair. When he gets to my shoulders, his hands fumble with the buttons on my shirt before he can tear it away from my body.

He admires my breasts. Yes, I have to admit, they do look nice. Even to my eyes, they look much fuller than I remember. Must be the chilly air, which has stiffened my nipples. They seem darker and larger. When he takes one in his mouth, my heart beats harder in my chest. . . .

One hand cradles the back of my neck as he guides me down onto the chaise, while his other hand slips below the waistline of my pants, exploring, probing, inciting me to desire him all the more, if that's even possible. He wants me just as badly, I know, because his cock swells in his swim trunks to the point where it lifts them up. I can see it clearly defined—

The buzz of my cell stops us cold. Harry sits up with a groan. "Well . . . maybe it's for the best."

I stare down at my purse, but I don't make a move.

So he does. He stands up and wraps the towel around his waist again. The effect is silly:

Tent trunks.

I'd laugh if I weren't crying so hard.

He sits beside me and cradles my head to his chest, but the tears don't stop, can't stop. He takes my hand and examines each finger before stroking them lightly, kissing them from tips to palm.

We sit together like that for at least an hour, not saying a word. Finally he rises, pulling me up with him. He picks up the painting and studies it carefully. "Someday we'll be this happy again."

"I know."

I mean it.

2:40 p.m.

I am already in my house when I remember the cell call. I don't immediately recognize the number on the caller ID, so I hit the message button to hear Patti's voice, choked with heartbreak, informing me that Dad passed away early this morning, and that the funeral will take place on Monday. She also says she will leave it to me to inform Mother, and would welcome her at the funeral if that is my wish.

I take a deep breath and walk upstairs so that the children can't hear me sob.

An hour later, when I'm all cried out, I ring Mother's number.

Her telephone has caller ID, so when she barks, "What is it?" I know she knows who she's talking to.

"He's dead." Really, that's all I need to say.

Her response is to blow smoke into the receiver. Then: "Yeah, okay, so what? What am I supposed to do?"

"Forgive," I murmur. Then I hang up.

45

"It isn't tying himself to one woman that a man dreads
when he thinks of marrying; it's separating
himself from all the others."

—Helen Rowland

Monday, 30 Dec., 11:30 p.m.

No kid looks great all in black, including my own. It isn't a happy color.

But they do look appropriate, and that is what the occasion of my father's funeral calls for. It is a simple event. Apparently, toward the end he had only a handful of friends. Fueled by my mother's venom, most had abandoned him when he left her.

Worn down by her bitterness, eventually they abandoned her too. People prefer pleasantness. I don't blame them. If I hadn't felt so guilty, I would have left too.

Most of the mourners here don't know me. In fact, most don't even know *of* me. My father gave little in the way of history, because it hurt too much. If they knew about me, it's because he'd already determined that they would not pass judgment on events they had not lived through, but would trust that he'd done the best he could.

That is, in the best respect, true friendship.

Ted stands beside me, smiling and congenial and supportive.

I think he expected me to be a lot worse off than I am: I smile wanly, with glassy eyes. I know he's happy for me that I made my peace with my father before this day. But even if I hadn't, I now know that I could have counted on him to hold it together for me. For our children.

One of my hands is tucked inside Olivia's. The other grasps Patti's. Or I should say, she holds on to me, tightly.

My mother would hate seeing that.

But since I don't care what my mother thinks or feels, I let this woman who loved my father lean on me in her time of need. I don't know if, after all is said and done, she will take me up on my offer to stay in touch, to let her come by and watch her husband's grandchildren grow into the kinds of human beings who, I hope, would make him proud.

My guess, though, is yes. I'm glad of that. My children need to hear about their grandfather from someone who actually knew him and loved him passionately, as opposed to someone who hated him unconditionally.

As he is lowered into the ground, I throw a handful of sod onto his coffin and say a prayer for his soul.

I pray for my mother's soul as well.

Tuesday, 31 Dec., 9:00 p.m.

Ted and I have gone into the city for New Year's Eve. I'm calling this a new tradition. We live too close to San Francisco to become those people who never go beyond the cloistered claustrophobic borders of their own little towns.

Unfortunately, our advance reservations mean nothing to the hostess at Il Fornaio on Battery. By the time we're seated for our nine o'clock dinner reservation, it's going on eleven. It's already a forgone conclusion that we'll miss the fireworks taking place just a couple of blocks down along the Embarcadero. We are both starving, and Ted refuses to rush out the door: "Hey, we're paying through the nose for this meal. Besides, who wants to be jostled by a couple of thousand drunk, horny party animals?"

We make it home after midnight, but without seeing one flash of a rocket's red glare.

In fact, we didn't realize it was midnight until it was too late.

I wonder if Ted would have suggested that we kiss, had we known.

My guess is no.

Happy New Year.

Wednesday, 1 Jan., 9:15 a.m.

"Ah! So today's the big day! Three o'clock, am I right? Olivia must be excited." DeeDee, a vision in white wool, is standing at the bakery case perusing the cupcakes when I come in to pick up Olivia's birthday cake.

"Yes, she's very excited. I'm sure she was a pain with Tanner last night while we were in the city." I hand the salesclerk my confirmation ticket so that she can find the cake in the pickup locker.

DeeDee's plasticine smile wavers. "You went in to see the fireworks?"

I nod. I wonder if she had her kids for New Year's Eve, or if Harry was allowed visitation last night. I think of how many New Year's Eve celebrations he and DeeDee have spent together, and suddenly I'm jealous.

My only consolation is the knowledge that, last night, she wasn't with him either.

To cover up my joy at that thought, I shrug. "For us, it was a bust. We got out too late from dinner to see the fireworks."

"Your husband works downtown, doesn't he?"

"Yes. When he's not on the road. He travels for business too."

"I liked that. When I was married, I mean. It gave me time by myself." She looks at her reflection in the mirror behind the counter and smooths a line by her mouth that no one else can see.

With what I know about her now—about her liaisons with Max Karloff—I find it hard to smother my smile over such a smug statement.

The smirk dissolves from DeeDee's face. "What are you laughing about?"

"Nothing! Really. . . . I guess it just struck me as funny. I mean, when we fall in love and get married, we can't get enough of each other. Then over time, for whatever reason . . . well, you know."

"Yes, I know." DeeDee glares at a lemon cupcake. "Obviously, you do too."

Are my feelings for Harry so obvious? It's my turn to be wary. "What are you saying?"

"Just that no marriage is perfect." She turns to look me straight in the eye.

I don't know what she wants to hear from me. "All of life is a compromise. Even marriage. Especially marriage."

"But how much do you compromise away before it isn't the life you want to lead? Is it selfish to want something different altogether, even if it doesn't include him?"

I glance down at a tray of pink coconut snowballs and realize that just looking at them nauseates me. She doesn't have to justify her actions to me, but to Harry. "I . . . I really don't know the answer to that."

"Oh no? I'm guessing you know what it's like when one of the partners in a marriage falls out of love. Or maybe I'm being presumptuous." DeeDee hands the clerk a twenty-dollar bill and takes her cupcakes, then turns to leave.

But no. If she is to be judged by me, she will never have a better chance to make her case than now and here, surrounded by so many sweet temptations. "When you're in an unhappy marriage, it's hard to walk out the door. No one likes the unknown. No one wants to take the chance that what they're walking toward is worse than what they're running away from. But it's more fair. I love Harry, Lyssa. Enough to leave him."

As a parting gesture, she reaches into the bag and hands me one of her cupcakes. "Happy New Year. I really mean that. Here's to having your cake and eating it too."

New Year's Day

46

"When a man steals your wife, there is no better revenge than to let him keep her."

—Sacha Guitry

1:20 p.m.

Olivia's party is rocking. We always get a full house, but this year it seems to be bursting at the seams.

I love it.

Dressed in her favorite princess gown, Olivia flows from room to room, blushing and smiling at the happy-birthday shout-outs she gets from well-wishers of all ages. Following close on the heels of my little princess's Mary Janes is her very own court: six other soon-to-be six-year-olds in rich dark velvets and stiff iridescent satins, all flittering behind her, laughing, giggling, and hugging one another.

Temple is one of these. At this point in her life, she doesn't seem to miss being the center of attention. What goes around comes around again eventually. I'm sure that, when she's ready to retake the spotlight, it will welcome her back.

Take your time, baby.

She arrived late, mother and brother in tow. DeeDee hasn't walked over yet to acknowledge me, and I've been rushing around too much to greet her. I hope Ted did, because that takes me off the hook, at least for now. I was not surprised when

Max Karloff showed up a few minutes later and immediately cornered DeeDee. He's treating her like his prized possession, whereas she nods stiffly and seems distracted. I don't think she's ready to be seen in public with him. Who can blame her?

Jake has disappeared into the bowels of the basement play-room with Tanner and the other tweens. I've no doubt that soon one of the empty bottles will be snatched from the recycling bin for a game of spin the bottle. Besides tending bar, Ted is charged with periodic check-ins down there, to make sure things don't get out of hand.

"Do you think Tanner is scoring already?" His eyes open wide at the thought. "You know, going all the way?"

I slap him on the chest. "Get real. Were you 'going all the way' at his age?"

He ponders that for a moment. "Well, I'd like to think I was."

"Exactly. *Think* is the operative word here. Let's have no regrets today."

Even as I say it, I think, *Famous last words . . .*

"Well, aren't you quite the little hostess with the mostest!" Brooke skips her usual air kiss, opting instead for a real peck on the cheek. The clear gloss on her lips is appreciated, the kiss more so. "My God, woman, this place is packed to the rafters!"

"You're telling me." I fan myself with the mitt I'm using to pull yet another tray of stuffed mushrooms out of the oven. It's so hot in here that I can barely breathe. It doesn't help that I'm feeling a bit tipsy too. Too much wine, I guess. I lean on the counter and take a big gulp of air. "Thanks for coming, Brooke."

"What, are you kidding? I wouldn't have missed it for the world." She takes the tray from me and leads me out into the dining room by my elbow. "Besides," she whispers with a wink, "you're no longer in exile."

"What does that mean?"

"Don't tell me you haven't heard! Boy, have *you* been put on ice! Well, okay, but remember, you didn't hear it from me. . . ."

I take a seat. I can tell this is going to be long and juicy, which makes me think of bloody red steaks—

Which makes me want to barf. I grab Brooke's frozen-mojito glass and put it up against my cheek, just to cool off.

". . . Tammy was found in bed with him. Can you believe that? You can just imagine the—"

"Whoa—wait! What did you say? Tammy was in bed—with whom?"

"Why, Gerard Hardaway! Honey, haven't you heard a word I've been saying?"

"But how . . . where . . ."

"Margot got some anonymous tip. Ha! With her reputation, I'm surprised anyone cared enough to let her in on it. Anyhow, turns out their little affair had been going on since at least Thanksgiving. It was caught on some videocam and streamed to Margot in an e-mail. They were using his doctor's office for their little love trysts." She shudders since she can't frown. "Let me put it this way: that was some little surgical procedure he was doing on her!"

"Wow! I have been off the planet. So, does Charlie know now?"

"You betcha! *Big* brouhaha! And he called Bethany before Tammy had a chance to do it first. Talk about adding insult to injury."

"I'll say." I'm so stunned, I can't even think of moving. So Tammy found a more willing sperm donor! Wait until Harry hears this. . . .

"Okay, but it gets even better. Yesterday Isabelle saw Tammy at the drugstore buying—*get this*—an early home pregnancy test!" Brooke is so excited, she's squeaking.

316 | Josie Brown

It's giving me a headache. "If she's preggers, I guess she'll finally get the child she has always wanted."

"Yeah, but the primary objective was to have it along with moneybags Charlie, remember? Not with a guy who'll be paying his wife through the nose until his other kid turns twenty-one." Disgusted, Brooke shakes her head. "To think it all could have been done with a surrogate—*and* she'd have saved herself the extra pounds and the stretch marks."

Both of Brooke's sons were carried by other women, for just that reason. Appallingly, she's always surprised that more women haven't thought to do that.

So much for the idea that it's the journey, not the destination.

I shake my head in wonder. "But if it was Charlie's sperm that was the issue—"

"Hey, don't think Tammy didn't use that angle first! She tried to talk him into considering using another man's sperm, but he was adamant that the kid had to have his genes. Well, I guess this was her way around it." She grins wickedly. "That being said, Margot now considers *you* the board's prodigal daughter. Besides, none of the rest of us have the desire, or apparently the talent, to take over from her. That's why we've let her get away with all the tsuris she's caused all these years. Hey, speak of the devil! There she is now, with Colleen and Isabelle. And she's coming this way. So welcome back, *ma chérie*!"

I smile at my most unexpected guest and hold out my hand to greet her.

However, if Margot curtseys and kisses my ring, I will throw up for sure.

How will I break the news to her that I'm no longer interested in being her puppet president?

I won't worry about that now. I'm just going to enjoy her groveling.

3:06 p.m.

The crowd is at its peak. The adults, plied with booze and appetizers, are loose and animated. The children, though, are getting antsy for the main event: the cutting of the cake for Olivia and Santa, then opening gifts, both hers and whatever silliness Santa has in his bag for them.

The man hired to play Santa is surlier than I'd like. While he allows Olivia to sit on his lap as we serenade the two of them with a robust version of the birthday song, he actually blanches at the forkful of cake Olivia offers him after they blow out the candles. Turns out he's vegan, and chocolate cake with seven-minute egg-white icing is not on his diet. Ted is the only one who thinks this is funny. He captures it all on his new Flip Ultra camcorder.

Olivia is having too much fun to let Bad Santa harsh her mellow, but the fact that he's less than jolly has Temple a bit upset. She yanks on her mommy until DeeDee indulges her and picks her up. As Temple wraps her legs around her mother and clings to her neck for dear life, the collar on DeeDee's crisp white blouse is yanked down on one side. I don't think DeeDee likes this stranglehold, but there is nothing she can do but grin and bear it. In this crowd, she has no choice but to play the ever-indulgent mommy. In fact, she hasn't even noticed that the top button on her blouse has come undone.

And that's when I see it: *DeeDee is wearing my necklace.*

Not the blue enamel heart-and-key necklace that was under the Christmas tree for me, but the double heart Tiffany necklace that wasn't.

I try my hardest not to stare, but my eyes are drawn to it. So that my interest isn't too obvious, I don't look directly at her, but watch her reflection in the mirror over the sideboard.

318 | Josie Brown

If Ted did give it to her, that means only one thing: he is her lover.

As I cut cubes of cake and pass them forward, I try to fathom that idea, but I can't. In the first place, they are total opposites. He is outgoing and flirtatious. She is cool and demure. What would be the attraction?

But of course, that's it exactly. She provides the challenge Ted needs to be turned on, while Ted provides the naughty excitement her life was missing.

So that I don't hyperventilate, or leap across the room and tear the necklace off her throat, I try to think of all the logical reasons why this simply can't be true. In the first place, that necklace is mass-produced for Tiffany, and certainly DeeDee is no stranger to the shops in Palo Alto or, for that matter, along Union Square.

And then I hit on the most obvious reason of all for why it's such a ludicrous premise:

Ted doesn't have time for an affair.

Hell, he rarely has time for sex with me.

I laugh hysterically, not at the precious anecdote Colleen has just told me about little McGuyver, but at myself for even considering such nonsense about my husband and Harry's ex.

And yet, out of the corner of my eye, I watch the two of them. When their paths cross, they are polite but distant.

I breathe easier. . . .

And then it hits me, why he is always too tired for sex with me:

Because he's already having it with DeeDee.

I have to keep it together until the party is over and everyone has gone home. Then I'll take the time I need to think this through.

Better yet, I'll confront him with what I think I know.

And, of course, he will tell me I'm wrong.

And I can pretend I believe him.

In the meantime, I smile and circulate.

So does Max Karloff. Devoid of his cool blond arm charm, he goes off in search of new listing prey. Bev Bullworth has had plenty of time to watch him. In the past, she would have broken out in hives every time he pounced on a potential new listing—particularly if his target was one of her current clients—but tonight it seems she couldn't care less. In fact, instead of doing her usual sales pitch on unsuspecting partygoers, she only has eyes for Cal.

Cal, too, seems relaxed, tanned, and happy. I walk over to re-fill their wineglasses. "Happy New Year, you two. Missed you at the lighting of the tree. I take it you've been out of town?"

"My honey took the whole family to Cabo the week before Christmas." Bev is beaming. "Have you heard? Cal's just picked up a big new contract: Shriver Tectonics! Pete's company is investing in Cal's municipal satellite security system. Harry Wilder is putting the deal together." Happiness agrees with Bev. "It's a relief, let me tell you! Now we'll have enough money to renovate the house the way I've always wanted."

"Wow, that's great. Very exciting!" Why didn't Harry say something? I guess we've both had other things on our minds. "You're quite a dynamo, Bev. Between working full-time and taking on a renovation—"

She laughs. "With Cal taking on more work, you won't see my shingle out that often in the new year, Lyssa. I'll be having too much fun tearing apart our kitchen." She kisses her husband on the nose. "Cal convinced me to take it easy, when we were down in Cabo. It was like a second honeymoon—even with the kids there. It was Cal's idea that we bring Jake along to keep them company. He read that in an article somewhere." She puts her arm through her husband's. "Where did you see that, Cal? Wasn't it in *Redbook*?"

I stare at Cal. If that's the case, then Jake couldn't have been doing the break-ins. . . .

So, Harry was telling the truth. It wasn't Jake after all.

But why didn't Harry just tell me Jake was with the Bullworths?

Because I didn't give him time to.

Where is Harry, anyway?

Almost as if reading my mind, Cal puts his arm around me. "Speaking of Jake, I just saw Harry in the kitchen admiring your orchids."

47

"The difficulty with marriage is that we fall in love with
a personality, but must live with a character."

—Peter De Vries

4:10 p.m.

It's in full bloom," Harry says, staring at the candy cane
amaryllis. He has his back to me, but he knows I'm here,
watching him.

"I knew you'd come, friend." In order to resist the urge to go
to him, to hug his back, I stare at what's left of Olivia's cake.

"Lyssa, I wish I could be your friend, but I don't think you'll
feel that way about me. Not after what I'm about to tell you."
When he turns around, I realize by the look on his face that what
he has to say is breaking his heart. "DeeDee does have a lover—"

I take a deep breath. "Yes, I know. It's Ted."

Harry stares at me. "You do? But . . . how?"

"DeeDee is wearing a necklace I saw in a Tiffany box sitting
on Ted's desk—a surprise Christmas gift I thought was meant
for me." The tears start running down my face. "So, how did
you find out about Ted?"

He searches my eyes. "DeeDee's computer. Pete's community
database provided us with the raw data of telephone numbers,
e-mail addresses, and DMV tags, and the SATCOM provided
us with a way to track DeeDee. But we still had no clue as to

whom she was communicating with, until she moved back into the house. Then we were able to check her e-mails."

"But once you moved out, you weren't allowed to go back in—oh! The SATCOM system let you know whenever she left the vicinity, am I right?"

He nods. "She had the locks changed, but I used Jake's new key. Before Cal went out of town, he linked the system to Pete's computer and gave us a crash course on how to use it, so that we could keep up surveillance, in case we caught a break."

Suddenly it hits me. "The break-ins! You were the ones who called in the pot house! And it was you who wore the Seals hat when you broke into my house."

Harry nods. "Guilty as charged. We had a lot of hits and misses before DeeDee got the house back. At that point, we were down to just one or two possible men, one being Ted. I presumed he was a long shot, except that Olivia had mentioned to Temple that her father would be working late—again." He picks up my hand when he sees my frown, and gives it a kiss. "Since I knew you'd be out with the kids for the tree lighting, we went in. And that's how I learned that the messages were coming from Ted's e-mail address or cell number."

"Harry, what you did could have landed you in jail! Then you would never have gotten custody of Jake and Temple." I'm tearing up at just the thought of this.

"We were monitoring the police too, so we had a heads-up there."

"Still, that doesn't make it right."

He rolls his eyes. "You can spank me later."

I laugh through my tears. "Won't you be surprised if I take you up on that."

"Tammy would, but you're not the type." His smile is wicked. "But, hey, it paid off one way: Tammy got caught with Gerard."

"I just heard about it from Brooke." I shake my head in

wonder. "Congratulations! You actually scooped the biggest gossip in the Heights."

"I only wish I'd been there to see Margot's face when she played that video." Then his smile fades. "Lyssa, I just want you to know that I debated for the longest time whether to even tell you. I figured I'd take a lot of satisfaction from letting the wife of DeeDee's lover know what he's been up to. But that's because I never figured it would be you. As your friend, I wanted to tell you. But as the man who loves you with all his heart, I knew just how devastated you'd be." His eyes are dry and hollow. "Besides, I knew when you confronted Ted and when he realized he'd be losing you, he'd beg you to take him back. Lyssa, I know you well enough to believe you would have. And if that's the case, I wouldn't have lost you to Ted at all, because I never had you to begin with."

He's wrong.

My kiss tells him that, as does the way I stroke the back of his head, and how I wrap his hand in mine.

Ted and DeeDee. He had to have the one woman who was his biggest challenge. Anyone else would have been too easy.

I was too easy. What did Brooke say? Oh, yeah: scratch my belly and I'll follow you anywhere. . . .

"Seriously, Harry, if you wanted Ted's e-mail address, all you had to do was ask me what it was. I'd have given it to you."

"I know. But it was more than likely he had one or more you didn't even know about. Turns out that was the case. And, quite frankly, with you out caroling, I thought that, if he was her lover, I might luck out and catch them in the act."

The idea that Ted and DeeDee might have been screwing just a few doors away—or, even worse, in my house—makes me angry. I have to see them, now, together, with my own eyes.

I walk out of the kitchen into the living room, where I last saw Ted—what, maybe twenty minutes ago? But he's not there.

Neither is DeeDee.

Nor are they in the front yard. I push my way back into the house, ignoring the laughs and chatter around me, the shouts that invite me over, because Ted isn't there. I know I look like a madwoman as I run down into the playroom. Forget spin the bottle. The kids—Tanner, Jake, Laurel, Duke, Sabrina, and Natassia—are playing strip poker. Duke is the only one fully dressed. But of course: he is the statistician in the group, so he's playing the odds. Smart boy.

"Everybody, get dressed! Upstairs with your parents, NOW!" The girls screech and grab for their clothes. Everyone scatters like leaves in a windstorm.

I race up the stairway with Harry on my heels. Thank God Ted and DeeDee aren't in Olivia's room. There, she and her friends have divided her stuffed animals among them.

Tanner's room is empty, as is Mickey's. I find my younger son and a couple of his buddies playing video games in my bedroom. He looks guilty when I walk in: he didn't get my permission beforehand to be in there and use my television. Considering the activity in the playroom, I consider this the lesser of two evils. I wave to him that it's okay, and close the door quickly. I don't want him to see that I have been crying.

There will be plenty of time for that later.

There is only one other place they can be.

It's been raining a fine mist all day. That has kept all our guests inside. It's also made it convenient for Ted and DeeDee to break away. The shed's door is closed, but not locked. They don't hear it creak as I open it.

They are too busy kissing, too busy making love. Missionary style, of course.

Harry comes up behind me. He, too, can't help but stare. Learning the truth about DeeDee at this point is a hollow victory. There is no triumph in revealing their deceit. Simply more sadness.

Ted doesn't even have the courtesy to take his socks off. I'm sure, if there had been a television in the shed, it would be turned to the Lakers game.

Poor DeeDee.

Then again, I really don't need to feel sorry for her, because she's proudly wearing the gift I thought he'd bought for me.

Ted keeps humping, but DeeDee looks up. At first she is surprised to see us, but I can tell she's also relieved. Finally, the charade is over.

Ted catches DeeDee's gaze and follows it. But even before his eyes light on me, he realizes what has just happened. He scrambles off of her and reaches for his pants on the floor, but I'm already gone, running toward the house.

Harry runs after me.

So does Ted, grasping at the sides of his slacks to hold them up. But it is too late. When Ted reaches me, I throw off his arm and keep walking quickly toward our back door. He takes my hand again, but I fight him off.

When he tries it a third time, it's Harry who grabs his arm and turns him around. Ted takes the first swing, but misses. Harry's fist, however, slams into Ted's jaw. He staggers back, then falls like a house of cards.

DeeDee, who has just come out, runs to Ted. As she cradles his head, she cries soft tears. I've never seen her so tender. I've never seen her so human.

Harry is shaken as well. I don't know why, but this makes me feel nauseated. I double over and retch until I have nothing left in me. Harry holds my head until I stop.

When I stand up, he steadies me in his arms. "Lyssa, I realize this is all happening too fast, but I want to know: are you going to ask Ted for a divorce?"

Before I can even think about my answer, I retch again.

And then it hits me: *Oh, my God, I'm pregnant.*

New Year's Day

One Year Later

48

"Love does not begin and end the way we
seem to think it does."

—James A. Baldwin

M other was right about one thing: Nothing is perfect.
For many of us in Paradise Heights, the past year is
proof of that.

For Tammy, that means having the child she's always wanted, but raising it on her own. Gerard will, of course, ante up for child support, but he has chosen Margot's form of forgiveness, whatever that is. No doubt it will be sadistic, but I guess he figures that the devil you know is better than the devil you don't.

The same isn't true of the Paradise Heights Women's League board. With a president-elect candidate embroiled in, and I quote, "actions that may be construed as . . . indecent, lascivious, lecherous, salacious, obscene, wanton, or libidinous," with the president's husband, a void was created, only to be filled in the most surprising manner. Summer pushed for a full-member vote, as opposed to a board vote alone, on all league positions. Needless to say, both Margot and Tammy were ousted, along with Isabelle. However, Brooke and Colleen were asked to stay on, in order to ease the transition with the new blood, which includes Summer and Mallory. In fact, Brooke and Summer were co-presidents last year. Ironically, they made a cohesive team. Go figure.

The Shrivers are also going through a contentious divorce. Pete has some remorse, but he's holding firm against Masha's pleas for forgiveness—which started the moment she realized that Pete's bank account went with him, and that there was nothing she could do about that. Pete can thank the battery of attorneys who safeguard his estate for having the forethought to insist that she sign an airtight prenup prior to his wedding.

As for me, this truly will be a new year: new baby, plus a new husband and a new best friend, Harry.

I realized that life is too short to be unhappy in a marriage that isn't working. I guess DeeDee was right about that.

Too bad she wasn't right about Ted. Now that he can have her out in the open, he's convinced himself that she isn't what he wants after all. Besides, he enjoys being single again.

Will he ever find a relationship that satisfies him? For his sake, I hope so, but I doubt it. Everyone deserves to be loved. But you have to give it to get it in return.

Our children are sad about our divorce, but are proving to be resilient. They know both of us love them with all our hearts. And, ironically, they now see more of Ted than they did when he lived with us.

I've named my newborn son Jonathan, after my father. He wasn't planned, but he is loved all the same. He won't have the same relationship with his biological father that his older siblings do, but he'll have the love of two fathers. Harry and Ted are both good men.

Olivia's birthday party ended an hour ago. There was a smaller crowd this year, but that was to be expected. Those who are uncomfortable with the circumstances that precipitated the blending of our families—of our lives—sent their regrets.

Fine with us. We have none ourselves.

Besides, it's always good to know who your friends are. They are the people who don't pass judgment on how you choose to live your life.

As Jonathan sleeps in my arms, I move through our house here on Bougainvillea Boulevard, counting my blessings as I count heads for dinner. Olivia and Temple are upstairs, where they're teaching all the stuffed animals their addition and subtraction in a makeshift school. In the great room, the boys—Tanner, Mickey, and Jake—are sprawled over the sectional couch, watching the Rose Bowl game.

Harry is in there too. As I perch on the arm of my husband's chair, he pulls me and the baby down onto his lap so that he can cuddle us both.

"The turkey should be ready to come out of the oven in another half hour," he whispers in my ear before he kisses it.

"You made sure it's set to Bake, right?"

He laughs, then kisses me again. And again.

I love the adoration in his eyes.

It's interesting how much of life doesn't go according to plan.

But I'm in awe that, despite this, things have a way of working out for the best.

SECRET LIVES OF
HUSBANDS AND WIVES

JOSIE BROWN

INTRODUCTION

Lyssa Harper has it all: a comfortable home in the exclusive neighborhood of Paradise Heights, a handsome and successful husband, and beautiful kids. But bubbling beneath the exterior of her enviable life, and the lives of her close friends, is a web of gossip, cheating, lies, and scandal. When the neighborhood's most attractive power couple breaks up, Lyssa finds herself drawn to the newly single Harry Wilder. As the bond between Harry and Lyssa grows, rumors begin to spread, and the long-repressed tensions in the quiet enclave of Paradise Heights boil to the surface. Friends become enemies, charity events and middle-school basketball games become battlefields, and the secret lives of husbands and wives are finally exposed.

Questions and Topics for Discussion

1. The town of Paradise Heights is portrayed as an upscale enclave for mostly upper-income families. What did you think of the author's portrayal of the people in this town? Do you admire or condemn them? Envy them for all of their material wealth, or pity them for the emotional balance they lack? Or both?

2. Why do you think Lyssa is so drawn to Harry Wilder at the beginning of the novel? Does she really just feel sorry for him, or is she projecting her own childhood experience with divorce on his circumstance? How are both Lyssa's and Harry's experiences with divorce different, and how are they similar?

3. Lyssa spends most of her time socializing with the women who make up the executive board of the Paradise Heights Women's League. They are depicted mostly as villains in the novel—especially their ringleader, Margot. In fact, the league board is called "the Coven" by those less-popular mommies they've nicknamed "the Undesirables," and all of them have been given nicknames of fairy-tale witches. What, if anything, is attractive about the power wielded by the members of this cruel clique? From where do you think they derive their power?

4. Do you think that all the members of Paradise Heights Women's League are equally guilty of bad social behavior? Does a follower like, say, Colleen, who silently allows Margot to behave atrociously, deserve just as much blame as the queen bee herself?

5. At times, the character of Lyssa seems both needy and eager-to-please. Her friend Brooke likens her to a puppy, saying, "If someone scratched your belly, you'd never leave their lap" (page 262). How do you think Lyssa changes over the course of the novel? What role does her relationship with Harry play in that transformation?

6. Many of the adults in the novel seem less well-behaved than their children, and Lyssa spends a lot of time worrying about the example that she and the rest of the adults in her social circle are setting for their children. They get into fights at basketball games, and shamelessly throw themselves at the husbands of their friends. How did you feel about the way the adults in this novel conducted themselves? Have you personally witnessed similar behaviors in a social setting? Did you think less of Lyssa for surrounding herself with people who acted the way they did? Would you consider Lyssa a good parent?

7. What did you think of the way Ted withheld intimacy from Lyssa and then used it as a means of marking his territory when he became jealous of Lyssa's relationship with Harry? Did you find it odd that Lyssa admittedly enjoyed being used by Ted as a way of his proving his dominance over Harry?

8. At one point, Lyssa's mother questions her daughter's need to have married "The One." And DeeDee very pointedly remarks that, "no marriage is perfect." Almost every relationship in the novel is unstable. What do you think is the author's opinion of marriage? Would it surprise you to learn that she has been happily married to the same man

for more than twenty years, and that like her, he is a jour-
nalist who covers relationship trends?

9. Is it significant that DeeDee is the only one who admits—
and acts on the fact—that her marriage made her unhappy?

10. Lyssa is concerned that Harry may be labeled an "Undesirable" and, admittedly, dreads it for herself. Do you think
that the need for the approval and admiration of our peers
can ever be overcome? Can a person be truly happy with
themselves without some sort of recognition from others,
or will we always need to be noticed in order to be happy
with ourselves?

11. As a character, Lyssa can be a little judgmental. She is
quick to find fault with her friends and to point out when
they're in denial. And yet, she is blind to the problems in
her own life. Are most people better at finding faults with
others than at looking within? Why?

12. What is the significance of Lyssa's relationship with her
mother and father? How do you think the example of her
parents' marriage affected the way she handled her own
romantic relationships with both Ted and Harry? How
does the news that her father didn't abandon her help
Lyssa to reevaluate her views on love and relationships?

13. The Paradise Heights basketball team plays a game at a
rival school that displays a banner in its gym, reading: "We
Own You." How do you think the wealth of some of the
characters in this book influences their views of the world?
How does it affect their children?

14. Although the novel takes place in an exclusive community, a place where most people could never afford to live, are there certain commonalities you noticed between the characters in this book, and the less elite? What sorts of problems transcend class barriers?

15. How did you feel about the way the novel ended? Were you at all upset that Lyssa immediately jumped from a marriage with Ted to a marriage with Harry? Did you want her to strike out on her own and prove her independence? What did you think of the way Lyssa's relationship with Ted was concluded? Did you want him to get more of a comeuppance?

ENHANCE YOUR BOOK CLUB

- Each chapter begins with a quote about love and relationships. Which quote was your favorite? Did any hit particularly close to home? Have you received any advice in your own life that rivals the advice offered in these quotes?

- The mean-mommy clique is part of a long-hallowed literary and film tradition that depicts the cattiness with which some women treat one another. Watch, read, and discuss other books and movies that depict similarly icy relationships between women (e.g. anything by Jane Austen, Edit Wharton; *Jane Eyre*, *Cinderella*, *Mean Girls*, *Heathers*, *The Women*; etc.). Discuss how you think these portrayals of female-on-female emotional violence affect societal views of women.

- One of the many ways that women in this book jockey for social superiority is through their baking skills (think of DeeDee's gingerbread man triumph over Lyssa). Have a *friendly* bake-off of your own and see who can bake the best treat for your book club.

- Go to www.josiebrown.com for information on the author's previous novels, her reading events, and to download additional book club questions, or to invite her to teleconference with your book club.